LITTLE MAN, WHAT NOW?

Hans Fallada

English translation by Eric Sutton

Academy
Chicago
Publishers

Published by
Academy Chicago Publishers
213 West Institute Place
Chicago, IL 60610

© 1933 by Simon & Schuster
Published by arrangement with Simon & Schuster, Inc.

First paperback printing: October 1983
Second printing: April 1992

Printed and bound in the USA by The Haddon Craftsmen, Inc.

Library of Congress Cataloging-in-Publication Data

Fallada, Hans. 1893-1947.
    Little man, what now?

    Translation of: Kleiner Mann, was nun?
    I.   Title
PT2607.I6K613   1983   813'.912   83-15694
ISBN: 0-89733-086-2

Table of Contents

PRELUDE: *Young Hearts*

1. Pinneberg finds out something new about Bunny and makes a great decision 3

2. Mother Mörschel. Herr Mörschel. Karl Mörschel. Pinneberg meets the family 11

3. A little conversation at night about love and money . . 21

PART ONE: *The Little Town*

1. Marriage begins correctly with a wedding-trip but— do we need a saucepan? 31

2. Pinneberg grows mysterious and Bunny has some riddles to solve 36

3. The Pinnebergs pay a courtesy call 44

4. Bergmann and Kleinholz, and why Pinneberg must not be married 49

5. The master of the Pinneberg destiny 59

6. Lauterbach the Nazi, the demonic Schulz, and the husband-in-secret get into difficulties 65

7. Pea soup is prepared and a letter written; but the water is too thin 72

8. A pact is sworn. Still no pea soup 79

9. A Pinneberg excursion arouses interest in certain quarters 83

10. How Pinneberg strove with the Angel and with Marie Kleinholz and how it was too late 89

11. Herr Friedrichs, the smoked salmon, and Herr Bergmann 100

12. Bunny (in her apron) makes a call on her husband . . 108

Table of Contents

PART TWO: Berlin

1. Introducing Frau Mia Pinneberg 115
2. An imperial French bed and Herr Jachmann . . . 120
3. Simultaneous acquisition of a job and a father . . . 126
4. A despondent walk through the little Tiergarten . . 134
5. A salesman (with the assistance of Herr Heilbutt) is born 138
6. Pinneberg gets his pay, behaves badly to a salesman and becomes the possessor of a dressing-table 148
7. Bunny receives a visitor and views herself in the glass . 154
8. Some Pinneberg conjugal customs. Mother and son. Jachmann again to the rescue 161
9. Why the Pinnebergs will have to move 175
10. Happy consequences of a fainting-fit 179
11. Odd lodgings. Appearance of Master Puttbreese. Reappearance of Herr Jachmann 184
12. The pros and cons of a normal budget 190
13. Heilbutt thinks we have courage. But have we? . . 200
14. Suppose I never see her again 206
15. How babies are made 215
16. Pinneberg pays a visit and lets himself be tempted towards nudism 221
17. What Pinneberg thought about nudism and what Frau Nothnagel thought about it 227
18. Pinneberg's first deception of Bunny 236
19. Children are born to the Lords of Creation, and Bunny embraces Puttbreese 243

Table of Contents

20. The baby-carriage, the two hostile brethren and the Confinement Grant 255

21. Disappearance of a tower of strength 267

22. Jachmann sees ghosts. Rum without tea 276

23. Jachmann discovers the wholesome things of life . . 284

24. Jachmann as discoverer and the little man as king . . 289

25. The movies and life. Uncle Knilli abducts Jachmann . 299

26. The baby is ill. What can be the trouble? 304

27. The inquisitors and Fräulein Fischer. Another reprieve, Pinneberg! 313

28. Frau Mia again 319

29. The jig is up 327

EPILOGUE: Continuation

1. Should you steal wood? Bunny earns a great deal and gives her husband something to do 337

2. Man as woman. A matter of six marks 345

3. Why the Pinnebergs do not live at home. Joachim Heilbutt's Photograph Agency. Surprising news about Lehmann 353

4. How Pinneberg started it all. The forgotten butter and the policeman 365

5. A visitor in a taxi. Two sit waiting in the night. No chance with Bunny 372

6. A mysterious bush 380

PRELUDE
Young Hearts

*Pinneberg finds out something new about Bunny
and makes a great decision.*

FIVE minutes past four. A neatly dressed, fair-haired young man stands in front of No. 24 Rothenbaumstrasse.

At a quarter to four Bunny was to have been here to meet him. Pinneberg put his watch back in his pocket, and surveyed a brass plate affixed to the wall.

Dr. Sesam
Gynecologist
Consulting Hours: 9–12 and 4–6.

"Five minutes past four. If I light another cigarette Bunny is sure to dash right round the corner. I won't then. It's all going to cost me enough money as it is."

His eyes wandered away from the brass plate. There was only one row of houses on the Rothenbaumstrasse; beyond the roadway, beyond a strip of green grass, beyond the paved embankment, flowed the Strela, already quite a broad stream near to where it joins the Baltic. A fresh wind was blowing, the bushes swayed and bent, the trees rustled faintly.

That's the way to live, thought Pinneberg. I'm sure Sesam's got seven rooms. He must earn loads of money. I wonder what sort of rent he pays—two hundred marks, I suppose. Maybe three hundred. Ten minutes past four!

Pinneberg felt in his pocket, took a cigarette out of his case, lit it.

Bunny blew round the corner in a pleated white skirt and her art silk blouse, without a hat, her fair hair all dishevelled.

"Hullo, darling! I just couldn't make it. Mad?"

"Not a bit. Only we shall have to wait God knows how long. At least thirty people have gone in since I've been waiting."

"Well, they won't all have gone to see the doctor. Besides we've got an appointment."

"There, you see it was a good thing we made one."

"Of course it was. You're always right, darling."

On the staircase she took his head between her hands and kissed him tempestuously. "Oh, I'm so happy to have you again. Just think, it's nearly two weeks."

The door opened. On the dim landing a white-clad shadow stood before them, and rapped out, "Appointment? Down the hall!"

They walked to the door indicated, passed in and found themselves stranded amid red plush.

"Must be his own sitting-room," said Pinneberg. "What do you think of it? Pretty seedy, I say."

The door opened and another Sister came in. "Herr and Frau Pinneberg, please? The doctor says he won't keep you a moment. Perhaps I could take the particulars while you're waiting?"

"Certainly," says Pinneberg; and the Sister at once asked, "Age, please?"

"Twenty-three."

"Christian name?"

"Johannes." A pause: "Book-keeper." Then, more

4

readily: "Always in good health. The usual children's ailments, nothing else. Both healthy, as far as I know." Another pause. "Yes, mother still alive. No, father dead. Can't say what he died of."

And Bunny: "Twenty-two—Emma." Now *she* hesitated: "Maiden name Mörschel.—Always in good health. Both parents living, both in good health."

"Thank you, just one moment."

"What's all that for?" he grumbled, as the door closed again. "We only want to . . ."

"You'd have been glad if you hadn't had to say 'Bookkeeper.'"

"And you were a bit nervous about your maiden name, eh?" He laughed. "Emma Pinneberg, called Bunny née Mörschel."

"Oh, you keep quiet!—what do you suppose the Doctor will say?"

"I don't know. He's bound to help us—they say he's not like most doctors that way."

"Well, I didn't like the looks of that Sister much. I don't see why she should have to worry about whether our parents are in good health or not."

"I wonder how long they expect to keep us waiting here."

"Good afternoon," said a voice. In the doorway stood Dr. Sesam, the famous Dr. Sesam of whom it was whispered over half the city and a quarter of the province, that he had a large heart, and many people also said, a good heart. Anyhow, he had written a popular pamphlet on sexual problems, which was why Pinneberg had summoned up courage to write to him and ask an appointment for himself and Bunny.

5

Dr. Sesam looked for a letter on his writing table.

"You wrote to me, Herr Pinneberg. You can't afford to have any children yet, wasn't that it?"

"Yes," said Pinneberg, in a fearful state of embarrassment.

"You might—er—get ready to be examined," said the Doctor to Bunny, and then went on. "And now I suppose you want to know an absolutely safe preventive. An absolutely safe one." He laughed sceptically behind his gold spectacles.

"I read about it in your book," said Pinneberg. "There must be some way . . ."

"Well," said the Doctor, "it depends on the individual case you know, depends on the individual case. Now your wife . . ."

He looked up at her. She was partly undressed, but had started with her blouse and skirt. Her slim legs made her look very tall.

"Well, come along," said the Doctor. "No need to take your blouse off for that, little lady."

Bunny blushed deeply.

"All right, let it be. This way in. One moment, Herr Pinneberg."

The two went into the next room. Pinneberg watched them go. Sesam did not reach up to the "little lady's" shoulders. She looked lovely, Pinneberg thought, the finest girl in the world, the only girl for him. He worked in Ducherow, and she worked here in Platz, he saw her at the outside every two weeks and his joy in her was always fresh.

In the next room he heard the Doctor ask a question

now and again in a low tone, an instrument tinkled against
the edge of a glass; he recognized the sound from the
dentist's, not a pleasant sound.

Suddenly he started, never before had he heard that
tone from Bunny—she was saying in a high, clear voice,
"No, no, no!" And once again: "No!" And then, very
softly (but he heard) : "Oh God!"

Pinneberg took three steps towards the door. What was
this? He had sometimes heard that such doctors behaved
abominably to women. Then Dr. Sesam spoke again, but
he did not catch the words; and again he heard the clink
of the instrument.

A long silence.

The pair came back. Pinneberg looked anxiously at
Bunny, her eyes seemed so large, as though fear had
widened them. She was pale, but she smiled at him, an
anguished smile at first, then it broadened and spread over
her whole face, like an opening blossom. The Doctor
stood in the corner washing his hands. He glanced over
his shoulder at Pinneberg. Then he said briskly: "A
little too late for precautions, Herr Pinneberg. The door
is shut. Early in the second month, I should think."

Pinneberg caught his breath. He said quickly: "But,
Herr Doctor, it's impossible. We were so careful. It's
quite impossible. Tell him, Bunny."

"No possible doubt," said the Doctor. "And believe
me, Herr Pinneberg, a child is good for every marriage."

"Herr Doctor," said Pinneberg, and his lips quivered,
"Herr Doctor, I earn a hundred and eighty marks a
month."

A weary look came over Dr. Sesam's face.

7

"No," he said. "No. You may save yourself the trouble of asking. It's out of the question. You are both healthy. And your income isn't so bad. Not—so—bad."

"Herr Doctor," said Pinneberg feverishly.

Bunny stood behind him and stroked his hair.

"There, there, dear; it'll be all right."

"But it's quite impossible!" Pinneberg burst out, and then was silent. The Sister had come in.

"Herr Doctor is wanted on the telephone."

"You see," said the Doctor. "It won't be long before you're glad. When the child has arrived, come to me at once. Then we'll see about precautions. Don't depend on its being safe while she's feeding the baby. Well, then . . . Courage, young woman."

"May I?" said Pinneberg, pulling out a purse.

"Ah yes," said the Doctor, already in the doorway, and he looked appraisingly at the pair. "Fifteen marks, Sister."

"Fifteen," said Pinneberg, halting, and looked at the door. Dr. Sesam was already out of the room. He carefully extracted a twenty-mark note and took a receipt in exchange.

"Come, Bunny."

They went slowly down the staircase. On one of the landings Bunny stopped and took his hand between hers. "Don't be so sad! Please! It'll be all right."

"Yes, yes," he said, deep in thought.

They walked a little way along the Rothenbaumstrasse, and then turned into the Mainzerstrasse. Here were tall houses and many people, and hurrying motor cars, the evening papers were already being shouted, and no one noticed them.

"Not a bad income, he says, and takes fifteen marks from my hundred and eighty."

"I'll manage," said Bunny. "I'll manage."

"Dear!"

From the Mainzerstrasse they turned into the Krumperweg where it was suddenly quiet.

Bunny said, "Now I understand a lot of things."

"How do you mean?"

"Oh nothing, except that I always feel so rotten in the morning. And it was so funny too."

"But you must have noticed it."

"I kept on thinking it would be still all right. You never think of such a thing at once."

"Perhaps he's wrong."

"No. I don't think so. I don't see how he can be."

"Perhaps you'll be all right tomorrow. And I'll write that man such a letter—!" He sank into thought. He was composing the letter.

"I'll ask for my fifteen marks back too," said Pinneberg suddenly.

Bunny did not answer. She stepped carefully with the full breadth of her shoe, and looked cautiously before her as she walked. Everything was different now.

"Where are we going?" he asked suddenly.

"I must go home again," said Bunny. "I didn't tell mother I was going to stay out."

"Well, you might have spared me that," he said.

"Don't be angry, darling. I'll arrange to come out again about half past eight. What train are you catching?"

"The nine-thirty."

"I'll walk with you to the station."

9

"Is that all? What a life!"

The Lutjenstrasse is a real working-class street, always swarming with children, it's impossible to say goodbye properly there.

"Don't be so depressed, darling," she said, giving him her hand. "I'll manage."

"Yes, yes." He tried to smile. "You're an ace, Bunny, you'd come through anything."

"I'll be down at half past eight. I promise."

"Aren't you going to kiss me?"

"I really can't. Somebody would tell. Now cheer up."

"All right, Bunny. Don't you be depressed either. We'll get through somehow."

"Of course," she said. "I'm all right. Bye-bye till later."

She slipped up the dark staircase, her vanity-bag tapping against the banisters as she went. Pinneberg watched her twinkling legs. How many thousand times had Bunny vanished up that accursed staircase.

"Bunny!"

"Yes?" she said from above, peering over the banisters.

"Just a second!" He dashed up the staircase and gripped her shoulders. "Bunny!" he said, panting with excitement and breathlessness. "Emma Mörschel! Suppose we get married?"

2.

Mother Mörschel. Herr Mörschel. Karl Mörschel.
Pinneberg meets the family.

BUNNY said nothing. She freed herself from Pinneberg and sat down softly on a stair. Her legs had suddenly given way. She sat and looked up at her boy. "Darling, if only you would!"

Her eyes grew strangely bright. They were dark-blue eyes, flecked with green. Pinneberg became quite embarrassed with emotion.

"That's settled, Bunny," he said. "We will. And as soon as possible, eh?"

"But darling, you really needn't. I'll be all right. Except you're quite right it would be better for the baby to have a father."

"The baby? Oh yes, the baby."

He was silent for a moment. Should he tell Bunny that in his proposal of marriage he had not thought of the baby at all? He had merely reflected that on this fine summer evening it was very unpleasant to have to wait three hours in the street for her to come out. He said: "Do get up, Bunny. The stairs are sure to be dirty. Your nice white skirt . . ."

"Who cares about my skirt! All the skirts in the world don't matter to us. Oh darling, I'm so so happy!"

She jumped up and flung her arms round his neck. And the house was kind to them: of all the twenty households that went up and down those stairs, not one soul came past, though it was after five in the afternoon, in the rush hour, just when the breadwinner comes home, and all housewives hurry to fetch some forgotten little extra for supper.

At last Pinneberg freed himself and said: "But we can do this upstairs, now we're engaged. Come along."

"Do you want to go up at once?" asked Bunny doubtfully. "Don't you think I'd better prepare father and mother? They know nothing about you—"

"What must be done is best done at once," observed Pinneberg boldly, his mind still on the street he would have to tramp for three hours. "They're sure to like it, aren't they?"

"Well, yes," said Bunny thoughtfully. "Mother will be. Father, you know—well you mustn't mind him. He's fond of scolding people, but he doesn't mean it."

Bunny opened the door. A narrow passage-way. From behind a half-opened door, a voice: "Emma! Come here at once."

"Just a minute, mother. I must take my shoes off."

She took Pinneberg by the hand, and led him on tiptoe into a little room looking on the yard.

"Put your things down there. Yes, that's my bed; mother sleeps in the other one. Father and Karl sleep across there. Now come. Wait—your hair!"

She hurriedly drew a comb through the tangle.

The hearts of both were hammering. She took his hand, they crossed the passage, and pushed open the kitchen door. By the stove stood a woman with a round bent back, frying something in a pan. Pinneberg noticed a brown dress, a large blue apron.

12

The woman did not look up. "Run down to the cellar, Emma, and get some briquettes. I keep on telling Karl . . ."

"Mother," said Emma, "this is my friend Pinneberg from Ducherow. We want to get married."

The woman at the stove looked up. A brown face with a firm mouth, a sharp, dangerous mouth, a face with bright keen eyes and myriad wrinkles. The face of an old worker's wife.

She glanced at Pinneberg for an instant—a sharp and angry look. Then she turned again to her potato pancakes. "Silly little fool," said she. "Bringing your fellows home with you. Go and get some coal, my fire's going out."

"But, mother," said Bunny, trying to laugh, "he really wants to marry me."

The woman looked up. Slowly she said: "Haven't you gone yet? Do you want your face slapped?"

Bunny hurriedly pressed Pinneberg's hand. Then she picked up a basket, cried in her cheerful young voice: "I won't be long," and the outer door slammed.

Pinneberg looked cautiously across at Frau Mörschel, then at the window. All that could be seen was the summer sky and a few chimneys.

Frau Mörschel pushed the frying pan aside and began to shift the stove rings with much rattle and clatter. She stirred the fire with the poker, muttered under her breath.

"Beg your pardon?" said Pinneberg.

They were the first words he uttered in the Mörschel home.

He had better have said nothing. The woman was down on him like a vulture. In one hand she held the poker, in the other the potato fork, and brandished them both at

13

her visitor. But her aspect was not so evil as her face, in which every wrinkle quivered and twitched; and more evil still were her terrible and angry eyes.

"If you bring my girl to shame!" she cried savagely.

Pinneberg recoiled. "I want to marry Emma," he said nervously.

"You think I don't know what's up? For two weeks I stand here waiting. She'll tell me, I say, she'll bring the fellow here soon; I can wait." She stopped to breathe. "She's a good girl, I tell you, Emma is, she's not for you to play with. She's always been good-tempered. Never given me a cross word—do you want to bring her to shame?"

"No, no," whispered Pinneberg timidly.

"You do!" cried Frau Mörschel. "You do! For weeks now I have been wondering what's actually happened to her. What have you got to say for yourself, young man, eh?"

"We're young people," said Pinneberg softly.

"And to think that you—you have brought her to this." Suddenly she growled: "You men are all swine. Pah!"

"We're going to get married as soon as we can fix up about the papers," explained Pinneberg.

Frau Mörschel again stood at the stove, over the frizzling fat. "But how? What's your job?"

"I'm a book-keeper in a corn-merchant's office."

"Clerk, eh? I'd sooner you were a working man. What do you earn?"

"Hundred and eighty marks."

"After deductions?"

"No, they have to come off."

"Thought so. Not much. My daughter's not going up in the world." Sharply: "Don't get it into your head she'll

14

bring you anything. We're working people, our girls get nothing when they marry. Only the few pieces of linen they've bought for themselves."

"I understand that."

The woman suddenly grew angry again. "But you've got nothing either. You don't look like the saving sort. When a man goes about in a suit like that, he's got nothing left for anything else."

Pinneberg did not need to confess that she had about hit the mark, as at that moment Bunny came back with the coal. She was in the best of spirits. "Did she eat you up, poor darling?" she asked. "Mother's a regular tea-kettle, always boiling over."

"Mind what you say, you young snip, or you'll get something you're not looking for. Go in the bedroom and play. I want to speak to your father alone first."

"All right," said Bunny; "but have you asked my young man if he'd like some potato pancakes, to celebrate our engagement?"

"Out!" said Frau Mörschel. "And mind you don't lock the door, so I can see you aren't up to any mischief."

They sat on white chairs on either side of a little table.

"Mother's a plain working woman," said Bunny. "She's got a sharp tongue, but she doesn't mean what she says."

"Must be like father!" said Pinneberg with a grin. "Do you know, your mother knows exactly what the doctor told us today."

"Of course she knows. She always knows everything. I think she liked you."

"It didn't look like it."

"That's just her way. She must have someone to yell at. I never pay attention now."

15

For a moment there was silence. They looked into each other's eyes, their hands outstretched on the little table.

"We must buy ourselves rings," said Pinneberg reflectively.

"Of course we must. Which do you like best, shiny or dull?"

"Dull."

"Me too! We've got the same taste in everything, that's fine. What'll they cost?"

"I don't know. Thirty marks?"

"As much as that?"

"Are we having gold ones?"

"Of course we are. Let's measure our fingers."

He came close. They snapped a bit of thread off a reel. It was not so easy. Once the thread broke, and once it was too loose.

"It's unlucky to look at hands," said Bunny.

"But I'm not," he said. "I'm kissing them. I kiss your hands, Bunny. I kiss your hands."

Bony knuckles rapped on the door.

"In a minute," said Bunny, freeing herself. "Let's fix ourselves a bit. Father's always nagging."

At the kitchen table sat a tall man in gray trousers, gray waistcoat, and white flannelette shirt, without coat or collar: slippers on his feet. A lined yellow face, with little sharp eyes behind a pair of pince-nez, a gray moustache, and an almost white beard.

As Pinneberg and Emma came in, he let the *Volkstimme* drop.

"So you're the boy that wants to marry my daughter? Glad to hear it, sit down. You must take time to think it over, though."

Bunny had put on an apron and was helping her mother. Frau Mörschel said angrily: "I wonder where that young rascal's got to. Supper will be spoilt."

"Overtime," said Herr Mörschel laconically; and winking at Pinneberg, he added: "I suppose you work overtime sometimes, don't you?"

"Yes," said Pinneberg; "fairly often."

"But without pay—?"

"Unfortunately, yes. The boss says . . ."

Herr Mörschel went right on: "That's why I'd rather have a working man for my daughter. When my boy works overtime he gets paid for it."

"Herr Kleinholz says . . ." began Pinneberg afresh.

"What the bosses say, young man," observed Herr Mörschel, "we've known a long time. It doesn't interest us. What does interest us is what they do. Any wage agreement in your job?"

"I believe so."

"Belief belongs to religion. The worker has nothing to do with religion. There's sure to be an agreement; and you'll find it provides that overtime must be paid. Why should I have a son-in-law that doesn't get paid for overtime?"

Herr Mörschel, after planting this poser, leaned back complacently. Pinneberg shrugged his shoulders.

"Because you clerks are not organized," Herr Mörschel explained kindly. "Because you don't stick together and back each other up. So they treat you as they like."

"But I *am* organized," objected Pinneberg. "I belong to a Trades Union."

"Emma! Mother! Our young man belongs to a Trades Union! Who would have thought it? Well!" The tall

17

Mörschel cocked his head and observed his future son-in-law with half-closed eyes. "What's your Union called, my boy? Out with it."

"The German Employees' Union," said Pinneberg, more warmly.

Mörschel was so overcome that his tall form was quite convulsed. "The G.E.U.! Mother, Emma, hold me tight. And the lad calls that a Trades Union. The bosses kind of like it, don't they? God bless my soul, children, what a joke!"

"Look here," said Pinneberg, now furious. "You're quite wrong. We're not financed by the employers. We pay our contributions ourselves."

"Yes, and I can guess what your officers do with them. Well, Emma, you've found a grand lad, I must say."

Pinneberg looked appealingly at Emma, but she did not catch his eye.

"People like you, so I've heard," went on Mörschel, "think you're a cut above us working men."

"No."

"Yes. And why? Because you're paid by the month instead of the week. Because you work overtime without pay. Because you don't mind being paid under scale. Because you never go out on strike. Because you're always scabs."

"It's not just a question of money," said Pinneberg. "We think differently from most working men, our needs are different."

"Think different!" said Mörschel. "Think different! You think just like any proletarian."

"I believe not," said Pinneberg. "I, for instance . . ."

"You, for instance," said Mörschel, fixing him with an

18

evil leer. "You, for instance, have had an advance, eh?"

"Advance?"

"Yes. An advance on Emma. Not very nice behavior. Very proletarian habit, too."

"I . . ." began Pinneberg; he grew very red, and longed to pull the place about their ears.

Frau Mörschel said sharply: "No more from you, father. That's all over. Keep your nose out of it."

A knock. "There comes Karl," cried Bunny.

"Let's have supper, then, wife," said Mörschel. "But I'm right, son-in-law, you ask your parson. Very bad behavior."

A young man came in; young only in age, yellower and more bilious than his father. He growled: "Ev'nin'," took no notice of the guest, pulled off his jacket and waistcoat, and then his shirt. Pinneberg observed him with growing astonishment.

"Overtime?" asked the old man.

Karl Mörschel grunted.

"That will do, Karl," said Frau Mörschel. "Come and eat."

Karl let the tap run full on and began to wash very intensively. He was naked to the hips. Pinneberg felt a little embarrassed for Bunny, but she seemed not to notice it.

There was much that Pinneberg could not help noticing: the ugly earthenware plates, blackened and chipped, the half-cold oniony potato pancakes, the sour gherkins, the tepid bottled beer for the men, this dismal kitchen, Karl at the sink . . .

"That's Emma's young man," said Frau Mörschel. "They're going to be married soon."

"So she's done it, has she?" said Karl. "A bourgeois, eh? A working man wasn't good enough for her."

"You see," said Herr Mörschel, with great satisfaction.

"What do you mean by 'you see'?" snarled Karl. "Sooner an honest bourgeois any day than you Social Fascists."

"Social Fascists," raged the old man. "Who's a fascist, you little Soviet toady!"

"Who!" says Karl. "You damned old jingo . . ."

Pinneberg listened to these words with a certain satisfaction.

But the potato pancakes tasted no better.

In general it was not a very festive engagement dinner.

3.

A little conversation at night about love and money.

THEY sat in the kitchen, their backs against the cold stove. The door to the little kitchen balcony stood open, the curtain stirred faintly in the breeze. Outside—over a stifling yard, all asquawk with radios—hung the canopy of night, scattered with stars.

"I should like," said Pinneberg softly, pressing Bunny's hand, "to have a rather nice little home. You know what I mean—very bright, white curtains, everything always terribly clean."

"I understand," said Bunny. "It *is* horrid for you here. Karl and father always quarrelling, mother and father just as bad, mother always cheating over the housekeeping and the food . . . it's all horrid."

"But why are they like that? There are three people earning, you ought to be quite well off."

Bunny did not answer. She went on: "I don't really belong here. I've always been the drudge. When father and Karl come home, their day's work is over. But I have to start in to wash up and iron and sew and darn stockings. Oh, it isn't so much that," she cried. "I'd do that and not mind. But what I do mind is that it's all taken for granted. I just get pushed about and never a word of thanks, and Karl behaves as though he were helping to keep me, just because he pays more for his board than I do. I don't earn

21

much—you know what a shop-girl makes nowadays."

"It'll soon be over," said Pinneberg.

"Oh, it isn't that," she cried in despair. "It isn't really that. But you know, darling, they've always just despised me, and called me silly. Of course, I'm *not* very clever. There's a lot I don't understand. And then they keep telling me I'm not pretty."

"But you *are!*"

"You're the first that's ever said so."

An uncomfortable feeling crept over Pinneberg. Really, he thought, she oughtn't to tell me that. I always found her pretty. Maybe she isn't after all.

"Well, darling, I'm not going to worry you with complaints. I'll only tell you this one time, that I don't belong here, I belong only to you. And I'm so awfully grateful to you, not only because of the baby, but for taking the poor little drudge away."

"Dear," he said. "Dear!"

"No, wait a minute.—And when you say you want the place bright and clean, you must be a bit patient, I've never really learnt how to cook. And if I do anything wrong, you must tell me, and I'll never, never tell you any lies."

"Please, Bunny!"

"And we'll never, never quarrel. Darling, we'll be so happy, just the two of us alone. And the boy."

"Suppose it's a girl."

"It'll be a boy, a sweet little boy."

After a while they stood up and walked on to the balcony. Yes, there was the sky over the roofs, there were the stars. For a while they stood in silence, their hands on each other's shoulders. Then they came back to the nar-

row yard, the countless lit window-squares, the din of
jazz.

Silence.

"Darling," said Bunny softly: "I must ask you something."

"Yes?"

"Don't be angry."

"No."

"Have you saved anything?"

Pause.

"A bit," hesitatingly. "Have you?"

"A bit," and then, hurriedly: "only a very, very little
bit."

"How much?"

"You say first."

"I . . ."

"Tell me."

"It's really only a very little, perhaps less than you."

"I'm sure it's not."

"I'm sure it is."

Long pause.

"Ask me," he implored.

"Well then," drawing a deep breath, "is it more
than . . ."

"Than what?"

She laughed. "After all, why should I mind telling? I've
got a hundred and thirty marks in the savings bank."

To which he replied, slowly and proudly: "Four hundred and seventy."

"Fine," said Bunny. "We'll manage easily. Six hundred
marks. Darling, what a lot of money!"

"Well . . . I don't think it's so much. A bachelor's life is so expensive."

"And out of my hundred and twenty marks wages, I pay seventy for board and lodging."

"Takes a long time to save as much as that."

"Awfully long. Money comes in and then it's gone."

Pause.

"I don't think we'll be able to find a home at Ducherow at once," he said.

"Then we must take a furnished room."

"Yes, and we'll be able to save up more for furniture."

"A furnished room is pretty expensive, isn't it?"

"Well, let's figure it up."

"All right. Let's figure there's nothing in the bank."

"Yes, we mustn't touch that, we'll have to put some more by. Now, a hundred and eighty marks . . ."

"But you'll get more as a married man."

"I'm not so sure." He looked very embarrassed. "By the wage scale, perhaps, but my chief is so funny. Bunny, let's figure first with the hundred and eighty. If I can get more, so much the better."

"All right," she agreed. "First the deductions."

"Yes, they have to be paid anyway. Taxes, 6 marks, and Unemployment Insurance, 2 marks 70. Employees' Insurance, 4 marks. Sick benefit, 5 marks 40. Trades Union, 4 marks 50 . . ."

"Oh, that Union of yours isn't necessary."

Pinneberg said rather impatiently, "That'll do, thank you. I've had enough of that from your father."

"Oh, all right. That makes 22 marks 60 to come off before we begin. You don't need carfare?"

"Thank heaven, no."

"Well, that leaves 157 marks. What will the rent come to?"

"I don't know yet. Room and kitchen, furnished. 40 marks anyway."

"Say 45," said Bunny sagely. "That leaves 112 marks 40. Food?"

"Mother always says she needs 1 mark 50 a day per person."

"That's 90 a month."

"Which leaves 22 marks 40."

They looked at each other.

Bunny went on hurriedly: "And then we've nothing left for coal and nothing for gas. And nothing for light. And nothing for postage. And nothing for clothes. And nothing for underclothes. And nothing for shoes. And cup and saucers."

"Yes," he said, "and we must go to the movies sometimes; and take a little trip somewhere on Sunday. And I like a cigarette once in a while."

"And we want to save something."

"At least twenty marks a month."

"Thirty."

"But how?"

"Let's add up again."

"The insurance payments and so on will have to stand."

"And we can't get a room and a kitchen cheaper than what I said."

"Maybe five marks cheaper."

"Well, I'll see. We ought to take in a newspaper."

"Of course. But we might save on food, ten marks a month, perhaps."

They looked at each other again.

"Even then we can't manage. And there's nothing left for savings."

"Dear," she said, anxiously, "must you have your linen starched? I can't starch it for you myself."

"Yes, the boss insists on it. A shirt costs sixty pfennigs to starch, and a collar ten pfennigs."

"That's another five a month."

Pause.

"Well, let's add up again."

After a while: "Then knock another ten off the food. But I can't do it cheaper than that."

"But what do other people do?"

"I can't think. There must be plenty who've got less than we have."

"I don't understand it."

"We must be wrong somewhere. Let's add up again."

They added and added, but could come to no other result. "Look here," said Bunny suddenly. "When I marry I can get my Employees' Insurance paid out to me, can't I?"

"Fine," said he. "That's sure to come to a hundred and twenty marks."

"And your mother," she said. "You've never told me about her."

"There's nothing to tell," he said shortly. "I never write to her."

"I see," said Bunny.

They got up and walked to the balcony. The yard was almost dark now, the town had grown quiet. Far away a motor horn hooted.

Still plunged in his thoughts, he said: "It costs eighty pfennigs for a haircut."

26

"Oh, shut up," she said. "If others can do it we can too."

"Listen, Bunny. I won't give you any housekeeping money. At the beginning of the month we'll put all the money into a pot, and each of us take what we need."

"Yes," she said. "I've got a nice little blue earthenware pot that will just do. I'll show it you. Maybe I can learn to starch shirt-fronts."

"I'll give up five-pfennig cigarettes. You can get pretty good ones for three."

Suddenly she gave a little shriek: "But, darling, we've forgotten the baby! He'll cost money."

He reflected: "I don't think a little baby can cost much, can it? Besides we'll be drawing allowances when you're confined and while you're nursing it and we'll have less taxes to pay. I don't believe the first few years cost anything."

"I don't know," she said doubtfully.

In the doorway stood a white form.

"Aren't you ever going to bed?" asked Frau Mörschel. "You can get three hours' sleep still."

"Yes, mother."

"It's all right," said the old woman. "I'm sleeping with father tonight. Karl won't be back. Take him with you, he's your—" The door slammed before she could say what he was.

"But, please, I would rather not," said Pinneberg, a little offended. "It really is very awkward here, with your parents and all."

"My dear boy," she said laughing, "Karl was right. You are a bourgeois."

"Not a bit of it," he protested. "If it doesn't disturb

27

your parents." He hesitated again: "And supposing Dr. Sesam was wrong, I haven't got anything with me."

"Then let's go and sit down in the kitchen again," she suggested. "I feel so depressed."

"Of course I'll come, Bunny," he said penitently.

"But if you don't want to—?"

"I'm a fool, Bunny."

"Well," said Emma Mörschel, "we ought to make a fine pair."

"We'll soon find out," said Johannes Pinneberg.

PART ONE

The Little Town

*Marriage begins correctly with a wedding-trip
but—do we need a saucepan?*

THE 2 : 10 train that left Platz for Ducherow on that
Sunday afternoon of August, carried in a third-class non-
smoking compartment Herr and Frau Pinneberg, and in
its baggage-car a large basket-trunk containing Emma's
possessions, a sack with Emma's bedding—but only for
her own bed, the family could not spare more—and an
egg-chest with Emma's crockery.

There was only one other occupant of the compartment, a morose-looking personage who could not make up
his mind whether to read the paper, look at the landscape,
or stare at the young couple. He abruptly turned from
one to the other, and whenever the two thought they were
quite safe, they found themselves caught.

Pinneberg ostentatiously laid his right hand on his knee.
The ring shone encouragingly. But their fellow-traveller
just at that moment insisted on looking at the landscape.

"Looks nice, the ring does," said Pinneberg. "You
couldn't tell it was only gilt."

"Do you know it's funny about my ring. I keep on feeling and looking at it."

"That's because you aren't used to it yet. People who've
been married a long while don't notice it. They don't even
know when they've lost it."

"Not me," said Bunny indignantly. "I'll always know I'm wearing it."

"So will I," said Pinneberg. "It reminds me of you."

"And me of you."

They bent towards each other, nearer and nearer; and then jumped back as they caught the old creature's shameless eyes upon them.

"Not from Ducherow," whispered Pinneberg.

"Do you all know each other?"

"Pretty well—anyone that matters. I got to know them all when I was a salesman in Bergmann's Ladies and Gentlemen's Outfitters."

"Why did you give it up? It was really your sort of job."

"Had a scrap with the boss."

Bunny would have liked to enquire further, but she scented another abyss.

Pause.

"Dear," began Bunny again, "I'm so terribly excited about where we're going to live."

"Well, I hope you'll like it. There isn't much choice in Ducherow."

"Never mind, describe it again."

"Right," said he. "I've already said that it's quite outside the town. Right in the country. With the widow Scharrenhofer."

"What's she like?"

"I hardly know how to tell you. She puts on airs and says she's seen better days, but owing to the inflation . . . She wept all over me one day."

"Oh Lord!"

"She won't always do that. Besides she won't have a

chance—we're going to keep to ourselves, aren't we? We won't have anything to do with other people."

"Of course. But suppose she's very persistent?"

"I don't think she will be. She's really a fine old lady with white hair and all that. And she's terribly particular about her furniture; it's all very nice and belonged to her mother. We have to sit down very gently on the sofa, so as not to break the springs."

"If only I can remember," said Bunny, doubtfully. "But when I've got the blues and want to howl, I sit down hard—and I just won't think of those darn springs."

"You must," said Pinneberg sternly. "You've got to. And you can't wind up the clock under the glass case on the mantelpiece. Neither can I."

"Oh, let her take her old clock away! Let's get back to the rooms. You go up the staircase and there's the landing door and then . . ."

"Then comes a little hall, which we share. The first door on the left is our kitchen. That is, it isn't a real kitchen, it was originally only a sort of attic under the sloping roof, but there's a gas-cooker . . ."

"With two burners," completed Bunny gloomily. "And how I'm going to manage I don't know. You can't cook a meal on two burners. Mother has four."

"We'll have quite simple meals, two burners will be quite enough."

"Of course. Still, you want soup, don't you? First saucepan. Then meat; second saucepan. Vegetables; third saucepan. And potatoes; fourth saucepan. While I'm warming two saucepans on the two burners, the two others are getting cold. Well—?"

"Yes," he said, lost in thought, "I don't know

either." Then suddenly, in a flurry: "You'll need four saucepans!"

"I certainly shall," proudly. "And they won't be enough. I'll want a stewpan, too."

"Oh Lord, and I've only bought one pan for the whole business."

The merciless Bunny: "Then we must buy four more."

"But that means spending out of savings again."

"Can't be helped, darling. What must be, must be, we've got to have those saucepans."

"Well, I didn't think it was going to be like this," he said, sadly. "I thought we'd manage on what we have and save money; and here we're starting out at once by spending it."

"But since we must . . ."

"What do we need a stewpan for?" he said irritably. "I never eat stew. Imagine buying a whole saucepan just for a little bit of stew. Never!"

"And how am I going to roast, or . . ."

"And there's no running water in the kitchen," he said in despair. "You'll always have to go into Frau Scharrenhofer's kitchen for water."

From far away a marriage looks extraordinarily simple. Two people marry and have children. They live together, they are quite nice to each other, and try to get on in the world. Companionship, love, kindness, eating, drinking, sleeping, business, housekeeping, an excursion on Sundays, and a movie sometimes in the evening.

But from near at hand, the whole affair dissolves into a thousand individual problems. Marriage in some sense disappears into the background, it is taken for granted, it is the basis of everything: but what about this stewpan, for instance? The reality is the stewpan.

Dimly they both felt this. But these are not yet urgent problems; the saucepans were forgotten in their sudden realization that they were alone in the compartment. The morose personage had got out somewhere unobserved. The stewpan and the mantelpiece clock were forgotten, they fell into each other's arms; and the train rumbled on. From time to time they drew breath, and then they kissed again, until the slower movement of the train said: Ducherow.

"Oh dear! Already?"

*Pinneberg grows mysterious and Bunny has
some riddles to solve.*

"I'VE ordered a car," said Pinneberg hastily. "It would
have been too far for you to walk."

"You didn't! And we who want to save money! Why
only last Sunday we walked about Platz for two hours."

"But all your things!"

"A porter could have brought them. Or someone from
your firm. You must have workmen."

"No; that wouldn't do at all. Besides," he said hurriedly, as the train braked to a standstill, "we don't want
to behave as if we were married, but as if we had only
just met."

"But why?" asked Bunny in amazement. "We *are* married, aren't we?"

"Well," he said awkwardly, "it's because of the people
here. We haven't sent out any cards, and we haven't put
any notice in the paper. And if they see us they might very
well be offended, don't you see?"

"No, I don't. How on earth could people be offended
because we're married?"

"I'll explain all that later on. But not now. Are you
carrying your suitcase? Now please pretend you don't
know me very well."

Bunny glanced up doubtfully at this young man beside
her. He suddenly became elaborately polite, helped his

companion out of the carriage, said: "This is the main Ducherow station. There is also the local line to Maxfelde. This way, please." He preceded her down the steps from the platform, really a little too fast for a husband solicitous enough to order a car in case the walk should be too much for his wife—two or three steps ahead of her; and then out through a side exit, where a closed car waited.

"Good day, Herr Pinneberg," said the chauffeur. "Good day, Fräulein."

Pinneberg murmured hastily: "One moment, please. Perhaps you wouldn't mind getting in? I'll see about the bags."

Bunny surveyed the station square, with its small two-storied houses. Right opposite was the station hotel.

"Can't we have the hood off the car?" asked Bunny. "It's such a lovely day."

"I'm very sorry," said the chauffeur. "Herr Pinneberg particularly ordered a closed car. Otherwise I certainly shouldn't have the hood up on a day like this."

"All right, if Herr Pinneberg said so." She got in.

She saw him walking towards her behind the porter, who was pushing the trunk, the sack of bedding and the egg-box on his trolley. And because she had been looking at this man of hers for the last five minutes with quite different eyes, she was struck by the fact that he kept his right hand in his trouser pocket.

They drove off.

"There," he said, with rather an embarrassed laugh. "Now you'll get a view of the whole of Ducherow—really just one long street."

"You were going to explain why the people might be offended."

37

"Later on," he said. "We can't talk in the car. The roads are so bad in these parts."

She was silent. But another thing surprised her: he kept his head far back out of sight against the upholstery.

"There's your firm," she said. "Emil Kleinholz. Corn, Fodder, and Manures. Potatoes Wholesale and Retail. I can come and buy my potatoes from you."

"No, no," he said hastily. "That's an old sign-board. We don't sell potatoes retail any more."

"That's a pity," she said. "It would have been so nice if I could have come to your office and bought ten pounds of potatoes. I wouldn't have let on I was your wife, dear."

"Yes, it's a pity," he agreed. "It would have been nice."

She tapped her foot sharply on the floor of the car, and breathed in little snorts of indignation, but said no more.

They drove on. They must be out of the main street by now. Bunny saw written up: "Feldstrasse." They were in a road of single houses, all set in their gardens.

"Dear, it's lovely here," she said delightedly. "Look at all the flowers!"

The car began to jolt unmistakably.

"Now we're at Green End," he said.

"Green End?"

"Yes, our road's called Green End."

"Is this a road? I thought the man had missed his way."

On the left was a meadow fenced with barbed wire, tenanted by a few cows and a horse. On the right was a clover field, spread with clover now in blossom.

"Do open the window," she begged.

"But we're just there."

Where the meadow came to an end, the cleared ground

ended too. Here the town had planted its last monument, a lank and lofty erection, painted brown and yellow in front, the side walls being left unpainted in expectation of adjoining buildings.

"It's very nice inside," he said, glancing at Bunny's face.

"Well, let's go in. Of course it'll be fine for the baby. So healthy."

Pinneberg and the chauffeur picked up the wicker trunk. Bunny carried the egg-box. The chauffeur said he would go down again and get the sack.

The ground floor, where the shop was, smelt of cheese and potatoes. On the first floor the smell of cheese predominated; on the second floor it ruled undisputed; the top floor, again, was pervaded by the musty dank odor of potatoes.

"How is it there's no smell of cheese up here?"

But Pinneberg was already opening the door.

They crossed the tiny hall; it was very small indeed. A wardrobe stood on the left, a chest on the right. The men could hardly get the trunk through.

"Here!" Pinneberg pushed open a door.

Bunny stepped in and uttered a cry of bewilderment.

Then she threw everything she was carrying on to an old plush-covered sofa—the springs groaned under the impact of the egg-chest—ran to one of the four large, sunny windows in the long room, flung it open, and leaned out.

Below her was the road, a rough sandy track overgrown with grass and thistles. Opposite was the clover field, and now she could smell it; nothing smells so glorious as blossoming clover after a day of sunshine.

39

Beyond the clover field were other fields, yellow and green, and a few rye fields already under stubble. Then came a strip of deep green—meadows—and between the meadows and the alders and the poplars flowed the Strela, here quite a narrow little stream.

After Platz, thought Bunny, where I drudged and was so lonely and so wretched, with nothing to look at but a yard. Nothing but walls and stones. Here I can see right away into the distance.

Just then, at the window beside her, she caught sight of her young husband's beaming face.

"Look: you can really feel alive here."

She reached him her right hand out of her window, and he took it with his left.

"The whole summer!" she cried and described a half-circle with her free hand.

"Do you see the little train? That's the local line to Maxfelde," he said.

The chauffeur appeared from below. He had been into the shop, for he hailed them with a bottle of beer. The man carefully wiped the lip of the bottle with the palm of his hand, tipped his head back, cried, "Good health!" and drank.

"Your very best!" said Pinneberg, dropping Bunny's hand.

"There," said Bunny; "and now we'll have a look at the Chamber of Horrors."

They turned from gazing at the bright and placid country landscape to contemplate a room in which . . . Well, Bunny was really not spoilt, her highest ideal was the plain and unadorned furniture she had once seen in a

shop-window on the Mainzerstrasse at Platz. But
this!

"I think you'd better take my hand, darling," she said.
"I'm afraid I'll get stuck somewhere and not be able
to go back or forward."

"It's not so bad as all that," he said, rather hurt.
"There are some cosy little corners, I think."

They started on a tour of the room, but though they
mostly had to walk one in front of the other, Bunny would
not let go her lad's hand.

The room was a sort of cleft or passage, not particularly narrow, but very very long. Four-fifths of it was
stacked with upholstered furniture, walnut tables, over-
mantels, consoles, flower-stands, whatnots, and a large
parrot-cage (without parrot) ; in the remaining fifth there
were two beds and a wash basin. But the partition between the two sections of the room was what attracted
Bunny. It was not a screen or a curtain or anything of
that kind, but a sort of trellis-work contrivance reaching
from floor to ceiling. The slats were not just plain wooden
slats; they were made of walnut, grooved, and stained a
beautiful brown. To prevent the trellis looking bare it
was intertwined with artificial flowers, roses, narcissi, and
violets; and with long green paper garlands reminiscent
of festive beer-evenings.

"Oh Lord!" said Bunny, and sat down. She sat down
where she stood, encountering a rush-bottomed ebony
piano-stool that happened to be standing there, widowed
of its piano. Pinneberg looked on dumbly. He had really
been rather attracted when he took the place. The trellis
had seemed distinctly gay.

41

Suddenly Bunny's eyes began to sparkle, her legs recovered strength, she got up, approached the flowered
trellis, passed her finger over one of the slats.

"There." She held out a gray finger to Pinneberg.

"A little dusty," he said cautiously.

"A little!" Her eyes were blazing. "You'll let me have
a charwoman, I suppose? I shall want a woman here at
least five hours a day."

"What on earth for?"

"Who's going to keep all this clean, please? I might
have managed the ninety-three bits of furniture with all
their knobs and legs and ins-and-outs. Though it would
have been a wicked waste of time. But this trellis means
three hours' work a day. And the paper flowers."

She flicked at a rose. The rose fell off, millions of gray
specks of dust whirled after it through the sunlit room.

"You'll let me have a charwoman, won't you?" asked
Bunny, now a Bunny no more.

"But surely you could clean it up thoroughly once a
week?"

"Rubbish! And this is where the baby's got to grow
up. Can't you see him knocking himself about against all
this trash?"

"But I hope we'll have a place of our own before
then."

"Before then! And how's it going to be kept warm in
the winter? Two outer walls! Four windows! Half a
hundredweight of briquettes every day, and we'll be freez-
ing even then."

"But look here," he said, now rather roused, "a furnished place isn't the same as one's own, of course."

"I know that. But what do you think of it yourself? Do

42

you like it? Do you want to live here? Think of yourself coming back home and bumping about into all this stuff, and—ow! Just as I thought, the covers are stuck on with pins."

"But we won't find anything better."

"*I'll* find something better. When can we give notice?"

"September first. But—"

"For when?"

"September thirtieth. But—"

"Six weeks," she groaned. "Well, I'll manage to survive. I'm sorry the poor kid should have to go through it all as well. I thought I should be able to take him for nice walks into the country—no, I'll have to spend my time polishing the furniture."

"But we can't give notice at once."

"Of course we can. I'd like to do it now, today, this very minute!"

There she stood, resolute, flushed, aggressive, fury in her eyes.

Pinneberg said slowly: "Do you know, Bunny, I didn't think you were like this. I thought you were much gentler."

She laughed, flung her arms round his neck, stroked his hair. "Of course I'm quite different from what you thought, I know that too. Do you think a girl who went straight from school into business, and had to hold her own against my brother and my father and the bosses in the shop and the other girls, would be a little softie?"

He murmured something reflectively.

The clock, the famous glass-covered clock on the mantelpiece—flanked by a Cupid with a hammer and a glass thrush—gasped seven.

43

3.

The Pinnebergs pay a courtesy call.

SUPPER was over.

"Let's clear away now," said Bunny. "I can wash up early tomorrow morning. Now I'll collect the first lot of stuff and we'll go and see Frau Scharrenhofer."

"Do you really mean it—the very first evening?"

"She'd better know at once. Besides she could have come out long ago."

In the kitchen, really no more than a garret with a gas-cooker, Bunny merely said: "Well, six weeks don't last forever."

In the living-room Bunny got very busy. She took off all the covers and crochet and embroidery and laid them neatly together. "Quick, darling, a saucer. She shan't think we want to keep her pins."

At last: "There."

She laid the pile of covers over her arm and looked enquiringly about her: "You take the clock, dear."

"Shall I really—?"

"Take the clock. I'll go in front and open the doors for you." And she did so, quite unconcerned, first across the little hall, then into a cupboard-like room full of brooms and suchlike, then through a kitchen.

("There, darling, this is something like a kitchen. And I can only come here to get water!")

44

. . . Then through a bedroom, like an elongated towel, but with two beds.

("So she's kept her late husband's bed? Why couldn't we have slept here?")

. . . And then into a little room, almost entirely dark, the plush curtains drawn close across the single window.

Frau Pinneberg remained standing in the doorway, looking uncertainly into the darkness: "Good evening. We just came in to say good evening."

"One moment," said a tearful voice. "Just one moment. I'll turn on the light."

Behind Bunny, Pinneberg was busy at a table, she heard a faint whirr from the precious clock. He was disposing of it as expeditiously as he could.

All men are cowards, decided Bunny.

"I'll turn on the light at once," said the mournful voice, still from the same corner. "Are you the young people? I must just tidy myself first, I always cry a little in the evening."

"Is that so?" says Bunny. "But if we are disturbing you. We only wanted to . . ."

"No, I'll turn on the light. Please stay, young people. I'll tell you why I was crying, and I will turn on the light."

Then the light appeared: one faint electric bulb flush against the ceiling, a dim twilight shed on plush and velvet, pallid, deathly gray. In the gloom sat a tall bony woman, with a livid complexion, a long and reddish nose, bleary eyes, sparse gray hair, wearing a gray alpaca dress.

"The young people?" she said. "Come to see me, have you?" She gave Bunny a damp bony hand.

Bunny pressed her bundle close to her side. She hoped

45

the old creature would not see it with those dimmed and tearful eyes. She was glad that the lad had got rid of the clock, perhaps they could take it away again unnoticed. Bunny's courage had evaporated.

"We really don't want to disturb you," said Bunny.

"Of course you don't disturb me. No one comes to see me now. Ah yes, they came when my dear husband was alive. But it's a good thing he is dead."

"Was he very ill?" asked Bunny, and then felt quite shocked at her silly question.

But the old woman had not heard: "Young people," she said, "before the war we had a comfortable fifty thousand marks. And now the money is all gone. How can money go?" she asked anxiously. "An old woman can't spend all that?"

"The inflation," Pinneberg made the mild suggestion.

"It can't be all gone," said the old woman, unheeding. "I sit here and add. I've always put everything down. I sit and add. There it stands: a pound of butter, three thousand marks. Can a pound of butter cost three thousand marks?"

"In the inflation," began Bunny on her own account.

"I will tell you. I know now that my money was stolen. Someone who lodged here stole it. I sit and wonder who it was. But I cannot remember names, and so many have lived here since the war. I sit and rack my brains. His name will come back to me. He must have been very clever to falsify my accounts without my noticing. He changed three into three thousand, and I never noticed."

Bunny looked despairingly at Pinneberg. Pinneberg did not look up.

"Fifty thousand— How can fifty thousand all be

46

gone? I've sat here and added up all I bought in the years since my husband died; stockings and a few shirtwaists; I had a lovely trousseau, and I don't need much. Not five thousand, I tell you."

"But it was the depreciation of money," said Bunny in a fresh attempt.

"He robbed me," said the old woman. The bright tears trickled from her eyes. "I will show you the books, I noticed that the figures became quite different after a while —so many noughts."

She got up and went to the mahogany writing table.

"Please don't trouble," said Pinneberg and Bunny.

At that moment the awful thing happened: the clock, which Pinneberg had put down in the old woman's bedroom, stuttered nine quick strokes. The old woman stopped half-way. With raised head she peered into the darkness, listening with parted quivering lips.

"Yes?" she said, uneasily.

Bunny felt for Pinneberg's arm.

"That's the clock my husband gave me at our betrothal. But it used to be in the other room."

The clock had stopped striking.

"We wanted to ask you, Frau Scharrenhofer . . ." began Bunny.

The old woman did not hear; perhaps, indeed, she never listened to anything other people said. She opened the half-closed door: there stood the clock, unmistakable even in that dim light. "The young people have brought my clock back," she muttered. "The clock my husband gave me. The young people don't like being here. They will not stay. No one stays."

And as she spoke, the clock began to strike again, more

47

rapidly and even more gaspily than before, ten times, fifteen, twenty, thirty times.

"That comes from carrying it. It won't stand being carried now," whispered Pinneberg.

"Oh Lord, let's get out of this," implored Bunny.

They got up; but the old woman stood in the doorway, still staring at the clock, and would not let them pass. "It strikes," she whispered; "It goes on striking. And then it will not strike again. This is the last time I shall hear it. Everything goes from me. Three thousand marks for butter. When the clock struck, I always thought how my husband used to listen to it too."

The clock was silent.

"Please, Frau Scharrenhofer, I am very sorry to have touched your clock."

"It's my fault," sobbed Bunny. "It was really me."

"Go, young people, go away now. This had to be. Good night, young people."

The pair slipped past her, nervously, like two scared children.

Suddenly the woman called after them in a voice now clear and strong: "Don't forget to report to the police on Monday, or I'll get into trouble."

4.

Bergmann and Kleinholz, and why Pinneberg must not be married.

"Awful!" Bunny drew a deep breath.

"The old woman's mad from worry over her money."

"She is; and I . . ." The pair stood hand in hand in the darkness . . . "and I've got to be here all day for her to come in whenever she likes. No! No!"

"Don't get excited. She wasn't like this before."

"*Young people . . .*" repeated Bunny: "she said it so horribly, as if she had some secret we couldn't know about. Oh darling, I won't get like her? I won't get like her, shall I? I'm afraid."

"But you're Bunny," he said, and took her in his arms. She was so helpless, so tall and helpless. "You're Bunny, and you'll always be Bunny, how can you get like old Scharrenhofer?"

"I won't, will I? And it *can't* be good for the baby to go on living here. I won't have him frightened; his mother ought always to be cheerful, so that he'll be cheerful too."

"Yes, yes," he said, stroking her, rocking her in his arms. "That'll be all right, we'll manage, you'll see."

"Oh yes, you say so; but you don't promise we'll go away, and at once."

"But how can we? How can we afford to pay two rents for six weeks?"

"Oh, money!" said she. "Am I to be scared out of my wits and the baby born ugly for the sake of a few marks?"

"Yes, money," he said; "just money. It's hateful, but we can't do without it."

He rocked her in his arms. Suddenly he felt wise and old; things that had always seemed to matter did not matter now. He could be honest: "I haven't any talent, you know, Bunny. I won't get on in the world. We'll always have to struggle for money."

"Dear," she said. There was a lilt in her voice. "Dear."

The pair walked arm in arm to the open window and leaned out.

The country lay flooded in moonlight. Away to the right gleamed a small flickering point: the last gas lamp on the road. Before them lay the country, a clear bright expanse, flecked with soft deep shadows where the trees stood. It was so still they could hear the Strela rippling over its stony bed.

"How lovely it is," she said; "how peaceful."

"Yes, you can breathe here a little better than you could at home in Platz."

"At home? I'm not at Platz, and I don't belong to Platz any more. I'm at Green End, at the widow Scharrenhofer's."

"Where do I come in?"

"Oh you don't come in at all!"

. . . . . .

"Shall we go out again?"

"Not now, darling, let's rest for a bit. Besides there's something I want to ask you."

Now for it.

But she did not ask. She lay there by the window, her fair hair fluttering faintly in the evening breeze. He watched it.

"So peaceful," said Bunny.

"Come to bed, Bunny."

"Can't we stay up just a minute? We can sleep late to-morrow. And I want to ask you something."

"Go ahead!"

There was an irritated ring in his voice. Pinneberg took out a cigarette, lit it carefully, inhaled a deep draught of smoke, and said, but in a noticeably gentler tone: "What is it, Bunny?"

"Won't you tell me yourself?"

"I don't know what you want to ask."

"You know!"

"I *don't,* Bunny."

"You know!"

"Please be sensible. Do ask."

"You know!"

"All right, don't then."

"Darling, don't you remember when we sat in the kitchen at Platz? The day we got engaged. It was quite dark and so many stars and we walked out on the balcony."

"Yes," he said peevishly. "I remember all that."

"Don't you remember what we promised?"

"Good Lord, we talked about all sorts of things; you don't expect me to remember it all now."

There lay the moonlit country outspread before the gaze of Frau Pinneberg, née Mörschel. On the right the little gas lamp twinkled. Opposite, not far from the bank of the Strela, stood a clump of five or six trees. The Strela rippled through the darkness and the night breeze was very soft.

It seemed a shame to mar the peace and calm. But something bored into Bunny's mind like an insistent voice: all this contentment was a fraud and self-betrayal. She must not give way to it or she would find herself up to the ears in trouble.

Bunny abruptly turned her back to the landscape and said: "Yes, we did make each other a promise. We solemnly promised we would always be honest and have no secrets from each other."

"Pardon me, it wasn't quite that. That's what you promised me."

"And aren't you going to be honest?"

"Of course I am.—But there are things women don't need to know."

"Oh!" Bunny was quite taken aback. But she soon recovered herself and said quickly: "You gave the chauffeur five marks when the meter read two marks forty? Is that the kind of thing we women are not to know?"

"He carried the trunk and the sack upstairs."

"Two marks sixty for that? And why did you keep your right hand in your pocket so that people shouldn't see your ring? And why did the car have to have the hood up? And why wouldn't you go down with me to the shop just now? And why might people be offended because we're married? And why . . . ?"

"Bunny," he said; "Bunny, I'd rather you didn't."

"It's all so silly, dear," she answered. "You simply mustn't have any secrets from me. If we have secrets

52

from each other, we'll start telling lies, and then we'll
be just like everyone else."

"Yes, Bunny, but . . ."

"You can tell me everything, darling, everything. Even
if you call me Bunny, I'm not a fool. You've got nothing
to be ashamed of."

"Yes, yes, Bunny, but it isn't quite so simple, you know.
I would like to, but . . . it looks so silly, it sounds
so."

"Is it something to do with a girl?" she asked firmly.

"No. No. At least—not in the way you think."

"How, then? Tell me. I can't bear this much longer."

He hesitated. "Can't I tell you tomorrow?"

"Now! This very instant! Do you think I can sleep
when I'm racking my brains like this? It's something to
do with a girl, and yet it's nothing to do with a girl.
It sounds so *mysterious*."

"All right then, listen. I'll have to begin with Bergmann. I started in Bergmann's shop, you know."

"The outfitter's? Yes, I know. I should think that was
a much nicer job than selling potatoes and manures. Manures—do you really sell *dung?*"

"Look here, if you aren't going to be serious,
Bunny."

"I'm listening." She had sat down again on the
window-ledge. Her eyes wandered sometimes from her
young husband to the moonlit countryside.

"Well, then, in Bergmann's I was first salesman at a
hundred and seventy marks a month."

"First salesman at a hundred and seventy!"

"Do be quiet! I always had to wait on Herr Emil

53

Kleinholz. He needed a good many suits. He drinks, you know. He can't very well help it when he's doing business with the farmers. He can't stand much drink; and he falls down in the street and spoils his clothes."

"Nasty!"

"Listen. So I always had to wait on him, he wouldn't have anything to do with the boss or the boss's wife. They could never get him to buy a thing, but I could sell him quite a lot. And he often told me that if I ever wanted a change and got sick of working for Jews, he had a good clean Arian business and could offer me a good job as book-keeper, at better pay than I was getting then. I thought to myself: That's all very well. I know what I've got; Bergmann isn't a bad sort, always very decent to his employees."

"Then why on earth did you leave him for Kleinholz?"

"Oh well, there was a bit of trouble. It's the custom here at Ducherow, Bunny, for every firm to send an apprentice to the postoffice for the mail in the morning. Among them were others in our line of business: Stern and Neuwirth and Moses Minden. And the apprentices are strictly forbidden to show each other the letters. On every packet they have to cross out at once the name of the sender so that our competitors won't know from whom we buy. But the apprentices are all old friends from the Technical School, they get talking and they forget to cross out the names. And some of the firms, Moses Minden for instance, aren't above a little spying.

"Well, the Reichsbanner wanted to buy three hundred khaki tunics. And all the four firms were asked to submit bids. We knew the others were doing all they could to find out where we got our patterns. And we didn't trust the apprentices so I suggested to Bergmann that I should go and get the mail for the time being, myself."

"Well? And did they find out?" asked Bunny eagerly.

"No," he answered indignantly. "Of course not. If an apprentice had come within ten yards of my letters, I'd have clouted his head for him. *We* got the contract."

"Oh do hurry up, darling. I want to hear about this mysterious girl. Why did you leave Bergmann?"

"Yes, but I've just told you that there was some trouble over it," he said awkwardly. "I got the mail myself for a couple of weeks. The boss's wife liked this arrangement; I had nothing to do in the shop between eight and nine, and during the time I was out, the apprentices were able to clean up the place, so she just said: 'Herr Pinneberg had always better get the mail,' and I said; 'No, that's not my job. First salesmen don't carry parcels through the streets.' And she said: 'Oh yes they do'; And I said, 'No!' and finally we both lost our tempers and I said: 'I don't take orders from you. I was hired by the boss.' "

"And what did the boss say?"

"What could he say? He couldn't put his wife in the wrong. He did his best to persuade me, I wouldn't budge an inch and so—well, what could he say but: 'I'm afraid we'll have to part, Herr Pinneberg!' And I said—I was pretty hot about it: 'All right, we'll part the first of next month.' And he said: 'You'll think it over, Herr Pinneberg.' And I would have thought it over, but unfortunately Kleinholz came into the shop the same day and noticed that I was excited, and he got me to tell him the whole story, and arranged for me to come and see him that evening. We drank a lot of beer and brandy, and when I went home at night I was engaged as book-keeper at a hundred and eighty marks. And what did I know about book-keeping?"

Bunny said reflectively, "What about this girl business?"

"Ah, that was the trouble. I've lived in Ducherow for four years and I never knew Kleinholz wanted to marry off his daughter at any price. The mother's bad enough, she nags all day and trails around in a kimono. But the daughter Marie—she's a beast."

"And it was she you were to marry, poor darling?"

"It was she I *am* to marry. All Kleinholz's men are unmarried—there are three of us—but she's got her eye mainly on me."

"How old is Marie?"

"I don't know," he said shortly. "Yes I do. Thirty-two; or thirty-three. Anyhow it doesn't matter. I'm not marrying her now."

Bunny's voice was sympathetic. "Thirty-three—and you're only twenty-three. It's impossible!"

"It happens all the time," muttered Pinneberg.

Bunny looked up at his morose face.

"You must admit, darling, it *is* funny. Is she a good match?"

"Not even that. The business doesn't bring in much now. Old Kleinholz drinks too hard, and then he buys too dear and sells too cheap. Is that a way to run a business? And besides the boy will inherit it, he's only ten. Marie will only get a few thousand marks, if that much, which is nothing to run after."

"So that's that," said Bunny. "And you weren't going to tell me about it? And that's why you got married so secretly, with a closed car and your ring hand in your trouser pocket?"

"Yes. Oh Bunny, if it comes out that I'm married those women will have me on the pavement inside of a week, and then what?"

"You must go back to Bergmann."

"No, I couldn't do that. You see," he swallowed, then controlled his voice; "Bergmann prophesied that the Kleinholz job would go wrong. He said: 'Pinneberg, there's nowhere else for you to go in Ducherow. You'll come back to me and I'll take you back. But you'll have to beg for it. I'll let you hang about the Labor Exchange and my shop for a month, begging for work. I can't let you off after such cheek.' That's what Bergmann said, and I can't go back to him now. I won't do it."

"But you can see for yourself he was right."

"Bunny," Pinneberg implored, "please, dear Bunny, don't ask me! Of course he was right and I was a fool and it didn't matter in the least about the letters. If you kept at me I'd go and he'd take me back. But the boss's wife and the other salesman—that fool Mamlock— would never let me forget it and I'd never forgive you."

"No. No. I won't ask you to, don't worry. But surely it's bound to be known, however careful we are."

"It *mustn't* be! I did everything so secretly and now we're living out here and no one ever sees us together and even if we meet on the street, we won't know each other."

Bunny was silent for a while, then she said, "But we can't go on living here, you see that for yourself."

"Try, Bunny," he implored. "Till the first anyway. We can't give notice before then."

She reflected for a while before she agreed. She peered down that tunnel-like room, but could distinguish nothing, it was too dark.

"All right," she sighed. "I'll try. But you know yourself it can't go on. We'll never be happy here."

"Thank you, dear. And we'll manage somehow. But I mustn't lose my job."

"No, you mustn't lose your job."

They looked out once more over the silent moonlit country and went to bed. No need to draw the curtains. There was no one opposite. As they fell asleep they thought they could hear the faint rustle of the Strela.

5.

The master of the Pinneberg destiny.

MONDAY morning. Pinneberg's employer, Kleinholz (corn-merchant) and family were getting up. This was never a pleasant process on any morning. They were all in a specially bad temper at that hour and inclined to tell each other the truth. But Monday morning was the worst of all. On Sunday evenings the father was rather given to escapades which took their toll when he awoke.

Frau Emilie Kleinholz was not exactly a gentle character. So far as a man could be tamed, she had tamed her husband. The last few Sundays he had been behaving himself quite well. Emilie would shut the door, provide her husband with a bottle of beer for his supper, and then cheer him up with an allowance of brandy. The family evening would follow its usual course: the boy crawled about in a corner (he was a bit feeble-minded), the women sat at the table sewing (for Marie's trousseau), and father read the paper, occasionally suggesting, "Just one more drop, mother." To which Frau Kleinholz would invariably reply: "Father, think of the boy," and then pour a little more out of the bottle, or not, according to her husband's condition.

Thus had passed this last night. All had gone to bed about ten o'clock. About eleven Frau Kleinholz awoke.

59

In the next room she heard her daughter Marie's breathing, the familiar sounds of the boy, who slept at the foot of his father's bed, but father's snores were missing from the chorus.

Frau Kleinholz felt under her pillow; the house doorkey was there. Frau Kleinholz lit a candle; her husband was not there. Frau Kleinholz got up, Frau Kleinholz searched all through the house, Frau Kleinholz went down into the cellar, Frau Kleinholz walked across the yard (the toilet was in the yard) : not a sign of anyone. Finally she discovered that a window in the office, which she was quite certain she had closed and bolted, was half-open.

Frau Kleinholz became a prey to a raging tearing fury: a quarter of a bottle of brandy, a bottle of beer, wasted! Hurriedly she put on a few clothes, flung around her person a quilted lilac dressing gown, and sallied forth. He would certainly be drinking at Bruhn's pothouse at the corner of the street.

"Kleinholz: Corn-merchants" on the Market Square, was a fine old-established business. Emil was the third generation to possess it. It had grown into a sound and respected concern, with some three hundred customers of old standing, farmers and land-owners. When Emil Kleinholz said: "Franz, the cotton-seed cake is good to-day," Franz did not ask for a chemical analysis, he bought that cake, and behold, it was good.

But there was one snare in such a business; it had to be kept moist, being in its very nature a damp trade. Over every truckload of potatoes, every invoice, every sort of deal—beer, whiskey, brandy. All very well when a man's wife is his friend, when the home is happy and united, but it will not do at all when the wife is always nagging.

Frau Emilie Kleinholz had always nagged. She knew it was foolish, but Emilie was jealous, she had married a fine well-to-do man, and she herself had been a poor thing with hardly a penny; she had captured him from all the rest. So after four and thirty years of marriage she fought for him as she had done at the very beginning.

In her slippers and dressing gown she shuffled along to Bruhn's tavern at the corner. Her husband was not there. She could have asked politely whether he had been there, but that was beyond her. She told the landlord he was a brute and beast for selling drink to drunkards and threatened to report him for forcing liquor on his customers. Old Bruhn himself, a tall gray-beard, ran her out of his shop; she struggled furiously, but his was a firm and steady grip.

"There, young lady," says he.

There she stood in the market square of a small provincial town, with cobbled roadways, two-storied houses, some gabled and some square-fronted, all curtained and all dark. The gas lamps flared and flickered.

Go home? Emil would taunt her for days if she went to look for him and didn't find him. Find him she must, and drag him away from his boon companions, from all the gaieties he loved.

Suddenly it flashed upon her: there was a dance that evening at the Tivoli.

Just as she stood, in slippers and dressing gown, she made her way half across the town to the Tivoli. The cashier demanded a mark for entrance; she asked him if he wanted his ears boxed; he said no more.

She found herself in the dance hall, at first a trifle embarrassed, and peered at the crowd from behind a pillar; but she soon flared into fury. Yonder was her fair-bearded Emil, still a fine figure of a man, dancing—dancing with a little dark-haired bitch whom she did not know. The master of ceremonies said: "Madam—if you please—Madam!"

But this was an Act of God, a tornado, a volcanic eruption before which men are powerless. He stepped back. A passage opened and between two human walls she marched up to the one couple that still stumbled heedlessly round the hall.

Suddenly she slapped his face. "My little sweetie!" says he, not understanding. And then he understood.

She knew that she must now depart, and depart with dignity. She gave him her arm: "Time to go, Emil. Come now."

He went. Crushed, humbled, he shuffled out of the room on his wife's arm; like a great beaten dog he glanced round once at his smart little dark-haired companion from Stossel's fringe-factory, who hadn't had so much fun in her life, and had been hugely delighted with her gay, open-handed cavalier. He went; and she went. A car had suddenly appeared at the door: the management had had sufficient intelligence to realize that in such contingencies the best thing to do is to telephone for a car.

Emil Kleinholz went to sleep on the journey, nor did he awake when his wife, with the chauffeur's aid, carried him into the house and to the hated marriage-bed he had left in such eager anticipation just two hours before. He slept. His wife put out the light, lay for a while in darkness; she lit the light again, and looked at her husband, her handsome, reckless, fair-haired husband. Beneath those pale and sodden features she saw him as he once had been, gay and impudent, a lover who laughed at her when she boxed his ears for his shameless advances.

And so far as her little foolish brain could think, she thought of the road they had travelled since that day. Two children, a scarecrow of a daughter and a half-witted son. A decaying business, a dissipated husband—and what of herself?

Well, she could weep, and that she could do in darkness, and so save light, when so much was being wasted. She fell to wondering how much he had spent in those two hours; she lit the candle again, felt in his pocket-book, reckoned, added. Then she wept again, and at last went to sleep, as people always do at last go to sleep, after toothache and childbirth, after disaster, and the great joys that come so rarely.

Then came the first awakening about five o'clock, when she hurriedly gave the stable-man the key to the oats-bin; then the second at six, when the servant knocked and fetched the key to the larder. One more hour's sleep! One more hour's rest! Then the third and final awakening at a quarter to seven. The boy had to get off to school; her husband was still asleep. She looked into the bedroom again at a quarter past eight. He was awake, and feeling sick.

"Serves you right for always getting drunk," she said, and went away again.

He came down to coffee, dark, silent, dishevelled.

"A herring, Marie."

"You ought to be ashamed to make such a beast of

63

yourself," said his daughter tartly, before she fetched the herring.

"God damn it!" he roared. "I can't stand the sight of that girl much longer!"

"You're quite right, father," said his wife soothingly. "What are those three young fools for, eh?"

"Pinneberg's the best. He's the man."

"Of course. You just put the screws on a bit."

"I will."

Then he went across to his office: Johannes Pinneberg's employer, and master of his, of Bunny's, and of the yet unborn baby's destinies.

6.

*Lauterbach the Nazi, the demonic Schulz, and the
husband-in-secret get into difficulties.*

LAUTERBACH was first at the office: five minutes to eight.
Boredom rather than a sense of duty was responsible for
this punctuality. He was short, fat and fair-haired, with
huge red hands. Formerly a bailiff, he found that he preferred town life, and finally ended up in Ducherow with
Emil Kleinholz. There he became a sort of expert on
seeds and manures. The farmers were not overjoyed to
see him beside the wagon when they delivered potatoes.
He noticed at once when the potatoes were not properly
sorted and when they tried to pass off white Silesians
among the yellow Industrials. Otherwise he was not so
bad. He was not, indeed, to be bribed with drinks—the
Arian race should be preserved from such demoralizing
poisons—nor with cigars. He clapped the farmers on the
back, called them "Old scoundrels!" and knocked ten,
fifteen, twenty per cent off their prices. However, he wore
the Nazi badge, he had a repertoire of excellent jokes
about Jews, and told them all about the latest Storm
Detachment recruiting march to Buhrkow and Lensahn.
In a word, he was a good sound German, an enemy of the
Jews, the French, Reparations, Socialists and the Communist Party. Which made up for everything.

He soon realized that Ducherow was no better than

the country at providing employment for his spare time. He did not care about girls, and as the movies did not open till eight, and church service was over at half past ten, there was a long interval to be filled. It was thus he joined the Nazis.

The Nazis kept him interested. He was soon promoted to a Storm Detachment and in street fights proved himself an extraordinarily astute young man, who used his fists (and what happened to be in them) with an almost artistic feeling for effect. Lauterbach's yearning for life was satisfied; he could get a fight almost every Sunday and sometimes on a week-day in the evening.

When Pinneberg arrived punctually at eight, Lauterbach promptly greeted him with: "The Storm Detachments are to have new badges. Very neat, I call 'em. Up to now, you remember, we only had the storm number, sewn on to the tunic. Now we'll have an edging in two colors round the tunic collars. Get it? So you can see the numbers from behind. Now, suppose I'm in a row. All right. Right ahead of me is a guy getting beaten up. I look at the back of his collar. What do I see?—"

"Amazing." Pinneberg was sorting the Saturday waybills. "Was Munich 387536 a full truck-load?"

Schulz, the third of the trio, came in about ten minutes past eight. At his appearance Nazi badges and wheat way-bills were forgotten. The demonic Schulz, as brilliant as he was unreliable, Schulz who could reckon in his head the total of 285.85 hundredweight at 3 marks 85, quicker than Pinneberg could do the sum on paper; but a slave to women, an unscrupulous libertine who couldn't keep his hands off anything in skirts, the only man who had managed to snatch a kiss in passing from Marie Klein-

66

holz, out of sheer exuberance, without being pinned down to marry that lady on the spot.

Schulz, with his dark pomaded hair, yellow lined face, and great black shining eyes; Schulz, the dandy of Ducherow, with creased trousers and black felt hat (fifty centimeters in diameter), Schulz with his beringed and nicotine-stained fingers, Schulz, king of the servant-maids, idol of the shop-girls, for whom they waited of an evening outside the office, and over whom they quarrelled at dances.

Schulz said: " 'Morning"; carefully hung up his jacket on a coat-hanger, and surveyed his colleagues, first with sympathy, then with complete contempt. "You haven't heard anything, of course."

"I know," said Lauterbach. "A different servant-girl, but the same story."

"You're a couple of ignorant nit-wits. You sit here adding up way-bills, making up the accounts, and all the time . . ."

"What do you mean?"

"Emil . . . and Emilie . . . yesterday evening at the Tivoli."

"Do you mean he took her with him? Nonsense!"

Schulz sat down. "The clover samples should be out by now. Who's attending to that, you or Lauterbach?"

"You are."

"Not my job, thank you. Our little friend the agricultural expert had better see about it. Well, the old man was hopping around with that little dark-haired girl, Frieda, from the fringe-factory, I was only two steps away, when the old lady appeared. She came down on him like a ton of bricks—didn't have a thing on but a dressing gown and maybe her night-dress underneath."

"At the Tivoli—?"

"Take it easy, Schulz."

"True as I'm sitting here. There was a big dance on with the military band from Platz, Reichswehr in uniform, everything going full blast. All of a sudden who blows in but our Emilie, hauls off at the old man, yells at him for a drunken old swine."

Sensation in the Kleinholz office—interrupted by the entrance of Emil Kleinholz.

The trio leapt apart and sat down on their stools with much rustling of papers. Kleinholz contemplated three bent heads.

"Nothing to do, eh?" he rasped out. "What about firing one of you?"

The way-bills continued to receive absorbed attention.

"We hear a lot about rationalization these days. Where three are idle two might find enough work. What about you, Pinneberg? You're the youngest here." Pinneberg did not answer.

"Can't open your mouths, of course, any of you. But you found plenty to say about the old woman, didn't you? I've a good mind to kick you all into the street."

The swine's been listening, they thought, terror gripping at their hearts. Oh God, what did I say?

"We weren't talking about you at all, Herr Kleinholz," said Schulz, in a low tone, almost to himself.

"Well, and you?" said Kleinholz, turning on Lauterbach. But Lauterbach was not as nervous as his two colleagues. Lauterbach was one of those rare employees who don't care a hang whether they've got a job or not. Afraid? thought Lauterbach. With these fists? What

68

have I got to be afraid of? I can get a job as a groom or a porter. Clerk, indeed! Hooey!

Lauterbach looked fearlessly into the old man's bloodshot eyes. "Yes, Herr Kleinholz?"

Kleinholz banged on the railing before the clerk's desks until it quivered. "I'll fire one of this little crew! You'll see. And the other two needn't think they've got safe jobs. Plenty more where you came from. Go along with Kruse to the loft, Lauterbach, and get five tons of ground-nut cake meal into sacks. No, stop; let Schulz go; he looks like his own corpse again this morning, it'll do him good to lift the sacks."

Schulz disappeared without a word, delighted to have made his escape.

"You go to the station, Pinneberg, and look alive about it. Order four twenty-ton trucks for tomorrow morning, closed ones. We've got to get the wheat off to the mills."

"Very good, Herr Kleinholz," said Pinneberg, and dashed off. It was probably only old Kleinholz's hangover that made him talk like that. Still . . .

On his way back from the station to the office, he noticed someone walking along on the other side of the street; a girl, a woman . . . his wife.

Slowly he crossed the street.

Bunny came towards him, with a net bag in her hand. She hadn't noticed him. She stopped and looked into Brecht the butcher's shop-window. He came quite close to her, looked cautiously round and up at the houses. Nothing dangerous in sight.

"How's the shopping going, young lady?" he whispered over her shoulder, and shot past her, though he turned round once to look at her happy glowing face. If Frau

69

Brecht had caught sight of him from the shop-window, she knew him, he always bought his sausages there . . . it was very reckless of him, still, what could a man do with a wife like that? So she hadn't yet bought those saucepans, apparently, they must really be very careful about money.

The old man sat in the office: alone. Lauterbach was out: Schulz too. Bad, thought Pinneberg, very bad. But Kleinholz paid no attention to him. With his forehead in one hand, he slowly passed the other hand over page after page of the cash-book, as though spelling out the columns of figures.

Pinneberg sized up the situation and thought he would do best at the typewriter. When a man's typing, he reflected, he's pretty safe from interruption.

"We have the honor of enclosing a sample of our red clover, this year's crop, guaranteed, ninety-five per cent productive, ninety-nine per cent pure."

He felt a hand on his shoulder. "Just a moment, Pinneberg."

"I beg your pardon, Herr Kleinholz?" Pinneberg raised his fingers from the keys.

"Writing about the clover, eh? Leave that to Lauterbach."

"But . . ."

"All right about the trucks?"

"Quite all right, Herr Kleinholz."

"Well, we must get busy this afternoon and sack the corn. The women must help too—tie up the sacks."

"Yes, Herr Kleinholz."

"Marie's very handy at that sort of thing. She's handy at most things; not pretty, maybe, but useful."

"Certainly, Herr Kleinholz."

There they sat, one facing the other. A kind of lull fell upon the conversation. Herr Kleinholz wanted to let his words sink into the other's mind; they were to act as a sort of developer and show what picture was on the plate.

Pinneberg sat and stared gloomily at his master, as he squatted on his chair in a suit of heavy green tweed, and high boots.

"Yes, Pinneberg," began the boss once more. His voice sounded quite sentimental. "Have you thought it over? How do you feel about it?"

Pinneberg reflected nervously. But he knew of no way out. "About what, Herr Kleinholz?" he asked feebly.

"About this firing business," said his master, after a long pause. "Who would you let out if you were in my place?"

Pinneberg grew hot all over. What a brute the man was to torment him this way!

"That I can't say, Herr Kleinholz," he said uneasily. "I can't speak against my colleagues."

Herr Kleinholz was enjoying the situation. "You wouldn't fire yourself if you were me?"

"If I were you? Really, Herr Kleinholz, I can't . . ."

"Well," said Herr Kleinholz, getting up: "I'm sure you'll think it over. You're engaged by the month. That would mean notice on September 1st for October 1st, wouldn't it?"

Kleinholz walked out of the office to report to mother how he had put the screws on Pinneberg. Perhaps mother might give him a drink. He needed one.

7.

Pea soup is prepared and a letter written; but the water is too thin.

BUNNY quickly hung the bedding out of the windows to air and went out. Why didn't he say what he wanted for dinner? She didn't know what to get and she had no idea what he liked.

The possibilities diminished as she meditated, until at last there remained only—pea soup. Pea soup was easy, pea soup was cheap, pea soup would hold over till to-morrow.

How she envied the girls who had been taught to cook! Her mother had always chased her away from the stove, cursing her for a clumsy fool.

What did she need? Water; water she had. Also a saucepan. Peas, but how much? Half a pound would surely be enough for two people, peas go a long way. Salt? Herbs? A little fat. How much meat? What sort of meat anyway? Beef of course. Half a pound's sure to be enough. Peas are very nourishing, too much meat is unhealthy. Potatoes naturally.

It was very pleasant to stroll about on a week-day morning, the streets empty of people, the air still fresh though the sun was already hot.

A large yellow mail car hooted slowly across the market place. Perhaps he was sitting behind those very windows.

72

But he was not: ten minutes later he asked her over her shoulder how her shopping was getting on. The butcher's wife must certainly have noticed something, she was so funny, and asked thirty pfennigs a pound for soup bones, bare bones at that, without a scrap of meat on them, which ought to have been thrown in free. She'd write mother and ask whether this was right. No, better not, better manage by herself. But she must write to his mother. On her way home she began to compose the letter.

Old Scharrenhofer was evidently a night-walking ghost. The kitchen showed no sign that anything had been or ever would be cooked. All was blank and cold. In the room beyond there was not a sound. She put her peas on. Should she put the salt in at once? Better wait until they had boiled, then she could judge how much was wanted.

After that she must dust the furniture. It was hard work, even harder than Bunny had thought. Oh those awful paper roses, those garlands, some faded, some a poisonous green, this threadbare upholstery, all these nooks and corners and knobs and ornaments. She must finish by half past eleven so as to write her letter. He had from twelve until two for lunch but he could hardly be back before a quarter to one, as he had to report at the Town Hall.

At a quarter to twelve she was sitting at a small walnut writing table with a bit of yellow notepaper dating from her girlhood open in front of her: *"Frau Marie Pinneberg—Berlin N.W. 40—Spenerstrasse 92 II."*

It simply had to be written, even if Hans didn't get on with her and didn't approve the way she lived. After all, he was the only son, the only child. She had a right to be told about the marriage.

73

"Mother ought to be ashamed of herself," Pinneberg
had said.

"But, darling, she's been a widow for twenty years!"

"That makes no difference; and anyhow, it isn't always
the same man."

"But, my dear, you've had more girls than me."

"That's different."

"What will the baby say when he figures out when he
was born?"

"We don't know yet when he'll be born."

"Oh yes I do. The beginning of March."

"How do you know?"

"Never mind, I do. And I'm writing to your mother
because it's right I should."

"Do as you like but leave me out of it."

Bunny nibbled her pen. "Dear Madam" seemed so silly
and out of place. "Dear Frau Pinneberg"? But that's
what she was herself, and it didn't sound right either.
Her husband would certainly read the letter.

Oh well, thought Bunny, either she's like what he
thinks she is and then it doesn't matter how I write, or
she's a nice woman and in that case I'd sooner write as I
feel. So—

Dear mother: I am your new daughter-in-law Emma,
known as Bunny, and Hans and I got married the day before yesterday, on Saturday. We are very happy and
contented and should be glad to know that you are
pleased. We are getting on all right except that Hans had
unfortunately to leave his dress-shop, and now works in
the manure business, which we don't like so much.

With best regards from

Your Bunny.

She left a space for Hans to write his name beside hers.
She still had half an hour to spare so she picked up a
book she had bought last week. With furrowed brow she
pored over *Motherhood: The Sacred Miracle*.

*"Yes, these are the happy, sunny days, when baby
comes. Thus does divine Nature make good our human
imperfections."*

This didn't seem very clear; it didn't seem to have
much to do with her own little baby. Then came some
lines of poetry, which she read slowly to herself, several
times over:

> *Baby-mouth, baby-mouth,*
> *So wise a tiny thing;*
> *You can talk the talk of birds,*
> *Like Solomon the king.*

Bunny didn't wholly understand this either. But it
sounded cheerful; she leaned back in her chair—sometimes
her body felt so heavy—and repeated the lines to herself
with closed eyes: "Baby-mouth, baby-mouth."

A baby must be about the nicest thing in the world.
"Talk the talk of birds."

"Lunch!" shouted Hans from the landing outside. She
must have dozed off, she often felt so tired these days.

"My lunch," she reflected, and got up slowly.

"Table not set yet?" he asked.

"Won't be a minute, dear." She hurried into the kitchen.
"Can I bring the pot to the table? I'll use the tureen if
you like."

"What is there?"

"Pea soup."

"Fine. No, bring the pot. I'll set the table meanwhile."

Bunny poured out the soup. She looked a little worried. "Doesn't it seem a bit thin?"

"I'm sure it's all right," he said, cutting up the meat on the little plate.

She tasted it. "Heavens, how thin!—And I forgot the salt!"

He too let his spoon drop, and across the plates, across the thick brown enamel pot, their eyes met.

"And I meant it to be so good," wailed Bunny. "I got everything: half a pound of peas, half a pound of meat, a whole pound of bones—it should have turned out such a good soup!"

He got up and stirred the soup meditatively with the large enamel ladle: "I can feel something every once in a while. How much water did you use, Bunny?"

"It must be the peas! There's just nothing to them."

"How much water did you put in?"

"I filled up the pot."

"About five quarts—and half a pound of peas. I think, Bunny," he said mysteriously, "it's the water that's the trouble. The water is too thin."

"Really?" she asked gloomily. "Did I use too much? Five quarts? It was to last two days."

"Five quarts—I think that's too much for two days." Again he tasted. "Sorry, Bunny, but it's really only hot water."

"My poor darling, are you just starved? Shall I run and get a couple of eggs, and make fried eggs and potatoes? I know I can do that all right."

"Fine," says he. "I'll go get the eggs myself."

When he came back into the kitchen her eyes were wet,

and not from the onions that she had cut up into the potatoes.

She flung both arms round his neck: "Darling, I'm such an awful housewife. I should so like to have everything nice for you. And if the baby doesn't get proper food, he won't thrive."

"Do you mean now or later?" he asked, laughing. "Do you think you'll never learn?"

"There, you're teasing me now."

"I was just thinking about the soup on the way upstairs. There was nothing wrong with it except you used too much water. If you put it on again and let it boil for a while, the extra water will all boil away, and then we'll have some first-rate pea soup."

"Fine," she said beaming. "I'll do it this afternoon and we'll have a plateful each for supper."

They took their potatoes and fried eggs into the sitting-room. "Is it all right? Is that how you like it? I'm afraid it's very late. Can't you rest for a bit? You look so tired, dear."

"No. Not because it's late, but I couldn't sleep today. This fellow Kleinholz . . ."

He had for some time been debating whether he should tell her. But last night they had agreed there should be no more secrets between them. So he told her. Besides, it does a man good to relieve his mind.

"Well, what shall I do now?" he concluded. "If I say nothing, he'll certainly fire me on the first. Suppose I just tell him the truth? Suppose I tell him I'm married—he can't just turn me out on the street."

Bunny became her father's daughter. "He doesn't care," she said indignantly. "Maybe there used to be a few decent ones. But today, in these hard times when they have to carry on anyhow, they think their own men don't matter."

"Kleinholz really isn't a bad fellow," said Pinneberg. "He's just thoughtless. I might be able to put it right with him and explain about the baby and so . . ."

Bunny burst out: "Are you going to tell him that! A man who's trying to blackmail you? No, dear, you can't do it."

"But I must say something to the man."

"I should talk to the other two," said Bunny, after a pause. "Perhaps he's threatened them the same way. If you stick together he can't fire all three of you."

"It might work," he said, "if I could trust them. Lauterbach wouldn't let me down, he's too big a fool, but Schulz . . ."

Bunny believed in the solidarity of all workers. "They'll back you up, don't worry. No, darling, that's the best thing to do. I'm quite sure nothing will go wrong with us. Why should it? We work hard, we're careful, we aren't bad people, we want the baby—we want him very much, don't we? Why should things go wrong? It wouldn't make sense!"

8.

A pact is sworn. Still no pea soup.

IT was in the Kleinholz granary that afternoon that things came to a head. Kleinholz, after giving voice to a particularly nasty series of threats and insinuations, disappeared in the general direction of Emilie and the brandy bottle, leaving the three clerks staring at each other over their weighing-scales. The same fear lay at the heart of each of them.

"We ought to watch out for him one night when he's drunk," said the doughty Lauterbach, "and beat him up so he'll remember it. That'd help."

Said Schulz: "I'm sick of this place."

"Well then, let's do something," suggested Pinneberg. "Didn't he speak to you this morning?"

The three surveyed each other: and in their eyes was doubt, mistrust and constraint.

"I'll tell you something," said Pinneberg. "The first thing this morning he started on me about Marie, how clever she was—and that on the first of next month, as far as I understood, I should have to say whether I would let myself be fired, because I was the youngest, and Marie . . ."

"Yes, he spoke to me too. He said my being a Nazi gave him a lot of trouble."

79

"Me too. He complained because I take a girl out once in a while."

Pinneberg drew a deep breath: "Well, then?"

"How do you mean?"

"What are you going to say on the first of next month?"

"Say——?"

"Whether you want Marie?"

"Good God, no!"

"I'd go on the dole first!"

"Well then?"

"What do you mean?"

"Let's all make an agreement."

"What sort of agreement?"

"For instance: let's solemnly promise that we'll all three refuse Marie."

"But he won't say anything about her, Emil isn't such a fool as that."

"He can't fire us on account of Marie."

"Well, then, let's agree that if he fires one of us, the others will give notice too. On our honor."

The three surveyed each other with misgiving: each was considering his chances of being fired and whether it would pay him to give his word of honor.

"He certainly won't let all three of us go," urged Pinneberg.

"Pinneberg's right there," agreed Lauterbach. "He couldn't do that just now. I'll give my word."

"So will I. And you, Schulz?"

"I will too."

"All settled, then?"

"I promise."

"I promise."

How pleased Bunny will be, thought the lad. Safe for another month.

All three went back to their scales.

It was about eleven when Pinneberg got home. He found Bunny asleep, huddled in the corner of the sofa. Her face was the face of a child who had cried herself out. Her eyelids were still wet.

"Thank God you're here at last! I was so scared!"

"What for? What on earth could happen to me? I had to work overtime—I have to every three days or so."

"And I was so frightened! Are you very hungry?"

"I should say I am. There's a funny smell here, isn't there?"

"Funny—what do you mean?" Bunny sniffed. "Oh my pea soup!"

They both rushed into the kitchen where they were met by an appalling stench.

"Open the windows! Open the windows quick! Make a draught!"

"Turn the gas off first!"

When the atmosphere was a little clearer they both looked into the large pot.

"My lovely pea soup," whispered Bunny.

"Looks like charcoal."

"And all that lovely meat."

They stared into the pot, the bottom and sides of which were covered with a black, smelly, sticky paste.

"I put it on at five," Bunny told him: "I thought you'd be back at seven. So that all that water would boil away. And then you didn't come and I was so frightened and I forgot all about the stupid pot."

"That's spoilt too," said Pinneberg gloomily.

"Perhaps I can get it all off again," said Bunny doubtfully, "with the right sort of brush."

"All costs money," said Pinneberg shortly. "When I think of the money we've thrown away these last few days. And now all these pots and brushes and dinners; it would have paid for three weeks' food at a boarding-house.—It's all very well to cry, but it's true."

"And I took so much pains, dear," she sobbed out. "Only when I'm frightened about you, I can't think of food. If you had only come back half an hour earlier; we'd have turned off the gas-jet in time."

"Well, well," said Pinneberg, clapping the cover on to the pot. "It's all under the head of experience. I . . ." he stiffened heroically: "I make mistakes myself. No need to cry. And now—how about some food? I'm simply starved."

9.

A Pinneberg excursion arouses interest in certain quarters.

AT breakfast on the morning of Saturday, August thirtieth, Bunny had repeated: "Then you're sure to be free tomorrow. Let's take the train to Maxfelde."

"It's Lauterbach's turn at the stables," said Pinneberg. "We'll go tomorrow, I promise."

"And we'll take a row-boat and row across the Maxe lake, and up the Maxe river." She laughed.

"I've got to get back to the office—bye-bye, wife!"

"Bye-bye, husband!"

Then came Lauterbach to Pinneberg: "Listen, Pinneberg, we've got a recruiting march tomorrow, and my group-leader says I've absolutely got to be there. Will you do the stables for me?"

"Awfully sorry, Lauterbach, but I simply can't tomorrow. Any other time with pleasure. How about Schulz?"

"No, Schulz can't either. He's in a jam with some girl, over maintenance. Now, please—"

"This time I can't."

"But you never have anything on."

"Well, this time I have."

"I'll do two Sundays for you, Pinneberg."

"No, I won't do it. It's no good asking any more."

83

"Well, I think it's lousy of you—when I've had special orders."

That was the beginning: but there was more to come. Two hours later Kleinholz and Pinneberg were alone in the office, which was full of a summer hum and buzz of flies. The boss was very flushed, he had clearly had several drinks that day, and was in a good temper.

He began quite amiably: "Mind doing the stables for Lauterbach tomorrow, Pinneberg? He wants the day off."

Pinneberg looked up: "I'm awfully sorry, Herr Kleinholz. I can't tomorrow. I already told Lauterbach."

"Surely you can manage as usual, you've never had anything important on."

"I'm sorry I can't this time, Herr Kleinholz."

Herr Kleinholz stared fixedly at his book-keeper: "Look here, Pinneberg, I don't want any trouble from you. I've given Lauterbach his leave and I can't withdraw it now."

Pinneberg did not answer.

"You see, Pinneberg," went on Emil Kleinholz, again in a kindly tone, "Lauterbach isn't any too bright, I'll admit. But he's a Nazi and his group-leader is Rothsprack the miller. And Rothsprack is very useful to us when we want a job done quickly."

"But I really can't, Herr Kleinholz."

"I might have got Schulz," proceeded Kleinholz meditatively, "but he can't either. He's got to go to some family funeral tomorrow and afterward the property's to be distributed. So he must go, you see, or the others will hog the show."

(His confounded women! thought Pinneberg).

"Yes, Herr Kleinholz," he began.

But Kleinholz was wound up: "As far as I'm concerned, Herr Pinneberg, I'd gladly do the job—I never mind obliging, as you know."

"That's so, Herr Kleinholz."

"But tomorrow I can't either. I've got to go out to the country and see about getting in some orders for clover. We haven't sold any at all this year." He looked expectantly at Pinneberg. "I must go on a Sunday, Pinneberg, because I'm sure of finding the farmers at home."

"I just can't, Herr Kleinholz."

Kleinholz now dropped from the clouds. "But I've just explained that no one has the time except you."

"But I haven't the time, Herr Kleinholz."

"Herr Pinneberg. You surely don't suggest I should do the work for you tomorrow simply because you don't feel like it. What are you doing tomorrow?"

"I . . ." began Pinneberg: "I must . . ." He fell silent.

"I can't lose money over my clover, just because you're being awkward, Herr Pinneberg. Be reasonable!"

"I am being reasonable, Herr Kleinholz. Really I can't do it."

Herr Kleinholz got up and walked backwards to the door, glaring darkly at his book-keeper. "I am greatly disappointed in you, Herr Pinneberg," he said. "Greatly disappointed."

The door slammed.

. . . . . .

They were sitting in the Maxfelde train, crowded even though it left Ducherow at six. Maxfelde and the Maxe lake and the Maxe river were a disappointment. There

85

was too much noise and crowd and dust. Thousands of
people had come from Platz, their cars and tents stood
in hundreds by the lake side. The few boats had long since
been hired.

Pinneberg and his Emma are just married, their hearts
hungry for solitude. This turmoil is frightful.

"Let's get away somewhere," suggested Pinneberg:
"Where there are trees and water and hills."

"But where?"

"It doesn't matter. Away from here, anyway. We'll
find some place."

And they found a place. At first the forest path was
fairly broad and pretty well crowded with people; then
Bunny discovered a smell of mushrooms under the
beeches. She lured him deeper and deeper into the forest
until they suddenly found themselves on a stretch of grass
between two wooded slopes. They clambered up the other
side, hand in hand, and when they reached the top found
a glade that led them up and down hill further and further into the green solitude.

Slowly the sun climbed the sky and time and again the
sea wind from the distant Baltic rustled gloriously in the
tree tops. The sea wind used also to reach Platz, which
had been Bunny's home so long ago. She told her husband about the only summer holiday she had ever had:
nine days in Bavaria, four girls together.

He too became suddenly talkative: he told her how he
had always been alone and could not get on with his
mother. She had never bothered about him and he had
always been in the way of her love affairs. Hers was such
a dreadful job. It was a long time before he could bring
himself to confess it: she was a barmaid.

Bunny grew thoughtful again and found herself regretting her letter. A barmaid is really something rather special. She wasn't clear as to what they did, never yet having been in a bar, but what she had heard of the duties of such ladies didn't seem to suggest that one of them could be old enough to be her husband's mother. She had much better have written to her in more formal terms. However, it was now of course too late to ask Pinneberg about that.

For quite a while they walked along in silence, hand in hand. But just as this silence began to grow burdensome and seemed to be carrying them apart, Bunny said: "Darling, how happy we are!" and held up her face to be kissed.

At that moment it happened.

On the sandy road that ran along the edge of the forest a motor car slid up behind them, soft and silent as though on felt slippers. When the two noticed it and started awkwardly apart, it was already about abreast of them. Although they really ought to have been able to see the faces of the occupants of the car in profile only, these faces were turned fully towards them. They were astonished faces, stern and indignant faces.

Bunny didn't understand; she thought the people stared at them rather stupidly, as though they had never seen a kissing couple before. More especially she didn't understand why her husband suddenly flung away from her and made a deep bow towards the car.

Then, as though at a secret word of command, all the faces reverted to profile, nobody took any notice of Pinneberg's magnificent bow, and with a rasping hoot from the

87

horn the car speeded up, plunged into the forest, and with a flash of red enamel, vanished.

Pinneberg stood there, deadly pale, his hands in his pockets; "That's done for us, Bunny. He'll fire me tomorrow."

"Who will?"

"Kleinholz, of course. Good God, you didn't know? Those were the Kleinholzes!"

"Oh Lord!" said Bunny and drew a deep breath: "Well, that's a bit of bad luck."

And she took her tall young husband in her arms and comforted him as well as she could.

IO.

How Pinneberg strove with the Angel and with Marie Kleinholz and how it was too late.

EVERY Sunday is succeeded by its Monday.

At the corner of the market square Pinneberg looked about him. Yes, there came Kranz the town clerk. When the two men were about abreast they took off their hats.

When he had passed Pinneberg held out his right hand. The gold wedding ring glittered in the sun. Slowly Pinneberg slid the ring off his finger, slowly he felt for his pocket-book, and then, with an air of quick defiance, put it back. Erect he marched to meet his fate.

Fate was some time in arriving. Not even the punctual Lauterbach was in his place that Monday, and of the Kleinholz family nothing was to be seen.

At about a quarter past eight Schulz shuffled in, very yellow, very ill-tempered.

"Have a good Sunday, Schulz?"

"God damn it!" said Schulz, and burst out into a torrent of oaths; then, after a spell of gloomy silence, he rapped out savagely: "Remember I told you that about eight or nine months ago in Helldorf I went to a dance with a girl—and Christ! what a cow she was! Well, now she says I'm the father of the kid and must pay up. Me—can you imagine?—I spent the whole day yesterday in Helldorf, trying to find out who else she'd been with but

89

these damned farm-hands, they all stick together. But I'll make her swear to what she says, if she dares."

"And if she does dare?"

"I'll tell the judge just what happened. Look here, Pinneberg, what do you think yourself?—I danced with the girl twice, and then I said: It's so smoky in here, shall we go outside for a minute?—We only missed one dance —why does it have to be me? Bosh!"

"But if you can't prove anything?"

"She's lying, and the judge is sure to see it. Besides, Pinneberg, what can I do on the pay we get?"

"Today's the first of the month," said Pinneberg casually.

But Schulz did not hear; he merely groaned: "And I'm sick as a dog, I hoisted too many yesterday."

At twenty past eight Lauterbach came in.

A black eye: *one*. Left hand in a bandage: *two*. Face covered with scars: *three, four, five*. On the back of his head a black silk plaster, a pervasive reek of chloroform: *six, seven*. And what a nose, what a swollen, bloody nose! *eight*. Under-lip split and protruding like a negro's: *nine*. *Knock-out*, Lauterbach. Is this the reward of patriotism?

The other two danced round him in huge excitement.

"Boy, they sure got to you this time!"

"Oh Ernst, will you never learn!"

Lauterbach sat down, very stiff and cautious. "This is nothing. Wait till you see my back!"

"But why on earth?"

"Ah, that's the sort of man I am. I could have stayed at home today but I thought of all the work you fellows would have to do."

"And today's the day when one of us may be fired. It would be tough on the fellow who isn't there."

"Now then, none of that. We've given our word."

Emil Kleinholz came in.

Kleinholz was unfortunately sober that morning, so sober that he smelt the schnapps and beer on Schulz before he was through the door. He opened fire: "Ah, still nothing to do, gentlemen? Well, today's the day when I've got to give one of you notice." He grinned. "Work's scarce, eh?"

They crept humbly to their places. Second shot: "Well, my dear Schulz, I suppose it suits you very well to sleep off your jag in my office and get paid in good money for it? Pretty wet funeral, wasn't it?" He thought for an instant; then he had it. "I think you'd better get on the trailer behind the truck and go along to the mills. It's a bad road and braking that old trailer will be just the sort of exercise to put you right. I'll tell the driver to keep you at it."

Kleinholz laughed. Schulz was on his way to the door when Kleinholz shouted: "How are you going to manage without papers? Pinneberg, get the order-forms ready for Schulz, the fellow's too shaky to write this morning."

Pinneberg ran off, glad to have something to do.

"Just a moment, Herr Schulz," said Emil. "You can't be back before twelve, and I can only give you notice up till twelve, by our agreement. I still don't know which of you I'm going to fire, I'll have to think it over. . . . So I'll give you notice just as a precaution, that'll give you something to chew on the journey, and if you attend to that brake properly, you ought to be pretty sober by the time you get back, Schulz, my lad."

Schulz got up; his lips moved, but not a sound came. His face was always lined and yellow, but this morning he was a pitiable object.

"Get along now, and report to me when you get back. Then I'll tell you whether your notice holds or not."

Schulz went. The door closed: slowly and with a trembling hand, on which the wedding ring glittered, Pinneberg pushed the blotting pad away from him. Was it his turn now, or Lauterbach's?

At the first word he understood that the next was to be Lauterbach. To Lauterbach Kleinholz used quite another tone. Lauterbach was stupid but strong, and if goaded too far he simply hit out. You had to be careful with Lauterbach; but Emil knew how to manage him.

"I'm really sorry to see you in such a state, Herr Lauterbach. Black eye, purple nose, a mouth you can hardly talk out of, and an arm— You're here to do a full-time job, I'd have you remember; at any rate you want full-time pay for it, don't you?"

"Nothing wrong with my work," says Lauterbach.

"Take it easy, Herr Lauterbach. I suppose National Socialism is a very good thing, we shall be able to tell better after the next elections, but I don't see why I should have to pay for it."

"I'm perfectly capable."

"You may say so, Herr Lauterbach: but I don't quite believe it. Old Brommen hasn't turned up, so we'll have to clean the winter barley over again and I was going to ask you to work the clapper."

Now this was a really dirty trick, even for Emil. Apart from anything else, working the clapper was not a clerk's job at all, and besides it called for two very sound strong arms.

"You see," said Emil; "as I thought, you're an invalid. Go home, Herr Lauterbach, but you won't get any pay while you're away. It isn't a case of illness."

"I'll do it," said Lauterbach in a tone of savage defiance. "I'll turn the fan. Don't you be afraid, Herr Kleinholz!"

"Very well; I'll come up to you before twelve, Lauterbach, and tell you definitely whether you're fired or not."

Lauterbach muttered something unintelligible and departed.

Now it's my turn, thought Pinneberg. But to his surprise Kleinholz said in quite a friendly tone: "Those two fellows, Herr Pinneberg, are like dung and manure, nothing to choose between them."

Pinneberg did not answer.

"You look very festive today. Can't I find some dirty work for you to do? You might make up the Honow estate accounts to the 31st of August. And keep an eye on the straw consignments. They once sent hay straw instead of rye straw, and the load wasn't accepted."

"I know, Herr Kleinholz," said Pinneberg; "that was the truck that went to the racing stable at Karlshorst."

"Good for you," says Emil. "Quite right, Herr Pinneberg. If only all the others were like you. Get going. Good morning."

And he went.

Pinneberg's heart was glad within him. Oh Bunny!

93

We're safe; we needn't be afraid about my job and about the baby.

He got the file.

Suddenly, as though at a clap of thunder, he looked up: "And like a darned fool I've given my word to the others that we'll all give notice if he fires one of us. And I suggested it, God help me for a fool. I never thought of this. He'll simply fire all three of us!"

He jumped up and began to pace up and down the office.

This was Pinneberg's hour, his special hour, in which he wrestled with the Angel.

He would certainly get no other job in Ducherow; and as things were at present he wouldn't get a job anywhere else. He remembered that before he came to Bergmann he had been unemployed for three months. It was bad enough for him alone, and now there were two of them and a third expected. He thought of his two colleagues, whom he really heartily disliked. Both of them could stand being fired better than himself. He remembered that if he gave notice and Kleinholz let him go he would have no right to unemployment pay for quite a while, as a penalty for having given up a job. He thought of Bunny, of Bergmann, the old Jewish outfitter, of Marie Kleinholz, and suddenly of his mother. Then he thought of a picture from *Motherhood: The Sacred Miracle* depicting an embryo at three months, and he realized that the baby would be looking just like this—a little naked mole, horrible to think of. He thought of it for quite some time.

He grew very hot. He rushed to the window and stared out on to the market square. If only she would pass; and quickly! She was sure to pass that morning, she had said

she was going out to buy some meat. Oh Bunny! Dear
Bunny! Do come by!

The door opened and Marie Kleinholz appeared.

It was an ancient privilege of the Kleinholz women
that on Monday morning when no customers came in they
should be allowed to lay out their wash on the large table
in the office. And it was further these ladies' right to ask
the clerks to see that the table was clear. But in the great
excitement of that morning this had not been done.

Pinneberg jumped up: "Just a moment. I'm so sorry,
it'll be ready in a minute."

He threw samples of corn into pigeon-holes, piled up
the files on the window-ledge, and ran blindly about with
the corn tester.

"Hurry up, my good fellow," said Marie in a quarrelsome tone. "I'm waiting here with my wash."

"Just a moment," said Pinneberg very quietly.

"A moment indeed. It ought to have been done long
ago. But of course if you stand at the window looking out
at the girls."

Pinneberg thought it wiser not to answer. Marie
dumped her armful of wash down on to the now cleared
table.

"Why, the table's filthy! This stuff will be dirty again
at once. Where's the duster?"

"I don't know," said Pinneberg rather sharply, and
pretended to look for it.

"Every Saturday I hang up a fresh duster, and by
Monday it's gone. Someone must just steal the dusters. I
didn't think such girls would touch dusters, they'd think
themselves above it."

"Look here, Fräulein Kleinholz," began Pinneberg; but mastered himself, and with an "Oh well," sat down in his place to work.

"Yes, I thought you wouldn't have much to say for yourself. Fancy kissing a girl like that in a public road."

She waited a minute to see if her arrow stuck. Then: "Of course I only saw you kissing; whatever else you were doing I didn't see it. I only speak of what I saw."

Again she was silent. Pinneberg controlled himself with an effort. There wasn't much washing, and then she'd have to go.

"The creature looked frightfully common. So over-dressed."

Pause.

"Father said he'd seen her in the Palm Grotto as a waitress."

Again a pause.

"Well, many men like their women common, it actually attracts them, father says."

Again a pause.

"I'm sorry for you, Herr Pinneberg."

"And I for you," said Pinneberg.

A longer pause. Marie was rather disconcerted. At last she said:

"If you are insolent to me, Herr Pinneberg, I shall tell father and he'll throw you out."

"What do you mean insolent?" asked Pinneberg. "I said exactly what you said."

Silence reigned. It seemed final. Now and again could be heard the clatter of the sprinkler, when Marie Klein-

holz shook it, or the steel ruler clinking against the ink-
pot.

Suddenly Marie gave a shriek and dashed triumphantly
to the window: "There she goes! There she goes, the
little slut! Lord, how she's made up—disgusting, I call
it."

Pinneberg got up and looked out of the window. Passing down the street was Emma Pinneberg, his Bunny,
with her net-bag, the being he loved best in the world.

He stood and stared at Bunny until she reached the
corner and disappeared down the Station Road. He
turned and walked up to Fräulein Kleinholz. His face
looked stern and pale, his forehead was set and lined,
there was fire in his eyes.

"Look here, Fräulein Kleinholz!" By way of precaution
he plunged his hands in his trouser pockets, then he swallowed, and started again. "Look here, Fräulein Kleinholz, if you say anything like that again I'll smack your
face for you."

She tried to say something, her thin lips quivered, her
skinny bird-like head jerked towards him.

"Shut your mouth," he said roughly. "That's my wife,
understand!" He pulled his right hand out of his pocket
and waved his wedding ring under her nose. "And you
can count yourself lucky if you ever get to be as good a
woman as she is!"

With that Pinneberg turned away; he had said his say
and felt immensely relieved. Consequences—? Who
cared? He was ready for them all.

For quite a while there was silence; he glanced towards
Marie, but she did not see, she turned her poor little head
with its thin faded hair towards the window.

97

Then she sat down on a chair, laid her head on the table and began to cry as though her heart would break.

"For heaven's sake," said Pinneberg a little ashamed of his brutality (but not much); "don't take it so hard, I didn't mean it."

She cried and cried, and it probably did her some sort of good; and between her tears she stammered out that she couldn't help being like what she was and she had always thought him such a decent man, quite unlike the other two, and was he really married?—ah, not in church? well, she wouldn't tell her father, he needn't be afraid, if his wife came from hereabouts, she didn't look like it, and what she had said before she had only said to make him angry, the girl looked very nice.

This would have gone on for a long while if Frau Kleinholz's shrill voice had not suddenly burst in upon them: "Where's that wash, Marie? I want to get the ironing done."

With a cry of horror Marie leapt up, picked up her washing and ran out. But Pinneberg sat on, quite pleased with himself. He whistled a tune, energetically added up figures, and kept an eye on the window in case Bunny should pass on her way back. Perhaps she had passed already.

Time went on: it was eleven, then half past, then a quarter to twelve and Pinneberg sang: "Bunny, my darling, we're safe for another month." And all might have gone well, but at five minutes to twelve father Kleinholz came into the office, surveyed his book-keeper, walked to the window, stared into the street, and said in quite a human voice: "Well, Pinneberg, I've been in two minds about this. I'd sooner have kept you on, and let one of

98

the others go. But your refusal to turn up on Sunday just because you wanted to have the day out with a girl—that I can't forgive, and that's why I'm giving you notice."

"Herr Kleinholz—!" Pinneberg stiffened himself for a comprehensive explanation calculated to last till after twelve o'clock and thus beyond the time within which he could be dismissed. "Herr Kleinholz, I . . ."

But at that moment Emil Kleinholz cried out in a fury: "God damn it! There's that girl again. Your time's up on October 31st, Herr Pinneberg."

And before Johannes Pinneberg could say a word Emil was outside and the door had slammed. Pinneberg saw Bunny disappear round the corner of the market square, sighed deeply, looked at the clock. Three minutes to twelve. Two minutes to twelve saw Pinneberg dashing across the yard to the seed-corn shed. There he fell upon Lauterbach, and said breathlessly: "Lauterbach, go to Kleinholz at once and give him notice! Remember your promise! He's just fired me!"

Lauterbach first took his arm slowly from the crank of the fan, surveyed Pinneberg with astonishment, and said: "In the first place, it's a minute to twelve, and I couldn't give him notice before twelve: secondly, I should have to speak to Schulz first, and he isn't here. Thirdly, I've just heard from Marie that you're married, and if that's true, you've taken us all in. And fourthly . . ."

But what fourthly was, Pinneberg did not hear: the church clock, slowly and stroke by stroke, struck twelve.

II.

Herr Friedrichs, the smoked salmon, and Herr Bergmann.

THREE weeks later—a dull, cold, rainy September day, very windy—Pinneberg slowly shut the outer door of the branch office of the Clerks' Union. For a moment he stopped on the landing, vacantly contemplating a placarded appeal to clerical solidarity. He sighed deeply and walked down the staircase.

The fat personage with the flashing gold teeth had decisively demonstrated there was nothing to be done for him and that he must simply become a member of the unemployed. "You know yourself, Herr Pinneberg, what the prospects in textiles here in Ducherow are. Nothing open." Pause. Then, with increased emphasis: "And there won't be either."

Every appeal was met with a shrug of the fat shoulders. Finally Pinneberg played his last card and said softly, "We're expecting a child, Herr Friedrichs."

Friedrichs glanced up at his petitioner. His tone was more encouraging: "Ah well, children bring a blessing. So they say. You'll get your unemployment pay: how many have to manage with less? It will be all right; you'll see."

"But I must . . ."

Herr Friedrichs saw he must do something. "Well now listen, Pinneberg, I can see you're in a tough spot.

Look—I'll write your name down here on my memo pad: Pinneberg, Johannes, twenty-three, salesman, living at—? Where do you live?"

"Green End."

"Ah, right outside the town? Good. Membership number? Thank you." Herr Friedrichs looked thoughtfully at what he had written. "Now—here it goes, right near my inkwell so I can't miss it. When anything turns up I'll think of you first." Pinneberg tried to speak. "So I'm making an exception in your favor, Herr Pinneberg, it's really an injustice to the other members. I ask myself: Friedrichs, I say, why do you do this? Well, I can't help it—I can see you're in a bad way."

Herr Friedrichs screwed up his eyes, looked at the note, picked up a red pencil, added a large red exclamation mark. "There!" he said with satisfaction, and laid the paper beside the inkwell.

Pinneberg turned to go. "Then you'll really think of me, Herr Friedrichs, won't you?"

"I have the note. I have the note. Good morning, Herr Pinneberg."

. . . . . .

In the street Pinneberg stood irresolute. He really ought to go back to the office, he had only a couple of hours off to look for a job. But he loathed it, and most of all he loathed the sight of his two fellow clerks who had not given notice, who had never had any intention of giving notice, who asked sympathetically: "No job yet, Pinneberg? Better get up steam, you know how hungry kids get!"

"Swine!" said Pinneberg emphatically, turning toward the Public Gardens.

These cold bleak gardens with their desolate flower-beds and dreary puddles and a wind so fierce you couldn't even light a cigarette! Just as well, perhaps, he wouldn't have any cigarettes to smoke very soon. He cursed himself for a fool. Just his luck to have had to give up smoking six weeks after getting married!

Here he was at Green End. And when Green End petered out, there would be something else, something cheaper; but at any rate, four walls, a roof overhead, and warmth. And, of course, a wife. It was fine to lie in bed at night and feel someone breathing at your side. It was fine to read the paper while someone sat in the corner of the sofa, sewing and darning. It was fine to come home and find someone who said: "Good evening, darling. How were things today?" It was grand to have someone to care and work for—or, in this case, for whom he could care though he could not work. And it was wonderful to have someone to comfort.

Suddenly Pinneberg burst out laughing. That smoked salmon! That half pound of smoked salmon. Poor Bunny!

One evening just as they were sitting down to supper, Bunny said she couldn't eat, the sight of the food repelled her. But today in the grocer's window she had seen a smoked salmon, red and juicy; how she longed for some!

"Why didn't you bring some home with you?"

"But you don't know what it costs!"

Well, they talked and talked, of course it was absurd, much too dear, but if Bunny couldn't eat anything else . . . Supper could be delayed half an hour and Pinneberg would run into town at once.

Bunny wouldn't hear of it. She'd go herself. Walking was good for her, beside she'd be sitting here terrified that he might be buying the wrong salmon. She must see every slice of it cut with her own eyes.

"All right; you go."

"How much?"

"A quarter of a pound. No, half a pound as long as we're going in for luxury."

He leaned out of the window. She had a fine long vigorous stride, and looked very well in her blue frock. When she had disappeared round the corner of the road he began to pace up and down the room. He figured that when he had gone back and forth fifty times she'd be back. He went to the window. Right, Bunny was just going into the house, she hadn't looked up. Only two or three minutes more. He stood and waited. He thought he heard her at the door. Still no Bunny.

What had happened?

He opened the door to the little hall. There in the doorway stood Bunny, shrinking against the wall with tear-stained anguished face, and holding out a piece of sticky waxed paper—empty.

"What on earth's the matter, Bunny? Did you drop the salmon?"

"I ate it," she sobbed; "I ate it all by myself."

"You ate it all out of the paper? Without bread? The whole half pound? Bunny!"

"I ate it. All by myself."

"Come on in and tell me about it. There's nothing to cry about. Tell me just what happened. You bought the salmon."

"Yes, and I had a craving for it. I could hardly wait

while she was slicing and weighing it. As soon as I got
outside I went into the nearest doorway and took out a
slice—and it was gone."

"And then?"

"Yes, darling, I did that the whole way home. Whenever I passed a doorway I couldn't help stopping. At first
I didn't mean to cheat, I divided it exactly, half and
half. Then I thought one extra slice wouldn't matter.
And then I ate more and more of your share, but one
bit I managed to keep until I got here, just outside the
door."

"And you ate that too?"

"Yes, I ate that too; it's so awful of me, and now
you've got no salmon. But it isn't that I'm really bad."
She began to sob again. "It's my—my condition. I never
was greedy. And I'll simply die if the baby's greedy.
And . . . and . . . shall I run back to town now and
get some more salmon? I'll bring it back this time, I will
really."

He rocked her in his arms: "You great big baby. You
silly little girl—if it's nothing worse than that."

He comforted her and caressed her and wiped her
eyes; slowly they fell to kissing, and then it was evening,
and then it was night.

For some while now Pinneberg had left the wind-swept
Public Gardens.

He was walking through the streets of Ducherow with
a settled destination in his mind. He had not turned down
the road to the country nor was he on his way back to
Kleinholz's office. Pinneberg was marching along, Pinne-

berg had made a great decision. Pinneberg had discovered that his pride was folly; Pinneberg now knew that nothing mattered except Bunny and the baby. What did Pinneberg matter? Pinneberg could quite well humiliate himself provided the other two suffered no harm.

Pinneberg marched straight into Bergmann's shop, straight into the little dark bird-cage partitioned off the shop. There was the old man himself, drawing a letter off the copying press. It was still used in Bergmann's shop.

"*Nu*, Pinneberg," says Bergmann. "How's life?"

"Herr Bergmann," said Pinneberg breathlessly. "I was an awful fool ever to leave you. I beg your pardon, Herr Bergmann, and I came to say that I'll be glad to get the mail always."

"Stop!" cried Herr Bergmann. "Don't talk like that. You said something? I didn't hear it. Don't bother about begging my pardon, I won't take you back."

"Herr Bergmann!"

"Don't talk! Don't beg! Later on all you'll be is ashamed you did it. I won't take you back."

"But Herr Bergmann, you said at the time you'd let me hang around for a month till you took me back."

"Right, Herr Pinneberg, I said it—and am I sorry! I said it in anger because you were a nice young feller and I liked you—until the business about the letters—and you were going over to an old boozehound, a petticoat-chaser. Only because I lost my temper I said it."

"Herr Bergmann," began Pinneberg again. "I'm married now and we're going to have a baby. Kleinholz has dismissed me. What can I do? You know what it's like here in Ducherow. There's no work. Please take me back. You know I earn my salary."

"I know, I know." He shook his head.

"Do take me back, Herr Bergmann. Please."

The ugly little Jew shook his head again: "I can't take you back, Herr Pinneberg. Why? Because I can't."

"Oh Herr Bergmann!"

"It's not a simple business, marriage, and I see you're starting in early. Your wife—she's a good woman?"

"Herr Bergmann!"

"Yes, yes, I see. She should only be good always. Listen, Herr Pinneberg, what I'm telling you now is the plain truth. I'd like to take you back, but I can't, my wife won't have it. She flew up when you said you didn't take orders from her, and she won't forgive you. It's impossible for me to take you back; I am very sorry, Herr Pinneberg, but it's no use."

Pause. A long pause. Little Bergmann turned the copying press, took out the letter, looked it over.

"Yes, Herr Pinneberg," he said slowly.

"How would it be if I went to your wife?" whispered Pinneberg.

"It would be no good, no good at all. You know, Herr Pinneberg, my wife would ask you to come and see her, and then tell you to come again—she would think it over. But she wouldn't take you back, and I should have to tell you in the end it was no good. Women are like that, Herr Pinneberg. Ah well, you are young, what can you know? How long have you been married?"

"A little over four weeks."

"So you still figure by weeks. Well, you'll be a good husband, anyone can see that. You don't need to be ashamed of asking for anything, the great thing is to be always kind. Always be kind to your wife. You must always remember she's only a woman, and hasn't got very much sense. I'm sorry, Herr Pinneberg."

Slowly Pinneberg went out.

12.

Bunny (in her apron) makes a call on her husband.

FRIDAY September 26th. Bunny was cleaning up. A knock at the door. The postman appeared.

"Does Frau Pinneberg live here?"

"I'm Frau Pinneberg."

"Letter for you. Ought to be a plate up on the door. I can't smell where you live, can I?"

He vanished.

Bunny stood there, letter in hand, a large mauve envelope, addressed in a scrawling script. It was the first letter she had received since her marriage. She did not correspond with the family at Platz.

This letter was from Berlin and as Bunny turned it over and over, she noticed the name of the sender written on the back.

Mia Pinneberg. Berlin N. W. 40, Spenerstr. 92 II.

"Why, it's his mother. Mia not Marie. She hasn't been in much of a hurry."

Bunny did not open the letter. She put it down on the table and while she went on cleaning, kept looking at it. She would read it with him, when he got home. That would be best.

Suddenly Bunny threw away her duster. She had a presentiment that this was a great hour; she was sure of

108

it. She ran into the Scharrenhofer's kitchen and washed her hands under the tap. The old lady said something to her and Bunny mechanically said yes.

She plumped down into the corner of the sofa just in the way she had been told not to do (the springs creaked protestingly), picked up the letter, opened it.

She read it.

It wasn't quite clear.

She read it a second time.

She was on her legs; they were trembling a little, no matter, she must go along to Kleinholz's place and speak to the lad at once.

Oh Lord, thought she, I mustn't be too delighted or I shall upset baby. All sudden emotions were to be absolutely avoided, said *Motherhood: The Sacred Miracle.*

"But I can't avoid this—how can I?"

Kleinholz's office wore rather a sleepy air. The three clerks were sitting around, and Emil was sitting around too. There was really nothing to do that day. But while the clerks had to behave as if they were doing something, and that with feverish energy, Emil merely sat around wondering whether Emilie would let him have another drink. He had managed two already that morning.

Suddenly the door flew open, and a young woman with flying hair, flashing eyes, and rosy cheeks, but wearing a most unmistakable kitchen apron, burst in crying, "Darling, come out of here; I must speak to you at once!"

And as the four occupants stared at her in bewilderment, she suddenly recollected herself and said: "I beg your pardon, Herr Kleinholz; my name is Pinneberg, and I must speak to my husband at once."

Suddenly this self-contained young woman burst out

sobbing and said imploringly, "Do come at once, darling.
I . . ."

Emil growled out something, Lauterbach emitted a cat-
call, Schulz grinned insolently, Pinneberg looked fran-
tically embarrassed. He waved his hand in a sort of desperate gesture of apology as he went out of the door.

In the doorway outside the office, the broad doorway
through which the trucks passed with their sacks of corn
and potatoes, Bunny, still sobbing, fell on her husband's
neck: "Darling, I'm nearly crazy I'm so happy! We've
got a job. Read this!"

She pushed the mauve letter into his hand.

Pinneberg was shaking with agitation, he had no idea
what was up. He read:

My dear daughter-in-law, called Bunny: I expect the
boy is just as big a fool as ever, and you will have plenty
of trouble with him. It's simply silly, after the education
I gave him, that he should be working in "manures." He
must come here at once, and on October 1st take up a job
I have got for him in Mandel's Store. To begin with you
can live with me. Greetings from your mamma.

P.S. I meant to write you a month ago but I couldn't
manage it. You must telegraph when you're coming.

"Oh darling, darling, I'm so happy!"

"Yes, sweetheart, so am I. I don't know what Mamma
means with her education. Well, I won't say anything now.
Go at once and telegraph."

But it was a moment or two before they could tear
themselves apart.

Then Pinneberg went back into the office and sat down
stiffly, silent and portentous.

"Any news of a job?" asked Lauterbach.

Pinneberg answered indifferently: "I've got a position as first salesman in the Mandel Store in Berlin. Three hundred and fifty marks a month."

"Mandel?" said Lauterbach. "Jews, of course."

"Mandel?" said Emil Kleinholz. "Make sure it's a respectable firm. I should find out first if I were you."

"I once had a girl," said Schulz meditatively, "who screamed like that when she was a bit excited. Is your wife always so hysterical, Pinneberg?"

PART TWO

Berlin

I.

Introducing Frau Mia Pinneberg.

FRAU MIA PINNEBERG paced up and down the Stettin station platform. She had a flabby, rather full face, and strangely light blue eyes which looked bleached. She was very fair, with dark painted eyebrows—as a matter of fact she was a bit made up everywhere but that was because this station trip was a little unusual. Ordinarily at that hour of the day she was hardly presentable.

Bless the lad, she thought, quite touched; she knew she ought to feel touched, otherwise what was the sense of the whole business? She wondered whether he was still as foolish as ever. Of course he was. Who would marry a girl from Ducherow? She—his old mother—could have made a man of him, a really useful man. His wife . . . well, she might help around the house anyway. Jachmann was always saying the bills were too high. Perhaps she'd get rid of old Möller. Thank the Lord, here was the train.

She beamed at them: "You look splendid, dear. The coal trade seems a healthy business. Oh, you didn't deal in coal? Then why did you write and say you did? Now give me a nice kiss, my lip-stick's kiss-proof. You too, Bunny. You're not what I expected at all."

She surveyed her at arm's length.

Bunny smiled: "What did you think I'd be like, mamma?"

"Well, you know, a country girl, and with the name of Emma, and he calls you Bunny. You still wear flannel underclothes in Pomerania, don't you? Well, Hans, you've got something this time. Bunny, indeed! She's a Valkyrie, high-bosomed and proud-hearted, eh? Get that blush off your face—it makes me think of Ducherow."

"I never blush," laughed Bunny. "Why shouldn't I have a high bosom? And a proud heart too. Today, especially. Berlin! Mandel! And such a mother-in-law! But I haven't got any flannel underclothes."

"Ah, speaking of flannel—what about your things? You'd better have them delivered by van. Have you got any furniture?"

"No, we haven't been able to buy any yet."

"No hurry. I can let you have a gorgeous furnished room. A very good room, it really is. Money's better than furniture, any day. You've got plenty of that, I hope."

"Money?" grumbled Pinneberg. "Where from? What does Mandel pay?"

"Who? Mandel?"

"Yes. Mandel's Store. Where I've got the job."

"Did I say Mandel? I forgot. You must talk to Jachmann this evening. Jachmann knows everything."

"Jachmann—?"

"Let's take a taxi. I've got a little party on this evening and I'll be terribly late if we don't. Hans, there's the express office. Send nothing before eleven. I don't like anyone ringing my bell before eleven."

For a moment the two women were alone.

"You like to sleep late, mamma?"

116

"Of course. Don't you? Every sensible person does. I hope you don't start creeping about the place at eight o'clock."

"Of course I like sleeping late. But the lad has to get to business in good time."

"The lad? What lad? Oh, *him*. Hans you mean. His real name is Johannes, old Pinneberg insisted on it, he was like that.—Well, you needn't get up so early. It's just a superstition of theirs. They can perfectly well make their own coffee and bread and butter. But you must tell him to be as quiet as he can. He used to be terribly inconsiderate."

"Not to me!" said Bunny decisively. "To me he has always been the most considerate man in the world."

"How long have you been married—? Don't tell me, Bunny. *Bunny,* my God—I must think of something to call you. Fixed up, son? Now for a taxi."

Inside the cab Pinneberg said: "So you're giving a party this evening, mamma? Not—?"

"Now what's the matter?" said mamma in an encouraging tone. "Anything wrong. A party in your honor, you meant to say, didn't you? No, son, in the first place I haven't got enough cash for that and besides it isn't a party, it's business. Just business."

"But you don't still go to—?"

"Oh Lord, Bunny," cried his mother in despair. "What's to be done with the boy? Now he's upset again. He wants to know whether I still serve in a bar. When I'm eighty he'll ask me that. No, my boy, not for many years. I'm sure he's told you I served in a bar, that I was a barmaid. Didn't he? Tell me now!"

"Well, he did say something . . ."

"There!" said Frau Pinneberg triumphantly. "Do you know, my son Hans positively gloats over his mamma's wickedness. He's actually proud of his shame! Hans, Hans, if you were only illegitimate! No such luck, my boy, you were born in wedlock, and I was faithful to Pinneberg, God forgive me for a fool."

"Really, mamma," protested Pinneberg.

This is wonderful, thought Bunny. Much better than I thought. She isn't really a bad sort at all.

"Now I'll tell you all about it, Bunny. I wish I knew some other name for you. Well, about that bar. In the first place it was at least ten years ago, and then it was a large bar with four or five girls and a mixer. They always cheated over the drinks and wrote them down wrong and the bottles didn't agree in the morning, so I took the job to oblige the proprietor. I was in charge, you might say, sort of a manager."

"Then, darling, how can you . . ."

"Now I'll tell you what he's like. He comes and peeks through the curtain at the door."

"Didn't do anything of the kind!"

"You did, don't tell lies. And naturally with customers I knew well I sometimes drank a glass of champagne."

"Schnapps," said Pinneberg darkly.

"And a liqueur now and then. I suppose your wife takes a drink sometimes."

"My wife drinks no alcohol at all."

"Quite right, Bunny. Bad for the skin, worse for the stomach. Made me fat too, I'm sorry to say."

"What sort of business party have you got on today?" asked Pinneberg.

"Look at that, Bunny! Just like a police court magistrate. He was like that at fifteen! Who's been here drinking coffee? There was a cigarette-end in the ashtray! There's a son for you."

"But it was you that started about the party, mamma."

"Did I? Well, that's all about it. If I saw a face like yours there, I wouldn't enjoy it a bit. I'll let you off anyway."

"But what *is* all this?" asked Bunny bewildered. "We were all so happy just now."

"The fool always will bring up these disgusting stories about the bar!" said Frau Pinneberg in a fury. "For years and years he's been doing it!"

"Pardon me, I didn't start it. You did," said Pinneberg angrily.

Bunny looked from one to the other. This was a new person to her.

"And who is Jachmann?" asked Pinneberg, unmoved by all these outbursts; his voice did not sound pleasant.

"Jachmann?" Frau Pinneberg's pale eyes sparkled dangerously. "Jachmann's my lover at the moment, the man I sleep with. He represents your father for the time being and you'll have to show him proper respect." She snorted. "Hi, there's the grocer's. Driver, stop and wait!"

She jumped out of the taxi.

"There, Bunny," said Pinneberg in a tone of profound satisfaction. "That's my mother. I wanted to show her to you properly and I have."

"But how could you!" said Bunny, for the first time really angry with him.

2.

An imperial French bed and Herr Jachmann.

"THERE, that's your room," said Frau Pinneberg triumphantly.

She switched the light on and a reddish glow from the ceiling mingled with the light of the fading September day. She had said it was gorgeous; gorgeous it was. On a low dais stood a large bed of gilded wood adorned with cupids. Red silk quilt, white fur rug on the dais, a baldachino above. A show bed, a bed of state.

"Good Lord," cried Bunny. Then she said softly, "But this is much too grand for us. We're just ordinary people."

"It's quite genuine," said Frau Pinneberg proudly. "Louis XVI or rococo, I can't remember which. You must ask Jachmann, he gave it to me." (He gives her beds, thought Pinneberg.) "I've always let it until now. Looks lovely but it isn't very comfortable, you know. Mostly to foreigners. With the small room opposite I used to get two hundred a month for it. But who will pay that today? We'll say a hundred for you."

"I can't possibly pay a hundred marks rent, mamma."

"Why not? Do you call a hundred marks much for a room like that? I'll throw in the telephone."

"I don't want a telephone. I don't want a grand room. I don't even know what I'm going to earn and you talk about a hundred marks rent."

"Very well, let's have some coffee," said Frau Pinneberg switching off the light. "If you don't know what
you're going to earn you can very likely pay a hundred
marks. Your things will be put in here. And listen, Bunny.
My cleaning woman, old Möller, hasn't turned up today,
will you help me a little to get things ready? You won't
mind?"

"I'll be very glad to help, mamma," said Bunny, "but
I'm not a very good housewife."

The scene in the kitchen developed thus: Frau Pinneberg was sitting on a rather broken down wicker chair,
smoking one cigarette after another. The two younger
Pinnebergs were at the sink. Bunny washed, he dried.
There was an enormous amount to wash up: saucepans
full of remains, regiments of cups, squadrons of wineglasses, plates, quantities of knives and forks and spoons.
It looked like the inheritance of at least two weeks.

"Don't leave any fluff on the glasses, Hans. Jachmann
can't stand it. Ah, here he comes, maybe he can lend a
hand too."

The door opened, Herr Holger Jachmann came in.

"Whom have we here?" he asked, looking rather disconcerted.

Jachmann was a giant, Jachmann was quite different
from what the Pinnebergs had imagined. A tall fair man,
with a strong, cheerful and straightforward face, broad
shoulders, and even now, though it was getting on
towards winter, without jacket or waistcoat.

"Whom have we here?" he asked in astonishment
stopping in the doorway. "Has that old beast killed herself at last with our brandy?"

"Charming, Jachmann," said Frau Pinneberg, but

stayed quietly in her chair. "There you stand and stare. I must really make a note of how often you stand and stare. Considering I particularly told you I was expecting my son and daughter-in-law."

"You did not say one word about it, Pinneberg, not one word," said the giant emphatically. "This is the first I've even heard you had a son. And now a daughter-in-law. Gracious lady—" Bunny, at the sink, her hands all wet, had her hand kissed for the first time in her life— "gracious lady, I am charmed. Will you always be washing up here? Allow me." He removed a saucepan from her hand. "This seems a desperate case. Pinneberg has apparently been trying to produce boiled shoe-soles. If I remember rightly, and the late Möller hasn't taken it with her to her grave, there must be a bottle in the kitchen cupboard. I thank you, young man, we will wet our friendship in due course."

"Well, you may say what you like," came Frau Pinneberg's voice from the background, "and flirt with my daughter-in-law, but do you mean to tell me I never told you about my son? Why you got this son of mine a job in Mandel's by your own personal influence, to start on October first, which is tomorrow."

"I? Impossible." He grinned. "I wouldn't attempt such a thing in these days. What would result from such an attempt save grief?"

"Good God, what a man!" cried Frau Pinneberg. "You said it was all fixed up and that I was to send for him."

"You are completely and utterly in error, Pinneberg. I may perhaps have said I would see what could be done, or something of that kind—indeed I can easily con-

ceive myself doing it, but you certainly never said anything to me about a son. It's your damned vanity again.
Son—never heard you utter the word."

"Is that so!"

"And of course I never said the thing was fixed up. I
am a most scrupulous 'and orderly man in business
matters, almost pedantic in fact. I was with Lehmann of
Mandel's only the day before yesterday—he's the head
of the personnel department—and he'd have been certain
to say something about it. No, Pinneberg, no, just another of your air-castles."

The two young Pinnebergs, long since finished washing up, stood looking from mamma to Jachmann. But
Johannes Pinneberg was to be reckoned with. He cared
less than nothing for Jachmann, but he took three steps
towards his mother and said, pale and a little halting in
his speech, but very clearly:

"Mamma, does this mean that you got us here from
Ducherow and made us spend all this money on our
journey just to make fools of us? Just to let your grand
bedroom for a hundred marks? Simply because you
wanted someone to wash up? We're poor people, Bunny
and I, probably I shan't get any unemployment pay here,
and what—what—" suddenly he began to sob, "what in
the world is to become of us?"

"Now, now, now," said mamma; "no sense crying.
You can always go back to Ducherow. You've just heard,
and you too, Bunny, that it isn't my fault at all, and that
this man Jachmann has messed up the whole thing as
usual. Why, to listen to him you'd think everything was
all right and he was the most orderly man under the sun,
but really . . . There he stands and I bet he's for-

gotten that the Stoschussens are bringing three Dutchmen this evening and that he was to invite Müllensiefen
and Claire and Nina. And you were to bring new écarté
cards with you."

"Just listen to her," said the giant triumphantly.
"That's just like Pinneberg. She told me about the three
Dutchmen and that I was to get the girls. But about
Müllensiefen—not a word. What do we want Müllen-
siefen for?"

"And the écarté cards, my treasure?" asked Frau Pinneberg glaring at him.

"I've got them all right. In my overcoat. I think they
were there, at least, when I put it on. I'll go outside and
have a look."

"Herr Jachmann!" said Bunny suddenly, barring his
way. "Listen a moment. It doesn't matter to you a bit
whether we have a job or not. You can probably get jobs,
though, you are much cleverer than we are."

"Do you hear that, Pinneberg?" said Jachmann with
great satisfaction.

"But we're quite simple people. And we're very unhappy because my husband hasn't got a job. So I do
ask you to do all you possibly can to get us one."

"My dear young lady," said the huge man with great
emphasis: "I most certainly will. I'll get the young man
a job. What shall it be? How much does he need to earn
so that you can live?"

"But you know all about it," declared Frau Pinneberg.
"Salesman at Mandel's. Gentleman's outfitting department."

"Mandel's? Why go into a sweat shop? Besides, I
don't believe they pay more than five hundred a month."

"You're crazy," remarked Frau Pinneberg. "A salesman at five hundred? Two hundred; two hundred and fifty at the outside."

"That'll do," said Jachmann. "Look here, I'll speak to Manasse, we'll fix you up in a fine little shop in the west end, something really unique and out of the way. I will establish you, young woman, I will establish you firmly."

"I've got a bellyful of your establishments, I'm sick of them," said Frau Pinneberg.

"All we want is a job at the Union rate of wages, Herr Jachmann," Bunny said.

"Is that all? I've done it a hundred times. At Mandel's then. It's a mere matter of dropping in on old Lehmann, he's always ready to oblige."

"But you mustn't forget, Herr Jachmann. It must be at once."

"I'll talk to him tomorrow. Your husband can begin the day after. Word of honor."

"Thank you, Herr Jachmann, thank you very much."

"Quite all right, young woman, quite all right. And now I must really look for those écarté cards. I could have sworn I put on my overcoat as I left the house. And then I hung it up somewhere—but where, God knows. It's always the same trouble in the autumn; I can't get used to the thing, and I leave it hanging up. In the spring I'm always putting on other people's overcoats."

Jachmann vanished on the landing.

"And the man says he forgets nothing," observed Frau Pinneberg consolingly.

3.

Simultaneous acquisition of a job and a father.

JACHMANN was waiting for Pinneberg in front of the boys' and youths' clothing window.

"Ah, here you are. Don't look so tragic. Everything's shipshape. I've talked old Lehmann deaf, dumb and blind till he's absolutely wild about you.—Did we disturb you much last night?"

"A little," said Pinneberg hesitantly. "We aren't accustomed to it yet. Maybe it was the journey too. Am I to go and see Herr Lehmann now?"

"Oh, let the old man wait a bit. He'll be glad to get you. I had to make up a little story, of course. If he asks you any questions you know nothing whatever, you understand."

"Perhaps you wouldn't mind telling me what you said to him. I must know what it was."

"You won't get a word out of me. Anyone can see you couldn't bluff through a decent lie. No, you don't know a thing. Come over to the café for a while."

"No, really I'd rather not," said Pinneberg firmly. "I want to get the thing fixed up for certain. It's so important for myself and my wife."

"Important! Two hundred marks a month. Now, now, don't hold your mouth open like that. I didn't mean any harm. Listen." The enormous Jachmann laid his hand gently on little Pinneberg's shoulder. "I'm not just standing here talking nonsense, Pinneberg," said Jachmann. "You don't mind my being friends with your mother?"

"No . . . no . . ." said Pinneberg very slowly, wishing he were somewhere else.

"You see," said Jachmann in a voice that sounded really kindly, "the point is, Pinneberg, I'm the sort of man who puts his cards on the table. Any other man would have said, why should I say anything to this little p—pot. There, I can see that disturbs you. You really mustn't mind, Pinneberg, tell your wife not to mind either. No, that's unnecessary, your wife's not like you, I could see that at once. And when Pinneberg and I have a spat, don't think anything of it, that's the way we are—just a method of avoiding boredom, you understand. It's absurd of Pinneberg to ask a hundred marks for that old moth-eaten room, just don't give her the money, she'll only waste it in dissipation. And don't go into a sweat over the parties, they'll go on as long as fools exist. And one thing more, Pinneberg . . ." The great blusterer now became really likeable and in spite of his aversion Pinneberg was quite carried away. "One thing more, Pinneberg. Don't be in any rush to tell your mother you're expecting a child. I mean your wife, of course. Your mother thinks it's the worst thing that can happen, worse than rats, worse than bugs. You must have been one of her bad experiences. So say nothing. Lie if necessary. I'll figure out the best way to break the news. There's plenty of time. He hasn't started to grab the soap yet, has he?"

"Soap? What do you mean?"

"Well," grinned Jachmann; "when wifie's in the bath-tub and the baby makes a dash for the soap you'd better 'phone for the doctor. Taxi! Hi! Hi! Taxi!" roared the giant suddenly. "I ought to have been at the Alex half an hour ago." Through the cab-window he shouted, "Second court on the right, ask for Lehmann. Good luck! Kiss the young lady's hand for me. And remember—not a word out of you!"

Second court on the right. It was Mandel, Mandel all the way. An enormous store. Pinneberg had never worked in one a tenth or even a hundredth part as big as this. He would work very hard and do well, be patient, never lose his temper: Oh Bunny! Oh little Pinneberg!

Second court on the right, ground floor: Personnel Department. And another gigantic placard: "No Vacancies at Present." And a third: "Come in; Don't Knock." Pinneberg did so. He went in; he did not knock.

A railing; behind it five typewriters. Behind the five typewriters, five girls, of varying ages. All five looked up, all five looked down, all five went on hammering at their machines; none of them had noticed his entrance. Pinneberg stood for a while waiting. Then he said to one in a green blouse, sitting nearest to him: "Excuse me, Miss."

The green blouse looked as though she had just received an offer of rape, effective immediately.

"I would like to see Herr Lehmann."

"Notice outside."

"I don't understand, Miss."

The green blouse was highly indignant: "Read the notice outside. No vacancies."

"I did read it. But I've got an appointment with Herr
Lehmann. He expects me."

The young lady—Pinneberg noticed that she looked
really quite nice and polite and he wondered whether she
spoke to her chief as she spoke to her colleagues—the
young lady looked at him crossly and said: "Form!"
Then with real fury: "You must fill out a form!"

Pinneberg followed her eyes. On a desk in the corner
lay a writing block, and beside it was a pencil hanging
on a chain.

Herr ——— ⎫		Herr ———	
Frau ——— ⎬ wishes to see		Frau ———	
Fräulein ——— ⎭		Fräulein ———	

Purpose of interview (*be specific*) ———————

Pinneberg hesitated over *Purpose of interview—be
specific*. He wavered between: *Known* and *Employment*.
Probably the stern young lady would not pass either of
these. He wrote: *Jachmann*.

"Please, Miss."

"Put it down."

The form lay on the railing, the typewriters rattled,
Pinneberg waited.

Pinneberg wondered gloomily whether all the Man-
delians were like this. He waited. It seemed the thing
to do.

After a while a messenger in a gray uniform materialized.

"Form!" The young lady uttered a soprano bark.

The messenger picked up the form, read it, surveyed
Pinneberg, vanished.

This time Pinneberg did not have very long to wait. The messenger reappeared, said very politely: "Herr Lehmann will see you," led the way through the railing, across a passage and into an anteroom.

An elderly lady with a lemonish complexion (his private secretary, thought Pinneberg nervously) rose from her telephone, said with a resigned and melancholy air, "Herr Lehmann is expecting you," and opened a brown padded door.

He was in a gigantic room with one wall almost entirely windows. By the windows stood a mammoth writing table on which there was nothing but a telephone and a mammoth yellow pencil. Not a scrap of paper. Nothing. At one side of the writing table was a chair: empty. On the other side stood a small wicker chair, and on it— why this must be Herr Lehmann: a tall yellow man with a lined face, a short black beard and a sickly looking bald patch. Very dark round piercing eyes.

Pinneberg remained standing by the writing table. Spiritually, as it were, he stood at attention, hunched his shoulders and kept his head down, so as not to look too tall. For it was only *pro forma* that Herr Lehmann sat on a wicker chair; to indicate the abyss between them he ought really to have been sitting on the topmost rung of a step-ladder.

"Good morning," said Herr Pinneberg, in a quiet polite tone, and bowed.

Herr Lehmann decisively picked up the mammoth pencil and with care stood it upright.

Pinneberg waited.

"What is it you want?" said Herr Lehmann petulantly.

This was a facer.

130

"I . . . I thought . . . Herr Jachmann . . ." His breath vanished.

Herr Lehmann surveyed his visitor. "I'm not concerned with Herr Jachmann. I want to know what *you* want."

"I am applying," said Pinneberg, speaking very slowly, so as not to run out of breath again, "for the position of salesman."

Herr Lehmann put the pencil down: "We are not taking on anyone," he said decisively and waited.

Herr Lehmann was a very patient man. He waited. At last he said, again standing the pencil up on end: "Anything else?"

"Perhaps later on . . ." stammered Pinneberg.

"In times like these!" Herr Lehmann was all scorn.

Pinneberg's heart sank. Poor Bunny! He might as well go. Then Herr Lehmann said: "Show me your references."

Pinneberg's hands were trembling and he was honestly afraid. What was in Herr Lehmann's mind no one knew, but the Mandel store employed men by the thousand and Herr Lehmann was the chief of the Personnel Department and therefore a great man. Perhaps he was joking.

So Pinneberg nervously produced his papers: his apprenticeship certificate, his school record, his employment insurance card, his wage-tax card and finally his references from Wendheim, Bergmann and Kleinholz.

The references were all very good. Slowly, impassively Herr Lehmann read them. Then he looked up and seemed to be thinking. The giant pencil, it would appear, was forgotten.

Herr Lehmann spoke: "We do not deal in manures."

Caught! All poor Pinneberg could do was to stammer awkwardly: "I thought . . . in the men's outfitting, perhaps . . . that was only a temporary job. . . ."

Herr Lehmann was delighted with his observation. He repeated it: "No, we don't deal in manures. Nor potatoes," he added.

He might have gone on to corn and seeds, all mentioned on Emil's notepaper; but the potatoes hadn't seemed so apposite.

There followed a pause, during which Pinneberg hoped, despaired, hoped again.

"Well," said Herr Lehmann finally, laying his hand on the papers. "Well, we are not taking on any new employees. We can't. We are even laying off old ones."

That was that; the last word. But Herr Lehmann's hand was still lying on the papers; he had even placed the mammoth pencil on them.

"However," said Herr Lehmann. "However. We can always transfer men from our branches. Efficient men particularly. Are you efficient?"

Pinneberg whispered something; not a protest. But it satisfied Herr Lehmann.

"You, Herr Pinneberg, will be taken over from our branch in Breslau. You come from Breslau, don't you?"

Pinneberg whispered again, and again Herr Lehmann was satisfied.

"I suppose there's no one from Breslau in the men's outfitting department, where you will work, is there?"

Pinneberg murmured something.

"Good. Then you'll start tomorrow morning. You will report at eight-thirty in Fräulein Semmler's office outside, and sign the contract and the House Regulations.

Fräulein Semmler will tell you what to do. Good morning."

"Good morning," repeated Pinneberg. He bowed. He progressed backwards toward the door. As he was about to turn the knob Herr Lehmann whispered, loud enough to be heard across the room: "My best regards to your father. Tell your father I have taken you on. Tell Holger I expect to be free on Wednesday evening. Good morning. Good morning, Herr Pinneberg."

4.

A despondent walk through the little Tiergarten.

OUT on the street again Pinneberg felt dead tired, as if he had been over-working all day or had just narrowly escaped some mortal danger. His taut, tortured nerves went loose and dead. Slowly he turned his steps homeward.

So he had a father. And as the father was Jachmann and he was Pinneberg he must of course be illegitimate. All of which, it would seem, had been a great help with Herr Lehmann. This revolting beast of a Jachmann enables him, Pinneberg, to come suddenly from Breslau, from a branch store, and snatch a job. References: useless. Ability: useless. Good appearance: useless. Humility: useless. Everything useless—except this Jachmann!

Jachmann—who is Jachmann?

What had gone on last night in his mother's house? Laughter, shrieks of gaiety, carousal. In their imperial bed Bunny and he had huddled, closing their ears to the noise. They had said nothing; after all she was his mother; but there was something very funny about that party.

To get to the toilet Pinneberg had had to go through the sitting-room. And very cosy it had looked, with only a table lamp burning, and everybody sitting around on the two great divans. The women were very young, very smart, very elegant; and the Dutchmen—Dutchmen ought to be fair and fat, but these were dark and tall. They all sat around, drinking wine and smoking. And Holger Jachmann was walking about, in shirt-sleeves of course, saying: "Now, Nina, you needn't put on airs here." He didn't sound as kindly and jovial as usual.

And among them was Frau Mia Pinneberg. Well, she hadn't been so much out of the picture after all, she had made herself up marvellously, and perhaps looked just the tiniest bit older than the young women. She joined in the fun, that was all right enough, but what were they doing all night until four o'clock? There had indeed been a welcome silence for a long while, a faint distant murmur and then a sudden outburst of gaiety again for a quarter of an hour. True, they had been playing cards, playing as a business with the two young painted girls, Claire and Nina, and the three Dutchmen, for whom it had been intended to invite Müllensiefen, but in the end Jachmann's arts had sufficed. Perfectly regular, Pinneberg! Nothing to worry about. Still . . .

Still . . . If Pinneberg knew anyone he knew his mother. She had good reason for being furious at his mention of the bar. It was *not* ten years ago, it was five; he had *not* only peeked through the curtain, he had sat down at a table, three tables away from Frau Mia Pinneberg. But she had been too far gone to see him. Looking after a bar! It was herself needed looking after. At first she hadn't been able to deny it but talked wildly about some birthday party. In the course of time this birthday party with all its vulgarity and shamelessness had also been denied into oblivion. He had merely looked through the curtain and the managerial mother had been standing respectably behind the bar. That's the way things were then . . . what had he to look forward to now?

Pinneberg, Pinneberg!

Here was the little Tiergarten of his childhood, never very attractive, not at all to be compared with its big brother across the Spree, just a bare strip of green meadow. On this first of October, damp and disordered, lit by fitful glimpses of sunshine, swept by winds from every corner, littered with ugly brownish yellow leaves, it looked especially cheerless. It was not empty, it was far from empty. Masses of men in gray clothes and with pallid faces waited—for what they themselves did not know. No man now waits for work. Helplessly they stood about; they could not endure their homes, and what else was there to do but stand about?

But Pinneberg had to get home. Bunny would be there waiting for him. Still, he stopped, he stood about among the unemployed, walked on a few steps, stopped again. Outwardly Pinneberg did not belong to them; his outer husk was that of a respectable man. He was wearing his brown winter ulster which Bergmann had let him have for thirty-eight marks. And a hard black hat, also from Bergmann, rather old-fashioned, with an exaggerated brim, you can have it for three marks twenty, Pinneberg.

Hence outwardly Pinneberg did not belong to the unemployed.

He had just been to see Lehmann, personnel manager at Mandel's. He had asked for a job, he had got it. A simple business transaction. But Pinneberg had a kind of feeling that, in spite of this transaction, in spite of the fact that he was now a wage-earner once more, he belonged much more to these who did not earn than to those who earned a great deal. He was one of them: any day he might be standing here like them, and he could not help it. Nothing could protect him.

He was one of these millions. Ministers made speeches to him, admonished him to lead a life of self-denial and self-sacrifice, to be a good patriot, to put his money in the savings bank, to vote for the constitutional parties. Was he not one of these harmless, starving, and now hopeless animals huddled in the little Tiergarten? Three months of unemployment—and good-bye to his brown ulster. Good-bye to any prospects for the future. Perhaps Jachmann and Lehmann would have a row on Wednesday evening, and he would suddenly be found inefficient.

Perhaps he hadn't really got used to Bunny yet, but as he stood there looking at these men he hardly gave her a thought. You couldn't talk to her about things like this—she wouldn't understand. She might seem soft but really she was tougher than he was. She wouldn't be standing here, she belonged to the Social Democratic Party—but that was only for her father's sake. Her real place was with the Communists. She had a few simple ideas, men are only bad because they are made so, no one should judge another because he doesn't know what he would do himself, the rich always think that the poor don't feel things. Not that she'd ever thought them out. But you could see her heart was with the Communists.

And that was why you couldn't really talk to her. Well, he must go home, tell her that he'd got the job, all the reason in the world to be happy, he *was* happy. But behind his happiness lay the fear: Would it last? No. Of course it wouldn't last.

Then: how long would it last?

5.

*A salesman (with the assistance of Herr Heilbutt)
is born.*

HALF-PAST nine in the morning, October thirty-first.
Pinneberg is in the men's ready-to-wear department, sorting gray striped trousers. Not far away assistants Beer-
baum and Maiwald are brushing off coats. Maiwald,
sportsman that he is, is able to impart even to his present
occupation a touch of real competition. Best record to
date: one hundred and nine coats an hour, scrupulously
brushed (though possibly a little over-energetically).

A button broke under his hands and Jänecke, sub-
stituting for Kröpelin, gave him a first-class blowing up.
Kröpelin wouldn't have opened his mouth. Kröpelin was
the kind of man who understood that buttons sometimes
break. But Jänecke could become department head only
when Kröpelin ceased to be one: hence his sharp look-
out for the firm's interest.

"Eighty-seven, eighty-eight, eighty-nine, ninety . . ."
The assistants counted half-aloud.

Where were those trousers at seventeen seventy-five?
Pinneberg could have asked Kessler a few yards away.
But he didn't like Kessler. When Pinneberg joined, Kessler had observed very audibly: "Breslau, eh—? We
know all about that—another of Lehmann's little jobs."

Pinneberg kept on sorting trousers. It was very quiet
for a Friday. There had been only one customer, who

had bought a mechanic's overall. Kessler had of course waited on him, he had pushed himself forward, although it was the first salesman's, Heilbutt's, turn. But Heilbutt, being a gentleman, didn't mind that sort of thing. Besides Heilbutt sold quite enough as it was and he knew very well that in case of difficulty Kessler would go to him for help. That satisfied Heilbutt. It wouldn't have satisfied Pinneberg, but Pinneberg was not Heilbutt. Pinneberg could show his teeth; Heilbutt was much too refined to do any such thing.

At the moment Heilbutt was standing at a desk over some figures. Pinneberg watched him, wondering whether he should ask him about the missing trousers. It would be a good opportunity of getting into conversation with Heilbutt, but Pinneberg thought better of it. He had tried several times to talk to Heilbutt. But though the latter had always been faultlessly polite somehow the interview had frozen.

Pinneberg didn't want to force his company on the man, more especially as he admired him. Their acquaintance must come without effort, and come it would. A fantastic idea came into his head: he would ask Heilbutt to visit them at Spenerstrasse, that very evening if possible. He must show Heilbutt to his Bunny, and above all show his Bunny to Heilbutt. He had a Bunny. Who of the others could say as much?

Slowly the store awakened. For some while the assistants had been standing about bored and only officially on duty; then suddenly they began to sell. Wendt was busy, Lasch was selling, so was Heilbutt. And Kessler, too, though it had really been Pinneberg's turn. But Kessler was always so impatient. However, Pinneberg soon had his customer, a young student. But Pinneberg had no luck: the student, a youth with a duel-scarred face, asked, short and sharp, for a blue trench-coat.

It flashed through Pinneberg's brain: Not one in stock.

He maneuvered the student before a mirror: "Blue trench-coat? Certainly, sir. Just try on this ulster a moment."

"I don't want an ulster."

"Certainly not. Just to get the size. There—looks quite smart, I think?"

"Doesn't look bad," said the student. "Show me a blue trench-coat."

"Sixty-nine fifty," said Pinneberg casually, feeling his way. "A special offer. Would have been ninety last winter. Woven lining. Pure wool."

"Very good," said the student, "only I want a trench-coat."

Slowly, reluctantly Pinneberg removed the smart ulster. "I don't think you'll find anything to suit you as well as this. Blue trench-coats are really quite out of fashion. They've become so common."

"Will you be kind enough to show me one," said the student emphatically: "or don't you want to sell me a trench-coat?"

"But of course, of course, anything you like." And he smiled just as the student had smiled when he asked his last question. "Only—" He reflected feverishly. He might as well try it—it wasn't really a lie. "Only, I can't sell you a blue trench-coat." Pause. "We haven't got any more trench-coats."

"Why on earth didn't you tell me that before?"

"Because I wanted to convince you how well that

ulster suited you. You see," said Pinneberg, in a lower tone and with a deprecating smile; "I only wanted to show you how much better it is than a blue trench-coat. That was just a fad, but this ulster . . ."

Pinneberg looked at it affectionately, stroked its sleeves, hung it over the hanger, was about to replace it.

"Just a second. I didn't say it looked bad, did I?"

"It certainly doesn't." Pinneberg helped his customer into the coat again. "An ulster always looks so distinguished. May I show you some more ulsters, sir? Or" (he felt he could risk it) "a light trench-coat?"

"Oh, then you have some light trench-coats?" said the student, angrily.

Pinneberg coolly walked over to another stand.

Here hung a yellowish green trench-coat; it had been twice reduced in price and everyone who tried it on somehow looked comic or grotesque.

"Here is something." Pinneberg flung the coat over his arm. "Light trench-coat, sir. Thirty-five marks."

The student slipped his arms into the sleeves. "Thirty-five?" he asked in astonishment.

"Yes," loftily. "Coats of this type are very modestly priced."

The student surveyed himself in a mirror. "Appalling," he muttered.

"It is a trench-coat," said Pinneberg bravely.

The transaction ended with the sale of the ulster at sixty-nine fifty.

Well, that's that, thought Pinneberg. He threw a quick glance round the department. The others were still selling or just starting to sell. Only Kessler and himself were unoccupied. Kessler therefore was the next. Pinneberg would not push himself forward. Then a strange thing happened. Step by step Kessler retreated against the array of garments on the walls, almost as though trying to hide. Pinneberg glanced at the entrance. There appeared first a lady, then another lady, both in the thirties, then another lady, rather older, the mother or mother-in-law, and fourthly a man, with a moustache, pale blue eyes and a head like an egg. You cowardly fool, thought Pinneberg indignantly, of course you'd run away.

"What may I have the pleasure of showing you?" He let his eyes rest for a moment on each of the four faces so that none should feel neglected.

One of the ladies said sharply: "My husband wants an evening suit. Please, Franz, tell the man yourself what you want."

"I want . . ."

"I don't much like the look of what you have here," said the second lady in the thirties.

"I told you don't go to Mandel's," said the older lady. "Obermeyer's is the place for that."

". . . an evening suit," concluded the man with the little pale blue eyes.

"Dinner-jacket?" asked Pinneberg cautiously. He tried to distribute the question equally among the three ladies, without quite leaving out the gentleman.

"Dinner-jacket!" The ladies were indignant.

The straw-blonde said: "My husband has a dinner-jacket of course. We want an evening suit."

"A dark jacket," said the gentleman mildly.

"With striped trousers," said the dark one, who

seemed to be the sister-in-law—but the wife's sister-in-law, so that as the gentleman's sister she had prior rights over him.

"Thank you, madam," says Pinneberg.

"We should certainly have found what we wanted at Obermeyer's," said the older lady.

"No, that won't do," said the lady, as Pinneberg produced a jacket.

"What did you expect at such a place?"

"We might as well have a look. Let us see something else, young man."

"Try that on, Franz."

"But Else, really—! That jacket . . ."

"Well what do you think, mother?"

"I shan't say anything, don't ask me, I shan't say anything. You'll say afterwards I chose the suit."

"Perhaps you'd raise your shoulders a little, sir?"

"Don't you raise your shoulders on any account, Franz! My husband's shoulders are always like that. You must find something to suit them."

"Turn round, Franz."

"Quite impossible."

"Now for goodness' sake do show us a decent jacket."

"How do you like this, madam?"

"The material seems very light."

"Madam notices everything. The material does come out rather light. How would this one suit?"

"That looks better. Is it pure wool?"

"Pure wool, madam. And a quilted lining, as you see."

"I like that one."

"Really, Else, how can you possibly like such a thing? Franz, surely you don't . . ."

"You see there's nothing fit to look at here. No one goes to Mandel's."

"Just try on this one, Franz."

Franz seemed to be getting balky.

"What on earth do you mean, Franz? Do you want an evening suit, or do I?"

"You do."

Pinneberg interposed carefully: "Would madam kindly look at this one? Quiet but very smart." Pinneberg had decided to concentrate on Else the straw-blonde.

"I think that's very nice. How much is it?"

"Sixty, I'm afraid. Quite an exclusive article. It isn't everybody's coat."

"Very dear."

"Else, don't be so silly! He showed us that one before."

"I know that as well as you do, my dear child. Now, Franz, please try this on again."

"No," said Egg-head venomously. "I don't want a suit at all. It was just you who said I did."

"Please do, Franz."

"I shall go out of the store if you're going to make a scene."

"So shall I. Else always wants her own way at any price."

General uproar. During these mutual courtesies the coats are flung and pushed about the counter.

Pinneberg tried in vain to get in a word. In his extremity he threw a glance round the shop and saw Heilbutt; the two men's eyes met.

At the same moment Pinneberg did something desperate. He said to Egg-head: "Your coat, please, sir."

He helped the gentleman into the disputed sixty-mark coat and then said hurriedly: "Beg your pardon, my mistake." He added ecstatically: "How well you look in it, sir!"

"Yes, Else, if you really think . . ."

"I always said that coat . . ."

"What do you say, Franz?"

"What's the price?"

"Sixty, madam."

"Perfectly ridiculous! Sixty, in these days? And especially at a shop like Mandel's."

A soft but resolute voice near Pinneberg said: "Ah, one of our smartest evening coats. An excellent choice."

Silence.

The ladies looked at Herr Heilbutt. There he stood, tall, dark, tanned, and distinguished.

"A very exceptional coat," said Herr Heilbutt after a pause. Then he bowed and departed. Perhaps—who knows—it was Herr Mandel himself.

"For sixty marks you have a right to demand something worth while," came the old lady's peevish voice; not quite so peevish as before.

"Do you like it too, Franz?" asked Else.

"After all, it's for you to say."

"Well, yes," says Franz.

"If there is a pair of trousers that will do," began the sister-in-law.

But nothing went wrong over the trousers. The party were soon in agreement, even to the extent of choosing an expensive pair which brought the bill to more than ninety-five marks. The old lady again adverted to Obermeyer's but no one listened.

Pinneberg threw in an extra bow at the cash desk. Then he went back to his place, as proud as a general after winning a battle, and as exhausted as one of his soldiers. Heilbutt was standing by a pile of trousers. He looked at Pinneberg.

"Thank you," said Pinneberg; "you saved the day."

"Not at all," said Heilbutt; "you would have pulled it through anyway. Oh yes you would. You're a born salesman, Pinneberg."

Pinneberg's heart swelled with happiness. "Do you really think so, Heilbutt? Do you really think I'm a born salesman?"

"But you know that yourself, Pinneberg. It amuses you to sell things."

"The people amuse me," said Pinneberg. "I always want to find out what sort of people they are and how to get them into the right buying mood." He drew a deep breath. "I nearly always pull it off."

"I've noticed that, Pinneberg," said Heilbutt.

Heilbutt smiled.

"Ah, now you're laughing, Heilbutt. Yes, now you're laughing at me. Of course now I come to think of it, they bought it because you impressed them so."

"Nonsense," said Heilbutt. "Utter nonsense, Pinneberg. You yourself know quite well that no one buys anything for that reason. I did perhaps speed matters up a bit."

"You certainly did, Heilbutt." Now was the moment to strike. "By the way, I have a great favor to ask of you, Heilbutt."

Heilbutt was rather taken aback. "Eh? Certainly, Pinneberg."

"I wonder if you'd come and see us," said Pinneberg. Heilbutt was even more taken aback. "I told my wife so much about you, and she'd so much like to meet you. Would you have time some evening? A very plain supper, of course."

Heilbutt smiled again, but it was a delightful smile, from the corners of his eyes. "Of course I will, Pinneberg. I had no idea it would amuse you. I shall be glad to come sometime."

Pinneberg asked hurriedly: "Would it . . . could you possibly manage this evening?"

"This very evening?" Heilbutt reflected. "I must think for a moment." He took a little leather notebook out of his pocket. "Wait now, tomorrow there's an evening class lecture on Greek sculpture at the University. You know, of course . . ." Pinneberg nodded. "And the day after, it's my nudist culture evening. And the evening after that I've promised my young lady. No, so far as I can see, Pinneberg, I'm free this evening."

6.

Pinneberg gets his pay, behaves badly to a salesman and becomes the possessor of a dressing-table.

PINNEBERG stood outside Mandel's, one hand in his pocket grasping his pay envelope. He had been working for a month but during all that time had had no notion how much pay he would get. He knew now. A hundred and seventy marks net! Eighty marks less than Bunny had expected, sixty less than he had counted on in his gloomiest moments.

Damned robbers, what do they care how people like us are to live? They can get plenty more for less money. And for a hundred and seventy marks net we have to crawl and cringe. It would be a pretty tough job to manage on that in Berlin. Mamma would have to wait a while for her rent. A hundred marks: Jachmann was right, she must be a little cracked. However, they'd certainly have to give mamma something, she'd put on the screws, that's the way she was built.

A hundred and seventy marks—what would become of that lovely scheme of his, the big surprise for Bunny?

This is how it all started. One evening Bunny said, pointing to an empty corner of their imperial bedroom: "That's where we ought to have a dressing-table."

"But do we need one?" he asked in astonishment. His ambitions had never risen above beds, a leather armchair and an oak sideboard.

"Don't be crazy. Of course not. But wouldn't it be nice to have one? Don't look like that, dear, it's just an idea."

That began it. They did a lot of walking because it was good for Bunny. Now they had something to look at on their walks; they examined dressing-tables. They went on long explorations: there were various districts and side-streets where carpenters' and furniture makers' shops stood almost side by side.

Soon they had their favorites and chief among them was the shop of a certain Himmlisch in the Frankfurter Allee. The specialty of Himmlisch & Co. was bedrooms. "Himmlisch for Beds," ran the sign outside.

For several weeks a suite of bedroom furniture had stood in this shop-window; not too dear, seven hundred and ninety-five marks, including mattresses and real marble tops. And one of the pieces was a dressing-table of Caucasian walnut.

Each time they stood and looked at it with greater longing. It was a good hour and a half's walk each way. "Oh, if we could only buy something like that I think I'd scream for joy."

"Those who can buy such things," said Pinneberg sagely, "do not scream for joy."

They turned to go home. They always walked with Pinneberg's arm slipped through Bunny's so he could feel her breast, now growing fuller; it was like a soft and friendly refuge among all these vast streets, these countless strangers. And on this journey home Pinneberg conceived the idea of giving Bunny a surprise. After all, they had to begin sometime: if they had one piece of furniture the rest would have to follow. That was the reason for his getting off at four o'clock this Friday. Not a word to

Bunny—just have it sent home, he wouldn't know a thing about it.

One hundred and seventy marks! Out of the question, absolutely and entirely out of the question.

But men do not so easily desert their dreams. How could he go home this way with his paltry hundred and seventy marks? He must be in good spirits when he arrived, Bunny had counted so heavily on two hundred and fifty. He made his way towards the Frankfurter Allee. Farewell, Himmlisch for Beds! Never again would they look into that shop-window. What was the use?

There it was, the bedroom suite, the wonderful dressing-table. Funny how you could fall in love with such a thing; there were thousands of dressing-tables more or less like it but this—this was the only one.

Pinneberg surveyed it at length. He stepped back a little, then advanced and pressed his nose against the pane. Beautiful as ever! The mirror was a good one, too; it would be just wonderful to see Bunny sitting in front of it in the morning in her white and red wrap.

Pinneberg sighed gloomily and turned away. No: not for you, little man. Go home, little man, waste your money as you will and can and may, but leave things like this alone.

From the next street corner Pinneberg looked back once more. The shop-windows of Himmlisch for Beds were a glow of magical light. He could just make out his dressing-table.

Suddenly Pinneberg turned. Without hesitation, without so much as a glance at the piece of furniture, he made straight for the shop door.

The temper in which Johannes Pinneberg suddenly

found himself is not at all dissimilar to the mood in which a man commits robbery and murder or joins in a riot. Pinneberg happened to buy a dressing-table, but it comes to the same thing.

"Yes, sir?" The salesman was an elderly, gloomy personage with a few sardine-like wisps of hair plastered across his pallid skull.

"You have a bedroom suite in the window," stated Pinneberg. He was in a savage temper and his tone was intensely aggressive. "Caucasian walnut."

"Certainly, sir. Seven hundred and ninety-five marks. A real bargain. The last of a lot. We couldn't produce any more at the price. Today it would cost at least eleven hundred."

"I don't want to buy the whole suite," growled Pinneberg. "I want the dressing-table."

"A dressing-table? Might I trouble you to come upstairs? We keep single pieces on the second floor."

"I want that one!" said Pinneberg angrily, pointing with his finger. "That's the dressing-table I want to buy."

"Out of the suite? Out of the bedroom suite?" It gradually dawned on the salesman. "Very sorry, sir, but we can't break up the suite. We'd spoil it if we did that. But we have some very nice dressing-tables upstairs."

Pinneberg made a gesture of impatience.

"Almost exactly the same," added the salesman eagerly. "Can't I persuade you to look at them, sir—just to look at them?"

Pinneberg snorted. "This is a furniture factory, isn't it?"

"Yes." The salesman was disturbed.

"Well," said Pinneberg. "Then why not make another dressing-table? I intend to have that particular dressing-table, understand? So you'd better make one like it—or not sell me one at all, just as you please. There are plenty of places that give decent service."

While Pinneberg was talking and growing more and more excited, he felt inwardly that he was behaving just as badly as his most objectionable customers. He was being abominably offensive to an old, bewildered, worried man. But he couldn't help it, he was furious against everyone and everything. And unfortunately his only antagonist was this old shop assistant.

"One moment, please," he stammered. "I should just like to speak to the manager."

Pinneberg looked after him with pity and contempt. What's got into me? I ought to have brought Bunny with me. Bunny's never like this. I wonder why? She doesn't have an easy time of it.

The man came back. "You can have the dressing-table," he said shortly. His tone was much altered. "The price will be a hundred and twenty-five marks."

A hundred and twenty-five—that's just crazy. They're trying to put one over on me. The whole suite only costs seven hundred and ninety-five.

"I think that's too dear."

"Not at all. A first-class crystal mirror like that costs fifty marks."

"What can you do for me on instalments?"

Pinneberg had suddenly dwindled, the salesman had grown very large.

"We cannot consider instalments," said the salesman

152

in a superior tone, looking Pinneberg up and down. "It is a favor for us to sell you the article. We are counting on the fact, that, later on, you . . ."

I'm caught, thought Pinneberg in despair. I shouldn't have made so much fuss. The whole thing is lunacy—what will Bunny say?

Aloud: "Good. I'll take the dressing-table. But you'll have to deliver it today."

"Impossible. The men are through in fifteen minutes."

I can still get out of it—or I could have, if I hadn't talked so big.

"I must have it today," he insisted. "It's a present. Otherwise there's no point to it."

Heilbutt would be coming that evening and it would be nice if his friend could see this present for his wife.

"Just a moment," said the salesman, and disappeared again.

Maybe he'll tell me it can't be delivered and then I'll say I'm sorry but I have to have it today and I'll walk out quick. He planted himself near the door.

"The manager says he'll let you have a hand-cart and one of the boys to help. You'll have to fix up the kid with something—it's after hours."

"Yes," said Pinneberg slowly.

"It isn't heavy," said the salesman encouragingly. "If you don't mind giving a hand behind, the lad can pull the cart all right. Just keep an eye on the mirror. We'll have some sacking put around it."

"Right," said Pinneberg. "A hundred and twenty-five marks."

7.

*Bunny receives a visitor and views herself in
the glass.*

BUNNY was sitting in their imperial apartment, darning
socks. This is an occupation which makes most women
melancholy. But not Bunny. Bunny was figuring. He'd
bring two-fifty; fifty goes to mamma, which was really
much too much considering she worked for her five or six
hours every day; a hundred and thirty must do for everything else; which left seventy.

Bunny lay back for a moment to rest. She had been having a good deal of pain in her back lately. For sixty,
eighty, and a hundred marks she'd seen layettes for
sale at Kadewe's. That was nonsense, of course. She could
do a lot of sewing herself. It was certainly a pity that there
was no machine in the house—but then you wouldn't expect Frau Mia Pinneberg to own one.

She'd speak to Pinneberg about it this very evening and
go out shopping tomorrow. She couldn't feel easy in her
mind until she had actually got all she needed. He had
some other notions in his head, she knew that. He'd mentioned he was going to buy something—she was sure it
had something to do with her shabby blue overcoat—but
there was no hurry about that kind of thing, it was more
important to have everything ready for the great event.

Gently Frau Emma Pinneberg let her husband's socks

154

drop, and listened. Very gently she felt her body. Here; that was where she'd felt a movement. Yes, that made five times these last few days, five times the baby had moved. Contemptuously Bunny looked across to the table on which lay *Motherhood: The Sacred Miracle.* "*Exactly halfway through the period of pregnancy the child first begins to stir within the mother's body. With joyous heart and wonder that is ever new the future mother listens to the baby's gentle taps.*"

Rubbish, thought Bunny. Gentle taps! The first time I thought I was being pinched by something that couldn't get out. Gentle taps! Bosh!

She smiled. Whatever it was she didn't mind. It was lovely. It was glorious. So he really was there; and now she must make him feel he was expected, joyfully expected, that everything was ready for him.

Bunny picked up the socks.

A ring at the front door bell. That's him, thought Bunny. Has he forgotten his key? No, it must be for mother, let her open it herself.

But she did not open it. Again the bell rang. Bunny sighed, and went out. Her mother-in-law's face, already half arrayed in war-paint, materialized in the door of the back sitting-room. "If it's anyone for me, Emma, show them into the little room. I'll be ready in a minute."

"Of course it's someone for you, Mamma." The head vanished and simultaneously with the third ring Bunny opened the door. Outside stood a dark gentleman in a light gray overcoat, hat in hand, a smile on his face.

"Frau Pinneberg?"

"She'll be right in. Won't you take your coat off? In here."

The gentleman was a little confused. "Isn't Herr Pinneberg in?" he asked, walking into the little room.

"Herr Pinneberg has been . . ." dead, Bunny was going to say. Then she suddenly remembered. "Ah, you want to see Herr *Pinneberg.* He'll be in any minute now."

"Strange." The gentleman did not seem at all offended —rather pleased. "He left Mandel's at four o'clock. But he first invited me to come here this evening. The name is Heilbutt."

Bunny was thunderstruck. So this is Herr Heilbutt. Left the store at four. Where on earth is he? There isn't a thing in the house and mamma will be butting in again at any moment.

"Goodness gracious, Herr Heilbutt. I don't know what you must think of me. Well, I'd better tell you right off that first I thought you meant my mother-in-law—her name's Pinneberg too."

"Correct," said Heilbutt with a smile of pleasure.

"And secondly my husband never told me he was going to invite you today. That's why I was so taken aback."

"Not at all," replied the impeccable Heilbutt.

"And besides I can't understand how if he left at four —and how did he get off at that time?—he isn't home yet."

"He had something he wanted to see about."

"The crazy boy must be buying me a winter coat somewhere!"

Heilbutt pondered for a moment: "I don't think so. He could get one at Mandel's at the employees' discount."

The door opened and with a large and cheerful smile Frau Mia Pinneberg sailed up to Heilbutt: "You must be

the Herr Seibold who 'phoned today about my advertisement. Would you mind, Emma——?"

Emma stood her ground: "This is Herr Heilbutt who
works with Hans at the store. He's come to see us."

Frau Mia Pinneberg beamed. "Oh I beg your pardon,
of course. Delighted, Herr Heilbutt."

Bunny heard the street-door being shut: "That must
be him!"

It was indeed. There he stood in the doorway, with one
end of the dressing-table in his hands, and the young
Himmlisch for Beds representative at the other end.

"Good evening, Mamma. Good evening, Heilbutt, very
glad to see you. Evening, Bunny. You might take a look at
our dressing-table. We were nearly run over by a bus on
the Alexanderplatz. I tell you I've lost twenty pounds getting here. Will someone open the door of our room?"

"But, darling——!"

"Did you bring the thing here yourself, Pinneberg?"

"In person," said Pinneberg.

"A dressing-table," said Frau Pinneberg cheerfully.
"You must be flush, my dears. Who on earth wants a
dressing-table in these days of bobbed hair?"

But Pinneberg did not hear. He had just successfully
trundled the object through the turmoil of the Berlin
streets; for the moment that was enough for him.

"Over there, in that corner, young fellow," he said to
the leaky-nosed apprentice. "The light's better there. We'll
have to shift one of the lamps. Now, my boy, we'll go
down and get the mirror. Excuse me just a moment. My
wife, Heilbutt," he said beaming. "I hope you like her."

"I can handle the mirror myself," said the lad.

"She's marvellous!" answered Heilbutt.

157

"The boy's quite mad today," was Frau Mia Pinneberg's judgment.

"No you don't," says Pinneberg. "I won't have you falling upstairs with my mirror!" He added in a mysterious whisper: "Real polished crystal, worth fifty marks by itself."

He disappeared with the boy.

"Well, I won't disturb you any longer at the moment," said Frau Pinneberg. "I suppose you'll be busy with the supper, Emma. Can I help you at all?"

"Good Lord—my supper!" Bunny was in despair.

"Remember," confirmed her mother-in-law as she swept out, "I'll be glad to help."

"Please don't trouble." Heilbutt laid a hand on Bunny's arm. "I didn't come here for supper."

The door opened again; and Pinneberg and the boy reappeared.

"Now we'll see what it really looks like. Lift your end a bit, young fellow. Got the screws? Wait a moment." He screwed, sweated and talked simultaneously and uninterruptedly. "A little more light here, I can't see properly. No, please, Heilbutt, don't go near it just yet. I want Bunny to see herself in the mirror before anyone. I haven't looked into it myself. Kept the cover on all the time. Here's three marks for yourself. Good night. Bunny, I want you to do something for me. Don't be ashamed on account of him—eh Heilbutt?"

"Why, of course not."

"Then put on your wrap. Just slip it on over your clothes. Please. That's the way I always imagined you, before the mirror in your wrap, and I wanted you to be the first to look into it. Please, Bunny."

"Dear," remonstrated Bunny, but she was naturally touched by so much ardor. "As you see, Herr Heilbutt, I must do what I'm told." She took her wrap out of the wardrobe.

"I feel very privileged," said Heilbutt. "And your husband is quite right: every mirror ought to reflect something specially pretty for the first time."

"Flatterer!" Bunny tossed her head.

"I assure you . . ."

"Bunny," said Pinneberg, looking from wife to reflection, from reflection to wife, "Bunny, I've dreamt of this. And now my dream's come true! Heilbutt, it may be a hard life and lousy pay and we're treated like dirt by the brutes that feed on us . . ."

"Even if we are," said Heilbutt, "we can, if we choose, remain untouched."

"Of course, I always knew that. But this is the kind of thing they can't take away from us. Let them do and say what they like, they can't stop me from standing here and watching my wife in her bath wrap look at herself in the mirror."

"Have I been on exhibition long enough?" asked Bunny.

"Is the mirror good? Does it show you up well? Many mirrors," he explained to Heilbutt, "make you look as green as a drowned corpse, not that I've seen any. Some flatten you out and others make you look all spotty. But this mirror's a good one, isn't it, Bunny?"

A knock at the door; it opened slightly and Frau Pinneberg's face appeared in the gap. "Have you a moment, Hans?"

"In a minute, Mamma."

159

"It's urgent." The door closed.

"She wants the rent," explained Bunny.

Pinneberg looked strangely overwrought: "She can take her rent and—"

"Darling!"

"She doesn't have to act that way," he said furiously. "She'll get her money all right."

"Yes, but mamma naturally thinks we've got loads of money, because we bought a dressing-table. And they pay very well at Mandel's, don't they, Herr Heilbutt?"

Heilbutt hesitated: "Well, it depends on your conception of good pay. Now I suppose a dressing-table like that—it must have cost at least sixty marks."

"Sixty. You're crazy, Heilbutt!" said Pinneberg in highest excitement. Then, as he noticed that Bunny was looking at him, he added: "I beg your pardon, Heilbutt, you couldn't know." He added in a loud voice: "There shall be no more talk about money for the whole evening; let's all go in the kitchen and see what we can find. I'm starved, myself."

"All right, darling, just as you like." But she looked at him very hard.

8.

Some Pinneberg conjugal customs.
Mother and son. Jachmann again to the rescue.

BEDTIME for the Pinnebergs. He undressed slowly and reflectively, occasionally stealing a glance at Bunny who
slipped out of her clothes in a twinkling. Pinneberg heaved
a profound sigh, then said, with surprising cheerfulness:
"How'd you like Heilbutt?"

"He's very nice." It was quite apparent that she had no
intention of talking about Heilbutt. The sigh was repeated.

Bunny had put on her night-dress and now, sitting on
the edge of the bed, was taking off her stockings. She laid
them on one of the wings of the dressing-table. Pinneberg
observed gloomily that she took no real note of where
she was putting them.

"What did you actually say to mamma about the rent?"
she asked suddenly.

"About the rent—? Oh nothing. Said I had no
money."

Pause.

Bunny hopped into bed, drew the blankets over her.
"Aren't you going to give her anything at all?"

"I don't know. I guess so. But not now."

Bunny was silent.

By this time he was in his night-shirt. As the switch was
near the door and couldn't be worked from the bed, it

161

was one of Pinneberg's conjugal duties to turn off the light before he got into bed. On the other hand Bunny liked to have her good-night kiss with the light still on. She liked to look at her husband at that moment. So Pinneberg would walk round the vast and princely bed until he reached the pillow on the other side, dispose of the good-night kiss, go back to the door, switch off the light, and so get into bed.

The good-night kiss itself fell into two parts, his and hers. His was pretty well established: three kisses on the mouth. Hers was subject to considerable variation: either she took his head in her hands and kissed him soundly; or she put her arm round his neck, drew his head down and, holding him tight, gave him one long kiss; or she laid her head against his chest and stroked his hair.

The casual male in him tried to disguise how much he disliked this prolonged demonstration; and he was never quite clear how far she saw through him or whether his coolness affected her at all.

This evening he wished the whole good-night business were over and for one moment played with the idea of "forgetting" it. But that would only make matters more complicated in the end. So, with as indifferent an air as he could muster, he walked round the bed, yawned heartily, said: "I'm awfully tired, my dear. Got a big day ahead of me. Good-night," and gave her the three kisses.

"Good-night, darling." She kissed him once warmly: "Sleep well." Her lips were especially soft and full and cool; at the moment Pinneberg would have raised no objection to a continuation. But life was already complicated enough. He mastered himself, turned, clicked the switch, jumped into bed.

"Good-night, Bunny."

"Good-night."

At first the room was always pitch dark; gradually the two windows would emerge as gray patches and the noises grow more distinct. They could hear the elevated, the whistle of a locomotive, a bus lumbering down the Paulstrasse. Suddenly from quite near-by—they both started up in bed—came a burst of laughter, followed by shouts, catcalls and giggles.

"Jachmann seems to be in good form again," said Pinneberg involuntarily.

"They had a whole case of wine sent in today from Kempinski's. Fifty bottles."

"God, they sure can tuck it away. All that good money wasted." He could have bitten his tongue. Here was Bunny's cue. She said nothing.

Long pause.

"Dear?"

"Yes?"

"Do you know what sort of ad mamma put in the paper?"

"Ad?"

"First she thought Heilbutt had come to see her and asked whether he was the gentleman who had 'phoned about her ad. Perhaps she's thinking about letting our room again."

"She can't do that without telling us. No, I don't think so. She's glad to have us."

"But if we don't pay any rent?"

"Please, Bunny! We are going to pay sometime."

"All the same I'd like to know how that ad read. Do you suppose it had anything to do with these evening parties?"

"How could it? People don't advertise evening parties."

"I don't understand it."

"Me neither. Well, good-night, Bunny."

"Good-night, dear."

Silence.

Pinneberg faced the door and Bunny the window. It was of course quite out of the question for Pinneberg to get to sleep. First, owing to the exciting good-night kiss his wife had given him a little while ago, and the fact that a woman lay tossing and turning in bed a foot away from him (how sweetly and softly she breathed). And secondly, there was the dressing-table. He would have done much better to confess.

"Darling," said Bunny in a very soft and gentle voice.

"Yes?" He was a little uneasy.

"May I come over to you for a minute?"

Silence. A pause of surprise.

"Why, of course, Bunny." He made room.

It was the fourth or fifth time during their marriage that Bunny had made such a request: and it cannot be urged that the question veiled a desire for further love-making. True, that was usually the result, but this was owing to the rather obvious conclusion that, in masculine fashion, Pinneberg finally drew from such a question.

With Bunny it was really only a continuation of her good-night kiss, a need for caresses, a longing for affection. Outside lay the wild wide world, full of tumult and hostility that boded them no good. She loved to think of the two of them lying side by side, like a little island of warmth.

Each of them at first felt the other's warmth as something strange, but suddenly that feeling vanished, and they

were one. And now it was the boy who pressed closer to
the girl beside him.

"Darling," said Bunny; "my darling. Sweetheart."

"Dear. Oh . . . Bunny dear."

He kissed her, and they were no duty kisses; how good
it was to kiss this mouth that seemed to blossom and ripen
beneath his lips.

But suddenly Pinneberg ceased his kisses, and left a
little gap between his and her body, so that only their
shoulders touched.

"Bunny," said Pinneberg from a full heart, "I've been
an awful idiot."

"Have you?" She was busy with her thoughts for a little while. Then she said: "What *did* that dressing-table
cost? But you needn't talk about it if you don't want to.
It's all right. You wanted to please me."

"Dear!" he said; and again they suddenly came together. Then he made up his mind, and the gap once more
appeared. "It cost a hundred and twenty-five marks."

Bunny said nothing.

"It sounds pretty steep but remember the mirror alone
would cost fifty marks."

"True," said Bunny. "The mirror *is* good. It's rather
beyond our means and we certainly don't need a dressing-
table for the next five or ten years, but it was I who put
the idea into your head. And it's very nice to have it. And
you're a lovely silly boy. And now you mustn't be cross if I
go about in my shabby winter coat for another year because the baby comes first."

"Oh you're so sweet!" The kisses were resumed. They
lay very close together, and perhaps no more might have
been said that evening, had not a sudden tumult burst from

the sitting-room—laughter, shouts and screams, a male voice speaking very quickly, and above it all, the protesting, rather peevish accents of Frau Mia Pinneberg.

"They're three parts tight again," said Pinneberg much annoyed.

"Mamma's in a bad temper," observed Bunny.

"Mamma always get quarrelsome when she's had a drop too much."

"Can't you give her the rent? Some of it anyway."

"I have," said Pinneberg resolutely, "only forty-two marks left."

"What!" Bunny started up in bed. Little she cared now for comfort, warmth, and love-making; she sat up straight as an arrow. "How much have you got left out of your wages?"

"Forty-two marks," said Pinneberg in a tiny voice. "Listen, Bunny."

But Bunny wasn't listening. This time the shock was too great. "Forty-two," she whispered, and began to add: "a hundred and twenty-five. Then you're getting only a hundred and sixty-seven marks. It isn't possible!"

"A hundred and seventy, I gave three marks to the boy."

Bunny fell upon the three marks: "What boy—?"

"The dressing-table boy."

"Well, then, a hundred and seventy. And you go and buy— Oh God, what will become of us, how are we going to live?"

"Bunny," implored the lad; "I know. I've been a damned fool. But it'll never happen again, I swear it won't. And soon we'll be getting a maternity grant."

"That will soon be gone if we go on like this. And what
about the baby? We've simply got to buy some things for
the baby. Now you've just got to listen to me. I wouldn't
care if the two of us had to live in a stable. But I won't
have the baby in need of anything for the first five or six
years of his life if I can help it. And you go and do a thing
like this!"

Pinneberg sat up too; Bunny had spoken in quite another voice, as though he whom she loved had ceased to
exist. Suppose he *was* only a little salesman who was only
too soon, it appeared, shown up as a little beast whose life
wasn't worth bothering about; and even admitting that his
very deepest love for Bunny had something impermanent
and earthbound about it—still, he was *somebody,* he was
Johannes Pinneberg. The whole value and meaning of his
life was at stake and he must hold fast to it, fight for it,
she couldn't take that away from him!

"Bunny, my darling Bunny, I know I've been a fool and
messed up everything but that's the way I am and you just
can't talk to me that way. I was always like that and that's
why you must stay with me and speak to me as if you loved
me and not as though I were just somebody to quarrel
with."

"But darling, I . . ."

He went on: this was his hour, thither from the outset
had the way inexorably led, he would not yield an inch.
"Bunny, you've simply got to forgive me. You know, deep
down inside you, that you aren't thinking about this any
more, that you could really laugh at your silly husband
when you look at that dressing-table."

"Darling . . ."

167

"No," he said, jumping out of bed. "I must turn on the light. I must see how you look when you're really forgiving me, so that later on I'll know."

He turned on the light, and hurried back to her. He did not get back into bed, but bent over her. Two faces met, strained, flushed, wide-eyed. Their hair mingled, their lips touched, through the yoke of her night-gown could be glimpsed the white, blue-veined loveliness of her breast.

How good it is here, he thought. How happy I am.

You great foolish crazy darling, she thought. You're mine, here, on my breast.

Suddenly her face began to glow, it grew brighter and brighter as though a sun were rising.

"Bunny!" He clutched at her. She seemed to be slipping from him, ever more distant and more radiant. "Bunny!"

She took his hand, laid it against her body : "Feel there; the baby just moved—he knocked. Can you feel it ? There he is again."

He, who could hear nothing, bent over her. Softly he laid his cheek against her body, so full and vigorous yet so soft.

"It's all right," whispered Bunny; "it's all right, my darling."

"Yes," he said, slipping closer into her arms, bending his face to hers. "I'm happier than I've ever been in my life. Oh, Bunny."

About midnight a bony finger rapped at the door.

"May I come in ?"

"Come in, Mamma," said Pinneberg loftily. "You're not disturbing us."

168

He gripped Bunny's shoulder to prevent her shrinking back to her side of the bed.

Frau Pinneberg came slowly in and surveyed the scene.

"I hope I'm not disturbing you. Your light was still on. But of course I didn't think you had already gone to bed. Are you sure I'm not disturbing you?" She sat down.

"Of course you aren't," said Pinneberg. "It doesn't matter in the least. Besides we're married."

Frau Pinneberg breathed heavily. In spite of her make-up she was clearly very flushed.

"Good Lord," muttered Frau Pinneberg—Bunny's night-gowns were so confoundedly open at the neck.— "What a breast the girl has. It isn't noticeable when she's dressed. You aren't going to have a baby, are you?"

"Oh no." Pinneberg contemplated his wife with the air of a connoisseur. "Bunny's always like that. Ever since she was a child."

"Darling," said Bunny warningly.

"You see, Emma," said Frau Pinneberg, with a sort of tearful indignation. "Your husband makes a fool of me. They all make fools of me. I've been out of the room at least five minutes, and I'm the hostess. But do you think anyone is asking where I am? No; they're all after those stupid little bitches Claire and Nina. And Holger has changed altogether these last few weeks. No one bothers about me."

A rather minor sob.

Bunny, embarrassed and sympathetic, would have got out of bed to go to her, but her husband held her fast.

"No, Bunny," he said inexorably, "it's the same old story. Just a drop too much, Mamma, that's all. It's the

169

old routine: first she cries, then she starts a row, then she cries again. Ever since I was a school-boy."

"Please, dear," whispered Bunny; "you mustn't say such things."

Frau Pinneberg said savagely: "I shouldn't talk too much about your school-days. I might tell your wife about the time when the policeman came along and found you fiddling around with that girl in the sand-bin."

"Go ahead, my wife knows all about it. You see, Bunny, now she's got to the quarrelsome stage."

"I won't listen to such talk," said Bunny with blazing eyes. "We're all no better than we should be, I know that too well, I had no one to look after me either. But for a son to speak to his mother like that."

"That'll do," said Pinneberg. "I didn't start it."

"And what about my rent?" asked Frau Pinneberg in a sudden fury, and plunged into her theme. "Today's the thirty-first, rent always has to be paid in advance and I haven't got a penny."

"You'll get it," said Pinneberg; "not today nor tomorrow. But you *will* get it—sometime."

"I must have it today, I must pay for the wine. No one asks me where I get my money from."

"Don't be so silly, Mamma. Nobody pays for wine in the middle of the night. And please remember that Bunny does all your work for you."

"I want my money," said Frau Pinneberg wearily. "I didn't suppose Bunny minded obliging me a bit now and again. I made some tea for you today—I didn't ask to be paid for doing that, did I?"

She looked very pale and got up unsteadily. "I'll be back again in a minute," she muttered, and staggered out.

"Now we'll put the light out at once," said Pinneberg. "It's a damned nuisance we can't lock the door. Oh Bunny, I wish the old woman hadn't come and disturbed us just at that moment."

"I can't bear it." He felt her whole body quiver. "I hate your speaking to mamma like that. After all, she's your mother, darling."

"Unfortunately she is," said the unmollifiable Pinneberg, "unfortunately she is; and because I know her so well, I know what she's like. You still fall for her, Bunny, because in the daytime when she's sober she's good company and sees a joke. But that's all put on. She doesn't really care for anyone—how long do you suppose she and Jachmann will keep going? He's no damn fool and he knows she's just making use of him. And she's getting too old to be much fun in bed."

"Darling," said Bunny very seriously. "I will not have you speaking of her in that way. You may be right and I may be a sentimental little fool, but I won't listen to it. I can't help thinking that the boy might one day speak like that of me."

"Of you?" His tone said everything. "The boy speak of you like that! But you're Bunny— God damn it, there she is again!—*We're asleep, Mamma!*" he roared.

"Dear children!" They were quite startled to hear Jachmann's voice this time, though in this case too the speaker was not entirely sober: "Dear children, excuse me a moment."

"Certainly," said Pinneberg. "But please go outside, Herr Jachmann."

"One moment, young lady, and I'll go away. You're a

171

married couple and so are we. Not officially, but in fact, and we certainly quarrel as if we were. Now why shouldn't we help each other?''

"Outside!" said Pinneberg.

"You're a charming woman," said Jachmann, sitting down heavily on the bed.

"It's me," said Pinneberg.

"No matter." Jachmann got up. "Being familiar with this room, I know that all I have to do is go around the bed . . ."

"Please leave the room," protested Pinneberg rather helplessly.

"All right, all right." Jachmann felt for the narrow passage between the basin and the wardrobe. "As a matter of fact I came about the rent."

"Oh God!" groaned both the Pinnebergs.

"Is that you, my dear?" called Jachmann. "Where are you? Turn the light on. Say 'Oh God' again." He stumbled across the room to the bed by the window.

"You know your mother keeps on cursing because you haven't yet paid the rent. She's been going on about it the whole evening. And now she's crying over it. So I thought to myself as I'd made such a lot of money these last few days why shouldn't I give some to the children instead of to the old lady? They'll give it to her, so it'll all come to the same thing. And then there'll be peace."

"Well, Herr Jachmann," Pinneberg began. "That's very kind of you."

"Not at all—damn it, what's this? A new piece of furniture? A mirror! Well, I like peace and quiet. Here, my dear, here's the money."

"I'm very sorry, Herr Jachmann," said Pinneberg happily, "that you should have gone all that way for nothing, but the bed's empty. My wife's in with me."

"Damn," muttered the giant.

From without came a tearful voice. "Holger! Where are you?"

"Quick, hide yourself. She's coming in," whispered Pinneberg.

A confused noise outside, the door opened. "Is Jachmann here?"

Frau Pinneberg turned on the light. Two pairs of eyes looked rather anxiously round, but he was not there; no doubt he was crouching behind the other bed.

"I wonder where he can be? He sometimes runs out into the street. He gets feeling too warm— Bless my soul!"

Pinneberg and Bunny followed mamma's eyes in dismay. However, it was not Holger she had discovered, but some bills, lying on Bunny's red silk eiderdown.

"Yes, mamma," said Bunny, who was the calmer of the pair. "We've just been talking it over. That's the rent for the next few weeks. Please take it."

Frau Mia Pinneberg took the money. "Three hundred marks," she said rather breathlessly. "Well, I'm glad you thought better of it. That'll be for October and November. Then there'll be a little bill for the gas and electric light. We can figure it out later. Right. Thank you. Goodnight."

She talked herself out of the room anxiously clutching her treasure.

From behind the further bed emerged Jachmann's radiant countenance. "What a woman!" he said. "Three hun-

173

dred marks for October and November is pretty good. Well, excuse me children, I must go and see after her. I'm curious to know what she'll say about the money. Also, she seems to be pretty well pickled. Well, anyway, good-night."

The Pinnebergs were left to each other.

9.

Why the Pinnebergs will have to move.

"Good morning," said Kessler. (But it wasn't; it was the beginning of a gloomy, gray November day.)

"Morning." Pinneberg did not look up.

"Still very dark today," said Kessler.

Pinneberg did not answer.

"Live in the Spenerstrasse, don't you, Pinneberg?"

"How do you know?"

"So I heard."

The fellow is after something, thought Pinneberg. If he'd only come out with it. Damn him!

"Married, aren't you?" said Kessler. "Marriage isn't an easy job these days. Any children?"

"I don't know," said Pinneberg savagely. "Why not do something instead of standing around here?"

"I don't know, eh? That's good." Kessler now rapped out his words with open insolence. "Pretty good when a father of a family says he doesn't know."

"Listen, Herr Kessler——!" said Pinneberg, raising his yard measure.

"Well, what's the matter? You said it; or didn't you? The main thing is whether Frau Mia knows."

"What?" shouted Pinneberg. The other assistants were staring at the pair. Involuntarily he lowered his voice.

"I'll give you a sock in the jaw if you don't watch out."

"What about these discreet introductions into distinguished society, eh?" asked Kessler contemptuously. "Don't try to take that line with me, my boy. What would Herr Jänecke say if I showed him that advertisement. A man who lets his wife put such filthy advertisements in the paper."

Pinneberg lost his head, let fly at Kessler's ear, then felt himself pinioned from behind. Heilbutt said quite coolly: "Don't be a fool, Pinneberg."

"I should like to know," said Kessler to those standing round, "what he's so excited about. A man who lets his wife advertise in a newspaper!"

"Come on, Kessler, out with it. What's this advertisement you're talking about? Let's see it."

General murmur of indignation: "Come on, let's see it, Kessler. You can't back out now."

"Very well, then, I'll read it," said Kessler; "though it's very painful to me to do so." And he unfolded a newspaper.

Kessler read it very nicely.

"Are you unhappy in your marriage? I can introduce you to a charming and unprejudiced circle of ladies. You will be delighted. Frau Mia Pinneberg, Spenerstrasse 92-II."

Kessler licked his lips over it: "You will be delighted. Well, what do you say to that?" He went on: "He told me definitely that he lived in the Spenerstrasse."

"I . . ." stuttered Pinneberg, who was as white as a sheet, "never . . ."

"Give me the paper," said Heilbutt suddenly, looking

176

really formidable in his anger. "Where? Here . . . Frau
Mia Pinneberg. Pinneberg, your wife's name isn't Mia,
is it?—your wife's name is—?"

"Emma," said Pinneberg tonelessly.

"That's for you, Kessler. It doesn't refer to Pinneberg's
wife. Pretty low, I think."

"Look here," said Kessler. "I won't stand this."

"And then," went on Heilbutt, "you can see that our
friend Pinneberg knows nothing about this business. You
live with a relative, don't you?"

"Yes," whispered Pinneberg.

"Well, then," said Heilbutt. "I can't be responsible for
all my relatives either."

Kessler, who began to find the general atmosphere of
disapproval rather uncomfortable, pulled himself together: "Then you ought to be grateful to me for calling
your attention to this disgusting business. It seems funny
you didn't know a thing about it."

"That's enough," said Heilbutt, and the rest obviously
agreed. "And now, gentlemen, as Herr Jänecke may come
in any moment, I think the only decent thing to do is not
to discuss the matter any more. I suggest it would be
rather disloyal, don't you agree?"

They all nodded.

Heilbutt took Kessler by the shoulder. The pair disappeared behind a row of ulsters. There they talked for quite
a while, mostly in whispers; Kessler could be heard protesting loudly once or twice, but finally he grew very quiet
and subdued.

"There, that's over," said Heilbutt, going back to Pinneberg. "He'll leave you in peace. Forgive me for speaking so familiarly to you just now. May I go on doing so?"

177

"Please do, if you like."

"Good. Well then, Kessler will leave you alone now, I've got him where I want him."

"I'm very grateful to you, Heilbutt. I knew nothing about it. I feel as if someone had hit me on the head."

"It's your mother, isn't it?"

"Yes. I never had much respect for her. But such a thing as this . . . no."

"Come, I don't think it's as bad as all that."

"Anyhow, I shall move."

"Yes, I certainly should. And as soon as you can. If only because of the others, now that they know all about it. It's quite possible they might go there out of curiosity."

Pinneberg shook himself: "God forbid. When I'm away I don't know what goes on. They play cards. I thought it was just card-playing. You know. Just playing cards. That's all. Just playing cards. . . ."

10.

Happy consequences of a fainting-fit.

BUNNY looked for a lodging, and Bunny walked up many many stairs. She did not find it so easy as she had done six months ago. Then a staircase was nothing—she went up it, ran up it, danced up it: hoop-la and she was at the top. But today she found herself stopping on a landing, her forehead covered with sweat, and her back aching badly.

So she walked and climbed stairs, enquired, and went on. She had to find something soon; her husband would not, she knew, hold out much longer.

Oh those landladies! Some, when Bunny asked for a furnished room with kitchen privileges, looked straight at her middle: "Expecting a baby, aren't you? Well, if we wanted to hear brats crying, we could make 'em ourselves."

And they slammed the door in her face.

Time and again everything seemed all right and the business almost settled, and Bunny thought thankfully that he could wake up next morning with his troubles over. Then when she said (for they didn't want to be thrown out after a week or two): "We're expecting a baby," the landlady's face grew very long and she replied: "No, my dear young lady, but please don't feel hurt. I'd love to have you, but my husband . . ."

The world is very large, Berlin is a very large city; there

must be nice people somewhere, surely a prospective baby ought to be a blessing, this is the era of the child.

"But we're expecting a baby."

"Oh that's all right. Guess we've got to have them. Except that children *do* spoil a place, what with all the washing, the steam, and so on, and our furniture is so good. And a child does scratch the polish. Yes, I'll take you. But I have to say eighty marks instead of fifty. Well, make it seventy."

"No, thank you," said Bunny.

She saw all sorts of nice places, bright, sunny, prettily furnished rooms, with gay clean curtains, and fresh cheerful wall-papers. And she thought of her baby.

Then some elderly woman would appear and look at the younger woman with a friendly eye when she whispered something about the expected baby—and indeed, for anyone with eyes in his head, it was a real joy to look at her. Then the older woman, surveying the blue and now very shabby coat, would say: "Yes, but I can't let it go for less than a hundred and twenty marks. You see the landlord gets eighty, and I have only my little pension, I must live."

Oh why, thought Bunny, haven't we got just a *little* more money. Then we shouldn't have to figure out every penny in this dreadful way. Everything would be so simple, life would look quite different, and we could just enjoy the baby without worrying about things.

In the evenings he was often already home waiting for her.

"Any luck?"

"Not yet. I have a feeling tomorrow's the day. Oh dear how cold my feet are!"

True, her feet really were cold and damp, but she only said this to take his mind off his disappointment. He took off her shoes and stockings and rubbed her feet with a towel.

"There!" he said with satisfaction. "Now they're warm again; put your slippers on."

"Fine," said she. "And tomorrow I'll certainly find something."

"You mustn't fuss," he said. "One day more or less doesn't matter. I haven't lost courage yet."

"No," she said. "I know."

But *she* soon lost courage. She tramped and tramped the streets, but what was the use? There was no reasonable lodging to be had for what they could afford.

She had now made her way further to the north and east: appalling barrack buildings, interminable, malodorous and noisy. Women opened the door: "You can see the room if you like, but you won't take it. It's not good enough for people like you."

She would look at a room with great patches of discoloration on the walls. "Yes, we used to have bugs, but we've got rid of them now with prussic acid." A shaky iron bedstead. "You can have a bedside rug if you like, except that it makes more work." A wooden table, two chairs, a few hooks in the wall. "Baby? As many as you like; I don't mind a couple of brats yelling about the place, I've got five of my own."

"I don't know," said Bunny doubtfully. "Perhaps I'll come back later."

"No, you won't," said the woman. "I know what you feel like. I had a good room once, it isn't easy to make up your mind."

No, it wasn't easy. This would mean the end, the surrender of their own lives. A dirty wooden table, he one side of it and she the other, in the bed a yelling child.

"Never!" said Bunny.

When she was tired or in pain, she said quite softly to herself: "Not yet."

One afternoon Bunny was standing in a small grocer's shop in the Spenerstrasse, buying a packet of Persil, half a pound of soft soap, a packet of bleaching soda.

Suddenly she felt faint, there was a black cloud before her eyes, and she had to hold on to the counter to prevent herself from falling.

"Hi! Emil!" cried the woman of the shop.

Bunny was given a chair and a cup of hot coffee; her vision returned and she whispered apologetically: "I've been walking about so much."

"You shouldn't do that. It's good for you to walk a little, but not too much."

"But I must," said Bunny despairingly: "I've got to find a place to live."

Suddenly her tongue was loosed and she told the pair all about her fruitless search. She felt she simply had to talk; with her husband she had always to be making the effort to keep cheerful.

The woman was tall and thin, with a yellow wrinkled face and black hair, and she looked rather forbidding. He was a fat red-faced fellow, shirt-sleeved, looming in the background.

"Yes, young woman," he said, "people feed the birds in the winter but we can starve to death."

"Nonsense," said the woman. "Think. Don't you know of anything?"

"Nonsense, eh? What do you expect me to know?"

"You know, Emil! Puttbreese!"

"Oh you mean rooms? Why didn't you say so?"

"Well, isn't his place empty?"

"Puttbreese? Does he want to let a place? What place?"

"Where he had the furniture store. You know."

"First I ever heard of it. Well, if he lets that hole, the young lady will never get to it up the hen-ladder. Not in her condition."

"Rubbish," said the woman. "Listen, dearie, you go and lie down for a couple of hours, and then come round again about four o'clock, and we'll go and see Puttbreese together."

"Oh thank you so much," said Bunny.

"If," said the shirt-sleeved gentleman, "the young lady takes that place, I'll eat a broom; a stiff broom, at one mark eighty-five."

"Rubbish," said his wife.

Bunny went home and lay down. "Puttbreese," she thought. "Puttbreese. The moment I heard the name, I knew it meant something good."

She went to sleep quite pleased about her little fainting-fit.

*Odd lodgings. Appearance of Master Puttbreese.
Re-appearance of Herr Jachmann.*

WHEN Pinneberg came home that evening an electric
flashlight suddenly shone in his eyes and a voice cried:
"Hands up!"

"What's the matter?" He was not in a very good
temper these days. "Where'd you get that flashlight?"

"We'll need it," cried Bunny delightedly. "In our new
palace the staircase lights don't work."

"You found a place?" he asked breathlessly. "Oh
Bunny, have you *really* found a place?"

"Yes," said Bunny triumphantly. "I really have. That
is, if you like it; I haven't actually taken it yet."

"Good God!" he said in terror. "Suppose someone
comes along and takes it before us."

"Don't worry—I've got an option till tonight. Hurry
up and eat your supper and we'll go round and look at it."

While eating he asked all sorts of questions but she
would tell him nothing. "No. You must see it yourself. I
do hope you'll like it."

They walked up the Spenerstrasse arm in arm and
turned in the direction of Alt-Moabit.

"A home," he murmured, "a real home for the two of
us."

"You may get a shock," said Bunny anxiously.

"Don't tease me."

A movie-house; beside it a doorway through which they walked into a yard. There are two kinds of yards and this was one of the other kind, more like a factory or a storehouse yard. A gas-jet flickered above a large double door like the door of a garage. On it was inscribed: "Karl Puttbreese: Furniture Stores."

Bunny pointed somewhere into the dark yard.

"The toilet's over there."

"Where?"

"There. The little door at the back."

"You're not fooling?"

"And this is our entrance," said Bunny, opening the garage door inscribed Puttbreese.

"No!"

They found themselves in a large shed crammed with old furniture. Overhead the dim glow of the little flashlight was lost in a network of rafters hung with spiders' webs.

"I hope," said Pinneberg, holding his breath, "this isn't our sitting-room."

"It's Herr Puttbreese's store-room. Herr Puttbreese is a carpenter and he also deals in old furniture. You wait and I'll show you everything. See the black wall at the back there, that doesn't quite reach to the roof? We have to go over that."

"Do we?"

"That's the movies—you saw it, didn't you?"

"I did," he said cautiously.

As they approached the torch flashed on to a narrow wooden stairway laid against the side of the wall. It was really more of a ladder than a staircase.

"Up there?" said Pinneberg doubtfully. "You, in your state?"

"I'll show you." She clambered up the steps. "Hold on tight."

The roof was close above their heads. They were in a sort of tunnel-vaulting; somewhere in the dim light to the left stood Puttbreese's furniture.

"Now follow me close or you'll fall down."

Bunny then opened a door, a real door this time, turned on a light, a real electric light, and said, "Here we are."

"Yes, here we are," said Pinneberg, and looked about him. "So this is it."

"This is it."

There were two rooms, or really only one, for the door between them had been removed. They were very low with thick beams across the whitewashed roof. That in which they stood was the bedroom, with two beds, a cupboard, a chair and a basin. That was all; no window. But further back was a fine round table and a gigantic white studded oil-cloth sofa, a writing desk and a sewing-table. All the furniture was old-fashioned mahogany; and there was also a carpet. There were pretty white curtains over the windows; three windows, all quite small, with square panes. It looked very cosy.

"Where's the kitchen?"

"There," said she, and opened the iron stove, which contained two ovens. "And the sink's right here."

"What's the rent?" He was still doubtful.

"Forty marks," she said; "but really nothing."

"What do you mean?"

"Well, with that staircase and the risk of fire he wouldn't be allowed to let it legally, of course."

"Well, I don't see you shinnying up here a couple of months from now."

"Leave that to me. The main thing is that you like the place."

"It's all right enough."

"You dumb idiot! We can be *alone* here—no one **can** interfere with what we do. It's *lovely*."

"Very well, dear. Then let's take it. It'll be your job **to** look after the place. I'm glad if you are."

"Of course I am," she said. "Come along."

"Young man," said Master Puttbreese, surveying Pinneberg and blinking his little blood-shot eyes. "Young man. I'm not of course taking any money for the place. You understand that."

"Yes," said Pinneberg.

"You understand that perfectly," said Puttbreese, raising his voice.

"Yes?" said Pinneberg encouragingly.

"Now then," said Bunny. "Put down twenty marks on the table."

"Right," said the Master appreciatively. "Good for you, my dear. The last half of November; quite correct. And don't you worry your head, young lady, about how you're going to get up there later on: if you get too fat and can't manage the chicken-ladder, I'll fix up a pulley and chair, and we'll haul you up; it'd be a pleasure for me."

"Well," laughed Bunny, "that's all right then."

"And when do we move in?" asked the Master.

The pair looked at each other.

"Today," said Pinneberg.

"Today," said Bunny.

"But how?"

"Look here," said Bunny turning to the Master. "Could you possibly lend us a hand-cart and give us a little help? There are only two boxes. Oh, and there's a dressing-table too."

"Dressing-table!" said the Master. "I would have placed bets on a baby-carriage. Well, you never know what to expect. All settled then?"

They departed with a hand-truck.

All went off excellently. Bunny packed with a positively gnome-like agility; Pinneberg stood at the door and held the handle against a possible intruder, as the usual party was going on in the dining-room. Master Puttbreese sat on the princely bed and said in amazement: "A gilt bed—I must tell my old woman about it, there's been some good work done in that bed, I'll bet."

Then the men carried down the dressing-table, Pinneberg with one hand only, in the other he held the mirror; and when they got back, the boxes were shut, the wardrobe gaping and empty, and the chest of drawers open.

"Off we go," said Pinneberg. Puttbreese grasped each of the two boxes at one end, and Bunny and the lad took the other. On the boxes lay a suitcase, Bunny's bag, and the egg-chest with the china.

"Forward march," said Puttbreese.

Bunny glanced behind her once; this was the first room she had had in Berlin, it was hard to leave it.

"One moment," cried Bunny. "The light!" She dropped the handle of her box.

It fell with a very audible bang. The suitcase made even more noise, but the egg-chest . . .

Puttbreese, though a little puzzled, had conscientiously obeyed the request for silence. Now his deepest bass rang out. "If they didn't hear that they deserve to lose their money."

The two Pinnebergs stared at the sitting-room door like detected criminals. The door opened and there stood Holger Jachmann flushed and smiling. The Pinnebergs stared at him fixedly; his expression changed, he closed the door behind him, took one step towards the little group.

"Herr Jachmann," said Bunny in an imploring whisper; "Herr Jachmann, we're moving. Please—but you know . . ."

Jachmann took another step. He spoke in quite a low voice: "In your condition you ought not to be carrying a box."

He took the box in one hand, the suitcase in the other.

"Now then."

"Herr Jachmann," said Bunny once again.

Jachmann said not another word; he carried the box in silence down stairs, silently he laid it on the cart, silently he shook hands with the Pinnebergs. He watched them disappear down the gray and foggy street; a cart with some odds and ends on it, a rather shabbily dressed woman who was going to have a baby, an insignificant youth, dressed with sham smartness, and a fat old boozer in a blue overall. Herr Jachmann, dinner-jacketed, smart, well-groomed, sighed heavily.

The pros and cons of a normal budget.

BEFORE Bunny lay a manuscript book, sheets of paper, a pen, a pencil and a ruler. She wrote, added, crossed something out, put it in again. She sighed, shook her head, sighed once more, thought: It isn't possible; and began to calculate again.

The room looked quite cosy with its deep beamed roof and warm brown mahogany furniture. It was in no way a modern room; "Be faithful unto death" worked in black and white beads on the wall seemed perfectly in keeping. Bunny, with her blue dress, her little machine-made lace collar, her soft face and straight nose, was part of the picture. It was pleasantly warm, the gusts of raw December wind that swept now and again against the windows only made it all the more snug.

Bunny had finished writing:

Normal Budget
of Johannes and Bunny Pinneberg
per month
Note: Under *no circumstances* to be exceeded!!!
Income:

Pay, per month, gross   200 RM

Expenses

a. Food
   Butter and margarine . . . .   10. —

Eggs	4. –
Vegetables	8. –
Meat	12. –
Sausage and cheese	5. –
Bread	10. –
Groceries	5. –
Fish	3. –
Fruit	5. –
	62. –

b. Other expenses:

Insurance and taxes	31.75
Union contributions	5.10
Rent	40. –
Car fare	9. –
Electricity	3. –
Coal and wood	5. –
Clothes	10. –
Shoes and repairs	4. –
Washing, mangling, and ironing	3. –
Cleaning materials	5. –
Cigarettes	3. –
Outings	3. –
Flowers	1.15
Replacements	8. –
Miscellaneous	3. –
	134. –
Total expenses	196 RM
Balance	4 RM

The undersigned solemnly agree that they will not under any circumstances or for any reason use money for any other purpose except as above or take more money out of the cash than that set out in the budget.

Berlin, November 30th.

Bunny hesitated: she could just see his face! Then she took the pen and signed her name. She folded the paper neatly and laid it in a drawer of the desk. From the middle drawer she took a capacious blue vase and shook out its contents on to the table. A few bills fell out, a few pieces of silver, a few copper coins. She counted it: a hundred marks exactly. She sighed gently, put the money in another drawer, replaced the vase.

Then she went to the door, switched off the electric light and sat down comfortably in the large wicker chair by the window, her hands in her lap, legs wide apart. Through the mica window of the stove a reddish glow gleamed on to the ceiling, flickered back and forth, stopped suddenly and quivered—only to re-commence its dance.

Bunny slept, sweet and long, lips parted, her head on one shoulder, a light quick cheerful sleep that raised and rocked her in its arms.

She leaped into full consciousness as he turned on the light and said: "Well, how are you? In the dark, Bunny? Baby left its card yet?"

"No. Not today so far. Good evening, husband."

"Good evening, wife."

They kissed.

He laid the table, she got the supper. She hesitated: "It's haddock and mustard sauce. They were so nice and cheap."

"Fine. I like fish every once in a while."

"You sound pretty cheerful. Have a good day? How's the Christmas rush?"

"Just beginning. People are still scared to buy."

"Did you sell much?"

"I was lucky—sold over five hundred marks. But—there's going to be a new arrangement."

"Nothing good, I suppose."

"They've got what they call an efficiency engineer. He's going to reorganize the whole works, make economies—all that sort of thing. Lasch heard he gets three thousand marks a month."

"That's what Mandel's calls economizing!"

"They're saying now every salesman will be marked down to sell so much goods, and if he doesn't—out he goes."

"Disgusting! Suppose customers don't come in or they haven't much money or they don't like the stuff. It oughtn't to be allowed."

"Well it is. They're crazy about it, say it's sensible and economical and a good way to find out who's no good. I think it's a lousy trick. Take Lasch, the poor kid. He says if they do that, and add up his sales book, he'll be so scared about not making his quota that he won't be able to sell a thing."

Bunny grew very warm. "Well, suppose he isn't such a good salesman—is that any reason why they have to take away his living and his whole happiness? Haven't the weaker got a right to exist? Do you have to value a man by the number of pairs of trousers he can sell?"

"Now Bunny, no need to go off the handle."

"I will! It makes me crazy just to think of it!"

"But of course they say they don't pay a man for being nice but for selling a lot of trousers."

"That isn't true, dear. They need to have decent people. But what they're doing, and the way they've treated the workers for a long while, and us too, will turn them all into wild beasts, as they'll find out one of these days."

"They certainly will," said Pinneberg. "Most of us are already Nazis."

"Thank you," said Bunny. "I know how we shall vote."

"Well—what? Communist?"

"You bet!"

"We'll think it over," said Pinneberg. "I always feel I should like to, and then I can't quite make up my mind. We don't have to anyway because just at the moment we've got a job."

Bunny surveyed her husband reflectively. "All right, darling, we'll talk it over again at the next election."

They abandoned the haddock. Bunny washed up quickly, Pinneberg dried.

"Have you been to see Puttbreese about the rent?" asked Bunny suddenly.

"All paid up."

"Then put the rest of the money away at once."

"Right." He opened the desk, took out the blue vase, felt in his pocket, took the money out of his purse, looked into the blue vase, and said in a bewildered voice: "But there's no more money in it!"

"No." Bunny looked firmly at her husband.

"But how's that? There must be some money there. It can't be all gone."

"It is," said Bunny. "It's all gone. Our savings are

gone and what we got from the Insurance is gone too. Every pfennig. From now on we live on your pay."

He grew more and more confused. He couldn't believe his Bunny was cheating him. "But I saw some money in the pot yesterday or the day before. There was certainly a fifty-mark note and a lot of smaller ones."

"There was a hundred marks."

"Then where is it?"

"Gone."

"But . . ." He grew suddenly angry. "Damn it, what have you bought? Out with it!"

"Nothing." But as he was on the point of blowing up entirely she added: "You don't understand, dear. I put it away safe; just imagine it doesn't exist. We must manage on your pay."

"But why put it away? If we say we won't spend any of it, that's just as good."

"But we do spend it."

"That's *your* story."

"Listen, dear, we always meant to manage on your pay, and even to save something, and where are our savings? Even our extra earnings have gone."

"But how?" He began to grumble. "It isn't as if we'd lived extravagantly."

"Yes," she said. "First there was when we were engaged, we were always running around."

"And that old brute Sesam with his fifteen marks— I'll never forget him, never."

"And the wedding, that cost money, too."

"And the first things we had to get. The saucepans and the knives and forks and the brushes and the sheets and my bed."

"And we spent a lot on excursions."

"And moving to Berlin."

"Yes, and then . . ." she broke off.

He continued bravely: "And the dressing-table."

"And the baby's outfit."

"And the crib."

"And a hundred marks still left," she added beaming.

"Seems to me we've done a lot." He was by now quite pleased. "Why all the fuss?"

"Yes." Her tone changed. "We did all we could, but we ought to've managed without our reserves. It was nice of you, dear, not to give me just so much for the house, but to let me take what I wanted from the blue pot. Still and all it made me careless and sometimes I went to the blue pot when it wasn't necessary—last month the veal cutlets and the bottle of Moselle weren't really necessary, for instance."

"The Moselle cost a mark. Don't you want us to have any fun at all?"

"It must be fun that doesn't cost anything."

"There's no such thing. If you want a little country air—money. If you want to hear a little music—money. Nothing without money."

"Museums, maybe . . ." she broke off suddenly. "Yes, I know, you can't always be going to museums and we never seem to find the right thing to look at. Anyway now we've got to budget and I've written down here what we'll need every month. All right?"

"Go ahead."

"You aren't sore?"

"Why should I be? I guess you're right. I'm terrible with money."

196

She showed him the paper. His forehead cleared as he began to read. "Normal budget—that's very good, Bunny. We'll stick to the normal budget no matter what happens."

He began to read it quickly through. "Food—that seems all right. Did you test it."

"Yes, I've been writing it down the last few weeks."

"Meat, twelve marks. Seems an awful lot."

"It's only forty pfennigs worth of meat a day for both of us. A lot less than you've been getting lately. We'll have to go without meat for two days at least."

"But what'll we eat?" he asked anxiously.

"All sorts of things. Lentils. Macaroni. Prunes and barley."

"Good Lord!" said he. "Just don't let me know when we're going to get tripe like that or I won't be any too happy about coming home."

She made a little wry grimace and then said briskly: "Right. We'll have them as seldom as possible. Only . . . if you don't like them very much, don't be cross. I'm always cross when you are and what's the use of anything if we're both going to be cross."

She nestled into his embrace—and then slipped away from him. "No, not now, darling. I want you to look at everything. Besides . . ."

"Besides what?"

"Oh nothing. I wasn't thinking. Later on. There's plenty of time."

This really made him uneasy. "What do you mean? Don't you want to any more?"

"Don't be silly. Of course I do, you know that."

"Then what did you mean?" he insisted.

197

"I meant something quite different," she said defensively. "In that book"—she glanced across at the desk—"it says that people oughtn't to so soon before the event. That the mother doesn't feel like it, and it isn't good for the child. . . . But . . ." she paused. . . . "I still feel like it."

"How long do we have to keep that up?" he asked suspiciously.

"Oh I don't know. Six or eight weeks."

He threw a devastating look at her and took the book from the desk.

"Oh never mind the old book," she cried. "It's a long time yet."

But he had found the passage. "Three months at least," he said, and his face fell.

"Well," she said. "I think it comes later with me than with most women. Now shut that dumb book."

But he went on reading, with raised eyebrows and forehead furrowed in amazement.

"Here's some more about abstinence," he said, now completely dumbfounded. "Eight more weeks while the baby's being fed. Well, say ten weeks and eight weeks, eighteen weeks—what do you suppose we married for?"

She looked at him with a smile and said nothing. He too began to smile. "Oh Lord," he said; "it's a funny world. I'd never have thought of all this." He grinned. "From now on, Emma Pinneberg, no exceeding the budget."

"Agreed. And now you'll have to get back to the budget really or everything is useless."

"Right. What's this? Cleaning materials?"

"Yes, soap and tooth-paste and your razor blades and benzine. Haircuts too."

"Haircuts? Excellent. Clothes, ten marks. It doesn't look as if we'd be getting any new clothes very soon."

"They're provided for too in the eight marks for replacements, though that's got to cover shoes as well; at most, a suit for you every second year, I thought, and a winter-coat for one of us every third year."

"Sounds good," he said. "But what's this? Three marks a month for outings? Where do you figure you'll go for three marks? The movies?"

"No," she said. "Here's *my* idea. Once in my life I'd like to go out *really*, like rich people do and not worry about money."

"On three marks?"

"We put it aside every month. And when we've really got together say twenty or thirty marks, then we'll have a real blowout."

He looked at her doubtfully, and a melancholy expression crept over his face. "Once a year?"

This time she noticed nothing: "Why not? The more we've saved the better it will be."

"Well," he said. "I never would have thought you'd enjoy anything of that kind."

"Why not? It's perfectly natural. I've never done anything like that in my life. Of course you know all about it from your bachelor days."

"You're quite right," he said slowly. He was silent. Suddenly he crashed his fists on to the table in a fury. "God damn it all!" he shouted, seized the pen and signed the normal budget.

13

Heilbutt thinks we have courage. But have we?

CHRISTMAS had come and gone. It was a quiet Christmas with a fir-tree in a pot, a tie, a shirt and a pair of rubbers for the lad; maternity stays and a bottle of Eau de Cologne for Bunny.

"I don't want you to lose your figure," he said. "I want to keep my pretty wife."

"Baby will be able to see the tree next year," said Bunny.

Generally speaking, December was a good month, and in spite of the Christmas festival the Pinnebergs' budget was not exceeded. They were as happy as snow kings and made plans as to how they would lay out their savings in the next few months.

But January was a gloomy, dark, depressed month. In December Herr Spannfuss, the efficiency engineer, had merely been looking around; in January he got busy. The sales-quota for the individual salesman was fixed, in the men's outfitting, at twenty times the man's monthly pay. Herr Spannfuss made a nice little speech on the subject. The arrangement was solely in the interests of the employees; every one of them now possessed the mathematical certainty that he was valued exactly in accordance with his deserts. No more of those attempts to curry favor with superiors which was so bad for the morale of a business. "Give me your sales-book," cried Herr Spannfuss, "and I will tell you what sort of man you are."

The assistants all pulled very long faces; and no doubt some intimates ventured a word or two to each other, but nothing was said openly.

However, there was a certain amount of murmuring at the end of January over the Kessler-Wendt transaction. Wendt had completed his quota by the twenty-fifth of the month. But on the twenty-ninth Kessler was three hundred marks short. When, therefore, on the thirtieth Wendt sold two suits one after the other, Kessler offered him five marks to be allowed to record the two sales on his own record. To which Wendt agreed.

All this was not known till later; Herr Spannfuss was the first to hear of it; how remained a mystery. Herr Wendt was asked to resign for taking advantage of a colleague's predicament while Herr Kessler got off with a warning.

As for Pinneberg he made his January quota comfortably and was inclined to be contemptuous of the whole scheme.

For February everyone expected a reduction in the quota, as February provided only twenty-four selling days as against twenty-seven in January. Besides the stock-taking sale took place in January. Certain bold spirits actually spoke to Herr Spannfuss about the matter, but he would not hear of any such proposals: "Whether you believe it or not, gentlemen, all your powers, mental and physical, are concentrated on this quota. Any diminution of the quota is a diminution of your capacity for work, which you would yourselves regret. I am confident that each of you will reach the quota and even exceed it."

And he looked at them all very hard and passed on. The consequences of these measures were not quite so moral as Spannfuss the idealist had contemplated. There was a general onslaught on customers, and many a client of the House of Mandel was rather surprised, as he strolled through the men's outfitting department, to see pallid, tense, obsequious faces appear on every side: "Please, sir, wouldn't you like—?"

It was oddly like a street of brothels, and every salesman was delighted when he could snap up one of his colleague's customers. Pinneberg had to join in with the rest of them.

On the twentieth he was very gloomy; he had been infected by the others, his self-confidence was gone, he had bungled two sales; he was no good.

She was in bed, she took him in her arms and held him close: his nerve was gone, he cried. She kept on saying: "Darling, even if you lose your job, don't lose your courage, don't give way. I'll never, never, never complain, I swear I won't."

Next day he was quieter, though still depressed. He told her a few days later that Heilbutt had transferred to him four hundred marks out of his own total, Heilbutt, the only one not infected by this fear psychosis, who went on his way as though there were no such things as sale quotas—and even took a poke at Spannfuss himself.

"Well, Herr Heilbutt," Herr Spannfuss had said with a smile; "I hear you are a man of great intelligence in your profession. May I ask if you have considered how economies are to be effected in this business?"

"Yes," said Heilbutt, his dark almond-shaped eyes

202

fixed on the dictator. "I have considered this question."

"And to what conclusion did you come?"

"I suggest the dismissal of all employees earning over four hundred a month."

Herr Spannfuss turned and went. But the whole department had positively exulted.

But, though Bunny rejoiced with her husband, she understood the black mood that lay back of his satisfaction. It was not only his anxiety over his business—indeed it was unlike him to be so easily affected by others; the trouble was that he had to do without her. She had grown so clumsy, so misshapen and heavy, that she had to be careful how she arranged herself and her burden when she lay down in bed, or she could not sleep.

The lad was used to her. She always noticed when he began to get restless, and now that he could no longer have her, he grew more often disturbed. How often was she tempted to tell him to go out and find himself a girl. If she did not say it it wasn't because she minded much for herself or grudged him a girl—once more it was simply a question of money. Just money. And in the last analysis it would have been useless. For she was aware of something else. It was no longer only her husband for whom she lived. When the lad told her his troubles, she listened, she comforted him, she backed him up; but in her heart of hearts she had to admit that she kept herself aloof from it all. She could not, she must not, upset the baby.

She went to bed; the light was still on, he was busy over something. She was glad to lie down, her back hurt her so. And now, as she lay, she pulled up her night-gown, and lay almost naked, looking at her burden.

"Darling," she cried. "Baby kicked me again just then, he's getting very lively, isn't he?"

"Yes?" he answered, and came hesitatingly up to her bed.

They both waited a moment or two. She cried again: "There! There!" Then she noticed that he was not looking there, but at her breast. She felt a shock as she realized how she had tormented him; she pulled down her night-dress, murmuring: "That's a stupid thing to do!"

"Never mind," said he. "I'm no better." And he went on with what he was doing in the half darkness.

So the time passed, and, ashamed as she felt sometimes, she could not help her eagerness to watch the infant tumbling within her. She wished she could have been alone, but they had only these two rooms with no door between them, so that each had to share the other's moods.

Once, and once only, Heilbutt came to visit them in their ship's cabin. It could now no longer be concealed that they were going to have a child, and it also became clear that the lad had never mentioned the matter to his friend. Bunny was surprised.

But Heilbutt was quite at home; he chaffed them a little, and asked some interested questions. He was sympathetic; he raised his tea-cup and said: "To baby's health!"

And then, when he had put his cup down again; "You've got courage."

In the evening when the pair were in bed Pinneberg said, "Did you hear Heilbutt say, 'You've got courage'?"

"Yes," said Bunny.

Then they were both silent.

But Bunny wondered for some while whether they

really had courage, or whether it was that their life would be utterly barren without the prospect of the baby. What else was there in life to gladden them? She would ask her lad sometime. But not just now.

14.

Suppose I never see her again.

SATURDAY afternoon he walked slowly up the Calvinstrasse, his overcoat unbuttoned to the light spring breeze. "Everything's easier when the weather is fine. I wish to God it would start!"

He crossed Alt-Moabit and a few steps further on a man offered him a bunch of lily of the valley; but the flower budget was exceeded.

At last he turned into the yard, through the garage door, up the ladder into the darkness. Bunny came to meet him with a smile. Whenever he came home it was always with the feeling that something must have happened; but nothing ever had. The event seemed as far off as ever, her body looked grotesque, stiff as a drum, her once white skin was covered with a hideous network of blue and red veins.

"Morning, wife," said Pinneberg, and gave her a kiss. "Kröpelin has really given me the afternoon off."

"Morning, husband. Fine. But don't start smoking. We're—dinner's just ready."

"Oh dear," said he; "and I was so longing for a cigarette. Isn't there a moment or two?"

"Of course," she said, and sat down on her chair. "How was it today?"

"Same old thing. And here?"

206

"Just the same too."

Pinneberg sighed. "Takes his time over it, doesn't he?"

"It can't last much longer."

"It seems pretty stupid," he went on after a pause, "for us not to know anybody. We ought to be able to ask. How can you be sure when labor starts? It might be just a stomach-ache."

"I think we'll know."

They began their dinner.

"Whee!" said Pinneberg. "Chops—? This is a Sunday dinner."

"Pork's so cheap just now," apologetically. "And I've cooked for tomorrow, so you . . . then we'll have more time to ourselves."

"I was thinking we might go for a slow walk in the Park. It's such a lovely day."

"Tomorrow morning, dear; tomorrow morning."

Then they started washing up. Bunny had a plate in her hand, when she suddenly opened her mouth and groaned. Her face grew pale, then gray, then very flushed.

"What is it, Bunny?" he asked anxiously, leading her to her chair.

"It's the labor," she whispered, and had no more time for him; she sat there, bent over, the plate still in her hand.

He stood, utterly non-plussed, he looked at the window, at the door, he wanted to run away, he patted her shoulders—should he get a doctor? Gently he took the plate out of her hand.

Bunny sat up again: her color came back, she wiped her face.

"Bunny," he whispered. "Darling Bunny."

"Yes." She smiled. "Now we must go. Last time there was an hour between the pains, and this time only forty minutes. I thought we'd finish washing up."

"And you said nothing about it, and let me smoke a cigarette!"

"There's plenty of time. When it's really near the pains come every few minutes."

"But you ought to have told me."

"But then you wouldn't have eaten a thing. You're always so washed out when you get back from the store."

She looked round the room. Upon her face there was a strange bright tremulous smile. "Yes, you'll have to wash up by yourself. And you'll keep our place nice and clean, won't you? It will mean a little work, but I love to think of it all neat and tidy."

"Bunny," was all he could find to say. "Dear Bunny."

"Well, let's go. You'd better go down first. I hope the pains won't come on just as I'm on the ladder."

"But," he began reproachfully, "you said only every forty minutes."

"You can't be sure. He may be in a hurry. If he takes his time he'll be a Sunday child."

They climbed down the stair-way. All went well.

Very slowly and sedately they walked through the lovely March sunshine. Some of the men stared unpleasantly at Bunny, some looked shocked, others merely grinned. The women all looked at them with quite a different, rather serious air; this was their business.

Pinneberg seemed to be thinking hard for a while, struggling with himself; finally he reached a decision. "That's settled," said he.

"What is it, dear?"

"No, I'll tell you later. Just before I leave you. I've made up my mind about something."

"Good," said she. "But there's no need for it. I like you very well as you are."

They had to cross a park, on the opposite side of which could be seen the gate of the hospital but it now became clear that she could not go on, and they made their way to a bench. Five—six women were sitting on it; they shifted along to make room, reacting to the situation immediately.

Bunny sat with her eyes closed, bent quite forward. Beside her stood Pinneberg, rather embarrassed and helpless, with her little suitcase in his hand.

A fat and rather deliquescent woman said in a deep voice: "Cheer up, dearie, if you can't stand it, they'll send a stretcher for you."

A young woman observed: "She'll have a cinch, the way she's made. She could do with a bit less fat."

The others stared at her with disapproval in their eyes.

"Every woman ought to be glad to have something round her ribs these days. You don't have to be nasty about it."

"I didn't mean anything of the kind," protested the young woman. But no one paid any more attention to her.

A dark, sharp-nosed woman observed meditatively: "That's the way it goes—all so that men may have their pleasure. We have to suffer."

Bunny had recovered. She looked round her like one awakening from sleep, into the row of women's faces, and tried to smile.

"All right now," she said. "I can go on, dear. Do you mind it very much?"

And all he could answer was: "Oh God."

Step by step the Pinnebergs went on.

"Darling," said Pinneberg timidly.

"What is it?"

"You don't believe what the old woman said, that it was just for my own pleasure?"

"Nonsense!" was Bunny's only answer, but she said it with such emphasis that he was quite relieved in mind. Here they were in the doorway, there was the fat porter.

"Confinement, eh? Office to the left."

"But," said the boy anxiously, "the labor's already started. Couldn't she be put to bed at once?"

Said the porter: "No need for hurry." Slowly they climbed a short staircase to the office. "We had one here a little while ago who thought she was going to pop in the waiting-room; she was in bed here for two weeks, went home again, and then it was another two weeks before anything happened—some of 'em can't count, I guess."

The office door opened, revealing a Sister sitting at a table. No one seemed very excited over the fact that the Pinnebergs had appeared with the intention of founding a real family, which, after all, is not so common these days as it used to be.

"Confinement?" asked the Sister likewise. "I'm not sure but I doubt if we have a bed vacant. If not we'll have to send you somewhere else. How often do the pains come? Can you still walk?"

"Look here . . ." Pinneberg was beginning to get really angry.

But the Sister was already at the telephone. She hung

up the receiver. "There won't be a bed free until tomorrow. But we can fix you up until then."

"One moment," said Pinneberg indignantly. "My wife has pains every quarter of an hour. She can't possibly be without a bed until tomorrow morning."

The Sister laughed; she looked at him and just laughed. "The first, isn't it?" Bunny nodded. "Well, you'll have to go into the confinement ward to begin with, of course, and then—" she turned sympathetically to Pinneberg— "if the baby arrives, there'll be a bed free." She added in an altered tone: "And now hurry up, young man, get the papers fixed up, and come back for your wife."

Fortunately the papers were soon disposed of: "No, you don't need to pay anything. Just sign here, to say that you surrender your rights to sick benefit. We get our money from the Insurance. That's all."

Bunny had just been through another attack.

"It's coming on slowly," said the Sister. "But I don't think it will be before tonight, at ten or eleven or so."

"So long?" said Bunny, with an anxious glance at the Sister. She wore quite a different expression now, thought Pinneberg, as though she were remote from all these people, even from him, and intent upon herself alone.

"Of course it may be sooner. You are a strong girl. It's often over in an hour or two but sometimes it lasts for more than twenty-four hours."

"Twenty-four hours," said Bunny, feeling very much alone. "Come along, dear."

They stood up and shuffled out. It developed that the confinement ward was at the back of the whole block of buildings, which seemed a very long way indeed. He would gladly have talked to Bunny and tried to take her mind off herself; she walked silently on, a mask on her face, and the worried wrinkle across her forehead that he knew so well. She must be thinking of those twenty-four hours.

He wanted to tell her what he thought of all this torment that she had to suffer. But he did not. Instead he merely said: "I wanted to talk to you a little. But nothing seems to come into my head, Bunny. I must try to think of something."

"Forget it, dear. And don't worry. Surely, what others have to endure isn't going to be too much for me."

"Well, yes," he said. "But——"

They had reached the confinement ward.

A tall fair-haired Sister in the hall turned as she saw the pair approach; perhaps she liked Bunny (all nice people liked Bunny) for she put her hand on her shoulder and said cheerfully: "Well, young woman, come to pay us a visit? That's right." And again the question—it seemed to be the main question here: "The first, eh?" Then to Pinneberg: "Now I must take your wife away from you. You needn't look so horrified, you can see her to say good-bye. And you must take all her things with you, nothing can be left here. Bring them back in a week's time when your wife goes home."

So saying, she disappeared with Bunny on her arm. Bunny nodded to him once more, over her shoulder, before she was absorbed into this child-bearing mechanism. Pinneberg waited outside.

Then he had again to give a number of personal details to an elderly gray-haired Sister who looked very stern. He found himself hoping that she would not have any

dealings with Bunny. She would certainly be angry if
Bunny did not do everything right. He tried, by behaving
very humbly, to win her sympathy, and was terribly
ashamed because he did not know the date of Bunny's
birthday. The Sister said: "As usual. No husband ever
knows."

But it would have been so nice if he could have been an
exception.

"Right. Now go and say good-bye to your wife."

He found himself in a long narrow room, crammed
with every sort of machine of which he could not even
guess the purpose. There sat Bunny in a long white night-
gown, smiling at him. She looked exactly like a little girl,
rosy-cheeked, with clear fair hair, and a faint air of being
ashamed of herself.

"Say good-bye to your wife," said the Senior Sister,
who was busy with something near the door.

The first thing that struck him was the cheerful blue
pattern printed on her night-gown. But when she put her
arms round his neck and drew his head down to her, he
saw that it was not a pattern but an inscription in round-
hand printed all over the garment: "Munic. Hospitals
Berlin."

The second thing that struck him was that there was a
very nasty smell about the place.

Bunny said: "Well, my dear, maybe this evening, and
certainly tomorrow morning. I'm so happy."

He whispered: "Bunny, I'll tell you one thing; I've
sworn that from now on I'll never smoke again on Saturday as long as I live, if all goes well."

The Sister called out: "Now Herr Pinneberg." To
Bunny she said: "Did the bowels work all right?"

Bunny flushed and nodded; not till then did he realize
that Bunny had been sitting on a commode while he had
been saying good-bye to her. He too blushed, though he
thought himself a fool for doing so.

"You can always ring up any time during the night,
Herr Pinneberg," said the Senior Sister. "Here are your
wife's things."

Pinneberg went slowly out feeling very unhappy: he
thought it was because for the first time in their married
life she had been entirely handed over to the charge of
other people, and because she was now enduring something that she had never endured before. "Perhaps a mid-
wife would have been better. Then I could have been with
her."

The park. No, the women were no longer sitting on
their bench. He wouldn't have minded, indeed he would
have been rather glad to have talked to one of them. Puttbreese was not at home either, so he could not talk to
him: he had to go alone up to his silent cabin-dwelling.

There he stood, in shirt-sleeves and Bunny's apron,
washing up again. Abruptly he said, aloud and very
slowly: "Suppose I never see her again. Things happen.
Often."

15.

How babies are made.

A QUARTER past five. It was little more than an hour since
he had left the hospital, and already there was nothing
more for him to do. He flung himself on to the great oil-
cloth sofa, and for a while, his face hidden in his hands,
lay motionless and silent. Yes, he was an insignificant little being, crying and struggling and elbowing to keep his
place in life; but did he deserve a place? He was nothing.
And because of him she must suffer torment. If he had
never . . . If he had not been . . . If only he had
never . . .

Lensahn, that was the name of the place, and there
were cheap Sunday excursion tickets there from Ducherow. One Saturday Pinneberg set forth, it was early summer, May or June. No, it was June. Bergmann had given
him the day off.

Lensahn is not very far from Platz. And so it happened that the little place was full of people, with radios
blaring from every restaurant garden and frenzied rev-
elry on the beach. Well, the virtue about the best kind of
beach is that it tempts you to go on and on. Pinneberg took
off his shoes and socks and strolled along the shore, bound
for nowhere.

He walked for a couple of hours until he saw no more
people, then sat down on the sand to smoke a cigarette.

He got up and went on. What a beach it was—so many curves and indentations. Sometimes it seemed as though there could be nothing beyond the next sandy headland, —as though you were walking straight into the sea. But the shore went on, sweeping inland in an infinite gentle curve. A great bay, scattered with white-maned waves, and another sandy headland in the distance.

Surely beyond that there could be nothing.

But there was: a bay, of course, and a human being walking towards him. He stared and frowned; a black speck at first, which then emerged as a person. But what were people doing out here? They ought to be at Lensahn.

As the figure approached, he observed it was a girl; barefooted, slim-legged, broad-shouldered, wearing a red silk blouse and a white pleated skirt.

It was getting on toward dusk and there was already a reddish glow in the sky.

"Good evening," said Pinneberg and he stopped and looked at her.

"Good evening," said Emma Mörschel and stopped and looked at him.

"I wouldn't go in that direction if I were you," he said, pointing behind him. "There's nothing but jazz, Fräulein, and half of them are drunk."

"Is that so?" she said. "And I wouldn't go in that direction"—and she too pointed—"either. It's just the same at Wiek."

"What'll we do then?" he laughed.

"What *can* we do?"

"We might have our supper here."

"If you like."

They clambered onto the dunes and sat in a hollow that encompassed them like a great friendly hand; the wind swept across the undulating dunes, and over their heads, away into the distance. They exchanged hard-boiled eggs and sausage sandwiches; he had coffee in his thermos, she had cocoa.

They chatted for a while and laughed. But they were mainly occupied in eating heartily, and they went on eating for quite a while. People were horrible, they agreed.

"Well I wouldn't be in Lensahn for anything," she said.

"Nor would I be at Wiek," said he.

"What'll we do?"

"We might have a swim."

The sun had set, but it was still light. They ran down into the soft surf, splashed each other and laughed. They were good citizens; they had brought bathing suits and towels. (Pinneberg had brought his landlady's.)

Later on they sat down and wondered again what to do.

"Shall we go?" she said.

"Yes, it's getting cold."

And they sat on in silence.

"Wiek or Lensahn?" she asked after a while.

"I don't care."

"Neither do I."

Another long silence. Their silence and their talk was filled with the rising murmur of the sea; the sound of it grew louder.

"Let's go," she said suddenly.

Very cautiously and gently he put his arm round her. He trembled; and so did she. The rustle of the waves grew louder.

He bent his head over her; her eyes were dark and shining hollows.

His lips were laid on hers; her mouth met his and her lips parted.

"Oh!" he said, drawing a deep breath.

His hand dropped gently from her shoulder, dropped until he felt her breast under the soft silk, firm and full. She made a slight movement.

"Please," he said softly.

Her breast slipped back into his hand.

And suddenly she said: "Yes. . . . Yes. . . . Yes. . . ."

It was like a cry of exaltation. It came deep out of her breast. She flung her arms round his neck, pressed her body against his. He felt her rushing toward him.

Three times she had said yes.

They did not so much as know each other's names.

There lay the sea; above them the sky—Bunny could see it very clearly—grew darker and darker, the stars came out, one after the other.

No, they knew nothing of each other, they merely felt that they were young and that it was good to love. They did not think of the baby.

And now he was on his way.

Around him the city roared. It had been glorious, it was still glorious—he had drawn first prize. The girl of the sand-hills had become the best wife in the world. But he could not claim to be the best husband.

Pinneberg got up slowly. He turned on the light and

looked at his watch. Seven o'clock. She was over there, three streets away from him. The time had come.

He put on his coat and ran across. "Where are you off to now?" the porter asked.

"Confinement wards. I . . ." But he did not need to explain.

"Straight ahead. Last building."

He walked past the various blocks; in all the windows there was light, and under each light lay four, six, eight beds. There they lay, hundreds, thousands, dying quickly or dying slowly, some even recovering, only to die later on.

In the corridor of the confinement wards the light was dim. The Senior Sister's room was empty. He stood and waited, feeling very awkward. A Sister came: "Yes?"

His name was Pinneberg, he would like to know . . .

"Pinneberg?" said the Sister. "One moment."

She went through a padded door. Immediately behind the door was another, also padded. That door she shut.

Pinneberg stood and waited.

Then a Sister hurried through the padded door, and after her another, dark-haired, short, very energetic.

"Herr Pinneberg? She's doing nicely. No, not yet. You might ring up again about twelv. . No, it's all going well."

Behind the padded door a cry rang out, no, not a cry, a shriek, a moan, a quick agonized wail of torment . . . it was not human, there was no human voice in such a sound. Then it died away.

Pinneberg had grown white as chalk. The Sister looked at him.

"Is it . . ." he stammered, "is that my wife?"

"No," said the Sister, "that is not your wife. Your wife has not got to that stage yet."

"Will my wife," asked Pinneberg, and his lips quivered, "will my wife shriek like that?"

The Sister looked at him again. Perhaps she thought it would be good for him to know; men weren't very nice to their wives these days. "Yes," she said, "the first labor is usually difficult."

Pinneberg stood and listened. But the place was still.

"About twelve then," said the Sister, and departed.

"Thank you very much, Sister," said he; but he kept on listening.

16.

*Pinneberg pays a visit and lets himself be
tempted towards nudism.*

FINALLY he had to go. Either there were no more
shrieks, or they had been cut off by the double padded
doors. However, now he knew that Bunny would shriek
like that. Well, it was natural enough, he supposed: you
had to pay for everything, why not this?

Pinneberg stood irresolute on the street. The lamps
were already lit, there was a festal glow around the Ufa
Theater, all this went on whether Bunny was there or
not. Whether there were Pinnebergs or not. That's an
idea not so easy to understand clearly, in fact almost
impossible.

Could he go home burdened with such thoughts?
There lay his empty dwelling, there stood the two beds
from which they had clasped hands at night across the
intervening gap; how good it was! Not tonight. Perhaps
never again. Where should he go?

No. Drinking cost money and besides he had to telephone again at eleven or twelve, and it would be disgraceful to be drunk when he called up. It would be
disgraceful to be drunk while Bunny was going through
her ordeal. He would not shirk; he would at least think
of Bunny shrieking, as he had been told she must.

But where should he go? Tramp the streets for four
hours? He passed the movies above which he lived, he

passed the end of the Spenerstrasse, where his mother lived. He couldn't go to the movies or visit his mother.

Here were the Criminal Courts, full of prisoners. Perhaps in cells people were sitting in torment behind those dark barred windows. You ought to know about such things, maybe life would be easier if you did; but you knew nothing. You went your own way, alone, and on a night like this—

Suddenly he knew what he would do. He looked at the clock. He looked at his watch; he must hurry, or the outer door would be shut before he arrived. He took a car for part of the way, then changed to another car. He was now feeling pleased with the prospect of his visit; with every mile placed between himself and the hospital, Bunny and the child-to-be faded farther and farther into the distance.

No, he was no hero, not in any respect. He was just an average young man. He did his duty, he thought it disgraceful to get drunk. But a man can pay a visit to a friend and even enjoy it—nothing disgraceful in that.

He was lucky. Heilbutt was having supper, and he would of course not have been Heilbutt if he had not been a little surprised at his late caller. "Pinneberg? Glad to see you. Have you had supper? No, of course not. It isn't eight o'clock yet. Sit down and join me."

He asked Pinneberg no questions. He didn't even ask why he had come. Quite annoying.

"It was a very good notion to come down. Look the place over. It's just the usual sort of den, hideous really, but I don't care. It doesn't worry me." He paused for a moment or two.

"Ah, you're looking at the nude photographs? I've got

rather a decent collection. And thereby hangs a tale. At first my landladies were horrified when I moved in and put the pictures up. Most of them were ready to run me out at once." He looked round the room. "Yes, there was always a row at first. Incredibly philistine, landladies." Pinneberg duly nodded. "But I persuaded them. One has to remember that, in itself, nudity is the only civilized thing. I managed to make them see it." Another pause. "My landlady here, for instance, you saw her—fat old creature—you can't imagine how wild she was! Put them in the cupboard, she'd say; gloat over them as much as you like, but not in front of me."

Heilbutt stared at Pinneberg: "But I convinced her. You see, Pinneberg, I'm a natural open-air man, I just said: All right, sleep on it, and if next morning you still want me to take away the pictures, I will. Coffee, please, at seven. Well, she knocks at seven; I say—'come in'; in she comes, the coffee tray in her hand, and there I am, perfectly naked, doing my exercises. I say to her— Now then, look at me, take a good look at me. Does it excite you? Or disturb you? Natural nakedness is without shame, and you aren't ashamed either. She's convinced. She says nothing more against the pictures, she thinks them perfectly all right."

Heilbutt looked straight in front of him: "People only need to know, Pinneberg, they've never been told properly. You ought to go in for it, Pinneberg, and your wife too. It would be good for you, Pinneberg."

"My wife," began Pinneberg. But Heilbutt was not to be checked—Heilbutt, so dark and self-possessed and dignified, had a bee in his bonnet, like everyone else. "Take these nudes, for instance. You won't see such a collection in all Berlin. There are firms that advertise nude photographs." He made a wry face. "Dozens of them; but they're no good; ugly models with ugly figures, no good at all. But these you see here were privately taken. Some are of ladies"—the voice grew solemn—"from the highest society, who accept our teaching." He raised his voice: "We are free men and women, Pinneberg."

"Yes, I should think so," said Pinneberg awkwardly.

"Do you believe," said Heilbutt, whispering almost in Pinneberg's ear, "that I could stand it all—the eternal selling of clothes, our idiotic colleagues and those filthy shop-walkers, and"—with a wave of his hand towards the window—"all the mess Germany is in, if I didn't have this? One might well despair, but I know that some day things will change. And this helps, Pinneberg, this helps. You ought to try it too, you and your wife." He did not wait for an answer; he got up and shouted to the door: "Frau Witt, you can clear away."

"Books," said Heilbutt, coming back, "and sport, and the theater, and girls and politics and everything that interests the others, are just narcotics—no use at all. In reality . . ."

"But . . ." began Pinneberg, and stopped, as Frau Witt had come into the room.

"Frau Witt," said Heilbutt, "this is my friend Pinneberg. I'm going to take him to one of our meetings tonight."

Frau Witt was a short round elderly woman. "Why not, Herr Heilbutt?" she said. "He ought to get a lot of fun out of it. Don't get scared," she said encouragingly to Pinneberg. "You don't have to undress if you don't want to. I didn't undress when Herr Heilbutt took me."

"I . . ." began Pinneberg.

"It's pretty funny," went on Frau Witt, "to see them all walking about naked, and talking to each other quite naked—old gentlemen with beards and spectacles and no clothes on. You feel pretty funny."

"You see," said Heilbutt, "but we don't feel awkward at all."

"Well," said the little round elderly Frau Witt: "I guess it's nice for the boys, all right. As for the girls, I don't quite understand them, but the young men of course find it a good stamping ground. They don't have to buy a pig in a poke."

"That's what you think," said Heilbutt curtly, obviously annoyed at this. "Perhaps you will clear away."

"Ah, you don't like me to say that, Herr Heilbutt." She collected the supper dishes. "But it's true all the same. Some of them don't think anything of going into the same locker together."

"You don't understand, Frau Witt," said Heilbutt. "Good evening, Frau Witt."

"Good evening, gentlemen," said Frau Witt, moving off with her tray, but she stopped for a moment in the doorway. "Of course I don't understand. But it's cheaper than going to a café, anyway." With that she disappeared.

"You can't be angry with her," he said; "the woman knows no better. Of course, Pinneberg, connections of that kind do happen, but then they happen everywhere when young people are together. That has nothing to do with our movement." He broke off. "Well, you'll see

225

for yourself. You can spare the time, can't you—you'll come along?"

"I really don't know," said Pinneberg, rather embarrassed. "I have to telephone very soon. My wife's in the hospital."

"Oh," he said sympathetically; then he understood. "Is it as near as that?"

"Yes, I took her there this afternoon. It's tonight. And Heilbutt . . ." he wanted to go on about his troubles, but Heilbutt broke in.

"You can telephone from the baths," said Heilbutt. "You don't think your wife would mind?"

"No, no, it isn't that. Only, it seems so crazy, there she is lying in the hospital—the confinement ward, it's called—and I don't think she'll have an easy time, I heard one woman shriek—it was awful."

"Yes, it's painful," said Heilbutt, with admirable composure, "but they all seem to go through with it. Besides, think how happy you'll be when it's over. And, as I said, you don't have to take your clothes off."

17.

*What Pinneberg thought about nudism and what
Frau Nothnagel thought about it.*

PINNEBERG had behind him the usual childhood with all
its disenchantments and revelations, and at least a dozen
love-affairs, without counting escapades. Then came
Bunny, and from the time following the scene on the dunes
there had been no one else. She had been the sweet and
delightful experience that had enriched his life.

Then they had married and they had often done what
in marriage is so easy and so near at hand; and it had
always been a good and pleasant thing, and a release of
pent-up energies, just as in earlier days, but no different
from what it then had been. Now, however, it had
changed, out of it had grown a bond between them, either
because Bunny was so fine a woman or from the habit
of marriage. Well the veils had come back, the illusions
were there once more. And now, as he made this pil-
grimage to the bathing establishment in the company of
his friend Heilbutt (whom he admired but now found
just a trifle absurd) he well knew that he had no desires
not connected with Bunny. He belonged to her as she
to him. He would feel no pleasure that had not its origin
and fulfilment in her, of that he was resolved.

It was therefore on the tip of his tongue to say to
Heilbutt: "Heilbutt, I'd sooner go to the hospital, I feel
a little nervous."

Just as an excuse, so as not to make a fool of himself.

But before he had been able to snatch a pause in Heilbutt's flow of talk, his mind became confused with visions of his home, the hospital ward, the baths full of naked women, the nude photographs—what little pointed breasts some girls had! He used to like them, but now since he had known Bunny's soft full bosom . . . There! —everything she was, was right. He would tell Heilbutt.

"Here we are," said Heilbutt.

Pinneberg looked up at the building. "Oh it's a real swimming bath. I thought . . ."

"You thought we had a place of our own; no, we aren't rich enough for that yet."

Pinneberg's heart began to hammer in his chest and he was horribly afraid. But for the time being nothing very terrifying happened. A gray female sat at the ticket-office and said: "Good evening, Joachim. Yours is number thirty-seven." She gave him a key with a number on it.

Pinneberg was very surprised to learn that Heilbutt's Christian name was Joachim.

"And this gentleman?"

"A guest," answered Heilbutt. "You won't bathe?"

"No," said Pinneberg rather awkwardly. "I'd rather not today."

"Just as you like," said Heilbutt smiling. "Just have a look around and perhaps you'll go and get a key later on."

They both went along the corridor behind the lockers. From the pool, which they could not yet see, could be heard laughter and splashes and shouts, there was the usual damp warm smell of a swimming pool. It all seemed

228

quite natural, and Pinneberg began to calm down a little. Suddenly the door of a locker opened, in the gap he saw something pink, and tried to look away. The door was opened wide and there stood a young feminine creature, clad in nothing at all, who said: "Here you are at last, Achim, I thought you were never coming."

"Allow me to introduce my friend Pinneberg. Herr Pinneberg—Fräulein Emma Coutureau."

Fräulein Coutereau made a little bow and held out her hand to Pinneberg like a princess. He looked at her, looked away.

"Delighted," said Fräulein Coutureau. She still had nothing on. "I hope we shall convince you that we're on the right path."

Pinneberg was saved—he caught sight of a telephone box: "I must telephone at once. Excuse me," he muttered, and dashed away.

Heilbutt called after him: "We're in thirty-seven."

"Well, one can lose all taste for it," he said to himself reflectively. "Perhaps one ought to be naked?"

He asked for Moabit 8650.

He waited and waited, and his heart began to throb again. Perhaps he would never see her any more.

The Sister said: "One moment. I will go and enquire. Who is it speaking? Pallenberg?"

"No, Pinneberg, Sister, Pinneberg."

"Pallenberg—that's what I said. One moment, please."

"Sister, Pinne . . ."

But she had gone.

"Are you still there, Herr Pinneberg?"

Thank heaven it was another Sister, he hoped it might be the one who was looking after Bunny.

"No, not quite yet. It may last about three or four hours still. You might ring up again about midnight."

"But is it all right?"

"All quite normal. About midnight, then, Herr Pinneberg."

He hung up the receiver, and had to go out, Heilbutt was waiting for him in thirty-seven—how on earth did he get the insane idea of coming here with him?

Pinneberg knocked at the door of number thirty-seven, and Heilbutt called out: "Come in." There they sat, side by side on the little bench, they seemed to have been really only talking; perhaps it was his fault, perhaps like Frau Witt he was quite spoilt for these things.

"Then let's go," said the naked Heilbutt, stretching. "Little close in here. You made it rather warm for me, Emma."

"No more than you did for me," laughed Fräulein Coutureau.

Pinneberg walked behind them, and again came to the conclusion that the whole thing was simply painful.

"What news of your wife?" said Heilbutt over his shoulder to Pinneberg. He explained to his companion: "Frau Pinneberg is in the hospital. She's going to have a baby today."

"Ah," said Fräulein Coutureau.

"Not yet over," said Pinneberg. "May last three or four hours longer."

"Then," said Heilbutt, with satisfaction, "you have an excellent opportunity to see everything."

Pinneberg had indeed an excellent opportunity of getting really angry with Heilbutt.

They were now beside the pool itself. Not many people, thought Pinneberg at first. But quite a crowd soon collected. A large group were standing on the spring-board, all incredibly naked, and one after another they walked along the plank and dived into the water. "I think," said Heilbutt, "you had better stay here. And if you want anything just wave."

With that the pair departed, and Pinneberg was left in his corner, secure and undisturbed. He watched what was happening on the spring-board. Heilbutt seemed to be a personage of some importance, they all hailed him with laughter and applause, and shouts of "Joachim" reached Pinneberg's ears.

Yes, among them were well-grown young men and girls, youthful creatures with straight lissom bodies; but they were greatly in the minority. The main contingent consisted of respectable elderly gentlemen and stout ladies. Pinneberg could well imagine them listening to a military band and drinking coffee; in this place they looked utterly improbable.

"I beg your pardon, sir," whispered a very polite voice behind him. "Are you a guest too?"

Pinneberg started and looked round. A sturdy, rather thick-set woman stood behind him (thank heaven fully clothed), wearing a pair of horn-rimmed spectacles on her rather prominent nose.

"Yes, I am a guest."

"So am I," said the lady, introducing herself; "Nothnagel is my name."

"Mine is Pinneberg."

"Very interesting here, isn't it?" she asked. "So unusual."

"Yes, very interesting," agreed Pinneberg.

"You were brought here by—" she paused and went on with almost portentous discretion—"a lady?"

"No, by a man friend."

"Ah, so was I. And may I ask whether you have decided yet?" pursued the lady.

"What about?"

"About joining. Have you decided to become a member?"

"No, not yet."

"Neither have I. This is the third time I've been here, but I haven't yet been able to make up my mind. It isn't so easy at my age."

She surveyed him cautiously. Pinneberg said: "No, it isn't at all easy."

She was delighted: "Well now, that's exactly what I always say to Max. Max is my friend. There—no, you can't see him just at the moment."

But Max was visible in a minute or two, a man of forty, good-looking, tanned, upstanding, dark, the pattern of an energetic business man.

"I always say to Max that it isn't so easy as he thinks, it isn't easy at all, especially for a woman." She again looked appealingly at Pinneberg, and there was nothing for it but to agree: "Yes, it's terribly difficult."

"There now! Max always says I must think of the business side of it—it's good for business, if I join. He's quite right, and he's done himself a lot of good by joining."

"Yes?" said Pinneberg politely. He was curious.

"Well, I can't see any reason why I shouldn't talk to

you about it. Max has a carpet and curtain agency. Business got worse and worse, and Max joined this society. When he can, he always joins an association of any size, and does business with his fellow-members. Naturally he gives them a good discount, but still he makes a decent profit, so he says. Yes, for Max, who's so good-looking and amusing and is so popular wherever he goes, it's quite easy. For me it's much more difficult."

She sighed deeply.

"Are you also in business?" asked Pinneberg.

"Yes," she said, looking up at him confidentially. "I'm also in business. But I don't do very well. I had a chocolate shop; it was quite a good business in a good position, but I haven't the talent for it. I've always had bad luck. Once I thought I would try and do better; I got a window-dresser, and paid him fifteen marks to dress my shop window; there was two hundred marks worth of stuff in it. And I was so pleased and excited that I forgot to let down the blinds, and the sun—it was summer time —shone into the window, and the chocolates were all melted when I noticed it at last. They were all ruined. I sold them to children for ten pfennigs a pound; just think, the most expensive chocolate creams for ten pfennigs a pound. Wasn't it dreadful?"

She looked at Pinneberg gloomily, and he felt quite gloomy too—both gloomy and amused; he had long since forgotten about the bathing.

"Didn't you have anyone who could have helped you a bit?"

"No, no one. Max didn't come along till later. I had then given up the business. And Max got me an agency in hygienic belts, hip-supports, and bust-bodices. It ought to

233

have been a very good agency, but I don't sell anything.
Or hardly anything."

"Yes, it's difficult these days," said Pinneberg.

"Isn't it?" she said gratefully. "It *is* difficult. I run
around all day long, upstairs and downstairs, and often I
don't sell five marks worth of stuff the whole day. Well,"
she went on, and tried to smile, "that isn't the worst—
people haven't got much money. But if only they weren't
so beastly to me. Do you know," she said cautiously, "I'm
Jewish—perhaps you noticed it?"

"No . . . not particularly," said Pinneberg awkwardly.

"You see, people do notice it. I always say to Max that
people notice it. I think people who are anti-Jew should
put up a placard on their doors, and then they wouldn't
be bothered. As it is, I never know what to expect. 'Take
your stuff away, you old Jewish sow,' someone said to
me, yesterday."

"Brute!" said Pinneberg savagely.

"I have often thought of leaving the Jewish church,
I'm not a very believing Jew; I eat pork and everything.
But I feel I can't do that now when everyone is so down
on the Jews."

"Quite right," said Pinneberg heartily. "I shouldn't do
that."

"Yes, and now Max thinks I ought to join this place,
and he's right; most of the women—I don't mean the
girls—do need supports for their hips and breasts. I know
what every woman here needs, and this is the third evening I've come. Max keeps on saying: 'Make up your
mind, Elsa; it's money for jam.' And I can't make up
my mind. Do you understand why that is?"

234

"Yes, I quite understand. I wouldn't be able to make up my mind either."

"Then you think I had better not join in spite of the business?"

"It is very hard to advise," said Pinneberg, looking at her reflectively. "You must know whether you think it absolutely necessary, and whether it will really be of service to you."

"Max would be angry if I said I wouldn't join. Anyhow, he has been so impatient with me lately that I'm afraid——"

But Pinneberg had a sudden fear that he might have to listen to this chapter of her life as well. She was a poor little gray creature, certainly, and as she talked he found himself hoping that he might not die soon, so that Bunny should be spared all this torment; he really could not conceive of any future for Frau Nothnagel. But he was already depressed enough that night, and he suddenly cut short what she was saying: "I must go and telephone. Excuse me."

And she said, very politely: "Of course; don't let me keep you."

And Pinneberg fled.

18.

Pinneberg's first deception of Bunny.

HE tramped all the long way from the outermost eastern district of the city to Alt-Moabit, in the north-west of Berlin. He might just as well walk, there was plenty of time until twelve o'clock, and he would save carfare. From time to time he found himself thinking of Bunny, of the Nothnagel, and also of Jänecke, who would soon be head of the department, as Herr Kröpelin was not in Herr Spannfuss's good books.

It was half-past eleven when he reached Alt-Moabit. He went into the nearest bar and ordered a drink. His purpose was to drink it very slowly, smoke two cigarettes and then telephone. By that time the half hour until midnight would be over.

Before the drink was on his table he jumped up and ran to the telephone box. He was suddenly aware that he already had the coin in his hand.

A man's voice answered him, and Pinneberg asked for the confinement ward. Then a long while passed, and a woman's voice replied, "Yes? Is that Herr Pinneberg?"

"Yes, Sister. Please."

"Twenty minutes ago. Everything went off splendidly. Child and mother both doing well. Congratulations."

"Thank God . . . and thank you so much, Sister."

Pinneberg suddenly felt radiant, a nightmare was lifted off his shoulders. "Tell me, Sister, what is it—a boy or a girl?"

"I'm sorry, Herr Pinneberg, but I can't tell you that, it's against the regulations."

Pinneberg dropped out of the clouds: "But how is that, Sister? I'm the father, surely you can tell me."

"I'm not allowed to, Herr Pinneberg; the mother has to tell the father herself."

"Oh," says Pinneberg, feeling quite abashed by so much forethought. "Can I come along to the hospital now?"

"Well I should think not! The doctor's with your wife at present. Tomorrow morning at eight."

Johannes Pinneberg walked out of the telephone booth like a man in a dream. He marched straight through the bar to the street and would have gone out if the barman had not taken him by the arm and said: "How about that drink, young feller?"

Pinneberg awoke and said very politely: "I'm very sorry," sat down at the table, took a gulp out of his glass, and said, as he saw the barman still looking at him indignantly: "You must excuse me; I have just heard on the telephone that I'm a father."

"That's different. That's enough to scare the pants off anybody. Girl or boy?"

"Boy," said Pinneberg boldly.

"It would be. They cost the most." He glanced at Pinneberg sitting huddled in his chair. "Well, just to cheer you up a little I'll set you up to the drink."

Pinneberg awoke once more and said: "Not at all! Not at all!" He put down a mark and dashed out.

237

A great light broke on the barman. "Why the damn fool's actually happy!"

Pinneberg was hardly three minutes away from home; but he walked on, past the movie, sunk deeply in his thoughts. In point of fact he was thinking how he could get some flowers by tomorrow morning at eight o'clock. But what can a man do when there are no flowers to be bought, and a man has no garden in which he can pick them? He steals them! And where can they be more conveniently stolen than from the gardens of Berlin, of which city he is a citizen, and in whose gardens he has a certain equity?

Thus Pinneberg set forth on a long nocturnal peregrination. He appeared in succession at the Grosser Stern, the Lützowplatz, the Nollendorfplatz, the Viktoria Luise Platz and the Prager Platz. Everywhere he stopped and surveyed the flower-beds. It was already the middle of March and there was hardly a flower to be seen: shameful. And such flowers as there were did not amount to much. A crocus or two, or a few snow-drops in the grass. Was that fit to offer Bunny? Pinneberg was disgusted with the city of Berlin.

He continued his wanderings; he made his way to the Nikolsburger Platz, then on to the Hindenburg Park, then to the Fehrbelliner Platz, the Olivaer Platz and the Savigny Platz. Nothing. Finally he raised his eyes from the ground and noticed a bush covered with golden blossom. Sprays, as golden as the sunlight, and without a green leaf; only yellow blossoms on the bare twigs. He did not stop to think. He did not even look round to see whether anyone was watching. He awoke from his reflections, leapt over the railing, ran across the grass, and broke off a whole branch of golden blossom. No one stopped him. Carrying the flowers in his hand he tramped the long way home. A kindly star must have shone upon the enraptured mortal, for he passed dozens of policemen before he climbed the ladder to his home in Alt-Moabit. He put the branch in the water-jug, flung himself on the bed and fell asleep in an instant.

He had of course forgotten to set the alarm and wind up the clock, but he awoke punctually at seven, lit the fire, made some coffee and heated his shaving water. He got out some clean clothes, made himself as neat as possible, and whistling earnestly, at ten minutes to eight took his branch of blossom out of the water-jug and set off.

With those radiant yellow blossoms in his hand he seemed to walk on air along the asphalt path between the hospital buildings, with not a thought for all the sick and dying that lay within.

A Sister greeted him: "Come in, please." He went through a white door into a long room and a moment later had the sense of many women's faces looking at him. But then he saw no more: right in front of him was Bunny, not in a bed but on a stretcher, with a soft, melting smile on her face. She whispered, as though from very far away: "Oh my dear."

Very gently he bent down over her and laid the stolen blossoms on the coverlet; "Bunny! Oh it's good to see you again!"

Slowly she raised her arms, and from them slipped the sleeves of the night-gown stamped with that odd blue lettering; white arms now so frail. But they found the way to his neck; "He's really here at last. It's a boy, darling."

Then he suddenly noticed he was crying—the tears came in dry convulsive sobs; and he said angrily: "Why haven't these women given you a bed? I'll raise hell with them!"

"There isn't a bed free," whispered Bunny. "I shall get one in two or three hours." She too was crying. "Ah, my dear, aren't you glad? You mustn't cry, it's all over now."

"Was it bad?" he asked. "Was it very bad? Did you . . . scream?"

"It's over now," she whispered, "and I've almost forgotten about it. But we won't have it happen again for quite a while, will we?"

A Sister spoke from the door: "If you want to see your son, Herr Pinneberg, come along now." Bunny smiled and said, "Give my love to our baby."

He walked behind the Sister into a long narrow room. Some more Sisters were standing there: they looked at him, but he was not embarrassed because he had cried and was still sobbing a little.

"Well, how does it feel to be a father?" asked a fat Sister with a double-bass voice.

But another—why, it was the Sister who had been so nice to Bunny yesterday, said: "What's the good of asking him that before he's seen his son?"

Pinneberg nodded and laughed.

Then the door into the next room opened, and the Sister who had called him stood in the doorway with a white bundle in her arms, and in the bundle was an ancient, ugly, wrinkled face, varnished red, with a pointed pear-shaped head that squealed and wailed and yelled.

Pinneberg became suddenly wide awake, and all his sins, from his earliest youth, came into his mind: his youthful abuses, the little girls in the sand-bins, and the four or five times that he had been very drunk.

And while the Sisters smiled at the little ancient wrinkled dwarf, the fear within him grew and grew. Bunny could certainly not have seen this baby. At last he could not contain himself, and he said with terror at his heart: "Sister, does he look all right? Do all new-born babies look like that?"

"Good gracious me," cried the Sister with the double-bass voice: "He isn't pleased with his son! You're much too nice for your father, baby."

But Pinneberg was still afraid: "Please, was there another child born here last night? There was? Then will you kindly show it to me . . . just so as I know what it looks like?"

"I never heard of such a thing," said the fair-haired Sister. "His is the nicest baby in the whole place, and he doesn't like it. Come along, young man, and have a look around." She opened the door into the next room, and went in with Pinneberg. There, indeed, in sixty or eighty beds, lay dwarfs and gnomes, old and wrinkled, pale and red. Pinneberg surveyed them anxiously. His mind was half at rest.

"But my child's got such a pointed head," he said in lingering doubt. "Doesn't that mean water on the brain?"

"Water on the brain!" cried the Sister, and began to laugh. "These fathers are really too much! They're born like that, you silly man, and the tops of their heads grow together later on. Now go to your wife and don't stay too long."

Pinneberg threw a last glance at his son, and went back to Bunny. Bunny beamed at him, and whispered: "Isn't he sweet, our baby? Isn't he lovely?"

"Yes," he whispered. "He's sweet! He's lovely!"

19.

Children are born to the Lords of Creation, and Bunny embraces Puttbreese.

A WEDNESDAY at the end of the month of March. Suit-case in hand, Pinneberg was walking slowly up Alt-Moabit; he turned in to the park. At that hour he should really have been on his way to work, but he was taking another day off.

In the gardens Pinneberg sat down for a while, there was plenty of time, he wasn't due till eight. He had been up since half-past four putting the room in order; he had actually scrubbed and polished the floor, and there were clean sheets on the beds. It was nice to have everything bright and clean, now that a new life, a different life, was to begin. There would be a child at home. All must be sunshine now.

It was pleasant here. The trees would soon be really green, the shrubs were green already. But later it would be nicer still and Bunny would sit with the baby in the big Tiergarten as soon as he was a little older. This lit-tle Tiergarten was too depressing: even at this early hour there were unemployed sitting about. Bunny took things so much to heart.

Well, up with the suitcase and on with you. Through the door, past the fat porter who at the word "confine-ment ward" replied quite mechanically: "Straight ahead, last building." A couple of taxis drove past, with men sitting inside, better off than himself, who could afford to have cars for their wives.

Confinement ward. Right, the taxis stopped. Should he take one? He stood there with the bag wondering what he should do; it wasn't far, but perhaps it was necessary, perhaps the Sisters would think it shocking of him not to take a taxi. Pinneberg stood and watched a taxi which had just arrived, sweeping up to the door with a flourish. The man said to the driver: "I shall be a few minutes."

"No," said Pinneberg to himself; "no, can't be done. But it isn't right, it really isn't right at all."

He walked into the hall, put down his bag, and waited. The men from the taxis had already disappeared, they were no doubt long since with their wives. Pinneberg stood there and waited. If he spoke to a Sister, she said hurriedly: "Back in one minute!" and ran off.

A sense of bitterness rose in his heart; he knew he was wrong, the Sisters obviously had no notion who had come in a cab and who had not—or had they? Why was he kept waiting here? He ought not to be kept waiting like this. Was he less important than the others? Was Bunny less important? Then he called himself an idiot for imagining such nonsense, of course all husbands were treated just the same. But his joy had gone. He stood there staring darkly into vacancy. Thus it began and thus it would go on; it was foolish to suppose that a new and brighter and more sunny life was now to start; it would go on exactly as hitherto. He and Bunny were used to it all; but he wished the child might be spared their troubles.

"Sister, please—."

"Just one minute—back at once."

Well, it didn't matter, he had the day off, a day that

he had so wanted to spend with Bunny. He could wait around here until ten or eleven; what he wanted was neither here nor there, it was of no consequence.

"Herr Pinneberg! It is Herr Pinneberg, isn't it? The suitcase, please. Where is the key? Right. Better go across at once to the Superintendent's office and get the papers. In the meantime your wife will be dressing."

"Right," said Pinneberg, took the form she gave him, and departed.

Now, he thought gloomily, there'll be more trouble. But he was wrong, everything went smoothly, he got his papers, signed something, and was free.

Then he stood in the corridor once more. The taxis were still waiting. Suddenly he caught sight of Bunny, still only half-dressed, passing from one door to another. She waved her hand and smiled: "Good morning, dear!"

Well it was still the same old Bunny anyway, however rotten life might be, she smiled and waved her hand: Good morning, dear. And she must be feeling pretty weak too, only two days ago she had fainted when she got up.

He stood and waited. There were several men standing there, waiting also—it had all been perfectly all right, of course, he had not been neglected in the least. They were very stupid to keep their taxis waiting so long, he couldn't bear to see money thrown away that way. The fathers were talking:

"It's a good thing I've got my mother-in-law at home just now. She does all the work for my wife."

"We've got a girl. The wife can't do everything, with such a small baby, and so soon after her confinement."

"I beg your pardon," said a fat gentleman in spectacles,

briskly: "A confinement is nothing to a healthy woman, in fact it's good for her. I told my wife that I would of course get her a girl, but I advised her not to have one. I said she would get well all the quicker, the more she had to do."

"I'm not so sure about that," said another doubtfully.

"But facts are facts," said the spectacled gentleman. "I've heard that in the country they have a baby and go out to the hay harvest next morning. All this fuss involves a weakening of morale. I'm very much against hospital treatment. My wife's been here for nine days, and the doctor didn't want her to go yet. 'I beg your pardon, Herr Doctor,' I said; 'this is my wife, and it is for me to say. What do you imagine my ancestors the Germani did with their women?' He turned red as a beet—I doubt that he had any Germani among *his* ancestors."

"Did your wife have a difficult time?"

"Difficult? My dear sir, the doctors were with her for five hours, and at two in the morning they sent for the head surgeon!"

"My wife was terribly torn; seventeen stitches!"

"My wife's a bit narrow too. This is our third but she's still narrow. Yes, it has its advantages. The doctors told her they had managed it this time, but the next time . . ."

The women appeared bearing long white packages in their arms, three women, five women, seven women, all with the same package, all with the same rather soft and melting smile.

The men are silent.

They look at their wives. Their expressions, lately so self-confident, become a little uncertain; they take a little step forward and then stop. They no longer appear to know each other. They look only at their wives, and the longish parcel that their wives are carrying: and they are all very embarrassed. Then suddenly they become very talkative: *Good morning, dear. . . . No, please let me. . . . You're looking splendid. . . . Quite well again. . . . Did you think I couldn't carry it? . . . All right, just as you say. . . . But the suitcase anyhow— where is it? . . . Why is it so light? Ah yes, of course you're wearing all your clothes. . . . Can you walk all right? A little shaky, eh? I've got a taxi outside. . . . Won't the little fellow be astonished when he rides in a taxi?—it will be a new experience. He won't notice it? Oh, don't say that. Why shouldn't it amuse him? . . .* While all this was going on Pinneberg stood beside his Bunny, saying only: "Oh it's good to have you back again!"

"Dear!" she said. "Are you happy? Did you have a hard time of it? Well, it's all over and done with. Oh how glad I'll be to get back home."

"It's all ready for you." He beamed at her. "Just wait till you see it.—Do you want to walk or shall I get a taxi—?"

"Nonsense. I'll enjoy a walk in the fresh air. And we've got time—you've got the day off, haven't you?"

Pinneberg took her arm and they walked out into the little yard in front of the building, as the taxis clattered off. Very slowly they made their way to the entrance gate, walking step by step as the taxis dashed past them. It doesn't matter, thought Pinneberg. I heard you talk, I know quite well it doesn't matter not having any money.

The porter had not even time to say good-bye to them, as he was standing talking to two people, a young man and a woman. It was obvious from her appearance what they wanted; and they heard the porter say: "Go to the Office first, please."

"They're starting," said Pinneberg dreamily, "and we're through."

They emerged from the gateway into the March sunlight and the March wind. For a moment Bunny stopped and looked up at the sky and the white, fleecy clouds sailing across it; she looked at the green of the trees and at the traffic on the street. For a moment she was silent.

"Yes?"

"Do you know," she began, and broke off. "No, nothing."

"Tell me; there was something on your mind."

"Oh it's too silly. Because I was outside again, you know. Inside the hospital you don't need to worry about a thing. And now everything depends on us alone." She hesitated. Then: "We're still very young. And we have no one."

"We have each other. And the baby."

"Yes, of course. But you understand?"

"Yes, yes, I understand. And I worry about it too. Life isn't very easy at Mandel's just now either. But it'll be all right."

"Of course it will."

They went arm in arm across the roadway and slowly step by step through the park.

"He doesn't move at all," said Pinneberg.

"He's asleep, of course. He was fed before we left."

"When do you have to feed him again."

"Every four hours."

Here they were at Master Puttbreese's furniture store,

and Puttbreese was there observing the approach of the trio.

"Well, did it go off all right, young woman?" he asked and blinked. "Did the old stork give you any bad pinches?"

"No, Master, thank you. It all went off very well."

"And how are you going to manage now?" asked the Master, jerking his head towards the ladder. "How are we going to carry the baby up, eh? A boy?"

"Of course."

"Well, how about that ladder?"

"Oh it'll be all right," said Bunny, looking rather doubtfully at the ladder. "I'm getting well very quickly."

"Look here, young woman, you put your arms round my neck, and I'll carry you up pick-a-back. Give your son to your husband, he'll get him to the top safely."

"It's quite impossible, of course . . ." began Pinneberg.

"What is?" asked the Master. "The rooms, do you mean? Can you find better ones? And can you pay for them? As far as I'm concerned, young man, you can clear out any day you like."

"I didn't mean that," said Pinneberg, hurriedly. "But you must admit it's a little hard."

"If you mean it's difficult for your wife to put her arms round my neck, then I agree with you," said Puttbreese angrily.

"Come along, Master," said Bunny. "Forward, march!"

And before Pinneberg knew what had happened, he found the long, firm package in his arms, Bunny laid her arms round the tipsy old carpenter's neck, he grasped her

249

gently round the behind, and said: "Tell me if I pinch,
and I'll let you go, young woman."

"You probably will—half way up," said Bunny laughing.

And with one hand clutching convulsively at the ladder
Pinneberg clambered up, rung by rung.

They stood alone in their room, Puttbreese had disappeared, they could hear him hammering below in his
shop; but they were alone, the door was closed.

Pinneberg stood there with his bundle in his arms, a
warm and motionless parcel. The room was bright and
cheerful, there were a few patches of sunshine on the
polished floor.

Bunny had flung her coat onto the bed. With light soft
steps she walked about the room, and Pinneberg watched
her.

She walked up and down, with soft quick fingers she
straightened one of the pictures. She banged the seat of
the sofa. She passed her hand over the bed. She went up
to the two primrose plants on the window ledge, and bent
over them very gently. She went up to the cupboard,
opened the door, looked inside, shut it again. She turned
on the tap at the sink, let the water run for a little, and
then turned it off.

Suddenly she laid her arm round Pinneberg's neck:
"I'm so glad," she whispered, "so very glad."

"Me too."

They stood for a while, quite silent, she with her arm
round his neck, and he holding the child. They looked
out of the windows, shadowed already by the faint green
of the tree-tops.

"How good it is," said Bunny.

"Yes," he said.

"Are you still carrying the baby?" she asked. "Put him on my bed. I'll get his crib ready at once."

Quickly she got the little woollen coverlet and spread the water-proof sheet. Then she cautiously opened the parcel. "He's asleep," she whispered. He too bent over the parcel; there he lay, her little son. His face was a little flushed, he had a worried air, and the hair on his head had grown a little lighter.

"I'm not sure," she said doubtfully. "I think I ought to get him dry first before putting him in his crib. He's sure to be wet."

"Must you disturb him?"

"And let him get sore? No, I must dry him. You wait, the Sister showed me how."

She folded a few diapers into triangles and then undid the parcel, very slowly. What tiny little limbs, they looked almost stunted, compared with the gigantic head. Pinneberg was rather shocked, and wanted to look away, but he knew he ought not to; he must not start like this, and the little being was, after all, his son.

Bunny bustled about, moving her lips as she did so: "How was it? Like that? Oh dear, how clumsy I am!"

The little creature had opened its eyes—eyes of a dim and tired blue, it opened its mouth, it began to shriek—no, to yell; a sort of helpless penetrating lamentable wail.

He looked on frowning. Bunny was very clumsy. So: pull the napkin through, that was clear, and then from the other side.

"Let me try," he said impatiently. "You'll never do it."

"Go ahead," she said with relief.

He took the diapers. It seemed so simple, the little

limbs hardly stirred. He would lay them on, then take the corners and draw them through.

"But they're all creased," said Bunny.

"Just you wait," said Pinneberg impatiently, more and more intent upon his task. The baby shrieked. The small bright room re-echoed with his yells, which were very loud and penetrating, tiny as his voice was. His body darkened to a deep red—surely he would soon need to take breath. Pinneberg could not help looking at him and the sight did not assist his efforts.

"Shall I try again?" said Bunny softly.

"If you think you can manage it."

This time she did manage it. All at once everything seemed to go smoothly.

"It's just nervousness," she said. "You soon get on to it."

The baby lay in its bed and shrieked in earnest.

"What are we to do?"

"Nothing at all," said Bunny. "Let him shriek. He'll be fed in two hours, and then he'll stop naturally."

"But we can't let him shriek like this for two hours?"

"Oh yes we can. It's good for him."

"And what about us?" Pinneberg felt inclined to ask but did not. He went to the window and looked out. In the room behind his son lay and yelled. Once more things were otherwise than Pinneberg had expected. He had intended to have a pleasant little breakfast with Bunny, indeed he had prepared one or two nice little dishes, but if the baby was going to yell like this. The whole room was full of it. He laid his head against the window panes.

Bunny stood beside him.

252

"Can't you carry him or rock him once in a while? It seems to me I've heard that's the thing to do when babies cry."

"Just you try," said Bunny indignantly. "You'll soon find yourself doing nothing else but walking up and down rocking the child."

"But I think we might the first day," implored Pinneberg. "We don't want him to be unhappy."

"Now listen to me," said Bunny energetically. "We're not going to start. The Sister said the best thing to do was let him cry himself out. He'll cry all through the first night. Probably." she corrected herself, with a glance at her husband. "He may not, of course. But he's not to be picked up on any account. Crying won't hurt him. And then he'll realize that he doesn't get anything by it."

"Well, all right," said Pinneberg; "it seems a little brutal."

"But, dear, it will only be the first two or three nights; and then we shall feel all the more relieved when he doesn't wake." A wheedling intonation crept into her voice: "The Sister said it was the only right thing to do. But out of a hundred parents, only three manage it. It would be so nice if we could."

"Maybe you're right," he said. "At night I can understand that he must learn to sleep. But now, in the daytime, I don't see why I shouldn't rock him a little."

"On no account," said Bunny; "absolutely not. Besides he doesn't know the difference between day and night."

"Don't talk so loud—you're sure to upset him again."

"He can't hear!" said Bunny triumphantly. "For the first few weeks we can make as much noise as we like."

"Well, really, I had no idea," said Pinneberg, quite horrified by Bunny's views.

But gradually the baby stopped crying and lay still. They had as nice a breakfast as he had hoped; and from time to time Pinneberg got up, went across to the crib, and looked at the child lying there open-mouthed. He crept across the room on tip-toe; it was quite useless for Bunny to tell him that nothing disturbed the baby. Then he sat down again and said to Bunny: "Do you know it's really very nice to have something to be glad about every day of your life."

"Of course," said Bunny.

"And when he begins to grow up and talk . . . When do children begin to speak?"

"Some at a year."

"As late as that? It'll be nice when I can tell him things. And when will he learn to walk?"

"Dear, it's all very slow work. First he learns to hold up his head, and then to sit, then to crawl, and last of all to walk."

"That's just what I said. Always something new. I'm so glad."

"And you can't imagine how happy I am. Oh, darling!"

20.

The baby-carriage, the two hostile brethren and the Confinement Grant.

IT was a Saturday evening, three days later. Pinneberg had just come home; he had stood by the crib for a moment looking down on the sleeping baby. He was now eating his supper with Bunny.

"Couldn't we both get out for a few minutes tomorrow?" he asked. "It's such lovely weather."

She looked at him doubtfully: "And leave the baby here alone?"

"But you can't stay indoors all the time until the baby can walk. You look quite pale already."

"It's true," she said slowly. "We must buy a baby-carriage."

"Of course." He added cautiously: "What will it cost?"

She shrugged her shoulders: "Oh it isn't only the carriage. We must have pillows and blankets for it."

A shock of fear came upon him: "But the money's all gone."

Her face fell. Suddenly something occurred to her: "You must get the money from the Sick-fund."

"Why I'd forgotten that," he cried. "Of course. But I can't go there myself. I can't ask for any more time off. And the lunch hour is too short."

"Then write."

"I will. At once. And I'll run right out and mail it. Listen," he said as he searched for the writing pad that they so seldom used. "What do you say, Bunny, if I got a paper to see whether anybody wants to sell a second-hand carriage?"

"Second-hand? For our baby?"

"We have to be economical."

"I'll have to see the child that used it before. Anybody's carriage won't do."

He sat down at once and wrote the letter to his Insurance Society, enclosing the discharge certificate from the hospital and various papers about the baby, and asking politely that the money due him, after deduction of the hospital charges, might be sent at once.

After a little hesitation, he underlined "at once." Then he underlined it again. "Very respectfully yours, Johannes Pinneberg."

On Sunday they bought a paper and found a few advertisements of carriages. Pinneberg went out and not far away saw an excellent one. He reported to Bunny: "The man's a conductor. But they seemed very decent. The child walks now, you see."

"What does the carriage look like?" demanded Bunny.

"Very nice. Almost new really."

"High or low wheels?"

But he was cautious: "Medium, I guess." Suddenly he had an inspiration: "There was white lace all round the coverlet."

"I can see I'll have to look it over myself," sighed Bunny.

When the baby had been fed and was lying peacefully

256

asleep in his crib, they got ready to go out. Bunny stopped
in the doorway, went back, looked at the sleeping child
and again walked to the door.

"I hate leaving him alone," she said, as they went
down.

"We'll be back in an hour and a half," he consoled her.
"He's fast asleep, and he can't move."

"I don't like it anyway."

The carriage had high wheels. It was very clean but
quite old-fashioned.

A small fair-haired child stood beside it surveying it
gravely. "It's his," explained the mother.

"Twenty-five marks is a lot of money for an old-
fashioned one like that," observed Bunny.

"I'll throw in the pillows," said the woman. "And the
horse-hair mattress. That cost eight marks alone."

Bunny was still doubtful.

"Twenty-four marks," said the conductor, with a
glance at his wife.

"It's really as good as new," said his wife. "And the
low wheels aren't so practical."

"What do you think?" asked Bunny, hesitating.

"Well," he said, "you can't go tramping around forever after baby-carriages."

"All right," said Bunny. "Twenty-four marks, with
coverlet and mattress."

The child cried bitterly when he saw his carriage leaving him. Bunny was rather reconciled to the old-fashioned
object when she observed the child so attached to it.

Pinneberg kept on putting his hand on the edge of it.
"Now we're really married," he said.

257

"We must always keep it downstairs in Puttbreese's furniture store. It isn't pretty."

"No," he said.

Pinneberg came home from Mandel's on Monday evening. "Have the Insurance people sent the money?"

"No, not yet," answered Bunny. "It's sure to come tomorrow."

But on Tuesday the money had not arrived, and it was almost the first of the month. Pinneberg's pay was spent, and of the hundred-mark reserve barely fifty marks were left.

"We can't touch that," said Bunny.

"No," said Pinneberg with rising irritation. "The money ought to be here. I'll run over tomorrow during lunch hour and stick a pin in them."

So he went; time was short, he had to miss his lunch, and it cost him forty pfennigs in fares; but he realized that he who has to pay out the money is not usually in such a hurry as he who has to receive it. He wouldn't make a fuss but just stir them up a bit.

Here comes the little man Pinneberg; he wants a hundred marks—or perhaps it will be a hundred and twenty, he has no idea what will remain after the hospital charges are deducted. He walks into a vast, resplendent edifice. He looks small and shabby in the mammoth hall. Pinneberg, my poor fellow, a hundred marks—? Here we deal in millions. The hundred marks are important to you? To us they are quite unimportant, well, no, that is not wholly true, as you will see later on. This building was in fact constructed out of your contributions, and those of people as small as you, but you are not to think of that now.

We use your contributions exactly as we are permitted to do by law.

It was a consolation to Pinneberg to observe that behind the railing were seated employees, in some sense colleagues of his own. Otherwise he might have been completely overwhelmed by all these sumptuous woods and marbles.

Pinneberg looked sharply about him; there was the right counter, letter P. No formidable bars or grating—just a young man sitting on the other side of the counter.

"Pinneberg, Johannes. Number 606,867. My wife has had a baby and I wrote to you about the benefit due."

The young man, busy over a card-index, did not look up. He reached out a hand: "Membership card."

"Here it is. I wrote to you."

"Birth-certificate."

Pinneberg said quietly: "But I wrote to you, and sent you all the papers I got from the hospital."

The young man looked up. "Well, what do you want then?"

"I want to ask if the matter has been settled. Whether the money has been sent. I need it."

"We all do."

Pinneberg asked still more quietly: "Has it been sent?"

"I don't know," said the young man. "If you applied for it in writing, your claim will have been dealt with by letter."

"Could you find out if it's been fixed up?"

"Everything here is dealt with promptly."

"But it ought to have reached me yesterday."

"Why yesterday? How do you know?"

"I reckoned up the time."

"Reckoned up the time! How can you know how matters are disposed of here? There are several departments."

Pinneberg said very quietly and firmly: "Would you mind finding out whether it's been settled or not?"

The young man looked at Pinneberg, Pinneberg looked at the young man. They were both very neatly dressed —Pinneberg had to be on account of his profession— they were both well washed and shaved, both had clean nails, both were employees.

But they were enemies, deadly enemies, for one of them sat behind the railing and the other stood in front of it.

"Nothing but useless bother," growled the young man. But he felt Pinneberg's eyes upon him, and disappeared into the background. In the background was a door, and through it the young man disappeared. Pinneberg watched him go. There was a notice above the door, and Pinneberg's sight was not good enough to read the inscription on it, but the longer he looked at it the more convinced he was that it read: "Men."

Inwardly he raged.

After quite a while, indeed after a very long while, the young man appeared through the same door.

Pinneberg looked at him anxiously, but the other would not raise his eyes. He sat down, picked up Pinneberg's membership card, laid it on the counter: "Your claim has been dealt with."

"Has the money been sent? Yesterday or today?"

"It has been dealt with in writing, I tell you."

"When, please?"

"Yesterday."

Pinneberg looked at the young man once more. He felt uneasy, he was sure that door led to the lavatories. "If I don't find that money at home, I tell you—!" he said threateningly.

But the young man noticed him no more. He was talking to his neighbor O about "crazy people."

Once again Pinneberg looked at his colleague, he had always known that something like this would happen, but he could not help feeling indignant. Then he looked at his watch; he would have to be quick and catch the train if he wanted to be on time at Mandel's.

Of course he had no luck. He was caught at the door; Herr Jänecke grabbed him as he dashed breathless into his own department. "Well, Herr Pinneberg," said Herr Jänecke. "Don't you take any interest in your work, eh?"

"I'm very sorry," said Pinneberg. "I was only at the Insurance Office about my wife's confinement."

"My dear Pinneberg," said Herr Jänecke with emphasis, "you've been telling me that for the past month. You've told some very good stories but perhaps you'll think of another one next time."

When Pinneberg got home that night he asked: "Money?"

Bunny shrugged her shoulders: "Nothing. But there's a letter from them."

Pinneberg could still hear the insolent tone in which the man had said, "It's been dealt with," as he tore open the letter. If he only had the fellow here!

It proved to be a letter, enclosing two sheets of enquiries to be answered: no, no money, no hurry about that.

A letter. Two pages of questions. Had he simply to sit down and fill in the answers? Oh no, nothing so easy as that. First get a Registrar's certificate of birth, as the hospital certificate was not adequate. Then sign the questionnaires, fill them in neatly (though they probably dealt with matters already in our card-index) : how much do you earn, when were you born, where do you live. Tabulated information of this kind is always handy.

Now comes the main point: to help settle matters in due course, get certificates showing what Societies you and your wife have belonged to during the last two years. We are well aware that doctors incline to the view that, in general, women carry children for nine months only, but it's just as well to make quite sure; so, for the last two years, please. Perhaps another office can be made responsible. And we trust, Herr Pinneberg, that you will not be inconvenienced by waiting for a settlement of your claim until the necessary information has been forwarded.

"The bastards," groaned Pinneberg.

And he sat down and wrote. His case was simple enough, he had only to write to the office in Ducherow; but Bunny had unfortunately subscribed to two offices at Platz, and who could say when they would see fit to answer?

Wait for a settlement until the necessary information has been forwarded.

And when these letters were written, and Bunny was sitting peacefully in her red bath-wrap, suckling the baby, who drank, and drank, and drank—Pinneberg once more dipped his pen in the ink-pot, and in his finest handwriting wrote a letter of complaint to the Control Office for private Benefit Societies.

No, it was not a letter of complaint, it was merely an enquiry: Could the Sick-benefit office make the payment of money due in respect of a confinement dependent on the provision of such information? And must it go back over the last two years?

Lastly a question: Can't you see that I get the money soon? I'm badly in need of it.

Bunny did not expect much from this letter. "They won't put themselves out over us," she said.

"But it's so unfair. Confinement allowances ought to be paid during the confinement. What's the sense in them otherwise?"

And Pinneberg seemed likely to gain his point: three days later he received a postcard to the effect that his representations had been the subject of enquiry, and that a further communication would be sent him in due course.

Then silence. The fifty marks were of course broken into, but then his pay came in, and again a hundred-mark note was put by. The money would surely come in any day now.

But neither did the money come, nor did the enquiry seem to have produced any result. What came in first were the certificates from the Sick-benefit offices at Ducherow and Platz. Pinneberg packed everything up together; the certificates, the questionnaires, the birth certificate, which Bunny had long since got from the Registrar. And he put it all in the mail.

"Now!" said he.

But in reality he had lost all sense of expectation, he

had been so infuriated that he had not been able to sleep. The whole thing was senseless; we can't do a thing; we're up against a stone wall; it'll never change.

Then came the money, it really came very promptly, immediately after the documents were sent in.

"You see," he said once more. Bunny saw, but she preferred to say nothing, as that only made him lose his temper.

"I wish I knew what enquiries the Control Office made. I expect those fellows in the office got it hot and heavy."

"I don't think they'll write again," said Bunny. "We've got the money."

Bunny seemed to be right; a week passed, and then another week. Then a third week. And a fourth week started.

"They won't write any more," said Bunny again.

But Bunny was wrong. In the fourth week they wrote; a very brief and dignified letter, to the effect that they regarded the matter as settled, as Herr Pinneberg had already received his money from the Office.

Was that all? What Pinneberg had asked was whether the Office had been justified in asking for all this information.

Yes, for the Control Office that was all. It was not considered necessary to answer his questions; he had his money.

But that was not all. One of their humblest representatives downstairs had shown Herr Pinneberg his proper place. It was time he was shown it by the really important and exalted gentlemen themselves. They wrote a letter to the Control Office about Pinneberg. The Control Office sent a copy of this letter to Herr Pinneberg. What did they say? That his complaint was unfounded. Well, that went without saying; they could say no less. But why was his complaint unfounded?

Because Herr Pinneberg was dilatory. Because Herr Pinneberg had got the Registrar's birth certificate on such and such a day and had not sent it to the Office until a week later.

"And they say nothing about all that information they wanted," groaned Pinneberg; "masses of it, and the certificates didn't come in until I had sent it in."

"You see," said Bunny.

"Yes I do see," said Pinneberg savagely. "They're swine. They misrepresent the facts, and make us look as if we'd complained about nothing. But now I'll . . ." He sank into a brooding silence.

"What?" asked Bunny.

"I'll write again to the Control Office," he said solemnly. "I shall say that so far as I am concerned the matter is not settled; that it is not merely a question of money, but that they have mis-stated the facts. That this must be put right. That we're human beings and must be treated like human beings."

"Oh, what's the use?"

"Are they to be allowed to behave as they like?" he asked angrily. "There they are, sitting in their palaces, all comfortable and safe and rich. And are they to say what they please about us? No, I won't stand it, I'll . . ."

"It's no use," said Bunny. "It won't do any good. Look how excited you are again. You have to work all day; they come quite fresh to their office and can take all the time they like and telephone to the people at the Control

Office, and they're much more in with each other than they are with you. They'll just laugh at you, and you'll make yourself sick."

"But you've got to do something," he shouted in despair. "I won't stand it any longer. Can't we ever say what we think? Are we going to be stepped on forever?"

"The people we could step on, we don't want to step on," said Bunny, taking the baby out of his crib, for his evening meal. "I know all about it from father. One man can do nothing. He just makes a fool of himself and they laugh at him."

"Well, I should like to . . ." persisted Pinneberg.

"Don't you do anything," said Bunny. "Just drop it."

And she looked so angry, that when Pinneberg happened to look at her for a moment, he was quite taken aback—he hardly recognized her face.

He walked to the window, looked out, and said in almost a whisper: "Next time I'll vote Communist."

But Bunny did not answer. The child fed contentedly.

21

Disappearance of a tower of strength.

IT was now April, a real capricious April, with sunshine, clouds, and showers of hail, green grass and daisies, budding shrubs and growing trees. Herr Spannfuss of Mandel's also began to blossom and to grow, and every day the salesmen in the Men's Outfitting had stories of some new efficiency scheme—usually involving one salesman's doing the work of two.

In these days Heilbutt often said to Pinneberg: "How are you getting on? What's your total?"

Pinneberg looked away, and when Heilbutt asked again: "Tell me your total. I'm well ahead," Pinneberg would say, with an embarrassed air: "Sixty."

And then they would arrange for Pinneberg to come along when Heilbutt had sold a suit or an overcoat and enter it on his own sales book.

But they had to be careful: Jänecke was always sniffing around, and Kessler, who would have given them away at once, was even worse.

But where are the days when Pinneberg regarded himself as a good salesman? Everything was different now. True, customers had never been so hard to manage. One day, for instance, a tall fat man came in with his wife and asked for an ulster: "Not to cost more than twenty-five marks, young man! Do you understand? A friend of mine got one for twenty, real English, pure wool 'and properly lined—understand?"

Pinneberg smiled a wan smile: "Perhaps the gentleman exaggerated his bargain a little. A real English ulster for twenty marks—"

"Look here, young man, you needn't tell me my friend was lying. I don't come here to have you insult my friends, do I?"

"I'm very sorry, sir," said Pinneberg humbly.

Kessler was watching, and Herr Jänecke was standing behind a coat rack a little way off to the right. But no one came to his help; and he sold nothing.

"Why do you annoy people?" asked Herr Jänecke mildly. "You never used to be like this, Herr Pinneberg." And Pinneberg knew it was true.

But since the damnable quotas had been introduced, everyone's nerve had given way. At the beginning of the month it wasn't so bad; people had money then and were inclined to buy, Pinneberg filled up his book and felt quite encouraged: "This month I certainly won't have to borrow from Heilbutt."

But then came a day, and perhaps another, when not a single customer appeared. "Tomorrow I'll have to sell three hundred marks," thought Pinneberg, as he left Mandel's in the evening. "Tomorrow I'll have to sell three hundred marks," was Pinneberg's last thought, when he had given Bunny her good-night kiss and lay in the darkness. It was hard to go to sleep with such a thought in his mind, and it was by no means the last waking thought.

"I'll have to sell three hundred marks today," was in his mind as he awoke, drank his coffee, walked to his work, entered the department. All day long: "Three hundred marks."

Then came a customer who wanted an overcoat—about eighty marks, a quarter of the total. Pinneberg pulled out all his stock, tried them on, fell into ecstasies over every coat. The more excited he became—oh God, if the fellow would only decide!—the more uninterested grew the customer. Pinneberg tried every device, he tried obsequiousness: "You have such excellent taste, sir, everything looks well on you." He realized that his customer was becoming uneasy and had begun to dislike him, but there was nothing he could do about it. Then the customer departed, saying he would think it over.

Pinneberg stood there, in a state of something like collapse; he knew he had bungled the affair, but it was fear that turned his heart sick—there were those two at home, it was hard enough to manage as things were, what would happen if—?

True, the worst had not yet come; Heilbutt was still there, Heilbutt, the best of all his colleagues, and he would say: "How much, Pinneberg—?"

He never gave him advice, never told him to pull himself together, he did not talk cleverly like Jänecke and Herr Spannfuss, he knew that Pinneberg was up to the job—but not just these days. Pinneberg was not very tough; he went soft under pressure.

No, he did not lose his courage, he always recovered himself, and there were good days when he was quite on his old level, and not one sale went wrong. He thought his fear was overcome.

And then his masters would pass by: "Can't you put a little more pep into your sales, Herr Pinneberg?" Or:

"Why are you selling no dark blue suits? Do *you* want them all kept in stock?"

No, there was no sense in minding what they said, but how could one help it? That very day Pinneberg had sold two hundred and fifty marks' worth. Spannfuss came along and said: "You look tired, Herr Pinneberg. Why don't you follow the example of the American salesmen? They look as bright in the evening as they do in the morning. Keep smiling. A tired-looking salesman is a poor ad for any business."

Pinneberg cursed him in his heart. But he made his little bow and kept on smiling, and his feeling of confidence had vanished.

As a matter of fact there were others worse off than he was. He knew of a few salesmen who had been summoned to the Staff Office and warned.

"He's had the first injection," they said on the floor. "He'll soon be dead."

For then the fear grew greater, the salesman knew that there would be only two more injections, and after that: unemployment, misery, charity, the end.

He had not yet been sent for, but without Heilbutt his hour would long since have been at hand. Heilbutt was his tower of strength, Heilbutt was unassailable, Heilbutt could say to Herr Jänecke: "Perhaps you'd like to teach me something about selling."

To which Herr Jänecke would reply: "I forbid you to use that tone to me, Herr Heilbutt."

But one day Heilbutt was missing; he had been in the department, and sold something, and then, in the middle of that April day he had vanished, and no one knew where.

Next day Heilbutt was still missing.

"If he isn't there tomorrow," said Pinneberg to Bunny, "I'll go right to his place when I leave the store."

But next day the mystery was solved. It was Herr Jänecke who condescended to explain to Pinneberg. "You were a friend of this—Heilbutt?"

"I still am," defiantly.

"Ah. Did you know that he had rather peculiar views?"

"Peculiar—?"

"Well—about nudity?"

"Yes," said Pinneberg with some hesitation. "He did tell me something about it. Some kind of Nudist Club."

"You don't happen to belong to it yourself, do you?"

"I? No."

"No, you're married, of course." Herr Jänecke paused for a moment. "Well, we've had to dismiss your friend Heilbutt. He was mixed up in a very nasty business."

"What!" said Pinneberg hotly. "I don't believe it!"

Herr Jänecke merely smiled: "My dear Herr Pinneberg, you have a very limited knowledge of human nature. I can see that from the way you sell." And he added emphatically: "A very nasty business. Herr Heilbutt allowed nude photographs of himself to be sold on the street."

"What!" cried Pinneberg. He had lived most of his life in Berlin, but he had never heard of anyone allowing nude photographs of himself to be sold on the street.

"Those are the facts," said Herr Jänecke. "It is very creditable of you to stand by your friend, though it hardly speaks very highly of your knowledge of human nature."

"I still don't understand," said Pinneberg. "Nude photographs in the street——?"

"Well, we can hardly be expected to employ a salesman whose photographs in the nude may have fallen into the hands of our customers, who might well be ladies. A man whose face was so unmistakable!" So saying, Herr Jänecke departed, with a friendly and almost encouraging smile, so far as the distance between them admitted of such familiarity.

No, Kessler could not give Pinneberg a copy of the nude photograph, glad as he would have been to see the effect on Pinneberg's face. Pinneberg did not see it until later, in the course of the morning. It was not merely the great event in the Men's Outfitting, the story had long since spread beyond the boundaries of that department; the Silk Stockings on the left, and the Toilet Requisites on the right were talking about nothing else, and passing the picture from hand to hand.

Thus it reached Pinneberg, who had been racking his brains the whole morning to figure out how nude photographs of Heilbutt could have been sold on the street. Well, it had not been quite so bad as that, Herr Jänecke was right and Herr Jänecke was wrong. It was a newspaper, one of those periodicals that maintain a doubtful existence between propaganda and pornography.

On the cover of the paper, in an oval frame, stood Heilbutt. It was a handsome photograph, obviously taken by an admirer, he was a fine figure of a man, just about to hurl a spear; and he had nothing on. It was undoubtedly very amusing for the little shop-girls, many of whom had been keen on Heilbutt, to see him so agreeably unveiled before their eyes. He certainly disappointed no expectations.

"Who buys papers like that?" said Pinneberg to Lasch. "No one ought to be fired for such a thing."

"Probably Kessler nosed it out," said Lasch. "At least the paper came from him. And he knew about it before anyone."

Pinneberg made up his mind to go and see Heilbutt, but not that evening. He must first talk over the affair with Bunny. For, good fellow as Pinneberg was, he didn't quite like the story, in spite of his regard for Heilbutt. He bought a copy of the paper and took it home to show Bunny.

"Of course you must go and see him," said she. "And don't you let people run him down."

"What do you think of him?" asked Pinneberg anxiously, a little jealous of his friend's handsome form.

"He's very well made," said Frau Pinneberg. "You're filling out a bit around the middle. And you haven't got such nice hands and feet."

Pinneberg was quite embarrassed. "Well, I think he looks great. Couldn't you fall in love with him?"

"I don't think so. Much too dark for me.—And then . . ." She put an arm round his neck and smiled at him: "I'm still in love with you."

"Still?" he asked. "Really?"

"Still," she said. "Really and truly."

The next evening Pinneberg went to see Heilbutt. The latter was not in the least embarrassed. "You know all about it, Pinneberg? Well, they'll find themselves in trouble for discharging me without notice. I've already put in a complaint to the Labor Court."

"Do you think you'll succeed?"

"Dead certain. I should have succeeded even if I had given permission for the picture to be published. But I can prove it was published without my consent. There's not a thing against me."

"Yes, but what then? You'll get three months' pay and be out of a job."

"My dear Pinneberg, I'll soon find something else, and if I don't I'll set up on my own. I'll manage all right."

"I'm quite sure you will. I hope you'll take me on when you have a business of your own."

"Of course, Pinneberg. Before anyone."

"But no quotas!"

"Not a quota! But how will you get on? It'll be a tough time. Can you get along by yourself?"

"I must," said Pinneberg with a confidence he did not feel. "These last few days I've done well. I'm a hundred and thirty marks ahead."

"Well, then," said Heilbutt, "maybe it's a good thing I've gone."

"Oh, no it isn't."

Well, time to go, Pinneberg, Johannes. It was funny, but after a while Heilbutt and he found nothing to talk about. Pinneberg was really much attached to Heilbutt, who was a thoroughly sound fellow, but he wasn't quite the genuine friend. You couldn't let yourself go with him.

And so it was some time before he again visited Heilbutt, indeed he had to be directly reminded of him by hearing people in the store say he had won his case against Mandel's.

But when Pinneberg got to Heilbutt's lodging, Heilbutt had vanished.

22

Jachmann sees ghosts. Rum without tea.

A LOVELY bright evening in late spring. Pinneberg had
finished his day's work, he emerged from Mandel's and
hurried off.

A hand was laid on his shoulder: "Pinneberg, I want
you."

"What the——!" said Pinneberg, not in the least
startled. "Herr Jachmann! I haven't seen you for an
age."

"Well, that shows a good conscience," said Jachmann
gloomily. "You didn't even start. Youth, Youth! How I
envy you!"

"Do you? I wish you could exchange three days with
me. At Mandel's."

"What do you mean, Mandel's? I wish I had your job.
It's safe and solid anyway," said Jachmann in a melancholy tone, and walked slowly on with Pinneberg.
"Things are pretty depressing these days. How's your
wife, my boy?"

"Very well," said Pinneberg. "There's a baby now."

"No! Really? A baby? That's very quick work. Can
you afford it? I envy you."

"We can't afford it," said Pinneberg, "but if we went
by that, people like us would never have any children."

"Right," said Jachmann, who had certainly not been

276

listening. "Be careful, Pinneberg! Do you mind if we look into this book-shop window?"

"Yes—?" said Pinneberg expectantly.

"That is a most valuable book," said Jachmann, in very audible tones. "I learnt a great deal from it." And softly: "Look to the left. Quietly, now, quietly."

"Yes—?" says Pinneberg once more; he found all this very mysterious and the gigantic Jachmann much altered. "What am I to look at—?"

"The fat old man with the spectacles and the curly beard, did you notice him?"

"Yes, of course," said Pinneberg. "He's walking away."

"Good," said Jachmann. "Just keep him in sight. And now talk to me in just an ordinary way. That is—don't mention any names, and especially not mine. Say something."

Pinneberg racked his brains. What was the matter? What was Jachmann up to? He hadn't said a word about his mother.

"Say something," said Jachmann urgently. "Talk about anything—it looks so silly if we walk along without a word."

Silly? thought Pinneberg. Then aloud: "The weather still keeps lovely, doesn't it, Herr . . ." and had almost blurted out the other's name.

"For God's sake be careful," whispered Jachmann; and then, raising his voice: "Yes, it certainly is fine weather."

"Not that a little rain would do any harm," continued Pinneberg, looking doubtfully at the back of the elderly gentleman three paces in front. "It's very dry."

"Rain would certainly do good," agreed Jachmann quickly. "But we don't want it just at the week-end, do we?"

"No, of course not. Not at the week-end."

That seemed to dispose of the subject. Not a thing came into his head. Once he threw a sidelong glance at Jachmann, and reflected that the man's familiar gaiety had gone. And he noticed that Jachmann too was anxiously surveying the gray back in front of them.

"For God's sake say something, Pinneberg," said Jachmann nervously. "You must surely have something to tell me. If I hadn't seen a man for six months, I should have something to say to him."

"You mentioned my name," said Pinneberg. "But where are we going?"

"Where? To your place. Where else? I'm going with you."

"Then we ought to have turned to the left just now," remarked Pinneberg. "I live in Alt-Moabit."

"Well, why on earth didn't you turn off to the left?" asked Jachmann angrily.

"I thought we wanted to follow the gray gentleman in front."

"Christ!" said the giant. "Don't you understand?"

"No."

"Then walk right on as if you were going home. I'll tell you all about it later. You must make conversation on the way."

"Very well, then, we turn off to the left again."

"Right; you lead the way, my lad," said Jachmann irritably. "How's your wife?"

"We've got a baby," said Pinneberg in despair. "She's

very well. Can't you tell me what really is the matter, Herr Jachmann? I can't make it out at all."

"Damn, now you've mentioned my name," said Jachmann savagely. "He's sure to follow us. Don't on any account look round."

Pinneberg said nothing, and after this outburst Jachmann, too, said nothing.

The traffic light was red, and they had to wait a moment.

"Can you still see him?" asked Jachmann anxiously.

"I thought I wasn't to . . . No, I can't see him any more. He's gone straight on."

"Ah!" said Jachmann, and there was a ring of infinite relief in his voice. "I must have been wrong. One often sees ghosts."

"Can't you tell me, Herr Jachmann—?" began Pinneberg.

"No," said Jachmann. "That is—I'll tell you later on. Later, of course. Now we'll go along to your place, and see your wife. So you've got a baby? Boy or girl? First-rate! Splendid! Did it all go well? Yes, of course it did; a woman like your wife wouldn't come to any harm. Do you know, Pinneberg, I've never understood how your mother could have had a son—it must have been an oversight on the part of heaven, not only of the indiarubber factories. There now—I'm sorry! But you know what I'm like. Is there a florist around here? Or would your wife rather have chocolates?"

"But really it isn't necessary, Herr Jachmann."

Jachmann had already vanished into a confectioner's. Two minutes afterwards he re-emerged: "Any idea what your wife likes best? Brandied cherries?"

279

"Nothing alcoholic, Herr Jachmann," said Pinneberg reproachfully. "My wife is nursing the baby."

"Of course, of course. No brandied cherries, then? I never knew that, I confess. A hard life." He had talked himself into the shop again.

After a while he again emerged, laden with a very substantial parcel.

"Herr Jachmann," said Pinneberg with misgiving; "What a lot of stuff! I don't know whether it will be good for my wife."

"Well, she needn't eat it all at once. The trouble is I don't know what she likes. There are so many kinds. And now watch out for a florist." Jachmann stopped for a moment and reflected: "I don't care to bring your wife any guillotined flowers, you know, I'd rather take her something in a pot. That's more suited to a young lady. Is she still as blonde as ever?"

"Herr Jachmann, please—."

But Herr Jachmann had gone; some time passed, and then he came back.

"A flower shop like that, Herr Pinneberg, would be just the thing for your wife. Somewhere in a good neighborhood, where stupid men appreciate being served by a pretty woman."

"Pretty?" said Pinneberg awkwardly. "I don't know about that, Herr Jachmann."

"Don't talk nonsense, Pinneberg, and don't talk about things you don't understand. I don't know, perhaps there is something you do understand? I suppose you admire the sort of woman you see in the movies— manicured beauties, all greed and stupidity inside, eh?"

"I haven't been to the movies for an age," said Pinneberg gloomily.

"Why not? You ought to go constantly, every evening if possible, so long as you can stand it. It gives a man self-confidence, though I never felt much need of that quality myself, I find other people such abysmal fools. So let's go to the films. Now! This very evening! What's showing, I wonder. We'll stop at the next . . ."

"But first," grinned Pinneberg, "you were going to buy my wife a flower shop?"

"Why, of course. A first-rate idea. Money invested that way would certainly bring in good interest. But . . ." and he sighed heavily; he collected two flower-pots and the parcel under one arm, and slipped his other arm through Pinneberg's . . . "but it can't be done, my lad. I'm in the soup."

"Then you oughtn't to be buying up all these shops for us," said Pinneberg indignantly.

"Don't talk rubbish! Not over money. I've got all the money I want; still. But I'm in the soup all the same. In other ways. We'll talk about that later on. I'll tell you and your Bunny. But there's just one thing." He bent towards Pinneberg, and whispered: "Your mother's a bad lot."

"I've always known it." Pinneberg was quite unimpressed.

"Oh you don't understand in the least," said Jachmann, taking his arm from Pinneberg's: "A bad lot, a real bitch, but a splendid woman. No, for the moment nothing doing with the flower shop."

"Is that because of the old man with the beard?" asked Pinneberg.

281

"Eh? What old man?" Jachmann laughed. "Ah, Pinneberg, I was just fooling. Didn't you understand that?"

"No," says Pinneberg; "and I don't believe you."

"Well, never mind. You'll see later on. And we'll go to the movies together this evening. No, not this evening, we'll have a quiet supper at home this evening—what have you got for supper?"

"Baked potatoes," said Pinneberg; "and a bloater."

"And what is there to drink?"

"Tea."

"With rum?"

"My wife drinks no alcohol."

"Of course! She's nursing the baby. That's marriage. Your wife drinks no alcohol. So you drink no alcohol either. Poor wretch!"

"But I don't like rum in my tea."

"You imagine you don't because you're married. If you were a bachelor you'd like it; these are just delusions of marriage. Now don't tell me I've never been married. But when I've been living with a woman, and found delusions coming into my head, such as rum without tea . . ."

"Rum without tea," repeated Pinneberg gravely.

The other did not notice: "Yes, or something of the kind, then I wash up the whole affair, once and for all, however painful it may be. Well then, baked potatoes, herrings."

"A bloater."

"A bloater, and tea. Listen, Pinneberg, I must just run into that shop; but this is absolutely the last."

And Jachmann vanished into a large and expensive grocer's shop.

When he re-appeared, Pinneberg said with emphasis: "Now I've got one thing more to say to you, Herr Jachmann."

"Yes?" said the giant. "Perhaps you wouldn't mind carrying a parcel for me."

"Hand it over. Now get this straight. The baby is a little over three months old. He can't hear or see a thing, and he doesn't play."

"Why are you telling me all this?"

"In case you should have the idea of going into a toy-shop, and buying my son a teddy-bear or a toy railway, you won't find me waiting for you outside."

"Toy-shop . . ." said Jachmann dreamily. "Teddy-bear . . . toy railway. . . . He talks like a regular father. Do we pass a toy-shop?"

Pinneberg began to laugh. "I'll run off and leave you, Herr Jachmann," he said.

"You really are a stupid fellow, Pinneberg," said Jachmann with a sigh, "when you consider that in a way I'm your father!"

23.

Jachmann discovers the wholesome things of life.

JACHMANN dutifully bent over the crib for a moment and said: "A marvellously pretty child, of course."

"Just like its mother," said Bunny.

"Just like its mother," answered Jachmann.

Then Jachmann unpacked, and at the sight of such a display of delicacies, Bunny politely said: "But you really shouldn't have bought all this, Herr Jachmann!"

Then they sat down and ate and drank (tea, indeed, but not baked potatoes and bloater); and then Jachmann leaned back and said comfortably: "So—and now for the best moment of all: the cigar."

But Bunny answered with unwonted energy: "Sorry; no one can smoke here on account of the baby."

"Are you serious?" asked Jachmann.

"Absolutely," answered Bunny decisively. But Holger Jachmann sighed so heavily that she suggested, "Why not do as my husband does, go out for a while on the roof and smoke out there?"

The pair were soon walking up and down outside. Pinneberg with his cigarette, Jachmann with his cigar. Both quite silent.

Up and down. Up and down. Silent and side by side. Taking advantage of the fact that a cigarette is shorter than a cigar, Pinneberg ran in to Bunny, and hurriedly told her all about this extraordinary affair.

"But what did he say?" asked Bunny.

"Nothing. He simply came along with me."

"Did you just happen to meet him?"

"I don't know. I think he was watching out for me."

"It's all very mysterious. What does he want here?"

"No idea. At first he'd got a notion some old man was after him."

"What do you mean—after him."

"The police, I think. And he's had a scrap with mother. I suppose it all fits in somehow."

"Ah," said Bunny. "And what else?"

"He said he wanted to go to the movies with us tomorrow night."

"Tomorrow? Does he mean to stay here? He can't stay here over night. We haven't got a bed for him and the sofa's too short."

"No, of course—but suppose he just sticks around?"

"In half an hour," said Bunny decisively, "I'm going to nurse the baby. And if you haven't told him by then, I will."

"There'll be trouble," said Pinneberg with a sigh. And he went out once more to the silent roof-walker.

After a while Holger Jachmann carefully trod out the remains of his cigar, sighed deeply, and said: "I often like to do a little thinking; mostly I prefer talking, but half an hour's thought now and again does one a lot of good."

Pinneberg was silent.

The giant sighed. "Well there's no use talking about it. You're quite right there. Shall we go in to your wife?"

They went in, and Jachmann, in radiant good humor, started his usual flow of talk. "Well, Frau Pinneberg, this is the oddest place to live in that I've ever seen. I've seen a good many, but a place so odd and so delightful too. It seems almost incredible that the police should have passed it."

"They haven't," observed Pinneberg. "We live here unofficially."

"Unofficially?"

"Yes, these rooms are really store-rooms, not living-rooms. And only the man who lets us the place knows that we live here. Officially we live on the street with the carpenter."

"Ah," said Jachmann, pondering. "So no one knows that you live here, not even the police?"

"No," said Pinneberg emphatically, and looked at Bunny.

"Good," said Jachmann. "Excellent." And he surveyed the room with a certain tender air.

"Herr Jachmann," said Bunny, and in that moment she was the angel with the sword: "I must nurse the baby and get him ready for the night."

"Good," said Jachmann. "Don't let me disturb you. And then I think we'd all better go to bed. I've been running about all day, I'm very tired. In the meantime I'll fix up this sofa with cushions and chairs."

The pair looked at each other. Then Pinneberg turned away and tapped on the window; his shoulders quivered. But Bunny said: "Don't you dare. I'll fix up the bed for you."

"Right," said Jachmann. "Then I can watch you nurse the baby. I've always wanted to see how it's done."

With furious resolution Bunny took her son out of the crib and began to undress him.

"You'd better come quite close, Herr Jachmann. Be sure you get a good view."

The baby began to scream.

"There; those are what are called binders. They don't smell very nice."

"That doesn't worry me," said Jachmann. "I was in the war."

Bunny let her shoulders drop: "Nothing seems to disturb you, Herr Jachmann," she said. "There, now we rub the diaper with oil, pure olive oil."

"Why do you do that?"

"So he won't get sore. My son never gets sore."

"My son never gets sore," said Jachmann dreamily. "Wonderful! My son has never told a lie. My son has never given me any trouble. I think it's marvellous how you manage those binders; as to the manner born. Yes, a born mother."

Bunny laughed: "That'll do, thank you. Just ask my husband what it was like the first day we were here. There, now you must turn around for a moment."

And while Jachmann obediently went to the window, and looked out at the dark and silent garden, and the branches of the trees swayed gently in the light from the window ("Look, just as if they were talking, Pinneberg")— Bunny slipped out of her dress and pulled the ribbons of her underclothes off her shoulders. Then she put on her bath-wrap and laid the child to her breast.

At the same instant he stopped yelling; with a deep sigh, almost a sob, he put his lips to her breast and began to suck. Bunny looked down at him; attracted by the sudden deep silence, the two men turned and looked silently at mother and child.

Not silently for long; Jachmann said: "Of course I've been all wrong, Pinneberg. The wholesome things . . ." He clapped his hands to his head: "Fool that I am!"

Then they went to bed.

24.

Jachmann as discoverer and the little man as king.

NEXT morning Pinneberg stood among his trousers, a little confused in mind. It wasn't very easy for a young married man to put up with such a lodger in so small a place. He could not help recalling how Jachmann had behaved that night when he brought the money for the rent, and how he had lurched across to Bunny's bed.

It was true that then he had had a lot to drink, and that last night he was quite different, really very nice indeed. He might be all sorts of a good fellow, but was he to be trusted?—that was the point.

But of course all was well when he got home, they looked at the baby, and he greeted the lodger, who was rummaging in a trunk by the window: "Evening, Herr Jachmann!"

"Evening, my boy," answered the other. "I must just . . ." He was at the door as he spoke, and they heard him clattering down the ladder.

"What was he like?" asked Pinneberg.

"Very nice," said Bunny. "He really is awfully nice. In the morning he was kind of nervous, kept on talking about your getting his trunks."

"And what did you say?"

"That he'd better ask you. He just mumbled something. Three times he ran down the ladder, and was back again in a minute or two. Then he rattled his key-ring to amuse the baby and sang songs. After that he just disappeared."

"So he's got over his fears."

"Then he came back with the trunks, and since then he's been singing like a lark; rummaging around in his trunks and stuffing papers into the stove. Yes, and he's made a discovery.

"He can't bear to hear the baby cry. It drives him frantic; he says he can't endure the thought of a baby being at war with the world. I told him he mustn't take it so much to heart—that the baby was just hungry. He said I was to feed him on the spot. And when I wouldn't he told me I was cruel. He said all this rubbish about training was going to parents' heads. Then he wanted to take him out for a walk—just imagine Jachmann with a baby-carriage in the park. And when I wouldn't let him, and the baby went on crying . . ."

She broke off, for, just as though he had heard her, the baby lifted up its voice, roared and yelled.

"There he is! And now you'll see what Jachmann discovered."

She got a chair and put it beside the crib. She put her bag on the chair; then she took the alarm clock and put it on the bag.

Pinneberg looked on intently.

The clock ticked with the real harsh tick of a kitchen alarm clock, quite near the baby's ear. But of course when the baby yelled, the insignificant sound was inaudible.

At first the baby went on yelling unceasingly, until he

had to stop for a moment to draw breath. Then he continued.

"He hasn't noticed it yet," whispered Bunny.

But perhaps he had. The next pause for taking breath came sooner and lasted longer. He seemed to be listening: Tick-tock-tick-tock.

Then he yelled again. But without real conviction. There he lay, rather red in the face from his exertions, a wisp of light fair hair across his skull, his absurd little mouth screwed up. He looked straight ahead, probably unseeing, his little fingers outspread on the coverlet. He certainly wanted to yell, he was hungry, something was rumbling in his belly, and when that happened, the trick was to scream. But now beside his ear there was a sound: Tick-tock, tick-tock. All the time.

No, not all the time. When he yelled, it wasn't there. When he stopped it came back. He tested it with an experimental howl: yes, tick-tock had gone. He was silent: tick-tock returned. Then he was quite silent, and listened; probably there was no more room in his brain for anything else: tick-tock, tick-tock.

"Seems to work," whispered Pinneberg. "Jachmann's quite a boy to have thought of it."

"Hi! Trying my discovery?" said the voice of Jachmann from the door. "Does it work?"

"Seems to," said Pinneberg. "The only question is—how long?"

"Well, my dear, how goes it? Does your good husband know of our programme? And does he approve?"

"I haven't told him yet. Listen, dear; Herr Jachmann has invited us to go out with him—in style. Night-club and bar; just think of it! And first to the movies!"

"Jachmann, you've done it!" exclaimed Pinneberg. "It's always been Bunny's ambition to go out once in style. Glorious!"

An hour later they were sitting in a box.

Darkness; then:

A bedroom, two heads on the pillow; a rosy young face, breathing softly, and a man, somewhat older and looking rather careworn, even when asleep.

Then appears the dial of the alarm clock, set for half-past six. The man begins to turn and toss in bed; still half-asleep, he reaches out for the clock; five minutes before the half hour. The man sighs, puts the clock back in its place, shuts his eyes again.

("Ah; sleeps till the last minute, I see," says Pinneberg disapprovingly.)

Then, at the end of the large bed, can be seen something white, a crib. In it lies a child, head on one arm, lips parted.

The alarm rings; the clapper can be seen hammering against the bell, savage, relentless, like a very devil. With a jerk the man leaps up, flings his legs over the edge of the bed. Thin, spindly legs, pitifully covered with black hair.

(The audience laughs. "Real cinema heroes," explains Jachmann, "oughtn't to have any hair on their legs. This film is going to be a flop.")

But perhaps the girl will save it. She is certainly marvellously pretty. As the alarm goes off, she sits up, the bed-clothes slip, her night-gown is a little undone, and, there is something like a faint ravishing glimpse of her breasts. Then, in an instant, she has pulled the bed-clothes firmly round her shoulders and snuggled down again.

("Pretty easy, isn't it?" says Jachmann sagely. "Five
minutes and she's showing you her breasts."

"Sure is a pretty girl," says Pinneberg.)

The man gets into his shirt and trousers, the child
sits up in bed and cries: "Papa—teddy!" The man gives
the child his teddy-bear, and then he wants a doll. But the
man has gone into the kitchen and put the kettle on, he's
a rather lean and meager sort of fellow. How he dashes
about! He gets the doll for the child, sets the breakfast, spreads the bread and butter, makes the tea, shaves
himself. The woman lies in bed, breathing sweetly.

Now the woman gets up, she really seems very nice,
she gets her hot water herself from the bathroom. The
man looks at the clock, plays with the child, pours the
tea into the cups and looks to see whether the milk is outside the door. No, but the paper is.

Now the woman is ready, she goes straight to her place
at the breakfast table. They both pick up a sheet of the
newspaper, a teacup, a piece of bread . . .

The child calls out from the bedroom: the doll has
fallen out of the bed, and the man runs to pick it up.

("This is stupid," says Bunny discontentedly.

"Something's got to happen soon."

Jachmann said one word only: "Money.")

Right enough. When the man comes back, the woman
has found an advertisement in the paper: she wants to
buy something. Then it begins: where is her housekeeping
money? Where is his pocket money? He shows his wallet;
she shows her purse. The calendar on the wall says 17.
The milkman knocks, and wants his money, the leaves of
the calendar whisk over and over;—18—19—20 . . .
until 31. The man sits with his head in his hand, a few

pennies are lying on the table beside the empty purses, the calendar flutters.

How pretty the woman is, she grows prettier than ever; she speaks softly to the man, strokes his hair, puts up her face to be kissed. How her eyes shine!

("What's the poor fool going to do now?" asks Pinneberg.)

Well, the man gets excited, he takes her in his arms, the advertisement appears and vanishes, near-by the child plays with its doll, the few pennies lie on the table, the woman sits on the man's lap.

The scene vanishes; and after a moment or two of pitch darkness the light slowly rises on a brilliant bank interior. There is the counter with its wire network, there are the packets of money, the grating is half-open, but not a soul is visible . . . fat packets of notes, cylinders of silver and copper, and a broken packet of hundred-mark notes, spread out fanwise . . .

("Money," says Jachmann composedly; "People always enjoy the sight of money."

Does Pinneberg hear? Does Bunny hear?)

Again it is dark . . . dark for a long time . . . very dark. One can hear the audience breathe—breathe long and deep. Bunny hears Pinneberg's breathing, he hears Bunny's.

Once more the screen grows light. No more agreeable glimpses, the woman is decently enveloped in a dressing-gown. The man is wearing his bowler hat and kissing the child good-bye. There he is, now, the little man, making his way through the great city, he jumps on a bus; how the people hurry along, how the traffic sweeps and surges past. The street signals flash red, green, and yellow, ten

294

thousand houses, a million windows, and people—always people, flicker past—he, the little man, has only the two-and-a-half room flat with a wife and child that he has left behind him. Nothing else.

A foolish wife perhaps, who cannot handle money, but after all there is so very little money to handle and he does not think her foolish. Before him, inexorable, stands his desk with its four foolish tall legs; to it he must go, thus is his fate mysteriously ordained. He cannot evade it.

No: of course he does not dare. For an instant the little cashier's hand hovers over the money like a sparrow-hawk above a dovecote, open-clawed. No, the hand closes, they are not claws, they are fingers. A little bank-cashier, not a bird of prey.

But see; this little bank-cashier has a friend; an honorary clerk at the bank, who is, of course, the son of a real bank director. And no one notices that this gentleman has seen that hawk-like hand. In the lunch hour the other takes his friend, the little cashier, aside, and says bluntly: "You need money." The other protests, denies it; but he comes home with his pockets full of money. But now, when he has pulled it out and laid it on the table, thinking his wife will be overjoyed—behold, his wife is quite indifferent, the money does not interest her in the least. What does interest her is her husband. She leads him to the sofa, she takes him in her arms. "How did you do it? Did you do it for my sake? Dear, I would never have believed it of you!"

He cannot bring himself to tell her the true story, no, he cannot do it—how she adores him all of a sudden!

295

He nods and is silent, and smiles meaningly . . . she is so passionate, so proud of him!

What a marvellous face this little actor has! This great actor, rather. Pinneberg has just seen that face as it was this morning, lying on the pillow beside his wife's, the weary lined face of a careworn man. And now here, in the presence of his wife whom he loves, and by whom for the first time in his life he is admired—his face is transfigured, all its crudities vanish, his happiness blossoms forth, glows like some vast flower in the sunshine. Poor little humble face, here is your chance, never will you be able to say—never—that you were always insignificant: today you are a king!

Yes, he has become a king, her king. Is he hungry? Do his feet ache from standing so long? She runs, she waits on him, he is so far above her, he has done this thing for her sake. Never will he have to get up first again and put the kettle on. He is a king.

Forgotten on the table lies the money.

("Look how he lies and smiles," whispers Pinneberg breathlessly to Bunny.

"Poor man," says Bunny. "He's bound to get into trouble. Is he really happy? Isn't he the least bit afraid?"

"This fellow Schlüter's a very fine actor," observes Jachmann.)

Of course, he is bound to be found out. The money cannot be forgotten forever. But his glory will survive the first great purchase and maybe the second. What ecstasy for the wife to be able to buy anything she pleases —anything! And what terror for the husband, who knows whence the money comes.

Then, on the third expedition, when the money is coming to an end, she sees a ring. Alas, there is not enough money. A glittering array of rings is spread before her, the salesman is not looking, he is serving two customers—look at her face as she nudges her husband: Take it!

Now she believes he will do anything for her sake. But he is only a little bank-cashier: he cannot do this, and he doesn't.

This she realizes, and says to the salesman: "We will come back again." A small gray figure, the little man, walks on beside her, and sees a vista of his life, a long, long life, to be spent in the company of this woman whom he loves and who expects him to do these things for her.

She is silent, peevishly, sullenly silent—suddenly she changes her mood, and suggests going to a restaurant with what money they have left, a bottle of wine is on the table, she flames and glows: "Tomorrow you must get some more."

That poor little gray face. And that radiant woman.

Even then he feels moved to tell the truth; but slowly and gravely he nods his consent.

How is he to manage? His friend cannot go on lending him money forever; after all, the money is really a gift, he says— No. And the little cashier tells his friend why he must have the money, and what his wife thinks of him. The friend laughs, gives him the money and says: You must introduce me to your wife.

And then the friend gets to know the wife, and of course he falls in love with her, but she has eyes only for her bold and reckless husband who will do anything for his wife. Then, out of jealousy, at the table in the restaurant where they are sitting, the friend tells her the truth.

The little man reappears from the cloak-room, and sits down, and she laughs in his face—an insolent and contemptuous laugh. And from that laugh he understands all : the treacherous friend and the faithless wife. His face changes, the eyes widen, two tears steal down his cheeks, his lips quiver.

They laugh.

He stands and looks at them.

He looks at them.

Perhaps this is the moment in which he is really capable of any deed, because his whole being has been destroyed. But he turns, and, with bowed head, shambles on his spindle legs towards the door.

"Oh Bunny," says Pinneberg, clasping her hand tightly. "I feel so afraid sometimes. And we're so alone."

Bunny nods gravely and says softly : "But we have each other." And then, in a quick and cheerful voice : "And he has the boy. The wife certainly won't take the child with her !"

25.

The movies and life.
Uncle Knilli abducts Jachmann.

It was really rather a gloomy little supper to which the three of them sat down in their bird-cage. Jachmann looked meditatively at his two grown-up children who seemed to take so little interest in the unwonted delicacies of yesterday's purchase.

But, contrary to his usual habit, he said nothing. Bunny cleared away and took up the baby, and then Holger Jachmann said: "Children, children, it's dreadful to see you like this. Don't pull such a long face over a stupid movie plot!"

Pinneberg said: "Of course we know it isn't all of it true to life, Herr Jachmann. There are no clerks like the man's friend and probably there's no one like the little cashier with the bowler hat. But the actor quite carried me away—what's his name—Schlüter, did you say?"

Jachmann began again: "But . . ."

Bunny said quickly: "I know what he means. He's right too."

"Life is just as dangerous as you let it be," said Jachmann. "You just have to keep things off you. If I had been the cashier, I should have simply gone home and got a divorce. And then I should have married again, a nice young girl . . . well, what's the sense of all this worrying? I propose that, as the baby seems to have had enough, we get ready as soon as possible. It's already after eleven. We could all use a little gaiety."

"I don't know." Pinneberg looked questioningly at Bunny. "Shall we go out after all? I don't feel much like it."

Bunny too shrugged her shoulders doubtfully.

Jachmann got furious. "No, I can't have this. We can't sit around here at home pulling long faces over a lot of nonsense we've seen on a screen. No, out we go! Pinneberg, you run out and drum up a taxi, while your Bunny puts on her best dress."

Pinneberg looked up doubtfully, but Bunny said: "Run along, dear; there's no arguing with him."

Pinneberg went out slowly; Jachmann, like the good fellow he was, dashed after him, and pressed something into his hand: "There, put that away. It's always unpleasant to go out with empty pockets. And here's a little silver too. And don't forget to give a little to your wife, women always need a bit of money. Now then, don't talk, hurry up with that cab!"

Pinneberg slowly descended the ladder, thinking: He's a nice fellow. But one never feels quite sure about him. That's why he's not *quite* all right. His hand closed on the notes. But when the taxi drew up in front of the house, he could not forbear putting his hand in his pocket and looking at them. "But this is just crazy. It's nearly a month's pay. He's mad. I must tell him at once."

But there was no opportunity; they were both waiting, and in the cab Bunny had to tell him that the baby had gone to sleep at once, and she wasn't worrying, or at least not much, and after all they weren't going to be out for so frightfully long. And where were they going to—?

"Listen, Herr Jachmann," began Pinneberg.

Jachmann said hurriedly: "I shan't take you to the west side, children. In the first place I'm too well-known there and that spoils half the fun, and besides it's nothing like so amusing. There's more going on in the Friedrichstadt than anywhere—well, you'll see."

The pair accepted Jachmann's proposal that they should first take a stroll down the Friedrichstrasse. They walked three abreast, Bunny in the middle, arm in arm with her two men. They were all in high good humor, and not merely stopped outside the Variétés, to admire the posters of the lovely ladies (who all somehow looked exactly alike), but stood and stared into almost every shop-window. Pinneberg found this rather tedious, but Jachmann was the best companion in the world. He could grow just as enthusiastic as Bunny over a knitted frock from Vienna, and could look at two and twenty hats in succession and give his opinion as to whether they would suit Bunny or not.

"Can't we go on now?" asked Pinneberg.

"Oh, these husbands," said Jachmann. "First, nothing is good enough for them, and then they get bored. However, I'm gradually getting thirsty. I propose we go right over now." He pointed diagonally across the road.

So they crossed and were almost at their destination when a car stopped behind them and a high voice squeaked: "Hullo, Jachmann, is that you?"

Jachmann turned and said in a startled voice: "Uncle Knilli—haven't they nabbed you yet—?" He broke off and said to the Pinnebergs: "Excuse me, I'll be back in a moment."

The car had pulled up quite close to the pavement. There stood Jachmann talking to a fat, yellow man with a face like a eunuch; and though they laughed together at first, their voices gradually sank and the conversation took on a more serious tone.

The Pinnebergs stood and waited. Five minutes, ten minutes; they looked into a shop-window, and when they had looked at everything there was to see, they kept on waiting.

"I think he might try to get away by now," growled Pinneberg. "Uncle Knilli he called the fellow, what odd people Jachmann seems to know——!"

"He certainly doesn't look very nice," agreed Bunny. "Why does he cheep like a bird or something?"

Pinneberg was going to explain when Jachmann came back and said: "I'm very sorry, children, but I can't take you out tonight. I must go with Uncle Knilli."

"Oh!" said Bunny doubtfully. "Herr Jachmann——!"

"Business. Business. But tomorrow midday at the latest I'll be with you again, children, punctually for dinner. And now look here, you go by yourselves. It'll be much nicer for you without me."

"Herr Jachmann," said Bunny once more. "Wouldn't it be better if you stayed with us tonight? I have a feeling . . ."

"No, I must go," said Jachmann. "Now you run along by yourselves. Any money left, Pinneberg?"

"Oh, that's enough, Jachmann," cried Pinneberg.

Jachmann muttered: "Oh all right. I only thought. Then tomorrow at midday."

The taxi sped away, and Pinneberg told his Bunny

302

about the hundred marks Jachmann had so lavishly pressed upon him an hour before.

"But you'll pay it back tomorrow," said Bunny energetically. "We'll go home now. Or do you want to go out?"

"Not on your life," said Pinneberg. "I never did. I'll return the money tomorrow."

But he did not. For a long, long time had passed, and Pinneberg's life had greatly changed, before they again saw Herr Holger Jachmann, who was to have been back so punctually to dinner at twelve o'clock.

26.

The baby is ill.
What can be the trouble?

"THE baby's yelling," said Bunny, quite unnecessarily.

"Yes," said Pinneberg, looking at the luminous dial of the alarm clock. "It's five minutes past three."

They listened, and then Bunny whispered again: "He never does that. And he can't be hungry."

"He'll soon stop. Let's see if we can't go to sleep again."

After a while Bunny said: "Shall I turn on the light? It's enough to break your heart, that crying."

But with regard to the baby Pinneberg was now a man of iron principle: "On no account! Do you hear?—on no account. We agreed we wouldn't pay any attention to him if he cried at night so that he'd know he had to sleep when it was dark."

"Yes, but . . ." began Bunny.

"On no account," said Pinneberg sternly. "If we start we'll be getting up nearly every night."

"But it's another kind of crying—I don't like the sound of it."

"It's no good, Bunny, you must be sensible."

They lay down again in the darkness. The crying went on without a pause, and of sleep there was naturally no question. Surely—surely it would stop, soon! No. Pinneberg wondered whether there was anything unusual about that crying. It wasn't temper, and it wasn't hunger; he knew the sound in both cases. Could he be in pain?

"Perhaps he's got a stomach-ache?" said Bunny softly.

"Why should he have a stomach-ache? Besides, what can we do for it? Nothing."

"I might make him some fennel tea. That seems to quiet him."

Pinneberg did not answer. Alas, it isn't so easy; he meant to do well by his baby. There were to be no mistakes made in his education, he was to grow up into the right kind of little boy.

"All right, get up and make him some."

But he got up almost quicker than Bunny. He turned on the light. The child was quiet for a moment as he saw the brightness, and then began again. His face was dark red.

"My little one," said Bunny, as she bent over him and lifted the small bundle out of the crib. "My little one, does it hurt? Show mother where it hurts."

Against the warmth of her body and rocked in her arms, the baby was silent. He sobbed, was silent, sobbed again.

Pinneberg, busy with the spirit stove, said triumphantly: "There you are! All he wanted was to be taken up."

Bunny paid no attention: she walked up and down, crooning one of the old old cradle songs from the shores of the Baltic, that she had brought with her from Platz.

The child lay still in her arms, staring at the ceiling with his bright blue eyes.

"There, the water's boiling," said Pinneberg ungraciously. "You make the tea yourself, I can't bother with it."

"Hold the baby." He walked up and down humming while his wife made the tea and waited for it to cool. Once the baby grabbed at his father's face, otherwise he lay as quiet as a mouse.

The baby swallowed very heartily from the teaspoon, but sometimes he let a drop fall, which his father gravely wiped away with his shirt-sleeve. "There, that's enough," he said. "He seems all right now."

The baby was again laid in his crib. Pinneberg threw a glance at the clock: "Just four. It's high time we went to bed if we want to get any sleep."

The light went out. The Pinnebergs went quietly to sleep.

And woke up again: the baby was bellowing.

Five minutes past four.

"There you are," said Pinneberg angrily. "If only we hadn't taken him up! Now he thinks that all he has to do is yell and we're at his service."

Bunny was Bunny: she quite understood that a man who had had to sell all day under the lash of a fixed quota was naturally nervous and touchy. Bunny did not say a word.

The baby screamed.

"Pleasant," said Pinneberg. "Very pleasant. How on earth I'm going to be able to get through my work to-day, I don't know." And after a while he burst out: "And I'm so far behind. God damn that noise!"

Bunny was silent. The baby cried.

Pinneberg tossed and turned. He listened. Yes, there was pain in that crying. And he also knew quite well that he had been talking nonsense just before, and that Bunny knew it too, and he was angry with himself for being so foolish. Now she could speak what was in her mind. She knew that with him the beginning was always difficult.

"Darling, didn't you think he was very feverish?"

"I didn't notice," growled Pinneberg.

"But his cheeks were so flushed."

"From crying."

"They were covered with round red spots. I wonder if he's ill."

"Why should he be?" asked Pinneberg. But in any case this was a new point of view, and he said, still none too graciously, "Well, turn on the light. There's no sense trying to go to sleep."

So they turned on the light. In his mother's arms he swallowed once and was quiet.

"There you are," said Pinneberg irritably. "I never heard of a pain that stopped the moment he was picked up."

"Feel his hands, they're so hot."

Said Pinneberg sharply: "That's from crying. I should be sweating all over if I yelled like that."

"But his hands really are very hot. I think he's ill."

Pinneberg felt the hands and his mood changed.

"Yes, they really are hot. I wonder if he's got a temperature?"

"It's so silly not to have a thermometer."

"We were always going to buy one, but it was the money."

"I'm sure he's got a temperature."

"It's just a bluff; put him in the crib, and you'll see, he'll cry."

"But . . ."

"Bunny, put him in the crib. Just to please me—put him in."

Bunny looked at her husband and put the baby in the crib. This time it was needless to put out the light, the baby started crying at once.

"There, you see." Pinneberg was triumphant. "And now take him out, and he'll be quiet at once."

Bunny took the baby out of the cot once more and her husband looked on expectantly. The baby went on crying.

Pinneberg stood rigid. After a while he said: "There you are. You've spoilt him by picking him up. What are we to do now for his lordship, please?"

"He's got a pain," said Bunny gently. She rocked him a little, and he fell silent; then he started again. "Darling, do go to bed, to please me. You might be able to catch a little sleep."

But it was no use. Now one lay down, and now the other, they carried him, they sang, they rocked him. Sometimes the crying subsided into a faint whimper, then it burst out again. The parents looked at each other across the crib.

"It's dreadful," said Pinneberg.

"He must be in agony!"

"How senseless it seems that such a little being should have to suffer so."

"And that I can do nothing for him." Suddenly Bunny cried out in her high clear voice: "Oh my precious, isn't there anything I can do for you?" The baby went on crying. "And he can't tell us! He can't even show us where it is. Where is it, sweet?"

"We're so stupid," said Pinneberg savagely. "We

know nothing. If only we knew something, perhaps we could help him."

"And I can't think of anyone we could ask."

"I'll go for a doctor," said Pinneberg, beginning to dress.

"You haven't got a certificate."

"He'll have to come. I'll get one later."

"No doctor will come now, at five in the morning. When they're rung up by the Sick-fund people, they all say it will be time enough in the morning."

"He *must* come!"

"Darling, if you brought him here, up this ladder, there'd be trouble. He'd certainly report us for living in such a place."

Pinneberg sat on the edge of the bed and looked gloomily at Bunny. "You're right there." He nodded. "We've got ourselves into a pretty mess, Frau Pinneberg. We never thought of that."

"You mustn't talk like that, dear. Things look bad now, but they'll get better."

"It's because," said Pinneberg, "we're people who don't count. We're quite alone. And the others are just exactly like us, they're alone too. We think ourselves a cut above the workers: I only wish we were working people. They call each other 'comrade,' and they really are comrades."

"I'm not so sure about that," said Bunny. "When I think of what father often told us and what he had to go through."

"Yes, of course," said Pinneberg. "I know they aren't very nice people. But at any rate they can say what they think."

309

The baby cried, they looked out of the window, the sun rose, it grew quite light, and they looked at each other; they were drawn and pale and tired. They clasped each other's hands.

They began to walk up and down again.

"I just don't know," said Bunny, "whether I ought to feed him or not. There may be something wrong with his insides!"

"Yes," he said despairingly. "What's to be done? It's nearly six."

"I know! I know!" cried Bunny in a sudden burst of energy. "When it's seven you can run round at once to the Infants' Clinic, and just ask one of the Sisters to come."

"Yes, I could do that. And I could still be in time at the store."

"And we'll let him go hungry till then. That can't do him any harm."

Punctually at seven o'clock a pallid young man with a very crooked necktie stumbled into the Municipal Infants' Clinic. There were notices everywhere: hours of consultation, so-and-so. This was certainly not one of them.

He stood and hesitated; Bunny was waiting, but he must not annoy the Sisters. Supposing they were asleep? What should he do?

A lady passed him, going down the stairs—she vaguely reminded him of Frau Nothnagel—this one too was elderly, fat, and Jewish.

Don't like the looks of her, thought Pinneberg. I won't ask her. Besides, she isn't a Sister.

The lady had gone one flight down. Suddenly she stopped and panted upstairs again. She stood in front of

310

Pinneberg and surveyed him. "Well, my young parent," she said, "what's the trouble?"

She smiled.

Those words and that smile! This was the right sort. How nice she was. Suddenly he realized that many people understood who he was, and what was the matter. An old Jewish nurse at a clinic, for instance—how many thousand fathers had wandered up and down that staircase. As he poured out his story, she merely nodded and said: "Yes, yes." Then she opened a door and called out: "Ella! Martha! Hannah!"

Heads appeared: "One of you go along with this young man, will you? They're worried about their baby."

The fat lady nodded to Pinneberg and said: "Good morning; I'm sure you will find it's all right."

In a minute or two a Sister came up and said: "Let's go along at once." In the meantime he was able to tell her all about it, and the Sister too seemed to think that all was well; she nodded and said: "It doesn't sound so bad. We'll see."

He was thankful that someone was coming who really did know about it; and even his anxiety about the ladder was needless. The Sister merely said: "At the mast-head, eh? After you, please," and clambered after him like an old sailor, carrying her leather bag.

Then Bunny and the Sister talked to each other in low tones, and looked at the baby, who was now of course perfectly quiet. Bunny suddenly called out to Pinneberg: "Hadn't you better go? You'll be late for work."

He growled out: "No, I'll wait. I might have to get something."

They unwrapped the utterly serene baby; they took his

311

temperature—no, no fever, just a fraction above normal; they carried him to the window and opened his mouth. He lay still, and suddenly the Sister uttered a word, and Bunny looked excitedly at something: then she cried out: "Darling, come over here. Our baby's cut his first tooth!"

Pinneberg came. He looked into the little naked mouth, at the pale pink gums, he followed Bunny's finger, and there was a tiny inflammation, a tiny swelling, and in it a glassy little point. Like a fishbone, thought Pinneberg, just like a fishbone.

But he did not say so, the two women looked at him so expectantly, and he said at last: "Well, well! So it's all right, then? The first tooth, eh?"

And after a time he asked meditatively: "How many are there to come?"

"Twenty," said the Sister.

"So many?" said Pinneberg. "And will he always cry like this?"

"It depends," said she encouragingly. "They don't all cry over every tooth."

"There," said Pinneberg; "if we had only known!" And suddenly he burst out laughing and clambered down the ladder.

27.

The inquisitors and Fräulein Fischer. Another reprieve, Pinneberg!

"TWENTY-SEVEN minutes late—Pinneberg," noted the porter. His face was impassive, every day some people came late. Many of them begged for mercy; this one merely looked pale.

Pinneberg compared the time on his own watch: "I make it twenty-four."

"Twenty-seven," said the porter decisively.

Jänecke, at any rate, was not in the department. Thank heaven the row wouldn't start at once.

But it did. There was Herr Kessler, always so concerned for the interests of the House of Mandel. He went up to Pinneberg: "You're to go at once to the Personnel Department; Herr Lehmann wants to see you."

Pinneberg felt he ought to say something just to show Kessler he was not afraid—although he was.

Kessler surveyed Pinneberg and grinned, not too obviously, but in his eyes the grin was unmistakable. He said nothing; he merely looked at Pinneberg.

Pinneberg went down to the ground floor, and across the yard. The elderly, yellowish secretary, Fräulein Semmler, was still at the door of Herr Lehmann's room. The door was ajar. She took one step towards Pinneberg and said: "Wait, please, Herr Pinneberg."

Then she picked up a file and opened it, stepped back

and again stood at the door, still of course reading the file.

From Herr Lehmann's room came voices; one of them sharp and precise: Herr Spannfuss's; then Jänecke's deep tones. A moment's silence, and a girl said something, rather faintly. She seemed to be crying.

Herr Jänecke's voice was audible: "So you admit in any cause, Fräulein Fischer, that you have been carrying on with Herr Matzdorf?"

Sobs.

"You must answer us," said Herr Jänecke, in a gently warning tone. "How can Herr Spannfuss form an opinion if you are obstinate?"

Pause.

"It's true, isn't it, Fräulein Fischer?" said Herr Jänecke patiently. "You have been having an affair with Herr Matzdorf?"

Sobs. Silence.

"You see! You see!" shouted Herr Jänecke with sudden energy. "It's true. We know all about it, but of course you would do yourself a great deal of good by a frank confession." A short pause, and then Herr Jänecke began again: "Now Fräulein Fischer, so far as I am aware, you were engaged here to sell stockings. Did you think you were engaged to have affairs with the other employees?"

No answer.

"And the consequences——?" Herr Jänecke rapped out harshly: "Did you not think of the consequences? You are only seventeen, Fräulein Fischer." Silence. Pinneberg made a step towards the door. Fräulein Semmler looked triumphantly at Pinneberg.

314

"Shut that door!" said Pinneberg furiously.

Then a girl's voice burst forth, sobbing, and almost in a shriek: "But I'm not having an affair with Herr Matzdorf—! I'm just friendly with him. I'm not . . . " the words were engulfed in tears.

"That is untrue," Pinneberg heard Herr Spannfuss say: "That is untrue. The letter states that you were seen coming out of a hotel."

The girl inside cried; "I never even met him in the store!"

"Come, come!" said Herr Spannfuss.

"No, I haven't! I certainly haven't. Herr Matzdorf is on the fourth floor and I am on the ground floor. We couldn't meet."

"And what about the lunch hour; in the canteen?"

"No, not even then," said Fräulein Fischer hurriedly. "Herr Matzdorf lunches at quite a different time."

"Indeed?" said Herr Jänecke. "You seem in any case to be pretty well informed on the subject."

"What I do outside the house is my business," cried the girl. She seemed to have stopped crying.

"There you are wrong," said Herr Spannfuss gravely. "That is quite a mistake, Fräulein. The Mandel Store clothes and feeds you, the Mandel Store provides the basis of your existence. It is only to be expected that in all the transactions of your life the Mandel Store should be considered first."

A long pause. Then: "You met in a hotel. You might have been seen there by any of our customers. That would have been painful for the customer, painful for yourself, and discreditable to the firm. You might—I must speak quite openly to you—you might have found

yourself with child, and according to the existing laws
we cannot discharge you for that reason—a further loss
to the firm. Your friend is burdened with maintenance,
for which his pay is not adequate, he is continually worried, and does his work badly—more loss to the firm.
You have," said Herr Spannfuss with emphasis, "acted
so prejudicially to the interests of the firm, that . . ."

A new and long pause. No. Fräulein Fischer remained
silent. Then Herr Lehmann said quickly: "As you have
offended against the interests of the firm, we are, by the
terms of paragraph seven of your contract, justified in
dismissing you without notice. We propose to make use
of this right. You are hereby dismissed without notice,
Fräulein Fischer."

Not a sound.

"Go to the outside office, and get them to give you
your papers and the wages due you."

"One moment," said Herr Jänecke. And he added
quickly, "You are not to imagine we are treating you un-
fairly: Herr Matzdorf will of course be dismissed without notice also."

Fräulein Semmler stood once more at her table, and
from Herr Lehmann's room appeared a girl with very
red eyes and a very pale face. She passed Pinneberg. "I
was to ask for my papers here," she said.

"Go in," said Fräulein Semmler to Pinneberg.

Pinneberg went in. His heart was hammering.

The three men looked at Pinneberg. Pinneberg took
two steps forward.

"Now listen, Pinneberg," said Spannfuss in quite a different voice. The tone of grave and paternal concern
had quite vanished, he was merely brutal: "You were

316

again half an hour late today. What the intention of this
conduct is I cannot conceive. Presumably you wish us to
understand that you view the House of Mandel with
complete indifference. Well, young man, it won't do—!"
And he waved his hand in the direction of the door.

Pinneberg had begun 'by thinking that nothing mattered, that he was bound to be fired. But suddenly hope
sprang up again, and he said very quietly and humbly:
"I beg your pardon, Herr Spannfuss, my child was ill
last night, and I had to run round and get a Sister."

He looked helplessly at the three men.

"Ah, your child," said Spannfuss; "so this time it was
your child that was ill. Four weeks ago—or was it ten?—
you were constantly away because of your wife. Two
weeks from now your grandmother will probably die, and
in a month your aunt will break her leg." He paused.
Then, with renewed energy: "You overestimate the interest that the Firm takes in your private life. Your
private life is without interest for the House of Mandel.
You will kindly arrange your affairs so that they can be
settled outside business hours." Again a pause, then:
"The Firm makes your private life possible, sir. The Firm
comes first, the Firm comes second, and the Firm comes
third, and then you can do what you like. You live by us,
sir, we have preserved you from anxiety about your
livelihood, do you realize that? You are punctual enough
in claiming your pay on the last day of the month."

He smiled faintly, and the other gentlemen smiled;
Pinneberg knew it would be a good thing if he too smiled
slightly, but with the best will in the world he could not.

In conclusion, Herr Spannfuss said: "Please understand that the next time you are late you will be dismissed

without notice. And you'll find out what it's like to live on the dole. There are plenty doing it. We understand each other, don't we, Herr Pinneberg?"

Pinneberg looked at him dumbly.

Herr Spannfuss smiled. "Your face is certainly very expressive, Herr Pinneberg, but I should like you to confirm your meaning orally. Do we understand each other?"

"Yes," said Pinneberg faintly.

28.

Frau Mia again.

BUNNY was darning stockings. The baby was in his crib
asleep. She felt gloomy, Hans had lately been in such a
bad mood, distraught and depressed, sometimes bursting
into fury, sometimes sunk in apathy. The other day she
had planned to give him a little treat by adding an egg
to his baked potatoes. When she brought it to the table
he flew into a rage and asked if they were millionaires.

After that he had been silent and depressed for some
days and had been very gentle with her; his whole behavior pleaded for pardon. There was no reason for
him to ask for pardon. They two were one, nothing
could come between them; a hasty word could cloud their
relations but not destroy them.

But in earlier days it had been quite different. They
were young, they were in love, a flash of radiance gleamed
through everything. They were still young, they loved
each other still—alas, perhaps they loved each other
more than ever, they had grown to share each other's
lives; but overhead the sky was dark—how could people
like them laugh? How could one laugh, really laugh in
such a world as this, a world of respectable and blunder-
ing captains of industry and little degraded down-trodden
people always trying to do their best?

319

She heard a commotion outside. It was Puttbreese in dispute with a woman.

Puttbreese called up to her. "Young woman! Frau Pinneberg!" he roared.

Bunny got up, walked across to the ladder and looked down. There stood her mother-in-law with Master Puttbreese. The pair of them did not seem to be getting on well.

"The old party wants to come up," said the Master, and trundled off to such purpose that he slammed the outer door and left them both in semi-darkness. But Bunny's eyes soon got used to it, below her she could distinguish the glimmer of the white fat face.

"Good day, Mamma, are you coming to pay us a visit? Hans is out."

"Do you propose to talk to me from up there? Or will you tell me how to get up?"

"The ladder, Mamma, right in front of you."

"Is that the only way?"

"Yes."

"I should very much like to know why you moved out of my apartment. Well, we'll talk about that."

The ladder was achieved without difficulty, Frau Pinneberg senior was pretty active. "Do you live here?"

"No, Mamma, over there, behind the door. Shall I show you?" She opened the door, and Frau Pinneberg came in and looked around. "Well, I suppose everyone knows best where they belong. I prefer the Spenerstrasse."

Bunny found herself longing for her husband's return. "Will you take your things off, Mamma?"

"No, thank you. I only came in for two minutes.

320

There's no occasion for me to call after the way you treated me."

"We were very sorry about it." said Bunny with hesitation.

"I wasn't," said Frau Pinneberg. "I shan't mention it. But it was pretty inconsiderate of you to leave me in the lurch, with no one in the house to do the work.—You've got a baby, haven't you?"

"Yes, he was born six months ago. His name is Horst."

"Horst! I suppose you couldn't have taken precautions, could you?"

Bunny looked steadily at her mother-in-law. She was going to tell a lie, but her eyes did not falter. "Yes, we could, but we didn't want to."

"Ah. Well, well. You must know best whether you can afford a baby. Personally, I think it rather unprincipled to bring a baby into the world on nothing. However, you can have a dozen for all I care, if it amuses you." She went to the crib and looked angrily down at the child. She was clearly out for a quarrel.

Frau Pinneberg looked up from the child.

"What is it? Boy or girl?"

"A boy," said Bunny. "Horst."

"Ah," said Frau Pinneberg. "I thought so. He looks just about as foolish as his father."

Bunny was silent.

"My dear child," Frau Pinneberg unbuttoned her jacket and sat down. "There's no sense in being sulky with me. I say what I think. Ah, there's the precious dressing-table. Seems to be your only piece of furniture. I often think one should be easier on that boy, he isn't quite right in the head." She sat down and stared at the wretched thing; it was a miracle that the veneer did not blister.

"When is Jachmann coming?" asked Frau Pinneberg suddenly, and with such sharpness that Bunny started. Frau Pinneberg was delighted. "You see I hear of everything; I found out your little hiding place—there's nothing I don't know. When is Jachmann coming?"

"Herr Jachmann," said Bunny, "was here for one or two nights many weeks ago. Since then he has not been here again."

"So!" said Frau Pinneberg contemptuously. "And where is he now?"

"I don't know."

"Oh, you don't know." Frau Pinneberg spoke more slowly, but her temper was rising. She pulled off her jacket: "How much does he pay you to keep your mouth shut?"

"I won't answer any such question."

"I'll put the police on to you, my dear child," said Frau Pinneberg; "then you'll soon answer. I suppose he told you there was a warrant out against him for fraud and cheating at cards, or did he say he was living here because he loved you?"

Bunny Pinneberg stood at the window. She was glad now that the lad would be back soon, she could not bring herself to turn his mother out. It was a job for Pinneberg.

"You'll soon see how he'll treat you. He swindles everyone; he can't help it. The way he's behaved to me . . ." Frau Pinneberg's voice had quite another ring.

"I haven't seen Herr Jachmann for more than two months."

"Bunny," said Frau Pinneberg; "Bunny, if you know where he is, do tell me, Bunny." She paused. "Bunny, do tell me where he is?"

Bunny turned and lóoked at her mother-in-law: "I don't know. Really I don't know, Mamma."

The pair surveyed each other.

"All right," said Frau Pinneberg. "I'll believe you. I do believe you, Bunny. Did he really only stay here for two nights?"

"I think only two."

"What did he say about me? Did he curse me out in style?"

Said Bunny: "Not a word. He didn't say anything about you to me."

"Ah," said her mother-in-law; "not a word. Well, your baby's a nice child. Can he talk yet?"

"At six months, Mamma?"

"No? Don't they talk at that age? I've forgotten everything—not that I ever knew very much. But—" She paused for quite a while. The pause grew longer and longer, there was something terrible in it—fury, fear, and menace.

"There!" cried Frau Pinneberg, pointing to the trunks lying on top of the cupboard. "Those are Jachmann's trunks, I know them. You liar, you shameless little liar—and I believed you. Where is he, when is he coming? You've stolen him for yourself, and that wretched husband of yours knows all about it. Liar!"

"Mamma!"

"They're my trunks. He owes me money, hundreds

323

and thousands of marks, the trunks belong to me. He'll
soon come if I've got the boxes."

She pulled a chair up to the cupboard.

"Mamma!" Bunny tried to hinder her.

"Let me go! They're my trunks!"

She got on to the chair and dragged at the handle of
the first trunk, but the cornice of the cupboard was in
the way.

"He left the trunks behind!" cried Bunny.

She did not hear. She dragged at the trunks and the
cornice broke off; the trunk slipped. It was rather heavy,
she could not hold it and it fell crashing against the crib.
The baby began to cry.

"Leave that alone at once!" cried Bunny with flashing
eyes, and ran to the child. "I'll throw you out."

"They're my trunks!"

Bunny held the weeping infant in her arms and mastered her fury; in half an hour she had to nurse him,
she must not get excited.

"Leave the trunks, Mamma," said Bunny; "they don't
belong to you and they must stay here." She started to
croon the old Baltic cradle song to her baby.

"Leave those trunks, Mamma," she called out again.

"He'll be pleased when he gets back to you tonight!"

The second trunk fell.

"Ah, there he is."

She turned to the door.

But it was not Jachmann.

"What's all this?" said Pinneberg quietly.

"Mamma," said Bunny, "wants to take away Herr
Jachmann's boxes. She says they belong to her. Herr
Jachmann owes her money."

"Mamma can fix that up with Herr Jachmann herself, the trunks must stay here." Bunny found herself admiring her husband's self-command.

"Of course," said Frau Pinneberg; "I might have known you'd stand by your wife. The Pinnebergs have always been fools. You ought to be ashamed of yourself, you poor idiot."

"Darling!" cried Bunny imploringly.

But it was not necessary. "I think it's time you went, Mamma," said Pinneberg. "No, leave the trunks alone. Do you think you can get them down the ladder by force? Just try. Did you want to say good-bye to my wife? You needn't trouble."

"I'll put the police on to you!"

"Look out, Mamma, there's a step here."

The door slammed, Bunny heard the clamor fade into the distance. "I hope it hasn't spoilt my milk." She unfastened her dress, the baby smiled and pursed his mouth.

While the child was feeding he came back. "She's gone now. I'm curious to see whether she'll put the police on to us. Tell me—how did she turn up?"

"You did that splendidly, dear," said Bunny. "I would never have thought it of you. You kept your temper so well."

He was quite embarrassed. "Nonsense. How did it happen? Tell me."

She told him.

"It's possible that Jachmann is wanted by the police. But if that is so, then mamma has something to do with it. In that case she won't send the police. Besides they would have been here before now."

The Pinnebergs sat and waited. The child fed, was put into his crib and went to sleep.

Pinneberg put the trunk back on top of the cupboard, got some glue from the Master and stuck the cornice on again. Bunny cooked the supper.

The police did not appear.

29.

The jig is up.

THE twenty-ninth of September. Tomorrow would be the thirtieth, and there is no thirty-first. Pinneberg's face was gloomy and rather gray. From time to time he took from his pocket a piece of paper on which he had noted down his daily totals. But really there was not much figuring to be done. The result remained the same. By tomorrow evening he would have to sell five hundred and twenty-three and a half marks' worth, to make his quota.

It was hopeless but he must make it somehow, or what would become of Bunny and the child? It was impossible—but when facts are stubborn, one hopes for a miracle. He was reminded of his very early days at school: Heinemann, whom he hated, was giving back the French exercises, and the school-boy Johannes Pinneberg was praying into his desk: "Oh God, please let me have only three mistakes." (He knew of seven for certain.)

The salesman, Johannes Pinneberg, prayed: "Oh God, please send me a customer who wants a dress suit. And an evening coat. And a . . . and . . ."

At that moment Kessler appeared: "Well, Pinneberg, how do your totals stand?"

Pinneberg did not look up: "Thanks. I'm okay."

"So-o-o," drawled Kessler. "Delighted to hear it. Because Jänecke told me you killed a sale yesterday, and

327

you were terribly behind with your total and he'd have
something to say to you."

Pinneberg said: "Thanks. Thanks. I suppose Jänecke
wanted to buck you up a little. How do you stand?"

"Oh, I'm set for the month. That's why I asked you.
I wanted to offer you some of my total."

Pinneberg stood silent. He loathed this cringing sneak.
He loathed him so heartily that he could not address a
word to him, or ask him the slightest favor. He said, after
a long pause: "So you're all right."

"Yes, I can take it easy. I don't need to sell a thing
these two days," said Kessler with pride, looking patron-
izingly at Pinneberg.

Perhaps Pinneberg would have opened his mouth and
asked for help, but at that moment a gentleman approached the two salesman.

"Would you kindly show me a house-jacket. Something
really warm and useful. The price does not matter so
much. But it must be in quiet colors."

The elderly gentleman had looked at both men and,
Pinneberg thought, more especially at him. So he said:
"Certainly, sir, if you'll please . . ."

But Kessler thrust himself between them: "Step this
way, sir. We have some excellent house-jackets in very
quiet styles. If you please, sir . . ." Pinneberg looked at
the two of them, and he thought: So Kessler has got his
total, and now he's pinching my customers. That would
have meant thirty marks.

Herr Jänecke came past: "Well, idle again? All the
others are selling except you. Looks to me as though you
really wanted to go on the dole."

Pinneberg looked at Herr Jänecke—and there ought

to have been fury in that look. But he was so helpless, so broken, he felt the tears coming into his eyes, as he whispered: "Herr Jänecke . . . Oh, Herr Jänecke . . ."

And even Herr Jänecke, the detested Jänecke, realized the poor man's helpless misery. He said encouragingly: "Now then, Pinneberg, don't give up. You'll be all right. After all we aren't so inhuman as not to listen to what you have to say. Anyone may have a run of bad luck."

Jänecke hurriedly stepped aside, as at that moment a gentleman who looked like a customer appeared, a man with an expressive face, a quick incisive face. No, he could not be a customer, he was wearing a suit made to measure; he would not want anything ready-made.

The man went straight up to Pinneberg (where had he seen him before?) and said, touching the brim of his hat:

"Good morning, sir, good morning. May I ask if you are the possessor of a lively fancy?"

He had an expressive voice; he rolled his R's, and seemed not to mind being overheard by others.

"Fancy stuffs," said Pinneberg, uneasily, "on the second floor."

The gentleman laughed, a sharply accented ha-ha-ha, his whole face, the whole man, laughed; and then, in an instant, he was again expressive and sonorous.

"I didn't mean that," said he. "What I meant was— if, for example, you looked at that press full of trousers, could you imagine a goldfinch sitting on it and singing?"

"Not very well," said Pinneberg with a pitiful smile; and racked his brain to remember where he had seen this buffoon.

"Not very well," said the gentleman. "I'm sorry for

that. Well, I don't suppose you have much to do with birds in your line." Once more he burst into his abrupt ha-ha-ha.

Pinneberg smiled too, although he was now growing nervous. Salesmen must not let themselves be chaffed in this way and they must gently but firmly get rid of drunken men.

"How can I serve you?" asked Pinneberg.

"Serve!" declaimed the other contemptuously. "Serve! No man ought to be another's servant! But one other thing. Suppose a young man should come into this store, from the Ackerstrasse, let us say, and being rather flush wants a complete new outfit—could you tell me, could you possibly imagine, what sort of things that young man would be likely to choose?"

"Very well indeed," said Pinneberg. "We often have customers like that."

"There you are! Why hide your light under a bushel? So you have imagination. What sort of material would be likely to appeal to this hypothetical young man from the Ackerstrasse?"

"As bright and striking as possible," said Pinneberg decisively. "Large checks. Very full trousers. Very waisted jacket. I could show you . . ."

"Excellent," said the other approvingly. "Excellent. Now let's have a look. This young man from the Ackerstrasse really has a great deal of money and wants an entirely new outfit."

"Certainly," said Pinneberg.

"One moment," said the other, and raised his hand. "I want you to have a picture in your mind. The young man will look like this when he comes in."

The gentleman's appearance completely changed. It was an insolent, vicious face that he now produced, and a cowardly, frightened face as well, with hunched shoulders and too short a neck.—It suggested a policeman's club somewhere in the background.

"And now when he has his nice suit on . . ."

In a flash the face had changed again. It was still impudent and shameless, but the flower had turned to the light, the warm bright sun had risen. He was smartly dressed, he could afford his fine clothes, and nothing mattered.

"Why," said Pinneberg breathlessly. "You must be Herr Schlüter! I've seen you on the screen. Why on earth didn't I notice it at once."

The actor was delighted: "I am indeed. What was the picture?"

"What *was* it called? You played a bank-cashier, and your wife thought you were embezzling money for her, when it was really your friend that was giving it to you."

"I remember," said the actor. "So you liked it? Good. And what part of my acting did you like best?"

"There was so much I liked . . . but perhaps the finest bit was when you came back to the table from the lavatory."

The actor nodded.

"And in the meantime the other man had told your wife that you hadn't stolen any money, and they were laughing at you. And suddenly you became quite small and shrunken, it was dreadful."

"Ah. So that was the best bit. And why did you think so?" asked the actor.

"Because—don't laugh at me—I felt it was so like us.
You see, sometimes we get to feeling that way too
and—"

"The voice of the people. However, I feel very much
honored, Herr—what is your name?"

"Pinneberg."

"The voice of the people, Pinneberg. Right, my
friend, and now we must turn to the serious affairs of
life and find that suit. The property clothes they showed
me were all rubbish: let's see now . . ."

And they looked. For half an hour, an hour, they over-
hauled the stock. They stood surrounded by piles of garments; Pinneberg had never enjoyed his work so much.

"Good fellow," muttered Schlüter the actor, from time
to time. He was a patient tryer-on; even after the fif-
teenth pair of trousers he was anxious to put on the six-
teenth.

"Very good fellow, Pinneberg," he muttered.

At last they had done, at last they had examined and
tried everything that might possibly suit the young man
from the Ackerstrasse. Pinneberg was in ecstasy, Pinneberg hoped Herr Schlüter might perhaps take more than
the one suit—perhaps the brown overcoat with the lilac
checks. Breathlessly he asked: "And what shall I put on
the account, Herr Schlüter?"

The actor raised his eyebrows: "Account? But I was
only looking at the stuff, you know. I'm certainly not
going to buy any of it. For God's sake don't make a face
like that. I have given you a bit of trouble, I know. I
will send you cards for my next first night. Are you married? I'll send two cards."

Pinneberg said hurriedly, in a low voice: "Herr

Schlüter, please,—buy something. You have so much
money, you earn so much, do please buy! If you go away
now without buying anything, they'll think it's my fault
and I'll be dismissed."

"This is absurd," said the actor. "Why on earth should
I buy this stuff? To please you? I never heard of such a
thing!"

"Herr Schlüter." Pinneberg's voice grew louder. "I
saw you on the screen. You see I've got a wife and a
child, too. The child is still quite little, and it would be a
bad business for him if I were dismissed."

"But God in heaven," said Herr Schlüter, "these
are your own private affairs. I can't be expected to buy
suits I don't want just to keep your child cheerful."

"Herr Schlüter," said Pinneberg. "Do it for my sake.
I've been serving you for an hour. Do at least buy the
one suit. It's pure cheviot, it will wear well, and I am
sure you will be pleased with it."

"Look here," said Herr Schlüter. "I'm getting tired
of this."

"Herr Schlüter," implored Pinneberg, laying his hand
on the actor's arm just as he was about to leave the
shop: "There is a quota fixed for us by the Firm, and we
have to make it, otherwise we're dismissed. I'm short by
five hundred marks. Please, please buy something. You—
you must know what we feel like!"

The actor lifted the salesman's hand from his arm.
He said very loudly: "Listen, my lad, I forbid you to
touch me. Your troubles are no concern of mine."

Suddenly Herr Jänecke appeared: "If you please. I am
the head of the department."

"I am Franz Schlüter, the actor."

Herr Jänecke bowed.

"You have very odd assistants here. They assault a customer to make him buy your stuff. The man says he is forced to do it. Somebody ought to write to the papers about it—these are blackmailing methods."

"The man is a very bad salesman," said Herr Jänecke. "He has been warned many times. I regret extremely that you should have come into contact with him. We will dismiss him, he is quite useless."

"Not at all, my dear sir, I don't ask you to do any such thing. He did take my arm."

"Took your arm? Herr Pinneberg, go at once to the Personnel Department and ask for your papers. And all this about the quota, Herr Schlüter, is quite false. Just two hours ago I told this man that if he could not reach it, not to mind. He has no complaints. An incompetent man. I beg a thousand pardons, Herr Schlüter."

Pinneberg stood there and looked after the two men.

He followed them with his eyes.

The jig was up.

EPILOGUE

Continuation

I.

Should you steal wood? Bunny earns a great deal and gives her husband something to do.

BUT no: life went on. Everything did. It was November, in the following year, fourteen months since Pinneberg had left his work at Mandel's. A dark, cold, damp November, all very well when the roof is sound. The roof of their hut was sound, Pinneberg had given it a fresh coating of tar a month before. He was now awake, the illuminated dial of the alarm clock showed a quarter to five. Pinneberg listened to the November rain hissing and rattling on the timber roof. It will keep the rain out, he thought. I've fixed it properly. The rain can't hurt us, anyway.

He was just about to turn round comfortably and go to sleep again, when it suddenly occurred to him that he had been awakened by a noise: the garden gate had clicked. Krymna would be knocking in a moment. Pinneberg took Bunny's arm as she lay beside him in the narrow iron bed and tried to awaken her gently. She started up and said; "What's the matter?"

Bunny had lost her joyful awakening of old days; if she was awakened at an unusual time, it was always for bad news.

"Don't talk too loud," whispered Pinneberg. "You'll wake the baby. It isn't five o'clock yet."

"What is it?" asked Bunny again, rather impatiently.

337

"Krymna's coming," whispered Pinneberg. "Shall I go with him?"

"No, no, no," said Bunny passionately. "That's settled, do you hear? I'll have no thieving."

"But . . ." pleaded Pinneberg.

There was a knock outside. A voice called: "Pinneberg!" And: "Are you coming, Pinneberg?"

Pinneberg jumped up and for a moment stood in doubt.

"So . . ." he began and listened.

Bunny did not answer.

"Pinneberg! Come out, you old rascal!" came the voice once more.

Pinneberg felt his way in the darkness on to the little porch, through the glass panes he could see the dark outline of the other man's form.

"At last! Coming or not?"

"I . . ." cried Pinneberg through the door, "I should like to."

"Then you aren't?"

"Look here, Krymna, I would, but my wife—you know how women are."

"Then you aren't," shouted Krymna from without. "Okay. We'll go alone."

Pinneberg looked after him. He could recognize Krymna's squat figure against the slightly lighter sky. The garden door slammed and Krymna was swallowed up by the night.

Pinneberg sighed once more. He was very cold, standing there in his shirt, and he knew he ought to go in. But there he stood and stared. From within the baby called out: "Da-Da! Ma-Ma!"

Softly Pinneberg felt his way back into the room.
"The baby must sleep," he said; "he must get a bit more
sleep." The child was breathing deeply, his father heard
him lying back in his bed. "Dolly," he whispered;
"Dolly!"

Pinneberg groped about the room in the darkness,
looking for the india rubber doll. The child had to have
it in his hand before he would fall asleep. He found the
doll. "Here's dolly, darling; hold him tight. And now go
to sleep." The child emitted a gurgle of satisfaction and
happiness and was soon asleep.

Pinneberg also went back to bed, and as he was so
cold, he tried to avoid any contact with Bunny, not wishing to alarm her.

There he lay, unsleeping, indeed it was then too late
for that to matter much. He thought of all manner of
things: whether Krymna was very angry with him for
refusing to go out and "look for" wood, and whether
Krymna could do him much harm in the neighborhood.
Then he wondered how they were going to afford briquettes, now that they would have no wood. He reflected
that he would have to go to town that day to draw the
dole. And then that he must also call on Puttbreese, to
pay him six marks. The old man did not want the money,
he would only spend it on drink; it made Pinneberg wild
to think of the way people wasted the money that others
so sorely needed. Pinneberg then reflected that Heilbutt
must also be paid his ten marks, and this would absorb all
the dole. How he was going to get food and fuel for
the coming week, heaven alone knew—or perhaps
didn't.

And so it went on, for weeks and weeks, months and months.

That was what was so ghastly—it just went on and on. Had he ever thought that it would end? The appalling thing was that it always went on, on and on, just the same . . . future there was none.

Gradually Pinneberg grew warm and sleepy. He would try to snatch a bit of sleep. Sleep was always a good thing. Then the alarm clock went off: seven o'clock. Pinneberg was awake at once, and the baby called out lustily: "Tick-tock! Tick-tock! Tick-tock!" over and over again, until the alarm was turned off. Bunny did not wake.

Pinneberg lit the tiny oil lamp with the blue glass globe; the day had begun, and in this first half hour he had a great deal to do. He was walking about in his shirt and trousers; the baby called out: "Ka-Ka." In response to this, Papa brought him a very precious toy, a cigarette box full of old playing cards. The little cast-iron stove and the fire were soon alight, he went to the pump in the garden, washed, made the coffee, cut the bread and spread it—while Bunny was still asleep.

As he did all this, Pinneberg thought of the film he had seen—a very long while ago. There, too, the wife lay asleep in bed, sweetly asleep, while the man ran around and did the chores—ah, but Bunny was not rosy, Bunny had to work all day, Bunny was pale and drawn, Bunny made their budget balance.

Pinneberg dressed the baby. Then he said, turning towards the bed; "Time to get up, Bunny."

340

"Yes," said she obediently, and began to dress. "What did Krymna say?"

"Oh, nothing, he was sore."

"I don't care. I won't have you mixed up with that sort of thing."

"Well," said Pinneberg cautiously. "It's quite safe, you know. There are always about six or eight of them go out to get wood. So the foresters don't interfere."

"Never mind," said Bunny. "We just don't do that sort of thing."

"And how are we going to get the money for the coal?"

"I've got another whole day's darning at the Krämers' today. That makes three marks. And tomorrow I may get a day's mending at the Rechlins'. That's another three marks. And the next week I've got three days' work fixed up already. I'm doing well here."

The room seemed to brighten as she spoke, the air was sweeter for her presence.

"It's such tiring work," he said. "Nine hours darning, for so little money."

"But you must figure in the food," she said. "I get a lot to eat at the Krämers'. I'll be able to bring some back for you in the evening."

"You must eat your own food," said Pinneberg.

"But I get such a lot at the Krämers'," said Bunny once more.

Day had come. The sun had risen. He blew out the lamp, they sat down to their coffee. The baby sat sometimes on his father's knee and sometimes on his mother's. He drank his milk, and ate his bread, and his eyes glowed with pleasure in the new day.

"If you go to town today," said Bunny, "you might bring back a quarter pound of good butter for him. I don't think all this margarine is doing him any good. He's cutting so many teeth."

"Oh, and I must take Puttbreese his six marks today."

"Yes, you must. Don't forget."

"And Heilbutt must have his ten marks. The day after tomorrow is the first of the month."

"Right," said Bunny.

"That finishes the dole money. I've got just enough for fares."

"I can give you another five marks," said Bunny. "I get three more today. So you can buy the butter, and you might see if you can get some bananas at five pfennigs on the Alex—the robbers charge fifteen here. As if anyone would pay such a price!"

"I will," he said. "Try not to be too late, I don't like the boy being left alone so long."

"I'll see what I can do. I imagine I can be back by half-past five. I suppose you'll start about one?"

"Yes," he said. "At two I have to be at the Labor Office."

"It'll be all right," she said. "It's not nice, I know, to leave the baby alone in the hut. But nothing has ever happened."

"No, and won't until it does."

"You mustn't talk like that," said she. "Why should we be always out of luck? Now I've got all this mending and darning to do, we aren't getting on so bad."

"No," he said slowly. "No, of course not."

"Oh my dear," she cried. "Things will improve one

of these days, I'm sure they will. Keep your chin up."

"I didn't marry," he said doggedly, "for you to keep me."

"Well, I'm not keeping you," she retorted. "Not on my three marks. Nonsense!" She reflected for a moment. "Listen, darling, you might do something for me." She hesitated. "It isn't very pleasant, but it would be a great help."

"Of course I will," he said. "What is it?"

"I did some mending three weeks ago at the Rusches' in the Gartenstrasse. Two days—six marks. I haven't had the money yet."

"You want me to go for it?"

"Yes, but you're not to make a scene, you must promise me that."

"No, no," he said. "I'll get the money all right."

"Right," said she. "That's a great relief.—And now I must go. Bye-bye, darling; bye-bye, little one."

"Bye-bye, my girl," said he. "Don't darn too hard. Two more pairs of stockings don't make much difference. Wave your hand, baby!"

"Bye-bye, baby," she said. "This evening we must really decide what we're going to plant in the garden next spring. We'll have such a lot of vegetables. I wish you'd think it over."

"Bless you, dear," he said. "I don't know what I should do without you. All right, I'll think it over. Bye-bye, wife."

"Bye-bye, husband."

He had the child on his arm, and they watched Bunny as she walked down the garden path. They called after her, they laughed, and waved. Then the garden gate

2.

Man as woman. A matter of six marks.

PINNEBERG put the baby on the floor, gave him a paper to look at, and prepared to clear up the room. It was a very large newspaper for such a small child, and it lasted quite a while, until the baby had spread it all over the floor. The room was very small, only nine feet by nine. It contained a bed, two chairs, a table, and the dressing-table.

The baby had discovered the pictures on the inner pages of the paper and was chuckling with delight. "Yes," said Pinneberg encouragingly. "Those are pictures, baby." Whatever the baby took for a man, he called "Da-Da," and the women were all "Ma-Ma." He was delighted because there were so many people in the paper.

Pinneberg hung the mattresses out of the window to air, tidied the room and went into the kitchen. This was just a strip cut off the other room, nine feet long, and four and a half feet wide, the stove was about the smallest ever made, with only one oven. It was Bunny's greatest affliction. Here too Pinneberg tidied and washed up and swept the floor, all of which he was happy to do. But his next occupation he did not enjoy at all; he set himself to peel potatoes and scrape carrots for dinner.

After a while Pinneberg had finished all he had to do. He went for a few moments into the garden and surveyed the landscape. The hut with its little glass-roofed porch seemed so tiny, the plot of land so large—almost a thousand square meters. But the soil looked in poor condition, no work had been done on it since Heilbutt had inherited the place, now three years ago. Perhaps the strawberries could still be saved, but a terrific amount of digging would be needed. The place was thick with weeds, couchgrass and thistles.

After the rain of the morning the sky had cleared, and there was a crisp feeling in the air. It would be good for the baby to get out.

Pinneberg went in again. "Now, baby, we'll go for a ride," he said, put on the child's woollen sweater and his gray waterproof leggings, and set his little white cap on his head.

"Ka-Ka! Ka-Ka!" came the child's eager cry. Pinneberg put the cigarette box with the playing cards into the baby's hand: he always had to hold something. On the porch stood the little cart which they had exchanged for the carriage that summer. "All aboard," said Pinneberg, and the baby got in.

Slowly they set forth. Pinneberg did not go the usual way, he did not want to pass Krymna's hut just then, there would only have been a quarrel which he was only too glad to avoid. But sometimes you couldn't sidestep it. On these three thousand little plots of land hardly fifty persons were left this winter; anyone who could raise the money for a room, or get himself taken in by relatives, had fled to the city to escape the cold and dirt and solitude.

346

Those that stayed, the poorest, the most enduring and courageous, felt somehow that they ought to hang together, but unluckily they did not hang together at all. They were either Communists or Nazis, and thus involved in constant quarrels and conflicts.

Pinneberg had never been able to make up his mind one way or the other; he had thought that this would be an easy way out of the dilemma, but it often appeared to be the hardest.

On some of the plots there was much busy sawing and chopping going on—these were the Communists who had been on the night expedition with Krymna. They quickly reduced the wood to kindling, so that when the forest-guard came along he would find no evidence. When Pinneberg politely said "Good-day," they growled a brusque "G'day" in answer. Pinneberg felt uneasy.

Finally they reached a respectable district of long sidewalks and rows of little villas. Pinneberg unhitched the straps of the cart. "Out with you!"

The baby looked at his father; in his blue eyes danced a little rogue.

"Out with you," said Pinneberg again, "and push your cart."

The baby surveyed his father, put a leg out of the cart, smiled, drew it back. Then he lay back as though about to fall asleep.

"Da-Da will go by himself."

The baby blinked.

Slowly Pinneberg went on, leaving cart and baby behind him. He walked on for ten paces, twenty paces: not a movement. He walked another ten paces, very slowly.

"Da-Da! Da-Da!"

Pinneberg turned: the child had got out of the cart but still made no attempt to follow his father, he held out the straps to be tied round him.

Pinneberg went back and tied the straps. This done, the child's sense of order was satisfied, and for quite a while he pushed the cart alongside his father. Soon they reached a bridge, beneath which a broad swift stream flowed across a meadow. After the rain the stream was full, and the turbid water surged along in swirling eddies.

Pinneberg left the cart standing above, and with the child's hand in his, walked down to the edge of the stream. They surveyed the speeding water. After a while Pinneberg said: "That's water, baby, nice water."

The child uttered a faint small sound of applause. Pinneberg repeated his words several times, to the baby's never-failing enjoyment.

It seemed to Pinneberg unfair that he should stand up so tall beside his boy, imparting information; so he crouched down on his heels.

The child, thinking this the right thing to do, imitated him. Thus they both sat for a while, and watched the water. Then they went on. The child was tired of pushing his cart; he walked by himself, first for a while beside his father and the cart; then he began to notice things and stop—chickens, or a shop-window, or the grating of a drain that caught his eye in the expanse of pavement.

Pinneberg waited a while; then he walked slowly on, stopped again, called and waved to the child who pattered on for a few short steps, laughed at his father, turned, and went back again to his grating.

This happened a few times, until Pinneberg was quite a distance in front, much too far—so the child thought. There the boy stood, shifting from one small leg to another, a very earnest look on his little face. He snatched at the edge of his woolly cap, and pulled it down over his face, so that he could no longer see. Then he called out: "Da-Da!"

Pinneberg looked around. There stood his little son in the middle of the street, his face quite covered with his cap, swaying on his little legs as though at any moment he might fall. Pinneberg rushed back to him, his heart pounding against his chest. He thought: That's pretty cute for one and a half: covering his eyes so that I'd have to go back for him.

He pulled the cap off the child's face. It beamed up at him. "Well, you are a little rascal and no mistake," said he.

Pinneberg said it over and over again, and the tears stood in his eyes.

Then they turned down the Gartenstrasse, towards the house of Rusch the manufacturer, whose wife had owed Bunny six marks for three weeks. Pinneberg repeated to himself his promise that he would not make a scene.

The villa stood in a garden, a little way back from the street; it was a large and pleasant villa with a large and pleasant orchard behind it. It looked very good to Pinneberg.

Slowly he became aware that no one had answered his ring. He tried it again.

A window was flung up, and a woman called out: "Nothing for beggars."

"My wife did some mending in your house," said
Pinneberg. "I have come to get the six marks."

"Come again tomorrow." The woman slammed the
window.

Pinneberg stood for a while considering how much
scope was left to him by his promise to Bunny. The baby
was sitting quietly in his cart as if aware that his father
was angry.

Pinneberg recollected the drudgery of eighteen hours
of darning and mending. He pressed his thumb firmly
against the bell-button. Several people passed and looked
at him. The baby did not utter a sound.

The window was flung open again. "If you don't get
away from the bell at once I'll call the police."

Pinneberg removed his thumb and shouted back: "I
wish you would. And I'll tell the policeman."

But the window was down again, and Pinneberg began
to ring once more. He had always been a quiet and peace-
able man, but these virtues had begun to collapse. As a
matter of fact, he would have been in a very awkward
position if a policeman had in fact appeared. But he did
not care. It was very cold, too, for the baby to sit so long
in his cart, but of that he did not think. Here stood the
little man, Pinneberg, ringing the bell at the house of
Rusch the manufacturer. He wanted his six marks and he
intended to get them.

The hall door opened and the woman came out. She
was wild with rage. She had two dogs on a leash, a black
and a gray. The beasts had understood that here was an
enemy, they tugged and growled ominously.

"I'll set the dogs on you if you don't go away at once."

"I want six marks from you."

The woman grew more furious when she saw the dogs were no help, as she could not really let them loose. They would have been over the railings in an instant and would have torn him to pieces. Pinneberg knew that as well as she did.

"You must be used to waiting," she said.

"I am," said Pinneberg, without moving.

"You're one of the unemployed," said the woman contemptuously; "I can see that quite well. I'll put the police on you for not reporting your wife's earnings."

"All right," said Pinneberg.

"And I'll take the taxes and sick insurance off your wife's six marks."

"If you do," said Pinneberg. "I'll come along tomorrow and make you show me the receipts."

"You wait until your wife comes and asks for some work!" shouted the woman.

"Six marks please," said Pinneberg.

"You impertinent ruffian!" said the woman. "If my husband was here . . ."

"Yes, but he isn't," said Pinneberg.

Here at last were the six marks. There they lay, two three-mark pieces, on the top of the railing. Pinneberg could not pick them up at once, the woman had first to take the dogs back to the house.

"Thank you very much," he said, taking off his hat.

The baby gurgled something. "Yes, money," cried Pinneberg. "Money, little one. And now it's home for us!"

He did not once look back at the woman and the villa, he slowly trundled off with the little cart; he felt dizzy and tired and sad.

The baby chattered and gurgled.

From time to time the father answered, but his voice now sounded different. Finally the baby, too, was silent.

3.

Why the Pinnebergs do not live at home. Joachim Heilbutt's Photograph Agency. Surprising news about Lehmann.

Two hours later Pinneberg had cooked the dinner for himself and the baby, they had eaten it together, and the baby had been put to bed. Now Pinneberg stood behind the half-open kitchen door and waited for the child to go to sleep. He kept on gurgling and calling out to his father. Pinneberg stood stock-still and was silent.

He ought long since to have started for the railway station; he must catch the one o'clock train if he was to arrive punctually to draw his dole. The idea of being unpunctual, even with the best reasons in the world, was unheard-of.

The baby kept on calling: "Da-Da."

Pinneberg could, of course, go. He had settled the child in his crib, and nothing could happen to him; but he felt easier in mind when the baby was asleep. It was not pleasant to think of him crying for five—perhaps six—hours until Bunny came home.

Pinneberg peered round the door. The baby was silent, he was asleep. Softly Pinneberg crept out of the hut and shut the door; for a moment he stood at the window and listened, in case the closing of the door had wakened the child. Silence.

He might still catch the train, though it was unlikely.

353

And yet he must catch it. Their main blunder had been, of course, in keeping their expensive lodging at Puttbreese's for a whole year after he had lost his job. Forty marks a month on an income of ninety. It was lunacy, but they had never been able to make up their minds to go. It meant giving up their last possession, their privacy and their companionship. Forty marks rent— it swallowed up Pinneberg's last month's wages and Jachmann's money, and then they could not pay, and yet must contrive to pay, and then—debts. Puttbreese at the door: "Well, young man, shall we start moving you at once? I promised you a free gratis removal as far as the street."

It was Bunny who always placated the Master.

"I know you'll pay, young woman," said Puttbreese. "But I don't think much of your husband—I'd have found a job long ago."

The struggle grew more bitter and the arrears accumulated and with them developed an impotent hatred of the man in the blue overall. Finally Pinneberg could not bear to go home. All day long he sat in some park or other, or wandered aimlessly through the streets staring into the shop-windows.

One day it occurred to him he might pay a visit to Heilbutt. It was not merely to pass the time that Pinneberg tried to track down Heilbutt; he was thinking just a little of a conversation he had once had with him, in which they had talked about Heilbutt having a business of his own, and how he would employ Pinneberg first of all.

Well, Heilbutt did not prove very difficult to find. He still lived in Berlin and was very respectably known to the authorities; only he had moved from the east side to midtown. "Joachim Heilbutt's Photograph Agency" was inscribed on his door.

Heilbutt had indeed got a business of his own; here was a man who had kept his end up and was making good. And he had been perfectly ready to employ his former friend and colleague. The post that Heilbutt had to offer was not a position with a salary, but one on a commission basis. It was a substantial commission, too; but after two days, Pinneberg, desperate as he was, resigned. He did not, indeed, question that there was money in it, only he was not the man to earn that money. No, it was not a matter of prudishness, he simply could not do the job.

Some while before, Heilbutt, on account of a nude photograph, had had to leave a position to which he was very well suited, and which was not without prospects. Other people, after such an affair, would have had no more dealings with such photographs. Heilbutt transformed them into the foundation-stone of his existence. He possessed an extraordinarily varied and valuable collection of such pictures, not of worn-out, slack-bodied professional models, but of fresh young girls and voluptuous women. Heilbutt started a business in nude photographs.

He was a cautious fellow—a trifle of retouching, or the substitution of another head was not so very costly, and no one could point to a photograph and say "that's so-and-so" though someone might say doubtfully "But isn't that so-and-so?"

He advertised his collection for despatch through the mails, but in this sphere there was too much competition. Though he did some business, the results were not bril-

liant. Direct sales, however, were wonderfully success-
ful. Heilbutt had three young men going about Berlin
(for two days the fourth had been Pinneberg). They
sold these photographs to certain girls, to certain landladies, to the porters of certain little hotels, and to lavatory attendants, male and female, in certain restaurants.
The business was a large one, and grew larger as Heilbutt found the kind of thing his customers wanted. It was
hardly to be conceived how great was the demand for
such material in a city of four millions; the sky was the
limit.

Yes, Heilbutt was sorry that his friend Pinneberg had
decided not to come in with him. Heilbutt reflected that
the best of women, owing to their very virtues, could
sometimes be a handicap. Pinneberg merely felt nause-
ated when an old lavatory attendant told him what his
customers had said about the last batch, and in what re-
spects the photographs must positively be made more distinct, and why and how. Heilbutt had once been a de-
fender of nudism, he raised no question, he merely said:
"I am a practical man, Pinneberg, I live as life is lived."

But he also said: "I won't be stepped on, Pinneberg.
I remain as I am, others must look after themselves."

No, there had been no quarrel. Heilbutt had entirely
understood his friend's attitude. "All right, it isn't your
job. But what are we to do with you?"

That was just like Heilbutt; he wanted to help. Here
was his friend, they were no longer intimates, indeed
they never really had been, but the man must be helped
somehow.

Suddenly Heilbutt thought of the hut outside Berlin,
some twenty-five miles away—in fact quite in the coun-

try, with a bit of land attached to it. "An aunt of mine left it to me, Pinneberg, three years ago. It's no good to me. You might as well live there and you'd be able to grow your own potatoes and vegetables."

"It would be great for the baby," Pinneberg had said. "Nothing like fresh air for children."

"You won't need to pay me any rent," Heilbutt had said. "It's just standing there empty, and you'll keep the garden in order. Only there are some taxes and road-charges and what not, that I have to keep on paying." Heilbutt calculated for a moment or two. "We might say ten marks a month. Or is that too much for you?"

"Not at all," said Pinneberg. "That's fine, Heilbutt."

Pinneberg reflected on all this as he sat in his train, the right train, which he had caught after all, and stared at his ticket. The ticket was yellow, and cost fifty pfennigs; the return also cost fifty pfennigs, and as Pinneberg had to call at the Labor Exchange twice a week, out of his eighteen marks' unemployed pay, two marks went on fares. This expense always made Pinneberg furious.

There were indeed cheap workman's tickets but to get them Pinneberg had to live where he really was living, and that he could not do. There was also a Labor Exchange near-by, where he could get his card stamped without having to waste money on fares, but for the same reason he could not use it: he did not officially live in the hut. For the purpose of the Labor Exchange Pinneberg lived in Puttbreese's establishment, today, tomorrow, and for all eternity, whether he could pay the rent or not.

Pinneberg hated to think, though he often did think,

how in the months of July and August he had run from
one place to another to get permission to move out of
Berlin, and to be transferred to the Labor Exchange in
his district.

"You will have to prove that there is a prospect of
work there, otherwise they won't accept you."

No, that he could not do. But he pointed out that he
would not get any work in Berlin either.

"You don't know that. In any case you lost your job
here and not there."

"But I save thirty marks rent a month."

"That's no business of ours."

"But my landlord here will throw me out very soon."

"Then the city authorities must find you another lodging. You only need to report to the police as without
one."

There was nothing to be done. The Pinnebergs still
lived officially in Berlin in Puttbreese's house, and Pinneberg had to travel to town twice each week to draw his
money. And every two weeks he had to visit the detested
Puttbreese and pay him six marks off his arrears of rent.

When Pinneberg had been sitting for an hour or so
in the train, he piled up all his afflictions in his mind and
they flared up into quite a pretty little blaze of anger,
hatred and bitterness. But it did not last. When he came
to push his way through the Labor Exchange in the gray
monotonous stream of his fellows—all kinds of faces
and all kinds of clothes, but in all their hearts the same
conflict, the same misery, the same bitterness . . . Oh,
what was the use? Why get excited? Tens of thousands
were worse off than he, tens of thousands had no such
wife to back them up, and they had, not one child, but

half a dozen. Move on, Pinneberg, my man, draw your money and clear out.

So Pinneberg went on, past the pay-desks and out on to the street; and he made his way along to Puttbreese. That personage was standing in his workshop cutting out a window-frame.

"Good morning, Master," said Pinneberg, trying to be polite to the enemy. "Have you taken to carpentry?"

"I can do everything, young man," said Puttbreese with a wink. "I'm not like some others I know."

"No, you certainly are not," agreed Pinneberg.

"How's the son?" asked Puttbreese. "What's he going to be?"

"I can't yet tell you exactly," said Pinneberg. "Here's the money."

"Six marks," said the Master examining it. "That leaves forty-two. Is the lady all right?"

"Quite all right," said Pinneberg.

"You say that as if you took some credit for it. You shouldn't, it has nothing to do with you."

"I don't," said Pinneberg peaceably. "Any letters?"

"Letters? Letters for you? About a job, you mean? A man was asking for you."

"A man?"

"Yes, a man, my lad. At least I think it was a man."

"What did he want?"

"No idea.—You aren't a Communist, are you?"

"I? No."

"That's funny. I should be, in your place."

"Are you a Communist, Master?"

"I? Not on your life. I'm a craftsman, how could I be a Communist?"

"What did the man want?"

"What man? Look here, I've had enough of him. He went on yarning here for half an hour. I gave him your address."

"The one in the country?"

"Of course. He knew this one already, didn't he?"

"But we had agreed . . ." said Pinneberg with emphasis.

"It's all right, my boy. You'll find your wife won't mind. You haven't got a ladder in your hut, have you? I'd pay you a visit if you had. Pretty legs your wife has."

"Damn you! For God's sake tell me what the man wanted."

"Why don't you leave off that collar?" sneered the Master. "It's filthy. Out of a job for a year and still going about in a celluloid collar. People like you are hopeless."

"Go to hell!" shouted Pinneberg, and slammed the workshop door.

Pinneberg's eyes were set with fury at having let the old man fool him again. Every time he went there he made up his mind he would only say a word or two and go; and this was what always happened. He was an idiot who would never learn, he deserved all he got.

Pinneberg stopped in front of a dress-shop window in which there was a large mirror. He looked himself up and down: no, not a pleasant sight. His light gray trousers were tar-stained from his labors on the hut roof, his overcoat was worn and faded, his shoes were in their last stages—Puttbreese was perfectly right, it was stupid to wear a collar with such clothes. He was just a broken-down creature without a job, anyone could see that twenty yards away. Pinneberg grabbed at his collar, tore it off, and stuffed it and his necktie into his coat-pocket. He did not now look very different, indeed he could hardly have looked much worse. Heilbutt would say nothing, though he would certainly stare.

A police car suddenly dashed past. So there had been another row with the Nazis or the Communists—the fellows had some courage left. He wished he still took a newspaper—you didn't know what was going on. All might be in perfect order in the land of Germany, he noticed nothing in his country hut. Well, well, if things were in such good shape, he would have noticed it.

Thus he mused as he walked; it was a cheerless way of passing the time, but what else was a man to do in a city where he was presumably expected to stay home and brood over his troubles?

He was glad when he climbed up the stairs to Heilbutt's abode. It was very nearly six o'clock, he hoped Bunny had got back by this time, the baby must be all right.

He rang the bell.

A girl opened the door, a very pretty girl in a silk blouse. She had not been there last month.

"I should like to see Herr Heilbutt. My name is Pinneberg." As the girl hesitated, he added sharply: "I am a friend of Herr Heilbutt's."

The girl let him into the hall. "Will you please wait a moment?"

The girl disappeared through a white enamelled door inscribed: "Office."

It was a very handsome hall, with red rugs on the

floor: not a hint of nude photographs on the walls, only strictly respectable pictures—etchings, thought Pinneberg, or woodcuts. It was indeed hardly imaginable that no more than a year and a half ago they had been both assistants at Mandel's, selling suits.

Here was Heilbutt. "Good evening, Pinneberg. Very glad to see you again. Come right in.—Marie," he said, "bring the tea into my study." No, they did not go into the office, it appeared that since his last visit Heilbutt had acquired not merely the young lady, but a study, with bookcases and Persian rugs and a gigantic writing table, a real gentleman's room, such as Pinneberg had always longed for and would never possess in this world.

"Sit down," said Heilbutt. "Have a cigarette. Ah, you're looking round the room. Yes, I've bought a few bits of furniture; I had to, you know. Of course it doesn't mean much to me. As you remember, at old Witt's . . ."

Pinneberg was in ecstasies. "I think it's lovely. All these books . . ."

"Oh, the books." Heilbutt's mind wasn't on the books. "How are you getting on in the country?"

"Very well. We like it very much, Heilbutt. And my wife has found some work, darning and mending, you know. We're doing a little better."

"Ah," said Heilbutt. "That's good. Put the tray down, Marie, I'll see to it. Thank you, no, there's nothing more. Help yourself, Pinneberg. Have one of those cakes, they go well with tea—I don't know if you like them. Tea doesn't interest me very much." He went on abruptly: "Very cold out in the country?"

"No, no," said Pinneberg hurriedly. "Not very. The little stove gives very good heat. The rooms are small, and the weather has been pretty mild. By the way, here's the rent, Heilbutt."

"Ah yes, the rent. Is it due again already?" Heilbutt took the note in his hand, folded it, but did not put it in his pocket. "By the way, you tarred the roof, didn't you, Pinneberg?"

"Yes, I did. And it was very good of you to pay me for doing it. It was when I was tarring it that I saw how leaky it was. It would have let in a lot of water during these autumn rains."

"And it's water-tight now?"

"Yes, thank heaven. It's quite sound now."

"Look here, Pinneberg, I read somewhere the other day . . . Do you keep the stove going all day?"

"No," said Pinneberg slowly, not quite understanding what Heilbutt meant. "We light it a while in the morning, and again in the afternoon, so as to have the place warm for the evening.—It isn't very cold yet."

"Do you happen to know what briquettes cost around there?" asked Heilbutt.

"I don't know exactly," said Pinneberg. "After the last emergency order they must be much cheaper. One sixty, perhaps? Or one fifty-five? No, I don't know."

"I noticed in some builder's paper the other day," said Heilbutt, fidgeting with the note, "that dry-rot soon gets into these little places if they are allowed to get damp. And I wanted to tell you to be careful to keep the place heated."

"Yes," said Pinneberg; "we could . . ."

"Well, that's what I meant to ask you. I don't want the place to get damaged. Would you mind keeping the stove lit all day, so the walls get thoroughly dry. I'll give

363

you this ten marks to begin with. On the first of next month you might perhaps bring me the coal bill as a receipt—?"

"No, no," said Pinneberg hastily, and swallowed. "It won't do, Heilbutt. You give me back the rent every time. You've helped us enough—even when I was at Mandel's."

"But Pinneberg!" said Heilbutt, in great astonishment. "Help?—why it's to my interest that the roof should be tarred and the place kept dry. There's no question of help. You're helping yourself."

Heilbutt shook his head and looked at Pinneberg.

"Heilbutt!" Pinneberg burst out. "I understand, you . . ."

"Listen," said Heilbutt. "Did I tell you whom I met from Mandel's the other day?"

"No," said Pinneberg. "But . . ."

"Didn't I?" said Heilbutt. "You'd never guess. I met Lehmann, our former chief, and head of the Personnel Department."

"Well?" said Pinneberg. "Did you speak to him?"

"Of course I did," said Heilbutt. "That is to say it was he who spoke to me. He poured his heart out."

"What on earth about?" asked Pinneberg. "He couldn't have had any troubles."

"He's been fired," said Heilbutt with emphasis. "Fired by Herr Spannfuss. Just like us."

"Good God!" ejaculated Pinneberg. "Lehmann fired! Heilbutt, you must tell me all about it. If I may, I'll take another cigarette."

4.

How Pinneberg started it all.
The forgotten butter and the policeman.

IT was about seven o'clock when Pinneberg again stepped
out on to the street. His conversation with Heilbutt had
cheered him up; he was tickled to death by the news, and
yet his heart was still heavy. So Lehmann had fallen.
Pinneberg well remembered the great Lehmann, the
exalted Herr Lehmann; he sat in solitary state behind
an empty writing table: "No, we don't deal in manure."

Lehmann made his slave Pinneberg tremble, then came
Herr Spannfuss and made his slave Lehmann tremble. A
day would come when that eminent sportsman Herr
Spannfuss would tremble too. That's the way the world
went; it was small consolation that all went the same way
in the end.

What had caused Herr Lehmann's fall? It was quite
clear; one Pinneberg had brought him down. Herr
Spannfuss had routed out the fact that the Head of
the Personnel Department, Lehmann, had exceeded his
powers in engaging favorites of his own. He had al-
leged that they came from branch establishments, from
Hamburg, Fulda, or Breslau; allegations that Spannfuss
had exposed.

As a matter of fact everyone knew that this was only
the pretext for dismissal. Favored persons were constantly being given jobs; Herr Spannfuss was in process

365

of staffing the business with his own creatures. But to do this undisturbed, it was essential to oust Herr Lehmann. What had for twenty years been common knowledge, now, in the twenty-first, filled the cup to overflowing: indeed Herr Lehmann had been guilty of actual forgery. He had had recorded in the man's personal file: "From the Breslau Branch," and the man came from the firm of Kleinholz at Ducherow. Lehmann might be grateful to Herr Spannfuss, as a criminal prosecution had been by no means beyond the bounds of possibility. Lehmann had better keep his mouth shut.

But Lehmann talked fast enough when he met his former subordinate Heilbutt! Had not Herr Heilbutt been a friend of that little man—what was his name again?—Pinneberg? They had pushed him on to the pavement all right—the stupid little fool. Because he hadn't sold his quota? Nonsense—after Heilbutt had gone, he was the only one who had more or less kept up with it. That was why he had aroused rather particular interest among the other assistants; that was why a letter had appeared among his personal papers, an anonymous letter, of course, to the effect that this Pinneberg belonged to a Nazi Storm Detachment.

Lehmann had always thought it was rubbish, since, if it had been true, how could Pinneberg have been friendly with Heilbutt? But it was quite useless to protest, Spannfuss would believe only Jänecke and Kessler; and besides it was almost notorious that Pinneberg was the man who had persistently drawn swastikas on the walls of the lavatories, scrawled "Down with the Jews," and depicted a fat Jew hanging on a gallows with the inscription: "Death of Herr Mandel." These drawings had ceased with Pinneberg's departure, and the lavatory walls were now immaculate—and a man like that had been engaged by Herr Lehmann as coming from Breslau.

Pinneberg walked on and on, until he reached the Friedrichstrasse, but anger and fury were becoming rather stale. Such had been his fate, he could rage against it if he liked, but to what purpose?

In former days Pinneberg had often walked down the Friedrichstrasse, it was an old haunt of his and he noticed how many more girls there were. For some time now, of course, they had not all been regulars, there had been much unfair competition in late years; even eighteen months ago he had heard in the shop that many wives of men out of work had gone on the streets to earn a few marks.

It was true—indeed it was obvious; many of them were so utterly without attraction or prospects of success, or, if they had any looks, greed, and greed for money, was written on their faces.

Pinneberg thought of Bunny and the boy. "We aren't so bad off," Bunny would often say. She was certainly right.

There still seemed a certain amount of excitement among the police, all the patrols were doubled, and every minute or two he passed a pair of officers parading the pavement. Pinneberg had nothing against the police, they had to exist, of course, especially the traffic police; but he could not help feeling that they looked irritatingly well-fed and clothed, and behaved, too, in rather a provocative way. They walked among the public like teachers among school-children during the play interval:—Behave properly, or—!

Well, let them be.

For the fourth time Pinneberg was pacing that section of the Friedrichstrasse that lies between the Leipziger and the Linden. He could not go home, he simply revolted at the thought. When he got home, everything was again at a dead end, life flickered into a dim and hopeless distance. But here something still might happen. It was true that the girls did not look at him; a man with so threadbare a coat, such dirty trousers and without a collar did not exist for the girls on the Friedrichstrasse. If he wanted anything of that kind, he had better go along to the Schlesischer; there they did not mind appearances so long as the man could pay. But did he want a girl?

Perhaps he did, he was not sure, he thought no more of the matter. He just wanted to tell some human being what his life had once been, the smart suits he had had, and talk about—

He had entirely forgotten the boy's butter and bananas, it was now nine o'clock and all the shops would be shut! Pinneberg was furious with himself, and even more sorry than angry; he could not go home empty-handed, what would Bunny think of him? Perhaps he could get something at the side-door of a shop. There was a great grocer's shop, radiantly illuminated. Pinneberg flattened his nose against the window. Perhaps there was still someone about. He must get that butter and bananas!

A voice behind him said in a low tone: "Move on please!"

Pinneberg started—he was really quite frightened. A policeman stood beside him.

Was the man speaking to him?

"Move on there, do you hear?" said the policeman, loudly now.

There were other people standing at the shop-window, well-dressed people, but to them the policeman had undoubtedly not addressed himself. He meant Pinneberg.

"What? But why—? Can't I—?"

He stammered; he simply did not understand.

"Are you going?" asked the policeman. "Or shall I—?"

The loop of his rubber club was slipped round his wrist, and he raised the weapon slightly.

Everyone stared at Pinneberg. Some passers-by had stopped, a little crowd began to collect. The people looked on expectantly, they took no sides in the matter; on the previous day shop-windows had been broken on the Friedrich and the Leipziger.

The policeman had dark eyebrows, bright resolute eyes, a straight nose, red cheeks, and an energetic moustache.

"Well?" said the policeman calmly.

Pinneberg tried to speak; Pinneberg looked at the policeman; his lips quivered, and he looked at the bystanders. A little group was standing round the window, well-dressed people, respectable people, people who earned money.

But in the mirror of the window still stood a lone figure, a pale phantom, collarless, clad in a shabby ulster and tar-smeared trousers.

Suddenly Pinneberg understood everything; in the presence of this policeman, these respectable persons, this gleaming window, he understood that he was outside it all, that he no longer belonged here and that he was rightly chased away; he had slipped into the abyss, and was engulfed. Order and cleanliness; they were of the past. So too were work and safe subsistence. And past too were progress and hope. Poverty was not merely misery, poverty was an offence, poverty was evil, poverty meant that a man was suspect.

"Do you want one on the bean?" asked the policeman.

Pinneberg obeyed; he was aware of nothing but a longing to hurry to the Friedrichstrasse station and catch his train and get back to Bunny.

Pinneberg was conscious of a blow on his shoulder, not a heavy blow, but just enough to land him in the gutter.

"Beat it!" said the policeman. "And be quick about it!"

Pinneberg went; he shuffled along in the gutter close to the curb and thought of a great many things, of fires and bombs and street shooting and how Bunny and the baby were done for: it was all over . . . but really his mind was vacant.

Pinneberg came to the junction of the Jägerstrasse and the Friedrichstrasse. He wanted to cross to the railway station, and so get home to Bunny and the baby. He began to feel himself a man again. The policeman gave him a push. "That's your way, young fellow." He pointed down the Jägerstrasse.

Once more Pinneberg tried to mutiny; he had to catch his train. "But I must . . ." he said.

"That's your way, I tell you," repeated the officer, and pushed him into the Jägerstrasse. "Get a move on." And he gave Pinneberg an emphatic shove in the desired direction.

Pinneberg began to run; he ran very fast, he realized

370

the men were no longer following him, but he did not dare look round. He ran along the roadway into the night, straight ahead, into the darkness, into the night that was not black enough to cover him.

After a long long time he slackened his step. He stopped and looked round. No one. Nothing. No police. Cautiously he raised one foot and placed it on the pavement. Then the other. He stood no longer in the roadway, he stood upon the pavement.

Then Pinneberg went on, step by step, through the city of Berlin. But it was nowhere very dark, and it was very difficult to slip past the policemen.

5.

A visitor in a taxi. Two sit waiting in the night.
No chance with Bunny.

On Street No. 87a, in front of allotment 375, a car
stopped, a taxi from Berlin. The chauffeur had for many
hours been sitting in Pinneberg's hut, in the little kitchen,
which he almost entirely filled.

They were still talking and talking, especially the fat
fair-haired man.

"I really don't understand where the lad can be. He's
always home by eight at the latest," said Bunny.

"He'll soon be here," said Jachmann. "How's the
young father, little mother?"

"Poor dear," said Bunny, "it's a bad time for him.
When a man's been out of work for fourteen
months . . ."

"Something will turn up," said Jachmann. "Now I'm
around again, you'll soon see something doing."

"Were you really away on a trip, Herr Jachmann?"

Jachmann stood up and walked over to the baby's bed.
"It's strange that a father can stay out when he's got
something like this waiting for him!"

"Oh God, Herr Jachmann," said Bunny. "Of course
the baby's lovely, but we can't think only of the baby.
You see I go out sewing by the day."

"You mustn't do that! It must stop at once!"

372

"I go out sewing by the day, and he looks after the house and the food and the child. He doesn't grumble, he's even glad to do it, but what sort of life is that for a man? Tell me, Jachmann, is this to go on forever, —men sitting at home and doing the house-work, and the women going out to work? It's impossible!"

"Come," said Jachmann. "How do you make that out? In the war the women did the work, and the men killed each other, and everyone thought it was all right. This arrangement is even better."

"Everyone didn't think it was all right."

"Well, nearly everyone, young woman. Man is like that, he learns nothing, he always does the same foolish things over again. I know I do too." Jachmann paused a moment. "I'm going back to your mother-in-law."

Bunny said slowly: "Well, Herr Jachmann, you ought to know best. Perhaps it isn't so foolish after all. She's very clever and amusing."

"Of course it's foolish," said Jachmann angrily. "It's damned foolish. You don't know what you're talking about, my dear. However . . ."

He sank into meditation.

After a long pause Bunny said: "You mustn't wait, Herr Jachmann. The ten o'clock train is through, too. I really believe he's gone on a bat tonight. He had quite a lot of money with him."

"What? A lot of money? Have you still got a lot of money?"

Bunny laughed: "What we call a lot, Jachmann. Twenty marks. Enough for a night out."

"Yes," said Jachmann gloomily.

And again there was a long silence.

373

After a while Jachmann raised his head: "Worrying, Bunny?"

"Of course I'm worrying. You'll soon see what these last two years have made of my husband. And he's really a decent boy."

"He is."

"I don't know why he's been made to suffer like this. And if he starts drinking . . ."

Jachmann reflected. "He won't do that. There's always been a kind of freshness about Pinneberg, and getting drunk is a nasty business—he won't drink. He might go off the path a little, but never really take to drink."

"The half-past ten train's come through," said Bunny. "I'm really worried now."

"Don't you worry," said Jachmann. "Pinneberg will win through."

"Through what?" asked Bunny angrily. "What is he to win through? There's no sense in what you say, it's just to comfort me. That's the worst of it—he sits around here in the country and has nothing to fight against. He can only wait—what for? What can happen? Nothing. Wait—that's all he has to do."

Jachmann surveyed her for a while. He had turned his great leonine head round towards Bunny and was looking her full in the face. "You mustn't be always thinking of the train, Bunny," he said. "Your man will come back again; he'll certainly come back."

"It isn't just the drink," said Bunny; "drink would be bad, but not so very bad. But you see he's so done in, that anything might happen to him—he went to see Puttbreese today, who was very likely rude to him, and that's the sort of thing that upsets him these days. He can't

374

stand much, you know. Jachmann, and he might . . ."

She gazed at him with large wide-open eyes. Suddenly they filled with tears, large bright tears that ran over her cheeks, the soft firm mouth began to quiver helplessly. "Jachmann," she whispered. "He might . . ."

Jachmann got up; he stood half behind her and grasped her by the shoulders: "No, my dear," he said; "that can't happen. He wouldn't do that."

"Anything can happen." She shook herself free. "You'd better go home. You're wasting your money keeping that taxi waiting. It's just one of our bad times."

Jachmann did not answer. He took two steps forward and two steps back. On the table lay the baby's tin cigarette box full of old playing cards. "What did you say," asked Jachmann, "that the boy called the cards?"

"What boy? Oh, the baby. Ka-Ka, he always says."

"Shall I lay the Ka-Ka, the cards, for you?" said Jachmann with a smile. "Just you wait, your future is quite different from what you think."

"Don't trouble," said Bunny. "There'll be some money coming to us—the dole for next week."

"I'm not very flush at the moment," said Jachmann; "but I can gladly let you have eighty or even ninety marks." He corrected himself: "Lend you, I mean, of course."

"That's very nice of you, Jachmann," said Bunny. "It would come in useful. But money doesn't help, you know. We'll get through. Money is no help at all. Work would help, and a little hope would help the boy. Money? No."

"Is it because I'm going back to your mother-in-law?" asked Jachmann, looking meditatively at Bunny.

"Partly," said Bunny; "that too. I have to keep everything from him that might torment him, Jachmann. You can understand that."

"I understand."

"But the main reason is because money really doesn't help. What's the advantage of being a little better off for six or eight weeks? None."

"Perhaps I could get a job for him," said Jachmann reflectively.

"Ah, Herr Jachmann," said Bunny, "you mean well. But don't go to any trouble; if he's to get another job, it mustn't be through fraud and lying. The lad must shake off his fears and feel himself free again."

"Well," said Jachmann gloomily, "if you want such luxury today, without fraud and lying, I can't find it for you!"

"You see," said Bunny eagerly; "the others steal wood for their fuel. I don't think it's so very wrong, you know; but I told the lad he wasn't to do it. He must not fall below himself, Jachmann, I won't have it. He must keep his self-respect. Luxury—yes, if you like, but it's our only luxury, we must stick to it, and we'll be all right, Jachmann."

"My dear," said Jachmann. "I . . ."

"Look at the baby in his crib—suppose things do improve again, and he pulls himself together and gets a job and some work that interests him, and earns money again. Then he'll always be thinking about what he was and what he did. It isn't the wood, Jachmann, it isn't the law; I don't think much of the law when we can be brought down to this state and no one suffer for it, while we have to go to jail for three marks' worth of wood."

"My dear . . ." Jachmann tried to begin again.

376

"But he can't do it," said Bunny energetically. "He's like his father. He gets nothing from his mother. Mamma has told me ten times over what an old stickler his father was. In his work as a lawyer's clerk, everything had to be just so and not otherwise. And it was exactly the same with his whole private life. If a bill came in during the morning, he went out and paid it the very same evening. He used to say that if he died, and the bill was overlooked, it might be said that he had been a dishonorable man. And he's just like that. So it isn't any luxury, Jachmann, he must stick to it, and if he often thinks he can do as the others do—he just can't. He must keep clean. And that's why I won't let him take any job that's shaky."

"What on earth am I doing here?" asked Jachmann. "Why am I sitting here? Nothing the matter with you, I suppose. You're quite right, my dear, you're dead right. I'll go home."

But he did not go, he did not even get up from his chair, he stared wide-eyed at Bunny. "This morning at six o'clock, Bunny," he said, "I was let out of jail. I've done a year, my dear."

"Jachmann," said Bunny, "since you stayed away that night, I've always supposed something of the kind had happened. Not at once, but it did occur to me. You see," —Bunny did not know exactly how to put it—"you are so . . ."

"Of course I am," said Jachmann.

"To the few people that you like, you're nice, and to all the rest you're probably not nice at all."

"Right," said Jachmann; "and I like you, my dear."

"And then you enjoy yourself, and you like having a lot of money and plenty going on, and you always need

377

to have something on hand—yes, that's your style. When
mamma told me there was a warrant out for you, I knew
at once I was right."

"And do you know who gave me away?"

"Mamma, wasn't it?"

"Of course. Frau Marie, called Mia Pinneberg. You
know, Bunny, I'd been off on my own a little, and
mamma's a devil when she's jealous. Well, mamma did a
little time too—not so very bad, only a month."

"And now you're going back to her? I understand.
You belong to each other."

"Right, my dear, we do. She's a splendid woman, all
the same, you know. I like her greed and her egotism.—
Did you know that she has more than thirty thousand
marks in the bank?"

"What? More than thirty thousand marks?"

"What did you suppose? She is a sensible woman. She
looks ahead. She thinks of old age. She's not going to be
dependent on anybody. No, I'm going back to her. For
anyone like me she's the best pal in the world, through
thick and thin, horse-stealing, and everything else."

Then there was silence for a while; after which Jachmann got up suddenly, and said: "Good-night, Bunny,
I'm off."

"Good-night, Jachmann, and I wish you the very, very
best of luck."

Jachmann shrugged his shoulders: "The cream's all
gone, Bunny, when a man's in the fifties; it's all skim milk
after that." He paused, and then said softly: "There's no
chance for me, Bunny, is there?"

Bunny smiled at him, out of the very depths of her

heart: "No, Jachmann, no good at all. The boy and I . . ."

"Don't you be afraid about the lad. He'll be here very soon. Bye-bye, Bunny, perhaps we'll meet again."

"Good-bye, Jachmann, I'm sure we will. When things are better. Now don't forget your trunks. They were the main point."

"Why so they were, my dear. Right as always; dead right."

6.

A mysterious bush.

BUNNY had gone into the garden with her visitor; the sleepy chauffeur could not get the chilled engine to start at once, and the two stood in silence beside the car. Then they shook hands again, and again said good-bye. Bunny watched the reflection of the headlights dwindle into the distance, for a time she could still hear the hum of the engine, then all was dark and silent.

The sky was clear and starry and there was a light frost. Among all the huts, so far as she could see, not a light was visible; only behind her, in the window of their own hut, shone the soft reddish glow of the oil lamp.

There Bunny stood, the baby slept—was she waiting? What was she waiting for? The last train was through, he could not now get back until tomorrow morning, he had gone off on a spree—one more affliction that she had not been spared. She had been spared nothing. She could go to bed and sleep. Or lie awake. It didn't matter.

Bunny did not go in. She stood there; in that silent night there was something that made her heart uneasy. Up yonder the familiar stars glittered in the chill air. The bushes in the garden and in the neighboring garden were crude compact masses of blackness, and the next hut stood like a great dark beast.

No wind, not a sound, nothing; far away in the distance

rumbled a train. There in that garden the silence was tense and still, and Bunny knew she was not alone. Someone was standing in the darkness, just as she was, motionless. Did he breathe? No, not a breath. And yet there was someone there.

There was an elderbush, there was another. Since when had there been something between them?

Bunny took a step forward, her heart was hammering, she said very quietly: "Darling, is that you?"

The bush, the bush that she had never noticed, was silent. Then it moved very slowly, and said, in a hoarse and halting voice: "Has he gone?"

"Yes, Jachmann's gone. Have you been waiting here long?"

Pinneberg did not answer.

For a while they stood silent; his face was not visible and yet, coming from that silent figure that confronted her, she was conscious of a waft of peril, something still darker than the night, something more menacing than this strange rigidity of the man she knew so well.

Bunny stood still, then she said lightly: "Shall we go in? I'm feeling cold."

He did not answer.

Something had happened. It was not that he'd been drinking, or at least it was not only that—he had perhaps been drinking too. Something else had happened, something worse.

There stood her husband, the boy whom she so loved, in the darkness, like a wounded beast not daring to come into the light. They had got him down at last.

"Jachmann only came to get his trunks. He's not coming back."

Pinneberg did not answer.

Once more they stood for a while: on the road beneath them, Bunny could hear a car, far away; then the hum of it approached, grew louder, and then gradually faded into silence. What should she say? If only he would speak!

"I've been doing some mending at the Krämers' today, you know."

He did not answer.

"At least—I didn't do any darning. She had a piece of material, and I cut out a house frock and made it up for her. She was very pleased; she's going to let me have her old sewing machine cheap and recommend me to all her friends. I get eight marks for making a dress, and sometimes ten."

She waited. She waited quite a while. Then she said cautiously: "Maybe we'll be making good money soon; our troubles may be over."

He moved slightly; then he again stood still and was silent.

Bunny waited, her heart was heavy within her, she felt very cold. She had no more words of comfort. She could do no more. Why should she struggle further? For what? He might as well have gone out to steal wood with the rest.

Once more she gazed up at the myriad stars. The heavens were still and solemn, but strange and vast and very far away. She said: "The boy kept asking for you all the afternoon."

No answer.

"Oh my darling!" she cried. "What is it? Do say just one word to your Bunny. Am I nothing to you any more? Are we—just alone?"

It was no good. He came no nearer, he said nothing; he seemed farther and farther away.

The cold had risen to Bunny's heart; it gripped her until she was chilled through and through. Behind her shone the warm red light of the hut window, where the baby was asleep. Alas, children depart also, they are ours only for a while—six years? Ten years? We are all of us alone.

She turned towards the red glow, she must go in— what else could she do?

Behind her a voice called from far away: "Bunny!"

She went on; it was no use, she went on.

"Bunny!"

She went on. There was the hut, there was the door, one step more and her hand was on the latch.

She felt herself held fast, he was gripping her, he sobbed, he stammered out: "Oh Bunny, do you know what they did to me? The police . . . they shoved me off the pavement . . . they chased me away. How can I ever look anybody in the face again!"

Suddenly the cold had gone, an infinite soft green wave raised her up, and him with her. They slid onwards, and the twinkling stars came very near. She whispered: "You can always look at me. Always and always. You're here with me and we're together."

The wave rose and rose. They lay on the sea-shore by night between Lensahn and Wiek, once more the stars were close above their heads. The wave rose higher and higher, from the polluted earth towards the stars.

Then they both went into the hut where the baby lay asleep.

A note about the Author of
"Little Man, What Now?"

HANS FALLADA was born in Pomerania in 1893, the son of a lawyer. He confesses to having been a moral reprobate in extreme youth and a very dull scholar as he grew older. At the age of twenty he found himself, obeying an instinct he had felt from childhood, an agricultural worker on a farm in Thuringia. He looks back to those hours with vegetables and cows as among the happiest of his life.

Then followed some years during which, as he says, he was "unfaithful to the land." He worked at a series of petty city jobs during which, it is probable, he gathered many of the impressions which later found their way into *Little Man, What Now?*

Between 1920 and 1922 he wrote his first two novels, one of which he admits is no longer readable; the other he still considers his most creative work.

The years that followed were years of poverty, distress, sickness, during which all thoughts of writing were given up. Then he married and gradually began to make a small place for himself as a journalist.

A chance meeting with the famous German publisher, Ernst Rowohlt, gave him his opportunity to come to Berlin. Here, when office work was over he worked at his first long novel (*Bauern, Bonzen und Bomben*) which met with considerable success and established him among the leading younger German writers. His next book was *Little Man, What Now?*

—ESSANDESS